M000283681

To Kill a Shadow

TO KILL A SHADOW

KATHERINE QUINN

This book is a work of fiction. Names, characters, places, and incidents are the product of the author's imagination or are used fictitiously. Any resemblance to actual events, locales, or persons, living or dead, is coincidental.

Copyright © 2023 by Katherine Quinn. All rights reserved, including the right to reproduce, distribute, or transmit in any form or by any means. For information regarding subsidiary rights, please contact the Publisher. Preview of *Last of the Talons* copyright © 2022 by Sophie Kim.

Entangled Publishing, LLC
644 Shrewsbury Commons Ave., STE 181
Shrewsbury, PA 17361
rights@entangledpublishing.com

Entangled Teen is an imprint of Entangled Publishing, LLC.

Visit our website at www.entangledpublishing.com.

Edited by Jen Bouvier
Cover design by LJ Anderson, Mayhem Cover Creations
Cover images by Polina Bottalova/Gettyimages
Interior map art and proclamation art by Andrés Aguirre Jurado
Interior design by Toni Kerr

ISBN: 978-1-64937-431-8
ISBN: 978-1-64937-663-3 (OwlCrate Edition)
Ebook ISBN: 978-1-64937-437-0

Manufactured in the United States of America

First Edition December 2023

10 9 8 7 6 5 4 3 2 1

entangled teen
an imprint of Entangled Publishing LLC

*To all those who have known the weight of darkness
and still shine. You're stronger than you know.*

And to Q, my own personal sun

To Kill a Shadow is an exciting fast-paced romantic fantasy that ends on a hopeful note. However, the story includes elements that might not be suitable for all readers. The death of a loved one, murder, blood, spiders, fictional hallucinogens, suicide, vomiting, descriptions of past parental violence toward a child, and descriptions of past torture are mentioned in the novel. Readers who may be sensitive to these elements, please take note.

FORTUNA

MOON GOD'S TEMPLE

RAINA'S TEMPLE

THE MIST

THE MIST

REALM OF ASIDIA

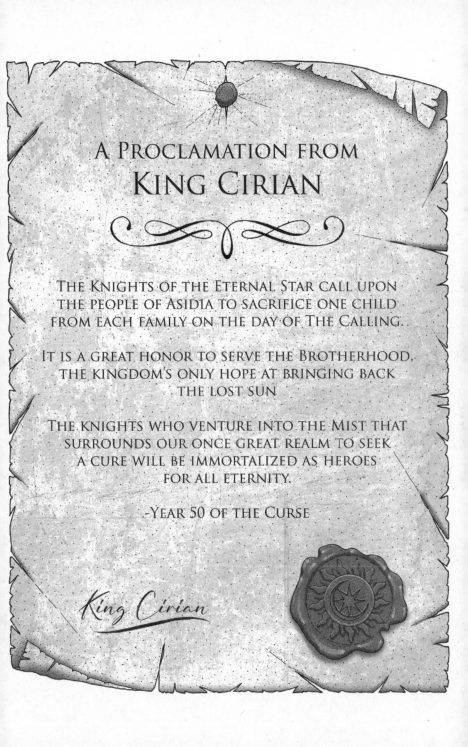

A Proclamation from
King Cirian

The Knights of the Eternal Star call upon the people of Asidia to sacrifice one child from each family on the day of The Calling.

It is a great honor to serve the Brotherhood, the kingdom's only hope at bringing back the lost sun

The knights who venture into the Mist that surrounds our once great realm to seek a cure will be immortalized as heroes for all eternity.

-Year 50 of the Curse

King Cirian

Chapter One

Kiara

The sun hasn't risen in days, and the people have begun to panic. I fear that if the sun and its goddess don't return, the world as we know it will delve deeper into the shadows.

Letter from Admiral Liand to King Brion,
year 1 of the curse

Few people knew that the night spoke.

Even fewer knew how to answer when it did.

Right then, it was taunting me. The hissing winds and the bloodred moon caused the hair on the back of my neck to rise, the crimson halo an omen of the cruel grief that would soon reach into my chest and make a home there.

A curse rumbled up my throat, drowned out by Liam's relentless snores across our shared room. Nothing could wake that boy, not even one of my colorful curses that turned Mother's ears red.

It was nearly morning, the telltale twittering of a starwing filtering through my cracked window. Some said starwings were the gods' spies, but I believed they were only birds, nothing more.

One of the creatures hopped onto my windowsill, its black feathers shimmering with speckles of purple, its downy underbelly a vibrant blue. It stared at me with its dark, beady eyes before taking flight, its melodious song trailing behind.

Apparently, I wasn't anyone worth spying on.

I returned my attention to my lap, my favorite dagger resting in my gloved hand.

As I twirled the handle, I cursed Raina, our glorious and forgotten Sun Goddess. If she hadn't left us to rot in the night, then today wouldn't be happening.

Liam wouldn't be taken. Not by *them*—

The damned Knights of the Eternal Star.

They'd sweep into our village and steal all eligible boys, forcing them to journey into the cursed lands—into the Mist. A place where no mortal would dare venture. After the Goddess Raina had left, the Mist had risen up like an incurable malady, and our arrogant king had been fighting for a cure ever since. With crops failing, and people starving, he was working against time to produce a solution. A solution he believed could be found where death bloomed.

I just thought him to be a fool.

Hope is a dangerous thing to possess.

"Do you ever sleep?"

I jerked against my headboard as Liam's long lashes fluttered open, his twin pools of blue eyeing me skeptically in the dim.

"No," I answered, flicking a match on the bedside table and reaching for the candle. The wick caught flame instantly, and Liam let out another grunt when the light hit his eyes.

"I already miss my bed." Liam groaned.

"You're *still* in bed." I chuckled, though it was strained. My red tresses brushed my cheeks as I shook my head.

"What time is it, Ki?"

While the mood was dour, it was impossible to stop the grin forming on my lips. Ki, the nickname Liam had gifted me with when he was little and couldn't say my full name, suited me like a fine leather coat, whereas Kiara sounded too...well, not *me*. Feminine and dainty. A girl with blooms woven into her hair and lips that fashioned pretty words. I was neither dainty nor well-spoken. Not that I ever wished to be.

My eyes drifted to the whirring timepiece beside my cot. "Around six."

"Gods, why must people insist upon waking at such a depraved hour?" Liam tugged the linens tighter, swaddled like a newborn babe.

"Of course you would say that. You'd be stuck in that bed all day if not for me nagging at you to get off your bum." Bounding across the cold planks, I catapulted onto his mattress with a defiant grin, the hinges beneath me squeaking in protest.

"Ki!" Liam griped, his scrawny body trapped below mine. He was a foot taller than my five feet two, but what I lacked in height, I made up for with solid muscle. Muscle I'd worked very hard to attain. The various bruises and scars dotting my body attested to that.

"Liammmmmm," I trilled, holding him in place while my fingers ruthlessly tickled his side. "Waaaake uuuuup." A squeal escaped his thin lips, his cheeks rosy with laughter.

The delightfully high-pitched sounds only fueled my merciless fingers.

"Ki, stop! I mean it!" Liam laughed so hard a snort slipped out, and my riotous cackles added to his.

"You're no fun." I sighed, pulling back to allow him room to breathe. Rocking back on my knees, I surveyed my brother, committing this moment to memory. But when my eyes fell to his chest, I tensed.

"I... I'm sorry, Liam," I whispered, all the glee sucked from my lungs.

His chest rose and fell in uneven and strained movements,

a slight rasp lining each shaking breath.

"It's fine." He smiled, but I didn't miss how his lips twitched at the corners.

"No, it's not. I shouldn't have been so careless. Not when you had another attack only two days ago."

Inhaling and exhaling with practiced care, Liam sought my eyes, his hand wrapping around mine. I hadn't felt his touch in over a decade, the leather encasing my fingers blocking his warmth. "Seriously. I'm okay. Though, you're still a pain in my ass."

"I'll delight in being a pain as long as you keep breathing." I scowled, fumbling to remove myself from the bed and smoothing down my simple black shift. I really should have known better.

"You can brew a pot of coffee to make it up to me," he crooned, the spark back in his eyes.

"Fine. But only because I nearly killed you." I grinned while Liam shook his head. I wasn't at all surprised when he threw a pillow at my back on my way out.

Tiptoeing into the kitchen, I went about boiling the water over the hearth, the single sunfire sconce casting a honeyed glow across thin wooden walls. Mined from the Rine Mountains in the north, the rare gems radiated golden yellow light. They cost a handful of silver each, and we were lucky enough to own *one* in our humble home.

I peered down at the brewing coffee, knowing it wouldn't help my nerves...even if it smelled divine.

What I *needed* was to train with Uncle Micah. My mother's older brother showed up in Cila mere days after the grisly attack that forced me to don the gloves I never removed. At the time, I'd been half alive, half cognizant, and there he was, a stranger that insisted he would train me to defend myself. He'd barely introduced himself before gazing at my hands and shaking his head at what he saw.

"We start tomorrow," he'd snapped, and it was only because of my grandmother's pleading that I listened. Supposedly, she'd been the one to implore him to come. With the entire village aware of what occurred, I would've become a target to more than ridicule. The attack was no ordinary one, and suspicion would inevitably follow me everywhere.

I hated Micah most days, but months turned into years, and those clandestine lessons became like a salve for the budding anger living just beneath my skin.

Today, on the day of the Calling, I'd never needed Micah more.

But there would be no sparring today, no knives and bloodied fists. No curses and sweat. Swallowing the need to lash out at some poor inanimate object, I curled my fingers around the handles of two steaming mugs as I crept across the groaning planks and back to our room.

Shoving inside, I thrust the cup into Liam's outstretched hands. "Here, you heathen."

All I received in thanks was an eye roll, and then he practically inhaled the scalding liquid, his eyes shut in content glee.

"Have I told you lately that you're a decent sister?" he asked when he came up for air.

A compliment? How unusual.

"You could tell me more often. It wouldn't hurt." My shoulders rose in a playful shrug before I indulged from my own cup. The liquid sloshed around the rim, its warm bitterness wetting my lips.

Liam downed an impressive gulp before setting the mug on the bedside table, the wood covered in faint rings from all the other times he'd never used a coaster. I could picture Mother's narrowed eyes now.

"Kiara," he began cautiously, and my stomach swelled with

ice. "I know what today will bring. There's no need to avoid it."
I was planning on avoiding it for as long as humanly possible. "I
am prepared to leave. I've already said my goodbyes."

To his friends. Our neighbors. His soon-to-be-former life.

"I love you, Liam."

If my words moved him, he didn't let on. He merely grunted
before retrieving his mug, gripping it until his knuckles shone
white. Maybe he did so out of awkwardness. Or shock. *I love you.*
I'd never spoken those words aloud.

He knew full well why I uttered them today.

"And I love you, Ki." His throat bobbed, as did mine.

Moments passed, hushed yet comfortable, neither of us
daring to speak. I sensed Liam's affection wash over me from
across the room, and I prayed he felt what my heart couldn't
bear to speak.

That was enough. It had to be.

"Ki—"

Thundering hoofbeats halted whatever he'd planned on
saying.

Lights flickered across the village, gleaming yellows casting
a hazy glow about the streets, a few pale sunfires dotting the
blur of burnt orange.

Liam's eyes hardened to steel. "It appears as though my
time has run out."

CHAPTER TWO

THE HAND OF DEATH

Year 49 of the curse

My blade pierced my brother's heart, cutting off his incessant screams.

He was not my brother by blood, but he might as well have been. We all were family, united by a common goal to save our people. We were supposed to end the curse. Bring back the sun.

I should have known better; family was nothing out here, not in the cursed lands. Not in the Mist.

Yanking my dagger free, I watched as he tumbled at my feet, his eyes wide and accusing. I didn't have the energy to shut them.

The ghostly fog crept about my ankles, winding around my calves and thighs. It reeked of desperation. The rottenness of death. It poked and prodded at my skin, pushing into my mind, its saccharine whispers caressing the deepest parts of a soul I didn't know I still possessed.

Glancing down into the obscurity, to where my brother's body lay shrouded in haze, my eyes landed upon my bloodstained hands. As if to taunt me, the luminous moon shone brighter, its mocking light illuminating the wet red that would never truly wash off.

The breeze shifted, plumes of white dancing up and down the length of my frame like a twisted lover's touch. But the whispers—the ones that urged me to do unspeakable things— were dissipating, the wind stealing the chaos and frenzy that had occupied my mind.

I blinked. The agonizing weight pressing against my chest throbbed as my gaze tore across the murky field.

I spotted limbs—an arm here, a severed leg there. A discarded boot soaked with blood. Unseeing eyes that caught the glint of the moon's light.

Dead. All my men were dead. And I was the last man standing.

My dagger dropped at my side.

And then I, too, fell to my knees.

"Commander," the rough, familiar voice of Lieutenant Harlow interrupted my waking nightmare. "We're nearly there."

I flinched atop my steed. I was surprised to see sunfire-warmed houses and a quaint square in the distance—all the markings of a traditional Asidian town—rather than the miles and miles of open land we'd been traversing the past few days since the last town. And the one before that, and the one before.

Each village we visited, we left behind empty voids and broken hearts.

Cila would be no different.

CHAPTER THREE

KIARA

Do not fear the dark
It was where we were born
And it is where we all shall die

PRAYERS OF THE MOON PRIESTESSES

Grief and heartache saturated Cila's square.

Milly, the seamstress, clutched her son Simon to her chest, her round cheeks flush and wet. Lola and Amelie, our neighbors, sandwiched their sixteen-year-old boy between them, the only sign of Tom being the tufts of raven hair poking out. Even Samuel, the stoic metalsmith, gripped his son Mikael by the arm, an uncharacteristic display of emotion playing across the older man's weathered face.

Mikael's sister, Lilah, caught my eye, her lovely brown eyes clouded with tears. She'd been my first love, my first *everything*, and yet, we hadn't spoken for months. I knew the reason well enough, and it had everything to do with the gossip surrounding me like a shroud—

Stay away.

Kiara's dangerous.

Cursed.

Slowly, Lilah's gaze traveled to Liam, and she bit her full bottom lip before giving me her back. Her apathy stung, but it didn't touch on the other emotions suffocating me today.

To their credit, my parents held back their tears, but judging from their red-rimmed eyes and the dark circles painting their lower lids, they'd shed their fair share of grief the night before.

Mother's black hair hung limply down her back, her head resting against my father's broad shoulder. Her delicate fingers squeezed the pendant tied around her throat, the chain tarnished and the face of the nameless Moon God spotted with age.

Often I wondered why she wore the charm of the Moon God when the day and its light was all she yearned for. Mother simply told me that sometimes it was best to pray to the gods you could see, for perhaps they might listen.

But the Moon God wouldn't help with our failing crops. None of the gods would. After Raina disappeared, all of the gods seemed to disappear, leaving us without direction or guidance. Leaving us a cursed land and people.

I followed my father's dark gaze to where Liam cut through the dense crowd of onlookers. His lifted chin and creased eyes radiated pride, an expression he rarely wore for his son.

I ground my teeth.

While Father would never admit it, I'd often see the glimmer of disappointment beneath his carefully constructed smile.

Liam found my eyes, and the spark glinting in his irises warmed the space in my heart reserved solely for him. With a final nod, he broke contact, marching into line with the others.

He was brave enough to meet the beginning of his demise with grace, and for that, I found him to be the most courageous person I'd ever known.

For the first time in a while, I genuinely missed my uncle. He'd left for the southern lands a week ago without any explanation. If he were here, he'd probably say something profound—or something harsh enough to snap me out of my stupor.

"It's *him*," Mother hissed into my ear, elbowing me gently.

I followed her vehement stare to a man more legend than flesh.

A man they claimed to have been disfigured by the grisly creatures roaming beyond the borders. Allegedly, he'd battled his way home to the capital of Sciona last winter, drenched in blood and reeking of death.

But that couldn't be anything more than gossip.

No one ventured deep into the Mist and returned. Yet, even as I assured myself, I couldn't help but admit that the commander's domineering presence could be felt from a distance.

Boldly, I drank him in.

He exposed no discernible features, his body and face encased entirely in thin onyx metal. All of them wore armor, but the commander's was covered in obsidian spikes, the tips glimmering in the erratic lighting of the torches that lined the square.

A wave of ice weighed my bones, slinking around my thudding heart and squeezing.

I shivered as phantom fingers traced down my spine, the mountain breeze tickling my ears like a whispered caress.

I sensed something here, in this square, that didn't…belong. A *feeling* my late grandmother would declare divine intuition. She died only last year, leaving a yawning void in my heart when she left. Aurora Adair was a force of nature, a formidable woman who believed in the impossibility that was faith.

"What's wrong?" Father's grip on my arm tightened as he peered down at me with concern.

"I'm fine," I ground out, swallowing hard. "I'm just—"

"Sad," Father finished for me, nodding to Liam. "I feel the same, Kiara."

But it wasn't *only* sadness I felt. No. What I felt was akin to waking from a dream, one that had thoroughly dug its claws into my mind, refusing to let go.

My eyes drifted back to the commander as if they were made to see only him.

I watched in fascination as the most feared man in Asidia ran his hands through his mare's wild mane, soothing the beast as it impatiently kicked at the stones.

My pulse hammered against my throat when he lifted his head, his gaze seeming to find me instantly. Almost as if I'd called his name.

I hissed, tearing my eyes away from the commander and directing them to the chipped cobblestones at my feet. I kept my head down until the names of the selected were shouted, and even then, I looked anywhere but at him.

Adam, a brawny seventeen-year-old, stepped up when his name sounded. A tawny leather string kept his fine raven hair from his face, his sharp features as foreboding as his protruding muscles.

I'd known him since we were young. Adam, and boys like him, trained their entire lives to join the Brotherhood of the Knights, even if they hadn't made this year mandatory for all eligible recruits.

I scoffed, my upper lip curling as I glared.

Liam looked visibly out of place beside the others—all tall, gangly limbs, purplish bruises painted below each glassy eye. I cringed at the fear swimming in his deep-blue irises.

He didn't belong there. Not with *them*. It wasn't fair. I would give anything to go in his place. Not that girls weren't allowed, not *officially*, but they hadn't called one girl's name at any of the previous gatherings.

Adam sidled up to Liam, a haughty sneer painting his wicked features.

Just yesterday, he'd cornered me and Liam outside the trading post with his buddies. I had grown used to the snickers and slurs; ever since my accident in the woods ten years ago, people gossiped, and none of it was kind. But when he'd set his vicious sights on my brother—shoving into his chest and calling him an invalid—I'd acted on instinct, punching him square in the face. Whereas I'd laughed when he'd doubled over in pain, Adam hadn't found me fracturing his nose all that amusing.

His nose was still swollen, and the bruises below his eyes had turned a ghastly yellow and purple. I smiled at him from across the street when he met my stare, his eyes narrowing into catlike slits.

I should have known my triumph wouldn't last.

My vindictive smile fell as Adam leaned to whisper into my brother's ears, his dark gaze never once leaving mine. My entire body became stone as Liam's handsome face morphed into a mask of fury. An emotion I'd never seen him wear.

Adam shot me a smug sneer as he pulled away, turning his body to face the commander and the Knights. The final name was being called, this nightmare nearing its end…but whatever vile poison Adam had spewed into Liam's ears had its intended effect.

One second Adam stood there, beaming with pride, and the next, he was a blur, knocked sideways by rushing limbs.

I thought I might have screamed Liam's name, but the world became muffled, the crowded square closing in on all sides.

Blood roared in my ears, and my legs instinctively picked up into a run, bringing me straight over to where Adam twisted my brother onto his back, pinning him to the dusty stones.

I definitely shouted a name, but this time it was Adam's. Or a very foul adjective in its place.

Every head in the crowd swiveled my way before whipping back to the scandalous scene unfolding.

"Adam!" I shouted, nearly upon them. Liam was gasping for air, swinging wildly at his opponent, who held him down with infuriating ease.

"Leave. Him. Alone."

Panting and clawing at the air now, I realized Liam wasn't swinging to strike but struggling to *breathe*.

Anger—raw and red and dipped in flames—overcame me.

And then I was in front of Adam, my fist colliding with his already bruised face. Even beneath the protection of my gloves, my knuckles stung from the impact.

Still I kept going, delivering another hit to his jaw, only satisfied when he pulled back, his bottom lip open and bleeding.

Droplets fell to the ashen stones, Adam's polished boots covered in crimson splatters.

There was a whirl of movement from the corner of my eye. Sparing a furtive glance, I spotted the commander raising a hand, instructing his scrambling men to stand down.

It appeared he wanted to see how this would all play out, and I was more than happy to put on a good show.

"You're going to pay for that," Adam snarled, barreling toward me, his eyes flashing with malice.

With a sly smirk, I ducked beneath his swinging arm, sidestepping his assault with my gloved hands clasped behind my back.

He was strong. Practically taller than two of me. But I was faster. Much, *much* faster.

He probably thought I'd gotten lucky yesterday at the general store, but now he would understand that I worked tirelessly for that *luck*.

Ducking once more, I avoided what would have been a painful blow, diving to the right and spinning before Adam even registered that he'd missed his target.

"Not so cocky now, eh?" I taunted, my copper hair slipping

free from my loose braid. A thin sheen of sweat lined my brow, and my pulse hammered against my throat.

Maybe I was just twisted, but the rush that came with the fight fueled me. Fighting made sense—it was a dance I could learn, a rhythm that soothed.

Adrenaline was better than any drink. Better than a stolen kiss or a cloudless sky. I thrived in its decadent chaos.

When my fist collided with his ribs, he let out a thunderous groan, his lungs emptied of oxygen. The hit wouldn't do much to stop him, but before he could counter, I bowed and kicked my legs, sweeping him clear off his feet—

Into the exact position he had put Liam in.

"You look so much better down there." I hovered above Adam, whose hands were flat against the pale stones, his chest rising and falling with rage. My own breath remained even and assured.

The hair on the back of my neck prickled, and I dared a hasty peek over my shoulder.

As Adam scrambled to his feet, his dignity all but decimated, I found the obsidian helmet of the commander trained my way. I couldn't see a single shred of flesh, his eyes concealed beneath long jagged slats, but I *felt* his gaze.

Goose bumps broke out along my arm, and an unfamiliar wave of uncertainty swam across my skin. Unlike the icy dread that had consumed me earlier, this cold *burned*.

When heavy boots pounded the stones, I forced my eyes from the commander, focusing instead on my brutish opponent. Grunting, I jabbed left, ducked, and then gracefully spun, delivering a blow to the back of Adam's head.

He toppled to the pavement, crashing to his knees as his head bowed forward. The image of Adam's face smashed against the stones would be a memory I'd forever cherish.

Vindictive delight practically radiated from my every pore.

I smiled at the sight of the drool pooling from Adam's mouth, how it mingled with his blood.

He was well and truly out.

I squeezed my eyes. The fight was over. Liam was safe. Adam was deliciously shamed.

But now, it was time to face what I'd done.

Spinning on the heels of my worn leather boots, I faced the Knights, avoiding the whispering crowd that was likely to gossip about this for years to come.

The commander hadn't moved an inch. Every Knight behind him merely faded away, a blur of armor and metal and pointy ends.

"Name?"

I nearly stumbled back in awe. The mighty commander deigned to speak. And his voice...it was smooth and deep, like red wine on a winter's evening.

"Kiara Frey," I answered, shoulders squared and chin raised. I might regret this moment for the rest of my days, but I wouldn't cower. Not even before the likes of *him*. The Hand of Death.

The commander remained frozen. A statue. Lifeless.

I understood why many feared him. He had the vexing gift of rousing terror without moving a muscle. An enviable trait.

My breathing hitched, and as time dragged, my poor heart threatened to combust. My lips parted when he spoke—

"Add her."

What?

My mouth gaped. That was...unheard of, never before done. Women didn't fight. Not in the last half century, at least—

Arms grabbed me before I could comprehend what on this godsforsaken earth was happening.

I hardly registered the fingers digging into my skin, likely leaving bruises that would dot my pale flesh in sickly purples and blues. I didn't take in all the familiar faces in the crowd, nor had I been allowed one final look at my parents or my brother, who hadn't been returned to the ranks.

I didn't have a chance to say goodbye, not as two Knights clad in heavy armor hauled up an unconscious Adam and tossed him on a wagon. Not as fifteen other boys surrounded me on all sides like a falling wave.

All I saw was the commander, and I could sense the cruel smile hiding beneath his helmet.

I was being taken by the Knights of the Eternal Star—

Chosen by the Hand of Death himself.

Chapter Four

The Hand of Death

Do not bother returning until you have what I need.

**Letter from King Cirian to the Hand of Death,
year 50 of the curse**

The girl would make a fine addition to our ranks.

King Cirian had commanded me to find him warriors, and I'd managed to find one amid a horde of children.

Children that would soon die.

But maybe Kiara Frey would stand a chance.

Maybe she would do what all other Knights had failed to do...

And live.

Chapter Five

Kiara

The capital is a cold place. I feel the evil here, how it seeps through the winding streets and invades the black hearts of its people. With every inhale, I sense a presence of wicked intent, and I cannot wait to rid my lungs of its poison. We will not settle here, not when such a horrid place could infect the family we will be blessed to have.

We shall return in a fortnight.

Letter from Stella Frey to her mother, Aurora Adair, year 30 of the curse

There had been no time to wash off the blood.

Crusted red had dried on my black leather gloves, bits flaking away whenever I scrubbed a hand down the front of my tunic.

Every step I took away from my village and toward the capital of Asidia brought back the images. Those final moments of freedom repeated endlessly in my head. Within a blink of an eye, my entire life had been decided. Or what would be left of it.

Isn't this what you always wanted? I thought bitterly. To be anywhere from Cila, to be someone who wasn't tainted by something that happened a decade ago?

But when wishes turn into reality, they never leave you feeling how you pictured.

Right then, I was just numb.

We'd been walking for hours, and while overcome with exhaustion, I shoved on, pushing closer to the front of the line, to the helmeted commander.

The other recruits hadn't taken too kindly to the lone girl walking beside them. Only a dark-haired boy with a freckled nose trailed at my heels, a half smile on his face whenever I glanced in his direction. I scowled, twisting back to where the Commander of the Knights rode upon his black steed.

Glaring at the back of his head didn't have the intended effect, and he never once looked back. I was no one to him. A grunt.

Another four hours later, the bastard deigned to speak.

"Welcome to Sciona, lads." The commander twisted in his saddle, his helmeted head immediately landing in my direction like he'd known where I walked all along. I flinched. I couldn't see his eyes, but I felt his stare, searing into my skin and making a home.

Instinct told me to dip my chin, but Uncle Micah would have told me to never back down. *"Never lower your eyes in the face of death,"* he'd say during one of our many covert training sessions in the nearby woods. *"You shouldn't fear dying, only failure."*

Dying didn't sound too great either, though.

He finally turned away, aiming for the imposing gates of the capital.

I couldn't help but feel as if he'd branded me right then and there, my cheeks flushing warm. This was the man who had taken me from home and everything I knew. Yet the truth was, I was grateful; Liam would've been dead within weeks, had he been chosen. I, on the other hand, could survive this. My uncle had taught me well, even if his methods were less than humane.

Once, when I was thirteen, he'd shackled my wrists and placed a blindfold over my eyes, delivering me fifteen miles from home. It'd taken me two hours to pick the lock, and another eight to find my way home without the use of stars to guide me.

When there wasn't a choice, all one could do was fight or die. Besides, I had been molded into a warrior, and a warrior I would be.

Lifting my chin, I noted the royal-crested soldiers lining the walls, all shouting orders upon our arrival.

Flashes of crimson cloaks and muscled limbs worked to lift the spiked iron gate protecting the city from attack, not that there were any of those. King Cirian slaughtered anyone even remotely considered a threat. He'd butchered his predecessor, King Brion, with ease years after the curse fell and anarchy ensued. Not even the famed sun priests and priestesses dedicated to Raina strayed close to the capital, too fearful of the newly appointed ruler. They were rumored to be covertly hidden away in towns across the realm, supposedly awaiting the day their Goddess came back and they could return to their mysterious temple located somewhere in the southern mountains.

I imagined they'd given up their devotion long ago.

The recruits moved as a unit, assembling like lost children as the Knights ushered us through the gates. I felt like I was marching to my death, the cackling crows circling above doing little to dispel my growing anxiety. If the sight wasn't an omen from the gods, I didn't know what was.

The unnaturally large birds pecked at the severed heads decorating the rusted spires.

I wondered if they were so large because they were well fed, as I counted at least fifteen heads currently impaled on the wall. Some of the victims appeared fresh, others picked at so thoroughly that their features were unrecognizable. There was no mistaking what they were—a warning.

The stone-faced soldiers of the King's Guard wore deep-red tunics and black trousers, the royal crest—a crescent moon and star encircled by a sun—emblazoned across their chests. Most paid us no mind, all except those who spotted me among the horde of boys, my long, fiery hair an unwanted beacon.

To those who gawked, I smiled, waving my fingers.

No better way to unnerve a foe than a smile.

Trudging through the main gates, the commander guided us down a narrow street paved with more washed stone. Soaring townhomes constructed of brick lined each side, all painted in varying shades of gray.

Paying no heed to the ignorant passersby, I swiveled my head around the curving street, admiring the impressive straight lines and rigid architecture of the somber capital.

Intricate sunfire lampposts made of winding silver were erected every thirty feet, a potted charcoal fern positioned below each one.

I noted not one stone was out of place, the outsides of the homes pristine and well maintained. If not for all the gray and white, Sciona had the potential to be striking, charming even. Yet all I felt when looking at it was sadness. No children laughing and playing in the streets. No shouts of vendors and gossiping townspeople. Just the harsh gray and quiet.

After rounding a particularly warped bend, the imposing palace of Sciona came into view, the sight striking me like a rock to the stomach.

Towering hundreds of feet above our heads, a castle fashioned of opaque, dense glass touched the clouds. It was the color of moonshine, reminiscent of steel. Two immense twin spires rose into the sky, the tips sharper than any blade as they pierced the heavens. At its base, thousands of loose sunfires glowed, illuminating every sinister angle and trenchant edge.

Some might say it was beautiful.

I was not one of those people.

A Knight with dark auburn hair waved us beyond the palace's main gates to a gravel-lined garden brushing against the fortress's walls.

I ran my hand across one of the cold marble statues we passed.

Raina, the lost Goddess of the Sun, had been erected beside Arlo, God of Earth and Soil. His features were hard as if disappointed, though his face was weathered and wise, and in many ways, he reminded me of Micah. The muscled form of Lorian, God of Beasts and Prey, loomed before Silas, the Water God, with his lithe body and long limbs.

And in the center was the Moon God, his serene face a thing of haunting beauty. His true name had been lost or erased over the years, and no two books of lore referred to him the same way. Not even his famously eccentric priests and priestesses knew of his true appearance, and I'd often wondered how a whole realm could've forgotten. But stranger things had happened.

Of course, my idol was missing from the main gods and goddesses. Maliah, Goddess of Revenge and Redemption, was a force to be reckoned with, and certainly a hero to many warriors. But, like most of the less powerful deities, she wasn't given the credit she was due.

Beside the statues was an impressive fountain of a horse at a gallop, its front legs rearing as water splashed around its hooves. Etched across its massive back was the fiery insignia of the Sun Goddess, a polished dagger piercing a blazing sun—an emblem the Knights themselves had adopted.

The horse had to be Thea, Raina's legendary mare.

A hand grasped my gloved one, yanking me forward. The freckled lad who'd grinned at me earlier. I flinched, every nerve in my body electrified by the unaccustomed contact. Slowly, I pulled my hand from his grasp, but not before giving him a smile I knew didn't reach my eyes.

"Keep silent and follow me."

The order came from the auburn-haired Knight, the one who I guessed was second in command. Dismounting his steed, he gave a subtle nod, the rest of the men following suit. Stablehands appeared out of thin air, hastily reaching for the reins of the wearied mounts.

"Come," Second commanded, waving a hand.

He probably had some over-the-top manly name, like Hawk or Steel. I wondered if his face would crack if he smiled.

Maybe I'd test that theory.

Second guided us through a narrow archway next to the stables, sunfires held in dusty sconces illuminating the glass walls and painting the earthen floor a deep moss. We avoided the main entrance to the palace entirely, entering through a mysterious corridor where strapping Knights marched by on occasion, only stopping to dip their chin at Second.

After many minutes passed, the tunnel sloped downward, bringing us *below* the heart of the palace. The elected official from my home of Cila had gone to the palace just last year for the annual summit with the king. While he hadn't ventured below, he'd spoken of the many rumors floating around the capital.

Among the gossip of torture, clandestine parties, and other such debauchery, one rumor claimed that the Knights were kept underground like the king's grisly beasts. It appeared that the official had been right.

While I wondered what the rooms above held—the countless treasures and obscene luxury they likely boasted—I had the sneaking suspicion I wouldn't be permitted. The wealthy and the nobility of Sciona probably didn't wish to see the faces of the hardened warriors who protected their lives, content to live in ignorance. Still, my imagination flourished, even though I hardly cared for such excessive extravagance.

Another minute of marching, and the corridor opened into a circular room, a massive iron chandelier hanging from the center.

Hundreds of ivory-colored candles flickered from above, shining light upon the various weapons lining every inch of the daunting rotunda. The sight of so many swords and daggers and bows nearly brought a tear of joy to my eyes.

Maybe this wouldn't be so bad after all. Liam always said I needed to be more positive, so I supposed he'd be proud of me now.

The commander came to a halt directly below the chandelier, a dark shadow amid the flames. I wished he'd remove that cursed helmet.

"Listen up," Second shouted, his thunderous command sending chilling reverberations through my chest. Even the candles wavered at the sound of his voice. "You'll all be assigned a number and a bunk. Two changes of clothes await you, so take care of them. You will not be afforded more."

He scanned the shuffling crowd, assessing his new charges with distaste before he said, "You may address me as Lieutenant Harlow. I will lead you in your training here. Now, form a line before Brother Damian and Brother Carter. They will be giving you your number."

Okay, Second had a name. It was fitting. Frankly, Hawk might've been a smidge better.

The brown-haired boy who had yet to leave my side settled into line behind me.

"I heard what you did to that prick Adam," he whispered at my back. I didn't turn, so he continued, "The boys from your village said you moved like a shadow beast, and that he was on his ass in a minute."

A slight exaggeration. It had maybe taken three.

"I'm far from a shadow beast," I said on a shiver. My skills were above average, but nothing compared to the creatures that lived to serve the darkness. Supposedly able to adopt human forms, they were composed of nightmares and ash and were so swift they devoured the souls of their prey within a heartbeat.

"My name is Patrick." He shifted closer, even though the line hardly budged.

With a sigh, I turned around, finding that same half smile on his full lips. He looked so damn eager to make friends, I almost felt bad.

"Kiara. Friends call me Ki." Not that I had many of those. Only Liam. My heart twinged at the thought of never seeing him again, and I turned my back to Patrick before he could see my mask fall.

It didn't take long before we approached Damian and Carter, their faces stern and unyielding.

The former appeared to be in his mid-twenties, while the latter boasted a thick gray-and-brown beard and wrinkles creasing his brows. He reminded me of Cila's blacksmith, a man who scowled more than he smiled and tossed horseshoes at the children bold enough to enter his shop.

I immediately liked the older Knight.

"Twenty-six," Carter shouted, thrusting a slip of dusty-white parchment toward me, the number scrawled onto the paper in messy strokes. He spared me a curious glance, his cold blue eyes softening. One corner of his lips lifted, but then fell just as quickly. "Go on, then, lass." He jerked his shaved head to the right.

Patrick got twenty-seven and practically tripped on my heels to keep up.

A lengthy hallway stretched out before us, crimson-painted doors on either side, all flung open. Our room was the third door on the left at the end.

I wasn't at all surprised by the two dozen or so narrow cots with paper-thin pillows and moth-eaten blankets. I might be a highly trained fighter, but I still enjoyed a comfortable pillow, and these accommodations were hardly luxurious. Sighing, I snagged my pack of fresh clothing, eager for a bath.

My boots skidded over the stones, and Patrick bumped into my back with a thud.

Bath.

Gods, I hadn't thought this through. There was no way I'd strip in front of this sorry lot, and while my dignity was at an all-time low, it was still *somewhat* intact. There were also my hands to consider. The second the boys uncovered my secret, I'd have more to worry about than nakedness.

My fears flourished minutes later, my pulse racing at the sight in front of me.

The bath was a single pool in a dimly lit chamber, the water filtered out by whirring mechanics. Pine-scented soaps were distributed, and the boys shed their clothing without thought, flinging soiled linens to the side before rushing into the rectangular pool.

There was absolutely no way I would expose myself here. Privacy was nonexistent.

"Do you...do you need help? Well, not *help*, per se, but..." The awkwardness on Patrick's face was evident. I desperately needed to bathe, my skin and hair reeking of the road and all of its many, *many* smells.

"I'll pass on your *help*, Patrick," I replied with a grimace, striding over to where a lone Knight stood watch, his back pressed against the steel-colored wall behind him. He looked a year or two older than me, his face boyish and not yet scarred by the weight of Knighthood. He must be a newer initiate, which made sense as to why he'd be in charge of bath duty. I could tell by his narrowed stare that he wasn't pleased.

"Um, excuse me, sir," I began, waiting until his brown eyes flickered my way. "Is it possible to bathe after everyone has left?" With a rumbling sigh, he turned his head my direction. A moment later, his gaze fell to my chest, a tinge of pink dyeing his cheeks.

"Recruits who have wished to bathe privately in the past have chosen to do so after dinner. But be quick about it," he added gruffly, turning away and indicating that the conversation was clearly at an end.

I thanked every god I could think of.

Avoiding every naked body in the packed room overflowing with boys, I hastily made my way to our room, plopping onto my assigned cot with a groan.

If only Micah could see me now.

Knowing him, he'd probably laugh his head off.

Chapter Six

The Hand of Death

You won't see him coming before your throat is already slit and death is swallowing you in its embrace. If the Hand of Death had a soul, it was lost long ago.

Excerpt from The Legends of Asidia

I hadn't bothered to remove my muddied traveling clothes. Which worked in my favor, as seconds after entering my chambers, a slip of paper slid beneath the gap of my door.

There was no question as to who'd sent it.

Sighing, I walked to my armoire and retrieved my tools of destruction. I owned over twenty blades, all of varying sizes and used for different reasons: to warn, maim, or kill.

Tonight's mission would be quick.

I stole through the inner sanctum and slipped past the gates, my weapons concealed beneath my leather jacket. Not one person dared look my way.

I was death. And people with a decent head on their shoulders tended to avoid me.

I snuck through the servants' back entrance to a townhome in the richest part of the city. Only nobles and upper-class men and women lived in the eastern part of Sciona, their doors unlocked as if on a dare. No one robbed Cirian's chosen—except for me.

Too bad I would be taking a lot more than coin tonight.

Shutting off my mind, I grasped my dagger and went to work.

CHAPTER SEVEN

KIARA

I'm writing to you as if you might ever read this letter. What you did for me makes me want to hate you. Your actions resulted in my best friend being taken from me, and now I'm left alone in this backward town. It's ironic, as even as I write this pointless letter, I cannot help but miss you and wish I could pull you into one of the tight hugs you despise so much.

UNMAILED LETTER FROM LIAM FREY TO HIS SISTER, KIARA FREY, YEAR 50 OF THE CURSE

The hall where we dined on wild boar and seared salmon contained long wooden tables and narrow benches. The walls were built of stone, not glass like the upper portion of the palace, the dark slabs glittering in the light of several sunfires captured in sconces. I shivered, taking in the somber surroundings, noting they lacked the one constant I'd grown accustomed to over the years.

Asidia was home to a superstitious lot, and I supposed they had a right to be.

People in my village collected tiny marble statues of the gods, and most constructed altars devoted to Raina. Intricate tapestries and fine candles and countless detailed illustrations honored the immortals, and there wasn't one home devoid of such signs of faith—whether feigned or genuine.

Aside from the statues in the garden, I'd seen no other depictions of the gods in the Knights' sanctum, and while I wasn't particularly religious, I found I missed their familiar steadying presence.

Practically inhaling my meal, much to Patrick's obvious amusement, I leaned back, a hand resting contentedly on my belly. Weeks had passed since it had been anywhere near full. Perhaps I should've felt guilty for indulging when so many went without, but I was too content to feel shame.

"I can't," Patrick sighed, motioning to the food. "I'm entirely certain the boar is still alive."

I laughed as he wrinkled his nose. "You need to eat. Besides, it's not too bad and who knows when we'll next get such fine fare." I picked at his plate and shoved a piece in my mouth, beaming wickedly. He couldn't truly be serious—food was just as precious as coin lately.

Patrick pushed his plate toward me. "Then you can have mine. You deserve it after dealing with Adam."

I was prepared to protest, as we both needed our strength, but Patrick began finishing off his loaf of bread, seemingly satisfied. When he shot me a pointed look and raised a lone brow, I gave in and devoured the rest of his meal.

A part of me suspected he was simply being kind, and that part rebelled against accepting his offer. I wasn't accustomed to such generosity, but in the end, my stomach won out over my pride.

Before long, a gong sounded, our short-lived dinnertime at an abrupt end.

There was a mass of flailing bodies as everyone scrambled to the rooms, a few scuffles breaking out in the rush. All I could think about was finally wiping the grime off my body.

That, and the lack of an audience.

"Night, Ki," Patrick said, lying down on his cot. He pulled the thin blanket up to his chin, giving a little shiver from the chill.

"Goodnight," I replied, smirking as he struggled to find a comfortable spot. In a way, he reminded me of Liam, and for a moment, I pictured my brother resting in Patrick's place.

I was glad I was chosen. There was no more doubt.

After everyone settled for the evening, I wandered down the corridor to the bathing chamber. As promised, not a soul was in sight.

Thank the cruel, wicked gods.

My fingers worked at the tiny buttons of my shirt, eyes fluttering shut as crisp air kissed my bare skin. My trousers dropped to the stones, stiff from dried mud and other things I wished not to dwell too long on.

The final things to go were the gloves.

With a sigh, I peeled off the thick leather one finger at a time, my heart dropping into my stomach at the sight of the naked flesh. No matter how much time had passed, I'd never get used to it.

Raised welts rose up from my palms. They graced the back of my hands, each finger touched with the same harsh onyx and blue lines that spread across me like sickly veins.

Wasting no more precious time feeling sorry for myself, I padded to the edge of the pool, lowering onto the first rocky step. The opaque waters were warm, effervescent bubbles traversing along the perimeter as the filter whirred.

My lips curved into a hesitant smile—my first true smile of the day—and I drifted down the tapered stairs, wading through the water until it reached my shoulders. I let out a contented groan.

My life had gone to shit, but at least I'd be clean.

Taking my time washing, I mercilessly scrubbed each inch

of my body, using my nails in places where the mud refused to part. Once satisfied I'd rid myself of the foul stench of the road, I turned to my hair, lathering the cheap soap and kneading my scalp.

I lingered underwater longer than necessary when rinsing my hair, relishing the eerie silence. My heart thundered in my ears, the only sound in the murky stillness. Down there, I could imagine I was back home with Liam and Micah and my favorite stretch of woods. Beneath the safety of the water, I could pretend nothing had changed, even if change was all I'd yearned for.

My lungs refused to let me fantasize for long.

Bursting to the surface, I sucked in air, reality crushing me with every sharp inhale.

It was the growl of a curse that had me jerking my head around, my wet hair coiling around my shoulder. I couldn't help the gasp that escaped my lips.

Behind me, with his hands stilled on the button of his trousers, stood a bare-chested Knight.

I joined him in his cursing, dipping below the water and covering my breasts with my scarred hands—though that was hardly necessary, as I doubted he could see through the dense layer of mud and foam.

I was helpless to do anything but ogle him, my eyes traitorously slipping to his toned stomach, which I was stunned to see was covered in pink scars and raised lesions. They traveled across his rippling abs and dotted his pectorals, some of the wounds not fully healed.

But his face…

In the low light of the torches, I took in his features—a masterpiece and a thing of ruin. He was young, likely a year or two older than my eighteen years.

Straight raven hair tumbled across his forehead, playfully

curling around his ears. The hazy yellow glow of the flames highlighted his cutting jaw and high cheekbones, which could have been weapons all by themselves. And his lips, well, I'd never seen a man with such full lips before, yet somehow, they fit him well.

But it was the left side of his face that added to his unearthly beauty. Two red scars—starting above his eyebrow and ending at his razor-sharp cheekbone—cut across his eye, which was nearly devoid of a visible pupil and held a milky-blue hue. The color was unlike anything I'd ever seen before, but beneath the clouds of roiling ash and shadows, beyond the mystery of his stare, was a spark of fire, its light fighting to break free from the darkness. A look I sometimes recognized in my own reflection.

He captivated me wholly and without apology.

"What are you doing in here, recruit?" he barked, dropping his hands to his sides, a look of surprise granting him a boyish glow.

I squeaked in reply, water sloshing around me as I angled my feverish body, all the while scolding myself for admiring him.

"I was told I could come here after dinner and bathe. In *private*," I enunciated, regaining what little composure I had left.

There wasn't much to work with.

The Knight showed no visible reaction to my words, but his eyes flickered to the stone floor. I might have been mistaken, but his pallid cheeks appeared washed in pink.

"I see," he ground out, a note of agitation deepening his voice. Hesitantly, he raised his gaze, his tone severe as he said, "Well, I usually reserve this time for myself."

"Then it appears as though we have a problem." I spoke without thought, though fire burned in his brown eye as though he secretly enjoyed the challenge as much as I did.

He was a distraction, and gods knew I needed one.

He shoved his hands deep into his trouser pockets, leaning

back on his heels. I kept my attention on his brooding face, denying myself glimpses of his strapping physique.

I wondered who he was. If he were some grunt or an illustrious officer. Based off his many scars alone, I suspected he'd been with the Knights for some time.

"For a recruit, you're awfully brave," he muttered, his nostrils flaring slightly.

I shrugged. "Isn't that the whole point? If I wasn't brave, what use would I be to the king? Though, I suppose even the brave die out there."

His right eye darkened. "Perhaps brave isn't the right word for you, then," he remarked dryly, assessing me with cold detachment.

Cocking my head to the side, my smile grew shrewd, and I savored every thrum of my wildly beating heart. "If you're insinuating that I'm dim-witted, then maybe it's *you* who should embark on some inner reflection."

Dropping my hands from my chest, I rose dangerously close to the top of the dense water. That tinge of pink on his cheeks deepened.

I had his full attention.

The Knight held my gaze, his milky-blue eye a cloud of mystery. Something flashed across his face, and I might have believed it to be intrigue, had I been in my right mind.

I doubted a recruit had ever spoken to him this way, especially face-to-face. But a little scarring wasn't enough to frighten me, of all people, away, and the adrenaline that came with challenging him gave my lungs new life.

"I'm more than open to share." I smiled, feeling bold and altogether unhinged. "If you're still wishing to utilize your scheduled bath, that is." It was a taunt, nothing more, but my heart plummeted as I awaited his response.

"I take it back." His muscled arms rippled as he crossed

them over his chest. "I do believe there to be a third option, little recruit."

"And what is it you think now?"

The Knight and I faced off, neither one of us breaking contact. But I never received his answer. Instead, he turned around abruptly, giving me his equally muscled back. An onyx tattoo twisted around his shoulder, three interwoven circles with odd, vine-like branches curving around the loops. It was a shame he was too far away for me to get a decent look.

"I'll be back in five minutes. I expect this room to be empty upon my return."

I stared, open-mouthed, as he marched away, his steps heavy.

Either I hadn't learned my lesson, or I simply wasn't done playing, but I opened my mouth one more time.

"Wait!"

His boots froze, though he kept his back to me. It wasn't an altogether displeasing view, I hated to admit.

"What's your name?" *Besides Sir Tall-Rude-and-Growly?*

His shoulders tensed, the only sign he heard me. "Commander Jude Maddox."

Shit. All air rushed from my lungs.

The *commander*.

I'd just verbally sparred with the damned Hand of Death, the same man who'd taken me in place of Liam. I hadn't recognized him without his helmet.

"Five minutes, recruit, and this better not happen again."

And then Jude—Jude Maddox, Commander of the Knights— was gone, leaving me speechless for the first time in my life.

CHAPTER EIGHT

JUDE

Only through our devotion and prayer can we hope to appease the Sun Goddess Raina. And perhaps we can convince her to take mercy on our world. Darkness and its shadows feed off the light of souls, and the warriors of the night are so very hungry.

EXCERPT FROM ASIDIAN LORE: A TALE OF THE GODS

I should never have picked her.

I thundered down the hallway leading to the officers' rooms.

She hadn't known who I was at first, but she sure as hells did now. I wondered if she'd be so bold the next time we spoke. A part of me wished she would. Something had sparked to life in my chest at the challenge in her piercing amber eyes, and a piece of myself I'd long ago believed dead had taken a deep breath.

Kiara.

A pretty name for a lethal fighter. The second I'd seen her toss that bully over her shoulder in Cila, I'd known she'd make a better soldier than her brother. I hadn't witnessed such fire, such passion, during a brawl in years, and the way she moved, like smoke on the breeze, had my heart thundering in my ears.

"Rough day?"

I glanced over my shoulder. Isiah quickened his pace to catch up with me, a sheen of sweat lining his brow.

"You could say that," I grumbled, refraining from rolling my eyes. I'd known the man for years, and he understood me better than any of the other pricks bearing the sacred emblem. He also knew when not to push. Now was such a time.

After the swift killing of Lord Paldyn—a would-be rebel sympathizer—all I'd wanted was to be alone and wash the shame from my body. What I hadn't expected was to come across *her*, the damned girl who had thoroughly unsettled me, her shrewd eyes digging into my skin, judging me as if she'd known exactly what I had done but an hour before.

"Tomorrow will be fun, then." Isiah snickered, slowing his pace before stopping at his door and crossing his broad arms. "Better get some rest, Maddox." He cocked a dark brow and added, "You look like shit."

I grunted but said nothing, and Isiah's laughter followed me down the hall and past the door leading into the commander's suite.

The room was sparse and neat, just how I liked things. Orderly. Uncomplicated. My life didn't leave much room for anything other than cold efficiency.

But tonight... Tonight had been the first time in years I'd felt that old and familiar heat flare in my chest, that blissful warmth. It both soothed and pissed me off.

I'd been living in a constant state of numbness since losing all of my men to the Mist last year. After the atrocities I'd committed, after I had allowed the influence of the cursed lands to consume me, I felt like nothing more than a fraud. And in my mind, I hardly deserved the basic decency of feeling anything else.

I didn't even bother undressing before flinging myself on the bed, the hinges squeaking beneath me. Tomorrow would be far from *fun*. And something told me recruiting the defiant fighter would be a mistake I'd rue for years to come.

T hat evening, well into my second hour of failed sleep, a sweeping rush of soothing frost, a whisper of a breeze, weighed my lids.

A hint of mint and forest skies breathed into my lungs, the scent as familiar as it was startling. Sleep had finally embraced me, although it wasn't peace I found beneath the veil of unconsciousness.

The Mist scaled the walls of my mind like tendrils of trapped smoke inside a vase. Swirls of ash and silver lightning leaped among the bluish plumes, the current sending shivers up and down my spine.

Why did I always have to come back to this place? I couldn't even escape it in my dreams.

Bone-white branches rose like gnarled blooms from the ground, leaves of silver and blue glinting in the light of the moon. If I didn't know any better, I would've thought it beautiful. But I knew the truth, had lived through the horrors concealed in the thick brush.

I ambled uncertainly ahead, and with every step forward, the burning in my chest heightened, changing and morphing into something new. Something frightening.

Clouds of ash glided away as an ethereal silhouette loomed in the distance. I came to an abrupt halt.

A charcoal hood draped low across her pallid face, the only visible part of her being a pointed chin. A bone-chilling breeze picked up the ends of her cloak, revealing a golden lining that blinded with brilliance. My feet ceased to move, the sight of the gilded cloak stealing my breath in the most unusual of ways.

Such a shade. Such mesmerizing, golden beauty.

The woman before me, a mixture of shadows and light, tugged gently at the hood that covered her. I ached to see her face, to regard the mysteries that lay beneath the disguise of obscurity. My heart beat impossibly fast, and the heat I began to crave swept into my chest like the welcome touch of a lover.

All around us, the ivory and blue wisps pirouetted and spun like fine spider silk, the clouds flashing as lightning battled to be released. I yearned for the spark, the power I felt coursing between us. Me and this wraith.

A warning, delivered by a voice that was everywhere and nowhere all at once, bellowed into the dying night.

Beware the black heart. For it stings, stings, stings when kissed by a lover's blade.

My chest rumbled, and a scream fought to be released. The cryptic warning echoed, causing the blood in my veins to freeze.

A death so slow, lips so sweet. One taste, and a thousand deaths you shall receive.

"Maddox." My name sounded from somewhere in the smog, a muffled echo. "Wake up, commander."

The woman's hands trembled as she began to lower her hood, the ominous voice still ringing in my ears. I held my breath, eager to see her face—

"Jude."

My eyes shot open.

Isiah hovered over my bed, watching me in that knowing way of his.

His steel-colored eyes creased at the sides, and I could swear the man saw into my soul and to the darkness that lay beneath.

He never shied away though, not in all the years we'd been together, not even when I snapped at him. He'd merely grunt and leave me to sulk, and then show up the next day with coffee and freshly baked goods from the palace kitchens. I suspected the sweets were more for him, though.

"The recruits are ready," he said. "I told Harlow you'd arrive shortly, but he seems impatient today. Impatient and grumpy."

"He's always impatient, and he's rarely *not* grumpy," I replied, rising from bed and shaking off my nightmare and the cloaked woman whose face I'd been denied. I yanked my old shirt off and snatched a fresh one, going about dressing. "Harlow smiles less than I do."

This earned me a laugh, and I *almost* smiled.

"Gods, you're both insufferable." Isiah ruffled my hair like he did when I was younger, and I glowered. He was about a decade older than I, and he often acted as if I were his pesky little brother instead of Asidia's most illustrious assassin.

"Well, hurry up, then, and try not to frighten off too many recruits today," he added over his shoulder, leaving the room.

I'd argue I did no such thing, but then I caught sight of my reflection in the mirror above my dresser. Sighing, I ran a hand through my disorderly hair.

She *wasn't afraid of you.*

The thought came unbidden, and against my will, I returned to the bathing suite, to the girl who'd stared at my face in wonder, not in fear, and…smiled. *That* had been the most unsettling part.

Shoving away from the dresser with another scowl, I grabbed my boots and yanked them on before heading out the door.

Today, Harlow would line the recruits up in the ring and get a feel for their strengths. I'd watch from afar, noting who stood out and who might be qualified to join our ranks. The lieutenant was unrelenting, worse than I, but he would prepare them for what was to come.

When I reached the outskirts of the ring, I leaned against the walls of the corridor, hiding myself in the shadows.

I always did like this room the best.

The massive chandelier dangling from the ceiling illuminated every inch of the space in an incandescent glow. The finely crafted weapons bracketed to the walls beckoned me closer, but I held my ground and crossed my arms against my chest.

There had to be around thirty bows and over a hundred various designs of daggers and swords. Some shone with jewels embedded in the hilts; others were leaner and deadly. I never wasted time on the ornamental blades, drawn more to the austere steel that could slice through bone without useless baubles.

Boots pounded as Harlow entered the ring, the subtle red in his hair shining like a halo of fire. I tore my attention from the weapons with reluctance and focused on the huddling boys watching the lieutenant with fear in their eyes.

Good. They should be afraid.

"Recruits!" Harlow barked, stopping in the very center of the ring. "I hope you're all rested, for today begins your training."

A lull fell over the crowd of boys, about forty in number.

"Every week," Harlow began, clasping his hands behind his back as he strode leisurely around the trembling trainees, "your number will diminish."

A flash of red caught my eye. *Kiara.* Her vibrant hair had her standing out from the rest, and I was unable to look anywhere else. At her side, a tall, freckled boy pushed closer, whispering something in her ear. Her lips quirked at whatever he said, and I noted how her eyes traveled to the wall of weapons.

That damned heat I'd felt last night resurfaced.

Harlow continued. "Only the best will serve the Knights of the Eternal Star, and those we deem unworthy will be sent to work in the Guard." One corner of his mouth curled in sick delight.

Kiara's face fell. Maybe she'd thought dismissal meant a return ticket home. The Guard boasted nothing but long, grueling days and certain death. The king had far too many enemies for soldiers to live a long life in his ranks. Not that the Knights offered much safety, either.

"Everyone. Backs to the walls," Harlow ordered, the recruits hastening to follow his instructions.

Harlow strolled about the room, scrutinizing the boys he passed with disdain. When he made it to Kiara, he wavered, thin lips twitching into an acrid smirk.

My breath caught, but he continued, passing her. I exhaled my disappointment. I'd selfishly wanted to see her fight again, to showcase the impressive skill that had captivated me. A memory that had yet to release me from its punishing and hypnotizing hold.

"You." Harlow pointed to a muscled lad with cropped black hair and rich brown skin. "In the center."

The boy stumbled hesitantly into the middle, his face a blank mask. Harlow pointed to a blond boy who reminded me of a cat. He had beady eyes the color of unpolished emeralds and a sly smile that contorted his already severe features.

Harlow whirled to them both, excitement lining his cunning eyes. "I'm sure most of you are familiar with the rumors. The legends of the Mist. Of what lies beyond it, *inside* of it. One thing the Knights pride themselves on is their honor."

Honor. I almost laughed. If only they knew the man who presided over the Knights. The king was far from honorable.

Harlow focused back on the two recruits. "We pride

ourselves on chivalry, honor, the old code. But"—he trailed off, meeting the stares of many a fearful boy—"we also know that to overcome what lies beyond, we must be relentless."

Kiara shifted in place, but her stare turned cold. Deadly.

I smiled, unexpected pride filling me.

"That being said"—Harlow jerked his head at both the smirking lad and his muscled opponent—"sometimes you will not be evenly paired. And there are no rules in the realm beyond our kingdom. You do *whatever* must be done."

No one spoke. Not even the asshole Kiara had beaten to a pulp back in her village. He'd been tossed on a wagon and brought here with the others.

Inside, I seethed. I would've sent him straight for the Guard, hells, probably even to the lower ranks of the Patrol, but the lieutenant had argued that we needed as many able-bodied recruits as possible.

Harlow motioned to the two in the center. "Face off. Do *whatever* you must do. There are no rules here in the ring." He gave them his back, retreating to the far side of the room, where he leaned against the stone like a king observing his subjects.

Judging by the way his attention darted back and forth, calculating where best to strike, I was sure that the boy with the feline smirk would make the initial move. But it was the muscled giant whose fist connected first.

It wasn't a hard hit, more like a testing one, and the aggressor appeared almost regretful. His eyes were gentle, the type that looked out of place among such rippling brawn and power. His opponent, whose name—Alec—was shouted above the crowd, didn't stay down for long.

Alec was quick to rise, bouncing on the balls of his feet as he lifted his arms to shield his face. Making no move to attack, he waited until his opponent lunged, a roar ripping from his throat.

There were chants of "Sam"—the larger boy's name—as well as whoops of encouragement from the recruits watching, the arena pulsating with a bloodthirsty energy.

Sam, clearly so sure he would take Alec down, never saw the smaller boy's feet. With a near-graceful sweep of his lean legs, Alec skillfully made Sam fall to the floor with a resounding thud.

I grimaced. His tailbone would be sore for the rest of the day.

Alec didn't slow as he jumped on Sam's torso, straddling him and delivering a rapid set of punches to his handsome face. The boy at Kiara's side averted his eyes, glancing down at his boots, and she sidled closer, almost as if in comfort.

Only when Sam called out in surrender did Alec cease his assault. Quick as the feline I'd likened him to, he jumped to his feet, twisting to face an unsmiling Harlow.

The foreboding lieutenant merely jerked his head and ordered the pair to remove themselves from the ring, compelling a friend of Sam's to rush in and help him stumble back into place. Alec leaned against the wall, a victorious smirk struggling to make an appearance, though he seemed to purposely avoid staring at the boy he'd decorated with bruises.

Once the ring cleared, Harlow resumed his unnerving saunter about the room, looking for his next pair of victims. Kiara's eyes lit up when he slowed near her, and her gloved hands formed into fists as a smile curved her mouth.

She wanted to fight. Not that it should've surprised me.

But then Harlow's focus landed on her companion, and all of her excitement dissipated.

"You."

Her mouth fell open in protest, but the boy shoved his way forward, taking his spot with a kind of bravery that I knew he didn't feel.

Harlow's astute gaze missed nothing. Certainly not the subtle concern causing Kiara's brow to wrinkle.

"And you." He raised his lean finger inches from her heart. "Join your fellow recruit in the center."

I cursed silently. This wasn't what I'd hoped for when wishing to see Kiara fight again. She was obviously more skilled than her opponent. It didn't take a trained eye to see the disparity.

Genuine panic clouded the freckled boy's eyes, and his hands twitched nervously at his sides as he curled them into loose fists.

"Any day now, recruit," Harlow snapped.

Kiara took a step forward, directing a venomous gaze to him. I found myself taking a step as well, an inexplicable fear worming its way into my chest and weighing down my breaths.

Floating to the center of the ring, Kiara assumed the fluid stance belonging to the notorious warriors of the north, her feet spread slightly apart, her hands lightly held before her in loose fists. Her knowledge of their fighting style surprised me, and I wondered how she'd learned it trapped within the small village of Cila.

Her opponent supplied her with a meek smile. When he made a fist, his thumb incorrectly placed inside his clenched hand, Kiara shot one final glower at Harlow.

"Go on, recruits," he cooed. "Fight."

"It's okay, Ki," the boy urged. "Wounds heal."

Yes, wounds healed, but lost honor wasn't as easily mended.

Harlow had matched them unfairly on purpose. I'd seen him glancing Kiara's way the entire trek to the capital. I hadn't ruminated on why until now.

Kiara's friend shifted, bringing his fists to his face, protecting himself. She squeezed her eyes shut, taking in a sharp inhale that echoed in the too-quiet ring. I could practically hear her indecision, the rampant thoughts racing through her mind. It appeared as if Patrick had been the only boy to befriend her, and judging by the way her jaw clenched, she struggled with the order to bestow him harm.

Her lids suddenly snapped open.

Before Harlow could issue a warning, Kiara advanced, delivering two jabs to the boy's upper body. She held back her full force, that much was obvious, but even those softer blows sent him stumbling and falling onto his back.

Snickers filled the chamber as he feebly rose to his feet, resuming his defensive stance. Kiara cringed.

Closing in, she pummeled his chest, sweeping her legs beneath his and knocking him down for the second time in the span of a minute.

Dusting himself off, her friend climbed to his feet. Kiara flinched when she saw him grimace in pain.

"Recruit!" Harlow shouted, spittle flying from his lips. "I told you to fight. To fight without rules or mercy." He motioned between her and Patrick. "There are no friends in the Mist. There are only beasts that wish to claw your faces and taste your blood. And here you are, holding back."

He was right. I knew better than anyone.

Harlow advanced, his heavy boots echoing as he brought himself nose-to-nose with Kiara. Whether brave or just plain arrogant, she didn't relent, didn't turn away.

My heart rate picked up at the determination in her eyes, how she tilted her chin in defiance. I didn't realize I'd drifted closer until the light of the ring hit my face. I couldn't look away, let alone take in a full breath.

"No rules, eh?" she asked, her voice deepening to a violent timbre.

"No rules," Harlow echoed, much to her obvious delight. Her canines poked into her full bottom lip as she smiled.

"Good."

Ducking and swerving around the towering Knight, Kiara swiveled around to his back, serving him with a forceful punch to the ribs. For the first time since I'd known him, Harlow looked surprised.

His shock didn't last long.

Spinning around, he slammed his fist into Kiara's jaw, the force of it knocking her sideways.

A growl left me, but I forced myself to stay in the shadows. The sight of her bleeding face caused phantom flames to ignite within me, my very blood boiling. My nails dug into my palms as she righted herself, wiping the red from her still smiling mouth.

Harlow didn't pause before he attacked, but thankfully, she swerved at the last minute, his fist sailing an inch from her cheek. Bouncing on her feet, Kiara dodged another rapid attack, ducking and twisting as she readied for her own assault.

A powerful punch—right to Harlow's jaw. Exactly where he had struck her.

Delight crept up the back of my neck as a trickle of blood ran from Harlow's bottom lip, his ensuing grin revealing a set of bloody teeth.

Gods, she moved fast. But she was reckless, too reckless to survive long among the Knights. Her impulsivity would get her killed.

Before she could gloat, Harlow clenched his fists, his body a blur of strength and speed.

I could've sworn I heard bones crack as Kiara flew into the air.

The chamber swirled and tilted around me, the chandelier lights muddling together into one continuous line as I watched her tumble into a heap.

Her body hitting the earth was the only sound in the room aside from the thudding in my ears.

There were no snickers or whoops of encouragement from

the recruits. Just an oppressive silence.

I could no longer hold myself back. At the sight of her small form, broken and bleeding on the ground, my heart gave another sharp twinge, and an onslaught of rage drove me into the light of the pit.

Kiara's amber eyes locked on mine as if she knew where I'd been standing the entire time. The heat in my chest grew unbearable the longer I stared at her, and only when her lids fluttered shut did it vanish altogether...

Leaving nothing but frigid cold in its wake.

Chapter Nine

Kiara

So far, the girl appears strong. Maddox chose her,
just as you suspected he would.

Letter from Lieutenant Harlow to King Cirian,
year 50 of the curse

I awoke to a wide-eyed Patrick hovering over me.

"Damn, Ki," he said, nothing but a blur of brown curls and green eyes. They shone with a tangible concern.

"P-Patrick." My voice sounded garbled. That must have been one hells of a knockout.

"How are you feeling?" The three floating Patricks became two.

"I feel like I probably look," I grumbled, the pinch of anger from earlier resurfacing.

Patrick let out a strained chuckle. "Yeah, you don't look too good," he admitted, the coolness of his hand stinging my face. I jerked at the contact, a bolt of fire and unease racing along my jaw. His eyes narrowed into slits before he brightened for me once more.

I hated that look. It made me feel like a fraud. I'd still hurt him in the ring.

"Did I get some good hits in, at least?" I asked, my poor attempt at lightening the mood.

Gods, talking hurt.

"Yeah," he scoffed, shaking his head. "You got in a few." Patrick hunched over, and I saw the bucket he'd placed on a wobbly stool beside my cot. I hissed as he pressed a chilled rag against my bruised and bloodied face, my hands fisting the thin sheets.

I'd wanted to protect him. Somewhere between walking into the center of the fighting pit and Harlow's vicious decree, realization had struck me like...well, like a punch to the gut.

He'd been the only other recruit to approach me, the only person here who had made an effort to show me kindness, to smile and laugh with me. It didn't help that he shared similarities with my brother, who would've been just as kind to an outsider as Patrick had been.

It made me want to do everything possible to keep him safe. Or as safe as possible in the Knights' inner sanctum.

"How long have I been out?" I groaned as I pushed up into a sitting position, my head throbbing and burning. Black specks teased along the edges of my vision.

"An hour," Patrick answered, avoiding my glare. "I was worried about you. I'm shocked you're alive after going toe-to-toe with a trained Knight."

Harlow had wanted to get a rise from me, sure, but I would bet fifty silver coins he hadn't thought I'd *strike* him.

I was going to be the death of myself.

"I can't stay long." Patrick rose, the damp cloth slipping beneath the pink-tinged waters of the rusted bucket. "We have a few drills. Harlow only gave me permission to stay with you until you woke."

That was surprising. I'd thought he'd toss me out on the street or to the Guard the second I'd shut my eyes.

"Patrick." I stopped him before he could turn away. "I'm sorry for—"

"Don't even think about it," he chided, shaking his head. "I barely have a bruise. I knew you were holding back on me, and while you shouldn't have, I appreciate the thought." He was halfway across the room when he paused, a boyish smile spreading. "Now you *can't* get rid of me. I doubt anyone will mess with you after that display."

Patrick loped off, leaving me alone and aching, though my lips curled up at the sides.

Yep, just like Liam. I imagined the two of them would get along exceedingly well. If the handful of boring botany and books of lore tucked neatly below Pat's cot were any indication of their likeness, I wasn't sure what was.

They could keep those dusty tomes to themselves.

I rolled onto my side, wincing at the stinging in my jaw.

While my pride had been horribly bruised—along with my face—I regretted nothing. Harlow *had* said there were no rules. Besides, he hadn't played fair either.

He'd deserved that punch, and I hoped his jaw ached just as much as mine.

I lay back down on my cot, a cruel smile blossoming as I replayed the fight over and over again.

Give me your worst, Harlow.

After the other recruits were snoring peacefully in their beds, I found the strength to haul myself to the bathing suite.

I'd just set down my towel and gone to unbutton my blouse when I glimpsed a swathed bundle from the corner of my eye.

Abandoning my buttons, I ambled over to where a piece of

burlap was tied together with a string. It sat on a wooden stool in the corner of the chamber, and I would have overlooked it entirely if not for the bright red ribbon.

I undid the bow with aching fingers to reveal a clear glass jar.

Unscrewing the lid, I found a jellied ointment that smelled of mint and some medicinal scent. I was about to place the jar back when a slip of a note fluttered to the stone steps.

For your face, recruit.

The crude scrawl had been scribbled in haste with no initial or name indicating who it was from. Yet, I knew. I could practically hear the deep timbre of the commander's voice as though he'd whispered the words across my mind.

Why had he left this here for me?

I'd seen him just before I'd passed out, an unreadable expression marring his face, both of his fists clenched at his sides. He'd watched as I'd struck Harlow and disobeyed a direct order. He likely thought I deserved the punishment of being sent to the Guard, where I'd die at the hands of the king's enemies.

And yet—

Not thinking too long on the act of unexpected kindness, I promptly undressed, folding my clothes and laying my gloves atop the neat pile beside the jar of ointment.

When I finished my bath, feeling better, I dressed and slipped the jar and note inside my trouser pockets.

That night, nestled safely beneath my linens, I applied the ointment to my aching jaw and black eye. My monstrous headache gratefully turned into a dull throbbing.

As I'd slept most of the day, I stayed up most of the night, my arms crossed behind my head as I thought of all I had left behind.

I might have convinced myself I'd lost so much, but the truth, found sometime around midnight, was that I didn't have much waiting for me.

Liam was my brother and friend. Uncle Micah, my trainer. Most times I didn't think he even saw me as a person, only a weapon to be used and honed. He never embraced me as family should, and I'd gone my entire life wishing for just one look of approval. The closest I'd gotten to making him proud was the day I turned fourteen. I'd been late to our session and come across some lost travelers in the Pastoria Forest. A group of thieves had attacked, stealing their few possessions of worth.

I'd plunged into the chaos without thought, managing to defeat two of the four assailants. But the third was a man three times my size. He knocked me on my ass, and I lost consciousness.

When I woke, the travelers were gone, as were the thieves. And hovering above was Micah, his lips curled up at the corners. "You tried, even though you knew you'd fail," he'd said gruffly. "And that's what matters."

When he offered me his hand, I swore my heart leaped out of my chest.

Aside from Micah, I had my parents to consider, although I often felt their disappointment. They might feel love for me, but I was the child who'd made them social outcasts. No matter how hard they tried to hide it, I was the shame they carried, and no number of false smiles could disguise that truth.

It was an evening of brutal realization.

I remembered something my grandmother had once said when she'd caught me coming home with a split lip. I'd been twelve at the time, training with Micah in the woods, and it had been a particularly intense session of hand-to-hand.

Without a word, she'd motioned me into the kitchen, out of my parents' sight, and stooped to her knees, digging around beneath the sink.

When she'd finally reemerged, she'd held a miniature glass jar, the facets glinting in the light of the sunfire. She'd rubbed at the glass, drawing my attention to the pale scar in the shape of a crooked star that ran up the length of her right thumb. An old wound, she claimed, nothing special. Yet whenever I asked her about the odd mark, she'd hush me and tell me to quit being so nosy.

"This will help, Kiara," she'd said, sitting down at the table, medicine in hand. The jar had smelled like the wild trees and the full moon. It had also smelled of mint.

"One day, you will need jars and jars of this," she'd remarked, arching a thin brow while dabbing some of the cool jelly onto my busted lip. Being the little brat that I was, I'd rolled my eyes.

"You're going to get in trouble with that attitude of yours," she'd scolded, even though there was mirth in her voice. "But I think it will be your greatest weapon, child."

"My attitude? I prefer my dagger!" I'd brought the freshly sharpened blade up so that she could see.

Grandmother had given a riotous laugh. "That will help, of course." Her weathered fingers had closed around my wrist, forcing the hand that had clutched my dagger to my side. "But it's what's in here"—she'd tapped the side of my head—"that will get you through the darkest of nights."

I might have been young, but I'd recognized the look that had flashed across her seasoned face. It had been...pride.

"One day you'll see more than you ever thought possible." She'd cupped my face, her amber eyes reflecting my own. "You're the light in my life, Kiara. In more than one way."

I'd never known exactly what she'd meant by that, but those words had haunted me every day for five years.

Grandmother would want me to fight. To succeed. Even if I was surrounded by those soulless Knights. But she was right about one thing—

My attitude was by far my greatest weapon. One I would use to obliterate all doubts that women couldn't hold their own in battle. Couldn't be warriors.

Perhaps it was time to loosen my restraint, to unleash the girl I'd long ago imprisoned.

Fate might have brought me here, but from now on, I would be the one to choose my destiny.

Chapter Ten

Jude

There have been reports of missing people in the villages bordering the Mist. They vanish while the realm sleeps, leaving behind all they own. It is my belief that they are being taken. By whom, I have yet to discern.

Letter from Admiral Jarkon to King Cirian,
year 11 of the curse

I watched from the shadows as Kiara tiptoed back to her room, the jar of healing ointment clutched in her gloved hands. She appeared to never take off those gloves.

Thank the gods she hadn't been too stubborn to take my offering. There'd been a fifty-fifty chance.

The jar had cost me a week's worth of wages, and I wasn't sure why I'd bought it for her in the first place. It wasn't because she was a girl. Kiara could hold her own in any fight, and I imagined that, with her obvious history of combat training, she'd taken a few punches before.

Lying to myself did me no good. I knew the answer well enough.

She made your heart pound for the first time in years.

Fighting and killing had become my everyday life, and after

the initial years of slitting throats and performing whatever method of torture King Cirian requested of me, I no longer felt the same adrenaline. In fact, I hadn't felt much of anything, which had been fine by me. It made every vile act I committed a lot easier.

But now that my pulse was racing and my skin tingled as if microscopic raindrops fell upon me, I knew it would be much harder to shove that feeling down again.

My next stop would be far less pleasant, but entirely necessary.

Shoving off from the wall, I glided down the hallway to the officers' mess hall.

As he always did at this time of night, Harlow stood before the stove, brewing himself a cup of tea. My eyes flickered to the herbs he'd used, a brow raising at the label: dewberry and lavender.

Did Harlow have trouble sleeping as well? Did he close his eyes at night and think of all the criminal things our dear king forced us to do in the name of Asidia and *justice*?

"What do you want?" he snapped, not glancing over his shoulder. How he'd heard me approach was a mystery. I was known for my stealth.

Harlow had been here for as long as I could remember, and while the man often had my hackles rising, I respected him. He was fair, or as fair as men in this world could be.

"What are your plans for the girl?" I asked, trying to sound as bored as possible. My voice came out stiff and strained instead. Inwardly I cursed as I slid into an unoccupied seat next to a round table littered with unfinished card games and half-empty glasses of ale.

Harlow grunted and finished making his cup. "I'm thinking of sending her to the Guard, of course," he said, taking a seat across from mine. My fingers dug into the wood of the table.

"She clearly won't be able to follow orders, and that's going to cost lives. Perhaps the generals there will know what to do with her."

Taking a sip from his steaming mug, Harlow watched me over its rim, his green eyes narrowing in that assessing way of his. He might seem a brainless brute to others, but he played that role for a reason. His enemies would never see him coming when he eventually struck.

"Thoughts on that?" he pressured when I remained silent, pretending to pick at the dirt beneath my nails.

My left eye sparked with the barest flicker of light; once, twice, a third time. It did that occasionally, often leading to headaches.

"Eh." I raised a shoulder, cocking my head. "Might be a waste of a soldier. If what the king plans comes to fruition, we'll need competent fighters. Besides, you won't have to deal with her much longer."

The Mist and its lethal mysteries beckoned. As much as I didn't want to think about it, Kiara and the other recruits *would* likely be dead by the end of the month.

Harlow took another drink, this time indulging, forcing me to hold my breath before he set down the mug a minute later. Sure, I could override any decision he made, but that would look suspicious, and if I'd learned anything from my past, it was to never show anyone your hand.

"You have a point," he grated out, meeting both my eyes. Another reason I respected him; he didn't glance away when his gaze met the left side of my face. He pushed back in his seat and ran a hand through his shoulder-length hair. "She should still be punished, though."

I scoffed. "You were the one that said there were no rules."

One of his brows rose. "I've never known you to care so much about a recruit before, Maddox. What's so special about this one?" he asked. "And please tell me it's not because you haven't had the company of a woman for quite some time." That brow of his lifted even higher.

"My private life is not your problem. Thanks for the concern, though." I crossed my arms and leaned back, matching his posture. "But I haven't seen a fighter like that in ages, and yes, her skills impress me. Besides, isn't it punishment enough that she's the only girl surrounded by a bunch of boys with oversized egos?"

The chuckle that Harlow let out stunned me. "I suppose," he said, grasping his bruised jaw. "But don't expect me to take it easy on her, Maddox. She might be *impressive*, but she's trouble."

I sighed. She was trouble all right. "If she steps out of line again, blame it on me." The words were out of my mouth before I could contain them.

Where the hells had that come from?

If Harlow was just as surprised by my promise as I was, he didn't show it. He dipped his chin in agreement before bringing his cup to his mouth and taking another sip.

Later in my room, once I'd left Harlow to his tea, I shut my lids and surrendered to sleep.

I didn't dream of the Mist, or of the life leaving the eyes of those I'd killed.

I dreamed of pure, radiant light.

CHAPTER ELEVEN

KIARA

Our world will know only despair, should this curse endure.
We cannot survive without the sun, not for long. Already our
crops have been cut by half, and what little food grows is
hardly enough to feed a hungry people. My king, something
must be done, and soon, for I fear rebels will rise and
bring chaos to the land.

LETTER FROM ADMIRAL LIAND TO KING BRION,
YEAR 2 OF THE CURSE

During the ensuing days, Harlow barely glanced my way,
only acknowledging me if delivering an order.

Or a threat.

I'd been surprised I hadn't been removed from the inner
sanctum and tossed to the Guard, but I wasn't about to open
my mouth and question it.

Instead, I performed Harlow's vigorous sets—from push-
ups and sprints to broadsword training and archery. Where many
struggled, I excelled.

I'd been taken back to the forests of Cila with Micah, gaining
bruises and getting knocked off my feet beneath luminous
moons and starry skies. There was something calming about

returning to a routine.

A week of training passed quickly, and while most nights I found sleep the moment my head hit the pillow, tonight, it refused to find me.

I missed my brother and my training sessions with Micah, and my aching heart was restless.

What I needed was a distraction.

Back home, when sleep evaded, I'd lie on my back and watch the sky dance, pretending the glittering stars were listening to my every prayer. Ones where I'd fill the hole inside my chest with adventures and quests. Where I'd be only myself, and people would stare at me in awe rather than in distaste or fear. Maybe then, I wouldn't feel so hollow.

Unfortunately, I couldn't escape the sanctum and lose myself beneath a cloak of stars.

But I could try the next best thing.

Swinging my legs over the side of the cot, I slipped from the room, sneaking through the silent corridor on soft feet. Thankfully, there wasn't a soul drifting through the halls, not at such a late hour, and I was left alone to wander the Knights' innermost sanctum in peace.

After exploring the kitchens and peeking into a few of the private offices, I strayed into a restricted zone, a winding hallway reeking of salt and rot.

The corridor, lined with several locked doors—much to my dismay—narrowed the farther I ventured, but I didn't stop until I'd reached a dead end. An arched entryway with intricate suns beckoned me to a gilded handle in the shape of a crescent moon.

Unlike every other door I'd tried, this one was unlocked, the metal clicking loudly as I shoved my boot against the thick wood. My breath caught as a groaning creak echoed down the curving corridor.

Bathed in white-hot adrenaline, I slipped into what appeared to be a library, a lone sunfire captured within a sconce saturating the large room with a buttery sheen.

Leather-bound books weighed down tall shelves, and haphazard stacks were piled on every available surface. And in the center, surrounded by the towering shelves, wooden tables and chairs were covered in blank pages and splattered ink.

Occasionally, I'd been known to pick up a book, but I found knives far more entertaining.

When the tips of my gloved fingers brushed against the spine of a muted emerald tome, my heart immediately fluttered at the contact. A low call, the muffled sound of a drumbeat, heavy and sacred, echoed in my mind, the pounding growing wild as I pulled the book from the shelf.

Gripping the tome, which lacked a title and author, I flipped open the dense cover and turned to a random page.

I read the first passage my eyes landed upon.

The Goddess Raina was born the day the earth was created.

The world, one that had been cast in darkness, was now glowing and brimming with color. Raina brought joy to the inhabitants of the earth, her light giving birth to new foods and crops and lush verdant trees and shrubs. Flowers blossomed, blooms of bright red and blue and yellow.

The people were well-fed and content, and the God Arlo was pleased.

I paused my reading, wondering what such vibrant flora might look like. Our land cultivated a few species of flowers, though most were dull in appearance. The closest to colorful was the infamous Midnight Bloom. Its velvety petals only opened for one hour each day, exposing its grayish lilac hue, the center a silvery blue that shimmered beneath the moon.

I imagined that Lorian, God of Beasts and Prey, had been

just as enraged by the goddess's absence, as his creatures suffered nearly as much as the humans. The lack of edible flora killed far too many innocent animals.

No one had seen Lorian in many years; the last appearance the god made had been atop his temple thirty years ago, surrounded by the small animals and vicious predators of his own creation. Apparently, Arlo had shown up and chased him back to wherever he'd been hiding for all these decades.

I continued reading.

Raina brought many years of peace and prosperity to the people, and they began to worship her unlike any other god before.

Arlo, whose vanity was immense, grew jealous of the Sun Goddess. He attempted to pluck her from the sky, but she always danced out of his reach. It wasn't until Raina had set her sights on one mortal man that Arlo's plans changed.

This mortal—

"There you are."

The book slipped from my grasp, tumbling to the stones, a single page breaking free. Twisting at the sound of the voice, I glimpsed the intruder's sadistic smile as he stepped into the light. The bruises I'd given him back in Cila had faded, much to my disappointment.

"Adam." I spoke his name like a curse. "What do you—"

I never got to finish my question—not when all the air had been sucked from my lungs.

My knees gave out as pain radiated across my body. Sinking to the floor, I clutched my tender stomach with both hands, my eyes flickering to where Adam's shadow stalked, his hand at his side, a wooden club held tightly in his grasp.

That bastard—

My vision swirled, taunting gray-black smoke lining the

edges of my eyes. Adam had struck me with a damned club.

"Still sore about Cila, are you?" I panted. "I'm sure the Knights got a kick out of me putting you in your place."

He'd gone too far and accosted my brother. No one messed with Liam, and I didn't care that my entire village had watched as I'd disgraced myself in front of the Knights.

It had brought me here in Liam's stead, so I was thankful.

While Adam seethed, I curled my hands into loose fists—

He struck again before I could act, pummeling me with all his strength, sending my body flailing backward and into a bookcase.

"You don't belong here," he bellowed as books rained down on my head. I hissed as each one fell, my skull stinging. "You always acted as though you were better than the rest of us. Better than *me*. But you don't look so high and mighty now. Maybe I can finally see what you hide beneath those gloves of yours."

I'm going to kill you, my mind retorted, even as panic had my body slumping down the bookcase. He couldn't see, he couldn't.

Weakly, I lifted my head and glowered, refusing to let Adam believe he'd won. "Is this because I denied your advances all those years?" I gave a scoff. Even with the label of pariah hanging over my head back home, Adam had still tried to corner me, using what he believed to be charm. When that hadn't worked, he'd resorted to taunts and threats. "You're nothing but a bully, Adam, and one who can't even throw a decent punch."

"Let's see if this"—he held up his club, giving it a skillful spin—"is better than one of my punches."

I couldn't breathe properly, and I was sure he'd managed to bruise a rib. The voice in my head screamed for me to stand, to do anything but accept defeat. But I was so very tired.

I exhaled, preparing for the pain that would surely follow.

But the blow never came.

My lids peeled open, boisterous grunts filling the room as two solid bodies collided. The shock of the crash echoed like irate thunder, the silhouettes wraithlike in the quivering light of the sunfire.

I was suddenly a spectator in a battle between shadows, my eyes wide as I watched them move like billowing plumes of smoke. A resounding thud sent one of the assailants down *hard*. Flashes of silver and swinging fists whirled, and then, there was no movement at all.

It ended just as suddenly as it had begun.

I automatically pushed back, my instincts urging me to get as far away from here as possible. If Adam succeeded—

The victor materialized, the sunfire casting ghoulish shadows across his scarred face. In the dimness, his injured eye glowed, an insidious blue and silver that sent shivers down my spine.

Jude.

I raised my chin to meet his imperfectly handsome face as he closed the gap between us. For once, my mouth didn't open and spill whatever nonsense came to mind. I was stunned into silence.

Beyond his frame, I made out Adam's unmoving body, his chest rising and falling slowly. He'd been knocked out cold.

Jude bent before me, his hands resting on his knees. The sunfire played across the severe features of his face, sharpening the angles of his jaw and cutting cheekbones. His hair shone a brilliant blue-black, and my fingers had the odd need to brush through the strands.

"You seem to attract trouble, recruit."

His voice sent a fluttering of tingles into my stomach, and I cursed the peculiar warmth that followed.

"I-I couldn't sleep," I stammered, which brought a touch of heat to my cheeks. Realizing I was still slouched in a defensive position, I straightened my shoulders.

Jude cocked his head to the side, his hair sliding out of his mismatched eyes. The faded red scars seemed to glow.

My chest was rising and falling rapidly, and his attention shifted, momentarily pausing on my gloved hands. I shoved them behind me, the hasty movement earning me a twinge of pain. I barely noticed it.

"You're not allowed in here," he scolded. His voice lilted at the end, and a sliver of amusement sparkled in his right eye.

This close to Jude, with my heart thumping and my thoughts scattered, I ignored his words and asked him what I'd wondered from that first day—the morning when they'd taken me.

"Why me?" My voice broke. "Why did you take me instead of my brother?" I shivered against my will, the chill in the air freezing my heated blood.

Jude seemed to consider, his lips turning down in a grimace. Gone was the playfulness, however subtle, replaced with his usual rigidness.

"Why?" I probed when he didn't reply, sitting up straighter and bringing my face inches from his. He reared back as though I were a venomous snake set to strike.

"Because you're a fighter," he gritted out, his jaw clenching. He was uncomfortable around me, though the reason why was not yet clear.

"But I'm a *girl*," I said derisively, raising an arched brow. "Women don't fight. We're docile creatures, don't you know?"

I recoiled as Jude let out a riotous laugh. The sound was so out of place with his features. And yet, it had the power to bring a smile to my lips.

"He smiles," I teased, knowing I was poking the beast. I didn't care. "And here I thought you would crack if you smiled. Shame."

Jude caught his breath, eyeing me from beneath thick lashes. "You'd have liked that, wouldn't you?"

"Immensely," I answered, unable to keep the smile from widening on my own face. "I've never seen someone shattered by a smile before, but I assume it would be a rather interesting spectacle."

He shook his head and my smile dipped. "As someone who *has* seen a person break and shatter to nothing but dust, I can tell you, it is far from interesting."

The lone survivor of the Mist. What terrors had he seen? What atrocities had he committed to simply survive? I hadn't asked about his scars, but I suspected he'd received them in the cursed lands.

Shame warmed my cheeks. I wanted to ask more, but he cut me off, a crease forming between his brow. "Would you have rather I taken your brother?"

"No." It was said without hesitation, without a doubt. "My brother has problems breathing. He wouldn't have lasted the trek to the capital."

Jude nodded, his left eye twitching. "I saw that." He looked at his boots. "He was hyperventilating after that prick"—he glanced at Adam's motionless body—"pushed him."

Gods. Liam would be dead if not for Jude selecting me. *Truly* dead.

Bile crept up my throat, and my eyes prickled with tears I wouldn't allow to fall. I didn't want to think about Liam, or how close I'd gotten to losing him.

"I always assumed girls weren't permitted into the ranks of the Knights," I said, changing topics. "I'm surprised they allowed it."

If Jude sensed me deflecting, he mercifully didn't show it.

"There's nothing that says you *can't*. Our king just so happens to believe that females are too...*delicate* to be warriors."

I made a face, and Jude hastily added, "But obviously he's misguided and ignorant. Besides, the decision is ultimately mine, and I saw potential." He tacked on the last part almost shyly.

But that couldn't be possible. Men like Jude weren't *shy*.

Instead, I grinned wide and said, "I'm elated to see you're not the misogynist pig I pegged you as."

"I'm not a—" He stopped when he glimpsed the smile on my lips. "Oh. Another joke?"

"See, you *do* get sarcasm and humor."

The corners of his lips fought to jerk upward, like he'd been out of practice and was just now relearning how to show joy. "I only get humor when it's actually funny."

"Then why are you trying not to smile?" I pressed, my pulse beginning to race.

He let out a noise somewhere between a groan and a sigh. "You make me regret my decision every day."

"Liar," I whispered, realizing I'd leaned forward.

His hot breath tickled my cheeks, my lips. My pounding heart seemed to stop beating entirely, as if eagerly waiting for his reaction.

His eyes once again fell to my lips. "Some lies should be believed," he said cryptically. His nostrils flared as he pushed back and to his feet. "And some rules should be followed as well."

Jude glanced around the library as if remembering where we were. As if remembering *who* he was there with.

"But you really shouldn't be in here, Kiara." His tone turned grave once more, the spell broken. I silently mourned its loss.

"Yes, sir." I gave a mock salute. "Thank you for—" My head tilted to a still unconscious Adam, who was a heap of muscle in the corner.

"I don't take that kind of behavior lightly, recruit."

"Good. He's an honorless cretin."

Jude nodded as though he understood.

His silence prompted me to rise on my trembling limbs, my

hands resting on the shelves behind me. I felt like I would fall over if not for the support.

"I'd try to get some rest," he whispered. "Tomorrow, you're training with me."

It sounded like a threat.

I met his mismatched eyes as I said, "Goodnight, Jude." His glare had me pausing, holding back a curse at my familiarity. "I mean, Commander Maddox," I corrected, and he nodded in approval.

I'd started to walk away when his broad hand wrapped around my wrist, stilling me. His calloused fingers touched the sensitive skin under the band of my glove, sending delicious heat shooting up and down the length of my arm. I lifted my chin, peering at him from beneath my lashes.

Hells, the way he stared right into my soul—

"Oh, and recruit?"

My roaring heartbeat muffled his voice. "Y-yes?"

Jude reached behind him, his eyes never once leaving mine. They pulled me in and demanded my devotion. It was like staring at the moon, at the endless sky, feeling nothing but possibilities and the promise of adventure.

A heavy tome pressed into my side, forcing me to lower my head, to break away from that penetrating stare that had my toes curling in my boots.

The book I'd been reading.

"Don't let anyone know you have that," he said, whisper-soft, his voice gravelly. His focus fell to where he grasped my wrist. Torturously, he peeled one finger away at a time, watching as he released me. A muscle in his jaw feathered.

"Thank you," I murmured, grateful I could form a coherent word at all. He'd gotten so close to my scars, and yet... I hadn't recoiled, hadn't shoved him away. I'd not even allowed Liam to get so close.

Jude's stare lingered on me for a moment longer, a moment where I could read the indecision in his eyes. Or the disbelief in them.

Tucking my new treasure against my chest, I quickly said, "Goodnight, commander," before racing off on unsteady feet toward the dorms.

I was out of breath by the time I slipped the tome beneath my pillow, right next to my jar of healing ointment. I lay back, crossing my arms below my head, nowhere near falling asleep.

I wasn't sure what had transpired in the library.

But it had been... It had been better than the adrenaline that had come with the fight, and I wasn't sure what terrified me more—

That I would soon journey into the Mist...or that I felt anything but hatred for Commander Jude Maddox.

CHAPTER TWELVE

JUDE

No one knows why Raina's absence cursed us, but there is one account by a lowly palace guard. His claims are unproven, but I hesitate to discuss the details with you in a letter. I request to speak with you in person when time permits.

LETTER FROM COMMANDER WILTON TO KING BRION,
YEAR I OF THE CURSE

My mother had given me that book.

It was one of two things I had of hers, and I'd been so pissed at her for abandoning me as a child that I'd shoved her book into the shared library. No one ever read it; if it didn't contain stories of war or the "art" of battle, not many of the Knights would touch it.

And of course, it had been the first book Kiara had selected.

I flipped over in bed, sleep not finding me. Not even my usual nightmares beckoned.

An hour earlier, I'd been thinking about the mother I'd never had. Wanting to torture myself, I'd journeyed to the library to seek her final farewell gift. When I had heard Kiara's muffled screams from behind the door, I'd sprinted without thought, only to come upon that spineless bastard beating her senseless.

Something had snapped inside me, and it had taken everything not to deliver the blow that would ensure he never opened his eyes again. I'd wanted to murder him, wanted to—

A knock sounded, interrupting my deadly thoughts.

At this hour, it could only be one thing.

Seconds later, a single piece of paper slipped through the crack of my door.

Kiara and how soft her skin had felt beneath my calloused fingers died away, replaced by the numbness I'd grown all too accustomed to. It flooded into my chest like poison, wiping away any of the warmth I'd felt back there in the library.

I felt nothing at all as I lit the candle beside my bed.

Rising, I padded over to the piece of paper left behind by one of the king's messengers.

One name had been scrawled upon the parchment.

Folding the note, I walked to the candle and allowed the flames to eat away at the evidence. Once it was nothing but ash, I turned toward my wardrobe. Shoving aside my Knight's uniform, I found what I searched for and began changing.

Lord Maurice Landon slept soundly in his king-sized bed, only his snores echoing in the too-big room. Tonight wasn't about sending a message, which meant less mess.

Stealing across the lord's chamber, I hovered above him, watching as he took his last breaths. The blade in my hand seemed to shudder in anticipation, eager to spill blood.

I'd make this quick, and then—

I spotted a pair of small feet poking out from beneath the covers, a child-sized lump positioned at the bottom of the bed.

Shit.

Landon had one son. He'd never remarried after his wife died, despite being nearly as rich as the king himself and the subject of many of the court ladies' attentions.

I paused, my hand beginning to tremble. If the child woke—

No. I'd told Cirian long ago that I drew the line at harming children, but even if he didn't wake during the act, the bustling of the new morning would rouse him eventually, and he would forever be traumatized by the memory of waking up in a bed full of blood.

I didn't have time for this, to hesitate, to grow a conscience.

My hand constricted around the hilt, inching closer to the slumbering lord, a man who'd likely pissed off Cirian by simply speaking up.

Many of the nobility wanted to overthrow a king more focused on self-image than on his own people, and they certainly weren't thrilled he hadn't lifted Asidia's curse. But they should know better than to fight a monster.

They should know that the monster would send *me*.

The blankets shifted, the child's form moving under the covers.

I aimed for the lord's throat with precision. I forced my eyes to stay open and watch as Lord Landon's eyes widened, as he choked and gasped on his own blood. I forced myself to watch all of it; the shock, the pain, the fear.

A thousand stones weighed in my chest. A stone for every murder I'd committed in the name of the king. I stepped back from the bed and the dying man in it.

The child hadn't stirred. He'd slept through the whole thing.

I was about to turn from the bed when a sharp pang of guilt stilled my feet.

Before I realized what I was doing, I was slowly moving the covers back, exposing a child no more than five. Curly black hair clung to his temples, a thin sheen of sweat lining his brow. He must've had a nightmare.

If only he knew that the real nightmare had just occurred.

After sheathing my blade, I slipped my arms beneath his tiny frame and brought him close to my chest. He felt so light and fragile in my arms. So easily breakable. I'd never held something so gently, as if he were made of glass.

His soft snores were the only sound as I crept out of the bedroom and down the hall. An open door on the left revealed a blue-painted room filled with bright wooden toys, a single bed shoved into the far corner. Moving beyond the threshold, I placed the boy on the mattress.

He stirred when I brought the thick comforter up to his chin, but sleep was too potent a lure, and his eyes remained shut.

I wondered if he had loved his father. He must have if he'd sought comfort in his room. My own father would've tossed me out with a curse and a slap. Shame sent my pulse hammering in my ears, and my eyes prickled and burned.

What was done was done, and I couldn't do a damn thing to change it now. It wouldn't have mattered anyway—if Cirian wanted Landon dead, he'd just send another assassin.

Twisting away from the child, I moved back to the lord's room and to the open window letting in the frigid air of Sciona. With one final glance toward the hall, I climbed over the window ledge. My feet hit the ground without a sound, and I took off into a sprint.

I might've spared his life, but he'd still wake without a father.

Tonight, there would be no dreaming of light. I deserved the darkness.

CHAPTER THIRTEEN

KIARA

He suspects nothing, though I can see the connection between
them grow. Wait for my orders.

LETTER SENT FROM SCIONA VIA MESSENGER
TO UNKNOWN RECIPIENT

Adam had been sent to the Patrol.

We'd been informed of his absence the following morning
by Jude himself, and many recruits didn't bother hiding their
gasps. The Patrol—a group comprised of the worst of the worst.
Men whom society eagerly sent away to safeguard the forests
that bordered the Mist. Essentially, it was a death sentence.

Jude made certain to avoid my eyes when he delivered the
news. I should've felt a twinge of sympathy. But I didn't. Adam
would never change his ways.

"Now"—after relaying Adam's fate, Jude set out for the
same corridor I followed last night, the recruits trailing in his
wake—"we will weed out the true Knights from the lot of you.
Those who have what it takes to survive out there."

An involuntary shudder worked its way down my spine at
how Jude's stare sharpened, the beast he was rumored to be
replacing the man I'd only begun to know.

Patrick pushed into my bruised side—a reminder of Adam's cruelty—making the already stifling corridor seem even more smothering. I shoved my gloved hands into my pockets, needing them to be far from his warmth.

"You will be separated into groups of five," Jude bellowed. "You will line up, right before each of these doors, and when I give the order, you will open them at the same time. I will not do you the favor of telling you what is expected."

Harlow, Carter, and a handsome man I learned to be Isiah—whose godlike stature had to be well over seven feet—wrangled the closest five into groups, ushering us before each plain wooden door. Carter grumbled the entire time, complaining about the "mess" they'd have to clean up afterward. Isiah scolded him, and the older Knight fell silent.

The word "mess" kept repeating in my head.

"Find another group, eh?"

I turned to find a russet-skinned boy standing to my right. He shooed away a stocky recruit who made for my side. "Go on then. I'm on her team."

My lips parted at the brazen display.

"I had to make sure I was in your group," the newcomer hissed, forcing my eyes to drift to his. They were a dazzling pale blue, ringed in a deeper shade of sapphire. "You've been kicking my ass all week," he added with a wink.

I arched a brow, my guard immediately up. "Does that bother you?"

He lifted both hands placatingly in the air. "It was a compliment. Though, it *does* bruise my tender ego, if only slightly. I'm Jake, if you care to know. Which you might, because I plan on making you my new best friend."

Patrick raised his gaze at that bold claim but didn't utter a word in reproach. My lips twitched upward. "And pray tell, Jake, why is that?"

His lean shoulders lifted carelessly, his entire persona a mix of untroubled cunning. "Because you're a mystery and, quite frankly, intimidating. Maybe it's the whole leather-gloved-always-scowling thing you got going on"—his eyes flickered to my hands—"but I suppose I've always been a sucker for a good mystery. And attracted to trouble."

My mouth opened to scold him, to say I wasn't some puzzle to be solved, but he cut me off.

"Plus, you look like someone with a few tricks up their sleeve and gods know, we need all the tricks to get ourselves out of the trenches." He shuddered dramatically, the blue in his irises sparking. "So, what do you say…?"

"Kiara. Or…Ki," I answered, shaking my head. I hated that I found this new recruit charming. "But don't get too comfortable," I warned. "*Friends* or not, I'll still kick your ass."

Jake beamed, twin dimples making an appearance. "Ah, I knew I'd like you."

"You two ready, or are you going to talk through this entire thing? Some of us would prefer not to die out there."

I jerked at Patrick's uncharacteristically gruff tone, his jaw set and eyes hard. He glared daggers at Jake before he seemed to regain his senses and soften his gaze.

"Oh, don't be such a—"

"On my order!" Jude's voice echoed like the clang of a sword against stone. It was time.

We weren't the strongest of the bunch, but I had a suspicion that brute strength might not be the only attribute we'd need. Besides, I wasn't about to kick anyone out now.

I attempted to inch closer to a sulking Patrick, but Jude barked his next command. A frenzy of hustling boots and frantic roars sounded through the corridor, all the doors banging at once.

I didn't know what to expect beyond, but complete darkness

was not it. Not a single sunfire or torch was lit.

Feigning bravery, I took a step into the vacuum of night, half expecting a shadow beast to jump out and devour me whole. Before I could turn around for the hallway, the doors thudded closed, a bolt sliding into place. Not a hint of light filtered beneath the thick door.

"That's not ominous or anything."

"Shhh, Jake," I scolded, narrowing my eyes in the pitch black. Thankfully, he complied, his silence accompanied by Patrick's ragged exhales a few feet away.

This was a test to see how we would react when one of our other senses was torn from us in the great blankness of the cursed lands. I forced my breathing to calm, ears straining for any sound, my tongue licking at my chapped lips.

Salt. I tasted salt. And the aroma of damp rock. But what I heard—

A coaxing hiss of water, the low murmur of a flowing stream, and the faint, grating sound of a growl.

My eyes fluttered open, my heart skipping with excitement. "There's something in here with us." Maybe I should have been more worried about shadow beasts than I thought.

I automatically reached for my blade, but we hadn't been instructed to carry them today, and my hands came away empty. I cursed.

"It's some type of cavern," Jake remarked, still pressed against me. While I would have shoved him away, his solid frame kept me from drifting, from losing the sensation of my body rooted to the slick rock below my boots.

"We need to follow the sound of the stream. Find our way out of here." I bit into the side of my cheek as I forced myself to take Jake's hand firmly. He gave a surprised jolt, and I shuddered, knowing there'd be no way around *not* touching. It took everything in me not to yank my hand away, the skin beneath the leather burning and itching.

"Everyone, form a chain and hold hands so we don't lose one another," I instructed, leaving no room for defiance.

"Aww, we're already holding hands," a new voice snickered to my right.

"Shut up, Nic," Jake snapped, though there was no bite to his tone. "This can't be worse than when we got lost in the mines back home."

So they knew one another. I wished I'd paid more attention to my group before, but it was too late now.

As the tenuous seconds ticked by, a breeze of winter wind whipped at my face. "Anyone else feel cold?"

"I'm sweating through my damned clothes. Probably looks like I just jumped into a lake. Which isn't a terrible look on me, might I add. The wet look really shows off my abs. As well as my best feature. According to Blake, that is. Oh, and Noah," Jake said, his fingers squeezing me.

"One-track mind." Nic snickered. "I bet you're more pissed no one can see you in all your glory than the fact we're lost in the dark."

"Quiet," Patrick snapped. Instantly, they complied, though I made out a snort from my right.

I grew lost in the rhythm of the trickling water and rush of a stream, though I should have known better than to relax. A minute later, I collided painfully with a solid stretch of unyielding rock, and the others bumped into one another with a chorus of groans.

My hands searched the wall blocking our path, my heart sinking as I realized we were facing a dead end. My mouth had just opened to suggest we go back the way we'd come and find another route when a great rumble shook the walls.

Spiked rocks tumbled from the roof, a sharp cascade of stinging rain. They pierced my scalp, arms, and shoulders. Heat swelled before the pain surfaced, my temples slick with my blood.

Jake let go of my hand, yelping alongside the others. The pattering of stone continued for a good many seconds, my bloodied arms protectively raised above my head as the cavern crumbled.

Silence reigned, all except for the ragged breaths that mingled with hearts pounding so fast I swore I heard them through their chests.

"Everyone all right?" I asked evenly, my jaw rigid from sustaining my air of control.

A wave of 'yeses' came at once, though they hardly sounded confident. And because of my earlier feeling, that there was more to this trial than it appeared, I suspected the falling stones were all a part of the plan.

Being here, trapped in this dank place, brought back unpleasant memories.

For a second, I was back in the Pastoria Forest, screaming in pain, my hands ruined. I heard the phantom calls of my father as he scooped me in his arms, blood dripping onto the ground and vanishing into the dark soil of Cila.

My knees wobbled, and unwanted tears burned my eyes. I had to get out of here. *Now*.

Sweat trickled down my spine as my inner panic reared its head, my anxiety churning viciously. I was about to start frantically pressing on the wall, hoping to find some miraculous way out of this nightmare, when I blinked and everything changed.

And by everything, I meant that I could *see*.

Fear immediately outweighed wonder.

It was as though the walls glimmered with crushed diamonds, and a yellowish hue highlighted the stones, though the light blurred every time I tried to focus on one particular spot.

I can see in the dark.

Or I was suffering from hallucinations. Yes, that felt more likely.

Swiveling around, I made out the path we'd taken, along with the pile of rocks blocking the exit. That yellowish glow continued to waver, and I rubbed at my eyes, wondering if something had gotten into them.

"What's wrong?" Jake asked at my side. How he sensed the sudden shift in my mood, I wasn't sure.

"Has it… You can't see anything, can you?" I whispered, yanking on his hand.

"Nope," came his reply. "I see only black. That's the entire point."

Patrick, Nic, and the unknown recruit agreed.

I twisted around, taking in Jake's exasperated expression, his dark brows pinched together. The sharp angles of his face were illuminated, though his eyes were cast in shadows. I could make out Patrick's broad figure hunched over, his hands moving over the loose rocks and seeking purchase.

And the long-haired boy I assumed to be Jake's friend, Nic, gazed stoically ahead, ghoulish shadows dancing beneath his eyes. The last recruit, skinny and short of stature, bowed his head, his mouth moving inaudibly, likely uttering some misbegotten prayer that wouldn't be answered.

So many questions danced across my mind, but I knew better than to waste this opportunity. Hallucination or gift from the gods, I'd take it.

"Follow my lead." I jerked on Jake's hand, ignoring the surge of unease causing my breath to stutter. Each time my fear pulsed, so did the light. They seemed to be connected.

"By all means, lead the way," he said, his lips quirking.

Heat spread down my arms and legs as I followed the path, which was lined with the same light leading the way forward.

Unfortunately, that path brought us to a dead end.

Focusing on the wall in front of me, I dropped to my knees and inspected the rock, noting just the barest hint of an opening.

"We dig here," I instructed the others. "I, uh, feel an opening," I lied. It wasn't as if I could explain why I'd been granted such otherworldly vision; all of it should've been impossible. "We have to move some debris. I think that stream we heard lies on the other side." I brought Jake's hands to the stones and he assisted Nic, who continued guiding the rest.

Their faces remained blank masks as we clawed at the dirt and jagged rocks, moving the debris behind us as we cleared the path. It took longer than I thought, but time was a fleeting thing in such a place. It could have been minutes or hours.

Wintry air rushed from the fissure, and the sweat on my brow grew cold. My heart skipped a beat as my vision wavered, the distorted light seeming to dim along with my adrenaline. Whatever miracle I'd been given waned. We had to hurry.

"We're almost there!" I cried merrily, ready to bathe the grime from my skin and feel the comfort of the torch and sunfire lights from above.

Jake dug earnestly, grunts echoing as the wall of stacked stone gave way to a passageway. It was narrow, barely large enough to fit through, but it would have to do. With an elated smile, I stepped through the void, pulling the chain of recruits behind me.

We were going down rather than up, but the rushing sound of water grew louder the farther down we traveled, and my hands grazed the cavern's wall to steady myself.

The opening brought us to a thin ledge, no more than two feet in width, the icy waters spraying my clothes as they churned against the jutting rock. I tapped my foot on the uneven landing, making sure it wouldn't crumble beneath my weight.

It didn't.

To the others, I said, "Keep close to the wall. There's a ledge."

Not waiting for their assent, I pressed my back against the coarse stone, the cave's craggy surface biting through my thin shirt.

We shuffled together, still linked, our heavy breathing drowned out by the whooshing waters. If anyone questioned how I'd brought us this far, no one voiced it, though I'd likely be harassed the moment we passed this loathsome trial.

Five minutes came and went, and my pulse was hammering in my neck. I wasn't going to be able to last much longer. I needed more light, more *air*. The sensation of being trapped crept into my bones and settled like a hive of bees beneath my flesh.

"All right, we're almost—"

A jerk on my hand sent me stumbling, swaying from side to side, my knees bending as my balance became nothing but a dream. There was a loud splash, the sound of a body striking the roaring waters, a cry, shrill and garbled.

Someone had fallen in.

"Help!" The forlorn plea was choked as water entered the boy's mouth.

My mind raced. There was something in those waters, something whose growls I'd first heard upon entry. It was massive, and knowing the Knights, it would be deadly.

"What do we do?" Patrick cried from down the line. Our trembling link of hands shook, the boys fighting to regain balance, composure. I felt guilty that I was thankful it wasn't him who'd fallen.

In a fit of terror, I realized the cavern was dimming.

The more I struggled to hold on to the light and clutch it

with both hands, the weaker it became. I let out a pained noise when a blanket of pure black cloaked the world.

The fallen recruit howled, his voice carried farther down the stream. The current wasn't strong, but it would rush him to where we couldn't reach.

"Hurry!" I roared, stepping briskly along the precipitous ledge, spiked adrenaline coursing through my icy veins.

There was resistance, but the rest of the boys followed, allowing me to lead, just as they had before. They trusted me, but now that I didn't have the advantage of sight, the sudden weight of their trust was crushing.

Our pace was graceless and frantic, but we hurried as quickly as we dared, jagged bits of stone scraping at the torn shirts on our backs. I could smell the tang of blood in the air, the bitterness of panic.

When the recruit let out a pain-filled scream, this one brimming with unbridled agony, two things happened.

First, I dropped Jake's hand.

Second, I made a run for it.

"Ki!" Jake called out.

They were slowing me down, and I understood that the recruit—whose name we hadn't had the decency to learn—was either drowning or being sucked under by…something.

The icy heat lit up my limbs, fire and resolve powering my motions.

Someone's life was in the balance, and I'd been the one to lead us this far. It was all I could think about. The blackness an afterthought as I scraped my exposed skin, my shirt clinging to my back in tatters.

I slowed as riotous splashing and mangled shouts sounded not far from me.

"Where are you?" I screamed into the void. I called three more times before I got my reply, though it was hardly an answer.

"I-it's… It's got me! My…l-leg!"

I possessed no weapons, nothing to use against a creature I couldn't even see. And yet, I didn't waste a second.

I dove into the water.

The surface hit me like bricks, the freezing temperature stifling any remaining warmth until only cold remained. Numbness.

When I came up for air, my gasps echoed, mingling with the recruit's frantic splashing and the beast who wished to make him his meal. His cries were coming just ahead, the current carrying me swiftly to the unlucky recruit, to whatever I was soon to fight.

My limbs were already growing weak, useless. The water was too cold, and it *burned*.

"H-help!"

A great wave splashed into my face, filling my mouth, my nostrils, with water. I could feel the movements, the recruit's thrusts and kicks as he fought.

"I'm here!" I choked, not sure if he could hear me over the roar. Over his struggle to live.

With one powerful kick, I was upon the beast, my fingers digging into scaled snake-like skin. The thing hissed, and a snap of teeth sounded next to my ears. From the feel of it, I was grabbing its thick middle, its raised bumps pressing into my hands.

With a guttural roar, I thrust myself upon its flailing back, a mighty tail clubbing my leg, spikes slicing through the cotton of my trousers. In the crushing dark, rushing water on either side, I climbed up its body, struggling to grip the slicked skin.

The recruit gasped for air, and there was more splashing. A minute later, I made out a stifled grunt, and then, I heard dripping water striking stone.

He'd made it to the bank.

"Help! S-she needs help!"

I could have sighed in relief. The recruit was safely on the ledge, but now I was the one stuck weaponless, straddling an underground river beast I couldn't even see.

Just my luck.

The damned thing let out a hiss, and this time, its teeth scraped my ear as it thrashed. I wound my hands around its neck, both holding on and attempting to choke the life from it.

The creature dove suddenly, its scaly body forcing me below the frigid waters. I hung on like a fool, my grip tightening, numbed fingers jabbing into the hollow of its throat.

The beast jerked from side to side, frantic to dislodge me.

If I let go, it would merely drag me back under, and the upper hand would be lost. It was either stay and fight or turn my back and get a row of teeth imprinted on my leg as the creature hauled me to the depths.

The last bubble of air escaped my lips. I didn't have much time before I would drown, all my energy having been spent merely holding on.

The creature wasn't dying, wasn't losing consciousness, and that meant I was failing. I could feel my limbs losing their grip, my heartbeat slowing painfully. It was happening so quickly, and yet, I could swear I'd been here, in the dark, fighting, all my life.

Right before death took me in its arms, an image came to me.

Maybe it was what everyone experienced right before they died—flashbacks of their lives—but I relished it, softening at the sweet memory.

It was a year before Grandmother had died.

She'd sat me down, her elbows propped on our worn kitchen table, her back slumped like the weight of the world lay upon her shoulders. She'd taken both my hands in her weathered ones, the wrinkly flesh comforting as it enveloped me. I'd felt safe. Happy. Loved.

"I won't always be here, my girl," she'd said, her voice thin, weary. "But I need you to always fight, even when they tell you that you've already lost. If you don't, then none of us stand a chance."

I'd assumed old age was ruining the sharpness of her mind, and I'd patted her hand, plastering a reassuring smile on my face.

But it wasn't what she'd said that day that filled me with warmth.

For just a second, I'd seen myself through the reflection of her eyes. Pure gold brilliance wavered around my face, snuffed out before it had time to truly bloom.

It was that spark, that flash that I saw now as I was losing consciousness, deep beneath the surface, clinging to a beast. And it was this memory, of the woman who owned my heart, that had my eyes bursting open, my fingertips blazing with electricity and the ferociousness of life.

I wouldn't lose. Not here, and not in a tomb of black.

Grabbing the creature with renewed strength, I dug my fingers into its throat, my muscles burning with the effort. The thing writhed and squirmed in my hold, trying frantically to free itself. Something was different this time around, my grip stronger, my pulse quicker.

Hard skin gave way, my fingers thrusting beneath scales, poking into muscle, and then deeper, into bone.

I could sense the beast's light fading, its life force leaving its body.

Gods, I could taste it, hear its thrumming energy departing this world. It emboldened me, gave me that final push I needed to end it all.

And then, there was nothing. No movement, its limbs heavy and stiff.

I yanked my fingers from its insides, shoving off its back.

Kicking to the surface, I broke free a moment later, gasping and gulping in air.

The fresh air seared my insides and burned my lungs, but I kicked and swam, struggling to breathe, to claw my way back to life. Several voices called my name, their shouts of encouragement all urging me closer.

I followed those cries, Patrick's despairing wails, my arms swinging and my legs moving to bring me to them. A strong hand grabbed my arm, and then there were more hands, all clutching different parts of me, tugging me to the ledge, hoisting me up, out of the waters that had nearly been my grave.

"Ki!" Patrick pressed me painfully to his chest, gripping the back of my neck to hold me in place. "I almost lost you." His arm slung around my hip, keeping me from toppling over and right back into the stream.

"We need to get her out of here!" Jake must have beckoned the others into motion, for the next moment, I was being gently dragged down the length of the ledge, my limbs shivering from the cold, my teeth chattering noisily.

It was more than the icy temperature of the stream that sent me drifting in and out of consciousness. Something had happened down there, in those mercilessly dark depths, and it had viciously sucked the life from my very bones.

Someone was talking about getting me into a hot bath, warming me up, but I was too lost to make out who it was. There was only Patrick's too-tight grip on me, the lone thing securing me to this plane.

I swam in and out of reality until the tunnel brightened, the wavering flames of torches a promise — a beacon.

"Almost there, Ki!" Patrick whispered in my ear. "Just hold tight."

CHAPTER FOURTEEN

JUDE

Salendons were bred for one purpose only: to kill. Silas, the
Water God, crafted them out of silt and the bones of the
dead—of those unlucky sailors who had drowned beneath his
waters. The god abandoned them once he learned they needed
air in their lungs and could be easily drowned.
It is said that he gifted them to Lorian.

EXCERPT FROM ASIDIAN LORE: A TALE OF THE GODS

A group of recruits emerged from the end of the tunnel, a
limp body carried in the arms of a gangly dark-haired boy.
His blue eyes were wide as he adjusted to the torches forming
a semi-circle around the exit, but he never ceased his relentless
pace.

I immediately tensed beside Isiah, Harlow, and Carter.

A pale face turned away from the boy's chest, her lids
fluttering.

Kiara.

She looked nearly dead, hardly able to move, to open her
eyes.

"She saved me," shouted a lad trailing behind. "I fell in, and
she fought, she f-fought whatever was down there." His voice

shook as violently as he did. "She was down there for too long," he added, and I recognized the guilt shrouding his features.

My feet were moving before I could stop myself. And I *should* have stopped myself.

Harlow was watching, always watching. He certainly didn't miss me as I ran for the boy carrying Kiara and scooped her into my arms before tucking her head against my heart.

She was so cold, her body lifeless in my arms.

I caught the lieutenant's steely gaze from across the room, a thousand questions swirling in those pools of green.

The damage was already done.

"Move aside," I shouted, shouldering past the other boys just arriving from the tunnel.

They were screaming about some monster attacking, and the one who'd claimed she had saved him sported a gruesome gash in his thigh. Harlow could deal with him.

Kiara shook, her teeth chattering, her eyes closed. She needed to get to the bathing suite, had to get warm. Instinctively, I pressed her deeper into the planes of my chest, wrapping an arm around her shoulders. She trembled even harder.

Shit, shit, shit, shit.

Barreling past a gaping and confused Isiah—who I was sure would ask me unwanted questions later—I stormed down the corridor and to the bath. I couldn't look down, too afraid of what I'd find.

Another death. Another body. Lifeless and forever frozen—

I kicked open the bathing suite's door and marched down the steps leading to the pool. I didn't waste time undressing or even pulling off my boots.

Kiara jerked when the warm water touched her skin, and she began mumbling something, her lips a shocking blue. Panicked, I submerged her, wetting her head, making sure her nose and mouth remained above the surface.

Wake the hells up, I ordered silently, gritting my teeth.

I'd picked her in Cila, and because of that choice, *my* choice, her death would be my fault. I'd killed so many others, but for some reason, I knew her death would be my final undoing. Kiara, although hardheaded and stubborn, reminded me of all that was light and good. I'd killed men before—too many men—but their hands had been dirty, at least to some degree.

All Kiara was guilty of was protecting her brother and getting chosen by me.

If I robbed the world of her light, there'd be no going back from that.

Like she'd heard my silent pleading, her lashes fluttered against her cheeks. I cursed, and her eyes opened into slits.

"There you are," I rasped, relief flooding me.

If it had been any other recruit, I'd have brought them here to warm up, but I sure as shit wouldn't have held them, rocking them back and forth beneath the heated water. And my pulse wouldn't be racing, panic flaring in my blood, causing fire to simmer inside me.

For the briefest of seconds, she turned her head to me, those bright, almost yellow, eyes cast in shadows. She blinked, unsure of where she was, but her body had settled, if only slightly.

"We need to get you warm, Kiara," I murmured, and one corner of her mouth lifted at the sound of my voice. It almost made me smile.

Her small hand grasped my biceps, her eyes lacking their typical shimmer. "Your arms feel good," she muttered, the words coming out as nothing but a choked whisper. Judging from her expression, she was clearly dazed and possibly delirious.

I released a bitter laugh and then said, "Stop flirting with me, recruit. Not when you nearly killed yourself."

The recruit with the gaping thigh wound said Kiara had

saved him, that she'd jumped into the water where the sharp-toothed salendons roamed. The king's monstrous pets.

I'd been on edge all morning knowing what they'd face. Yes, in the past, some of them had died in those murky depths, but never had I been as fearful as I'd been today.

Surprising, because after last night's *mission*, I didn't think I'd be able to feel anything at all.

Kiara shifted in my arms, her mouth falling open in fear when she realized she was nearly submerged.

The water. She'd almost drowned no more than five minutes ago. "I've got you. I won't let go."

At my promise, her body relaxed, but the arms she'd wound around my neck tightened. The weight there felt nice, too nice. I didn't deserve it.

I noticed she still wore those damned gloves, so I reached around to grasp her hand, about to pull off the material and allow her hands to warm. That's when she froze again, all the tension back.

"N-no," she whispered, digging her fingers deeper into my neck. "D-don't touch t-them."

She lifted her head, her eyelids struggling to stay open as I took in the severe edges of her face, the sunfires casting moving shadows below her eyes.

"Shhh, I won't," I promised, shifting my hand to rest beneath her back. I wasn't sure why she never took off those gloves, but there'd been genuine fear in her eyes when I prepared to remove them. It made me all the more curious to know the secrets she hid.

"I-I thought y-you d-didn't like to s-share your b-bath time," she chattered after many long moments. She loosened her grip on my neck, but her fierce stare left me no room to breathe.

"I made an exception, Kiara. Don't get used to it." I made my voice harder than it should have been, but she still smiled, gazing at me like I was her savior, a man worthy of her adoration.

"What happened down there?" My arms constricted, my fingers digging into her exposed flesh. The salendon had left her shirt in tatters, the scraps of it floating to the surface. I wanted to yell at her all of a sudden, to curse her selflessness. My nostrils flared, and my damned eye twitched.

"A recruit f-fell i-in," she managed to get out, her chattering easing. "S-something attacked. I k-killed it."

My eyes briefly shut in frustration. Careless, careless girl.

Now I *was* angry. Genuinely angry.

Reaching for her chin, I held her firmly in place so she'd understand my every word.

"Never do that again, Kiara," I said, my tone hard, biting. "Never risk yourself like that. Especially when you couldn't fucking see. When you didn't even know what the hells you were fighting." My voice rose, turning furious. What little calm I'd employed vanished.

"He would have d-died, and I c-could save him."

"You can't save everyone," I snapped. "In this world, you have to look out for yourself."

She shook her head weakly. "That's s-such a sad way of l-looking at things."

Every muscle in my body went rigid. I felt only my hands on her bare skin now, felt her hopeful stare pierce into my own, and cursed the undeniable hold this girl had on me.

I wanted to argue and say that my words were simply the truth, but my lips remained in a thin line.

The darkness hadn't tainted her yet, but it soon would.

"Besides," she continued, and I sucked in air through my teeth when one gloved hand fell to my chest, right above my thundering heart. "Knights t-take an oath to protect the p-people of the realm. How could I have l-let him d-die?"

"Some people aren't worth saving," I murmured.

The yellow of her irises sparked, and she narrowed in on me in a way that was all too telling. My teeth ground together, and I fought not to turn away first.

That hand of hers remained over my heart as she said, "I think I'm a good judge of c-character."

A brittle laugh left me, and she flinched. "Wait until you've entered the Mist, and then tell me if people are still worth saving. They'll do anything to save themselves. They'll stab you in the back even if they aren't in the Mist." She'd be naive to think otherwise.

"You're w-wrong," she snapped, dropping her hand from my chest altogether. I felt like she'd slapped me. "Yes, people are c-cruel, but if I did nothing, then I'd be just as b-bad as them."

Suddenly, I couldn't stand being in this pool, trapped with her in my arms. I couldn't handle how she stared at me. I shattered the moment in the only way I knew how.

"Don't disobey me again, Frey. Your only words should be 'Yes, sir,' when I give you an order."

Kiara flinched again. Even in her feverish state, she bristled at the command.

Why did her defiance cause my blood to boil, and not in a way that often led to death? No, this time it simmered beneath my skin, a delicious heat settling into my chest.

I *needed* her to get angry, to fight and show me that *life* in her eyes. Even if her anger was directed at me.

It was how she'd stay alive.

Kiara growled as she shoved against my chest. I forced myself to drop my arms and step back before fixing my face into a mask of apathy.

She swayed on her feet, but a rosy blush had finally colored her wan cheeks.

"You may be the commander," she said, "but you're a fool t-to think I'd let someone die if I could s-save them, order or not. Y-you don't know me at all."

She gave me her back, dismissing me.

My teeth ground together as my temper flared, and I curled my hands into fists.

Minutes passed, but she refused to turn, to give me the satisfaction of her gaze. So I stayed, fixed in place, my eyes eating holes in the walls. My anger didn't dissipate.

Why couldn't she understand that she'd almost died?

Images of a field of white haze filled my thoughts, of lifeless eyes and broken bodies. My brothers…all dead, all lost, because they'd dared to hope they might make a difference.

"You're a foolish child who knows nothing of the world," I snarled, breaking the eerie quiet that had befallen. "And you will die because of it."

I wanted to take back the words the second they stained the stifling air dividing us. They tasted acrid and vile on my tongue. Her shoulders stiffened. She didn't face me, but she did reply, her tone colder than the frozen mountains in the north.

"And you are an unfeeling, miserable bastard. And when you die, it will be alone."

I might as well have been punched in the gut.

How many times had people told me I was a prick? A cold-hearted shell of a man, only good at bloodying his hands for a corrupt king? I've been called every name in the book for the past five years, ever since I officially joined the Knights, and yet…

Why did it sting more when the jab came from her? I didn't know her, I shouldn't care.

Ripples of water rocked against my shoulders as I moved toward the steps and climbed out of the pool. I didn't pause before opening the double doors and slamming them shut behind me.

Something foreign twisted my gut, but I ignored it.

If I didn't get myself in check, I *would* die alone, as she'd so vehemently put it. But my death would occur out there in the cursed dark, where the Mist would swallow me up whole. Another soldier who dared to fight against the impossible.

CHAPTER FIFTEEN

KIARA

The commander is hesitant when it comes to the girl. I fear his attachment might become a problem.

LETTER FROM LIEUTENANT HARLOW TO KING CIRIAN, YEAR 50 OF THE CURSE

"Ki. You there?" Patrick was waving his hand in front of my face, his dark brows furrowed. He'd apologized multiple times for being short with me yesterday, and I was quick to forgive.

"I'm here," I said finally, shaking off the residual fog. After nearly drowning, I'd been living beneath a perpetual haze, wondering why I'd been able to see in a void of pure darkness.

So far, I had no good answer.

"Harlow is staring at you with a look I can only describe as annoyed."

I lifted my head across the dining hall and toward the thin-lipped lieutenant, finding his auburn hair tousled as though he'd spent hours running his hand through it. I could sense the immense displeasure radiating from his every pore.

"Eh, he's probably just angry I didn't drown," I remarked dryly, gulping down the last of my water. I slammed the empty cup on the table just as the gong sounded. More training awaited.

"Soooo." Jake knocked my shoulder, his tone suggesting mischief. "You ever gonna tell us what happened after the damned *Commander* of the Knights lifted you in his arms and personally brought you to the bath?"

Patrick choked on his water, and Nic snickered. Inwardly I groaned. I'd known this question was coming.

"He had to get her warm," Patrick offered, coming to my rescue. I gave him a grateful smile, and he winked. Under the table, his hand squeezed mine in reassurance.

"Yeah, totally normal behavior coming from our superior. You sure you don't want to tell us something, Ki?" Jake asked, waggling his dark brows suggestively.

"What can I say? I can't help the fact that I'm his favorite." I smiled as if I weren't inwardly panicking and my hands weren't growing slick with sweat. "Maybe if you trained harder, he'd pay you the same attention."

Jake held a hand to his chest in mock affront, and Pat rolled his eyes.

"Regardless, the man looked livid when he left the bath," Jake added, shoving the last of his meal in his already full mouth. "So maybe you aren't a favorite anymore."

Nic elbowed his friend, and they exchanged knowing grins. "You're just pissed he didn't carry *you* out of there in those muscular arms of his," he teased.

"Damn right I am," Jake scoffed, all smiles.

The gong sounded once more, and I used it as an excuse to drop all the talk of Jude and his oh-so-muscular arms.

"We better get to it then," I said quickly, shoving off from the table and following the other recruits. There was some residual teasing, which I expected, but I shut it out.

Once they saw they'd get no rise out of me, they hurried along as Isiah led us above the Knights' sanctum and to an open field. Today, we would be practicing archery.

Once the targets were set up, Carter assisted the less skilled recruits, demonstrating the proper stance and adjusting their fingers on the bow to perfection. He grumbled every so often when they failed to strike the mark, but when they did hit the bullseye, the man's eyes gleamed with pride.

When I nocked my arrow and aimed at the target, my thoughts ventured back to the topic at lunch. Nic had been right about one thing. The commander had been pissed, his face distorting into something unrecognizable. Of course, that image made me think about the harsh words we'd exchanged.

I released my arrow, missing the bullseye by a half inch.

Great. Now Jude was screwing up my aim.

It was only after dinner, when I shuffled after Patrick to the dorms, that I saw him.

Jude leaned into the shadows of the corridor, a wavering sunfire illuminating his scarred face. Both arms were crossed, his bare forearms rippling with muscle and painted with old wounds.

I paused there, in the middle of the hallway, ignoring the curses of the recruits who nearly stumbled into my back.

Jude had been livid because of one thing—my safety. I'd been equally as angry, but then again, no one had ever really cared about my safety before, certainly not to that extent. Instantly, I softened.

Maybe we both didn't know how to communicate properly. We were cut from the same cloth, and being friends—or whatever we were—was brand new.

We locked eyes.

I didn't mean what I said. I wondered if the sincerity of my gaze relayed such truth. If he could decipher what I couldn't say aloud.

Perhaps he grasped the coarse regret eating away at me, because Jude lifted his chin ever so slightly. And then he gave me a barely perceptible nod as if he, too, wished to apologize, his throat bobbing with the effort.

In our frozen moment of apology, where all else faded to dust, I recognized the pain etched into every crease, every taut muscle, and each scar he wore. I saw through the mask of apathy, a sliver of pure light shining through.

Maybe there was hope for us after all.

The following week was full of training exercises designed to assess our abilities. Since the first test, fifteen recruits had been sent to the Guard. A few had surrendered to the darkness of the cave, giving into their devastating fear, and the others —

Three recruits had died.

Devoured by those water-dwelling beasts that lived below the caverns of the palace. "Salendons," I believe they were called.

The fifth recruit I'd saved was one of those dismissed, and he seemed rather thankful for it. The poor boy, Lucas, had embraced me in a tight hug, uttering his gratitude ten times over before he'd been sent packing.

Harlow continued to appraise me as though I were the grit between his toes, a persistent scowl hardening his gaze. I wasn't bothered, not after so many years of training with Micah. Yet, there was something besides annoyance lingering behind his stare, and if I caught his eyes for too long, the intensity of that unnameable emotion had me hastily turning away, the hair on the back of my neck rising.

Carter and Isiah, on the other hand, were patient to a fault. Whenever Isiah smiled my way, I felt as if the very gods had blessed me. It was even rarer when Carter bestowed me with a look of pride, though his approval felt well earned when received.

And the commander… I didn't see him much, other than at dinner, and occasionally when he led the Knights into the meeting room. But he'd shut the grand mahogany doors behind him without a glance.

I wondered endlessly what they discussed in that room, if it had to do with the Mist and the curse of Asidia, and all the other secrets the king kept close to his chest.

My new friends and I speculated, but we knew nothing useful; the king had kept the realm's curse and the true nature of the Mist under wraps. He liked his people scared and compliant.

Jake, Nic, and Patrick were good distractions.

They'd only asked about my gloves once, and when I'd shot them a menacing glower and delivered threats of violence, they'd shut up. Maybe they'd done so because deep down, they knew it wasn't their place. Or they were truly terrified I'd knock them all on their asses. Either way, the subject hadn't been brought up again.

I was grateful they kept my mind busy, diverting my focus from Jude and thoughts of home. I'd learned that Jake and Nic hailed from a village about twenty miles away from Cila. They claimed they were basically brothers, having grown up in and out of one another's households since they were five.

Nic was the quieter of the two, but I had a feeling his silence had to do with leaving his girlfriend behind during The Calling. I sensed that the distance broke his heart, but a fraction of me envied him for what he shared with another, even if he'd been made to say goodbye.

My romantic life back home had been comprised of clandestine meetings, none of my partners willing to be seen with me when the town was awake. Lilah had been the only one to suggest meeting in public, but when the time came, she'd grown fearful and broken it off.

I'll never forget how hopeful I'd felt, nor would I forget the crushing weight of betrayal when she'd all but thrust a dagger into my heart over a year ago, walking by me as if she didn't know me, her gaggle of friends in tow, snickering behind their open palms. After that, I'd decided it was better to be alone. Even if I knew that to be a lie.

Many times, when I'd been struck by the suffocating loneliness, when I'd lie awake in bed and toss and turn, I'd wonder what it would be like to gift someone a piece of yourself and own a part of them in return. And when my plaguing thoughts grew too much, I'd sneak out of the dorms, my borrowed book tucked under my arm.

As I couldn't risk lighting a candle in the dorms, the bathing suite was where I'd curl up and read. I'd only sifted through half of the handwritten text, and most of it reiterated what we'd already been taught in school—the five central gods and goddesses, the kingdom's humble beginnings, and King Cirian's bloody rise to power just years after the curse had begun.

But it was tonight, after a particularly grueling session with Harlow and an exquisitely crafted longsword, that I opened to the next chapter.

The Breaking of the Sun

A mortal man captured the eye of the Sun Goddess during her midday rise. Young and ambitious, he prayed to the goddess from atop the tallest mountain in the kingdom. Presenting his last coin as an offering, he pleaded for a more influential life.

The goddess answered.

But when he saw her in her true form, luminous and ethereal before him, the young man tumbled to his knees, awestruck and reverent.

The goddess was ravishing; cascading hair of fire fell to her waist, her heart-shaped face featuring full lips and eyes that matched the rays of light she radiated.

Captivated, the man retracted his wish, claiming he only desired to remain in her presence for a little longer.

Raina, entranced by the mortal's adoration, urged him to stand. She decided to grant the man his wish, choosing to stay in her current form and dwell at his side.

Days turned to weeks, weeks to months, the goddess and the mortal consumed with one another's company. It didn't take long before they fell in love.

One day, while journeying to the southernmost region of the realm, the goddess fell from her horse, slicing open her leg. Light escaped from the wound, nearly blinding her lover. And yet, he raced over to her, shielding her light with a blanket.

Raina realized she was weakened and could no longer stay with the man during the day—a time when she was sorely missed in the heavens. She couldn't maintain the light and walk the earth, and a decision had to be made.

Devoted to the people she watched over, Raina made up her mind, much to her lover's dismay. She would depart from the world during the hours of light, returning when the moon graced the skies. This way, she could stay with the man she loved while still bringing life to the people who worshipped her below.

I paused here, a sudden pang of warning shooting across my chest. I could predict how this tale would end—in heartbreak or death. The scars hidden by my gloves throbbed as if in agreement.

Raina's love abided by her decision for many years, and she granted him the rare gift of everlasting life in return. This way, he would never grow old and die, and they could live out eternity together.

But as the years progressed, the mortal grew discontent. He grew greedy.

By this time, he had made a name for himself among the people. Quickly rising through the ranks of the Guard, he found himself in the company of the king. As he was clever and sharp, the king used his abilities, keeping him as an advisor.

Raina watched with a heavy heart as her lover grew more and more power-hungry with each passing sunset. One night, as she drifted down to earth, her lover was waiting for her—

"What are you doing in here this late?"

Just as it had in the library, the tome went flying out of my hands, tumbling to the stones, inches away from the pool's edge.

Turning my head, I found the commander, his face unreadable, an extra change of clothes swaddled under his arm. He must've been late for his bath. I hadn't even heard his footsteps.

"I was reading." Scrambling to recover the fallen tome, my gloved fingers wrapped around the wrinkled spine, yanking it protectively to my chest. "I couldn't light a candle in the dorms," I added softly, the commander taking a cautious step in my direction.

We hadn't spoken since that day in the pool, our words cutting and teeming with frustration and insecurity.

With feline grace, Jude placed his clothes beside the pool and glided over to where I rested, my back pressed against the damp chamber wall. He didn't stop until he was hovering over me, forcing me to crane my neck to meet him.

There was no emotion in his depthless eyes, nothing to give away what thoughts consumed him. I held my breath in wait, for once choosing silence over my forked tongue. Ironic how the very man I once thought I despised now rendered me speechless.

Crouching, his elbows digging into his muscled thighs, Jude

cocked his head, his attention drifting to the moss-green book still tucked to my chest like a newborn babe. His trenchant stare wholly unnerved me. Unable to hold it for much longer, I glanced down.

That's when I noticed the speckles of red covering his hands. *Blood.*

"Are you hurt?" I asked, about to reach for him, but Jude shoved his hands away, inching back on his heels.

"I'm fine," he ground out, his biting tone relaying that he was anything but *fine*.

Jude was shutting down before my very eyes, his features glazing over, his stare cooling to ice. I had to stop it.

"Well, you interrupted me right when it was getting good." I lifted the book. "Though I'm surprised such a serious man as yourself owns a book of gods and myths. I'd have assumed you'd prefer texts about combat strategies or how to properly brood while staring off into the distance."

The tautness of his face relaxed ever so slightly, and a gentle grin spread across his lips, shocking me. I would have fallen over had I not seen him smile before.

Serious Jude was handsome. But smiling Jude? He was absolutely mind-numbing.

Our petty fight fell to the back of my thoughts. I imagined he ignored the lingering awkwardness as well.

"Is that so?" he inquired, his right eye shining a brilliant honey. I couldn't stop looking at it, the way it changed hue with every blink. "Though, according to Isiah, I have mastered brooding already."

The tall Knight he was always seen with. Were they actually friends?

Clearing my throat, I adopted a visage of nonchalance, ignoring Jude and what his ever-changing eyes did to me. "How long have you known him?"

Jude settled against the wall, only a foot separating us. "Since I was fourteen. He's more like an older brother at this point. An *annoying* older brother." Something soft flickered across his face. It had me leaning closer, even though my heart twinged in my chest. I missed my own brother fiercely. He, too, was my only friend.

"I'd keep reading if I were you." He angled his chin to the book, changing topics before I could ask more about his life. "Sometimes the best part is the middle…before the ending can ruin it for you, that is."

"Was this yours?" My focus rested on what my hands clutched so dearly, a finger lovingly tracing the spine. I asked because his eyes sparked with interest whenever he saw it in my hands.

"It still *is* mine." His uninjured eye glinted roguishly in the torchlight. "I never said you could keep it."

"Too bad." I shrugged, meeting his stare, which was growing more and more heated. "I think I've grown rather attached over the past few days. *Foolish children* like me love lore such as this."

I'd meant the words to sound light and teasing. Instead, they came out soft and uncertain.

"You know I didn't mean that," he said on a sigh, muscles rippling in his taut jaw. "Those creatures, salendons, are deadly. The king trapped them below the palace years ago as his *pets*." Jude practically spit out the word, his disgust evident. "Diving in and wrestling with one wasn't your best idea. I thought you would've heard the growls and stayed as far from the water as possible."

One could only guess what the cruel king used his pets for, and I had a feeling it involved painful deaths for those who'd displeased him.

"Would you have preferred me to let that recruit die?" I crossed my arms defensively. We were so close, his knee touching mine. I could feel the heat emanating from his lean body, his warmth seeping through the thin cotton of my shirt.

"No, I suppose not," he said at last, his lips curling down. "You wouldn't be you if you'd allowed him to perish. If anything, I admire you for it. Even if it has me questioning your sanity."

I startled. "*Admire* me?" I let out a snort, completely ignoring the last part. "I'm stunned you'd say such a thing."

Jude shook his head, tangles of black falling into his eyes.

"While I am still, let's say, *irritated*, that you did it, I find myself unable to stay angry with you. Especially since your selflessness is an admirable trait for a Knight. And that's the entire purpose of those tests. To see who stands out among the lot as possible defenders for Asidia."

"Would you have been angry had it been anyone else?" My question was a whisper.

Seconds ticked by before he answered, his voice equally as soft. "No. I don't think I would have been." But before I could ask him *why*, why I was different in his eyes, Jude said, "I expect you to return that to me when you're finished. Take care of it in the meantime. And try *not* to toss it into the bath." His gaze drifted toward the whirring pool, where the tome almost had met its end minutes before.

"I wouldn't want to invite the wrath of the most feared man in the kingdom, all because of a book," I replied cheekily, the pressure on my chest dissipating.

"Most feared man, eh?" Jude repeated, one corner of his mouth curled up in delight. He liked that, didn't he? A man and his ego.

"Well, perhaps Harlow is the most feared. After training with you both, I'd say he might outdo you on the whole dangerous-and-brooding thing the two of you have going on." I waved my hand about his face as if to make my point.

This time, Jude laughed outright, pronounced dimples

playfully dotting both cheeks. My heart fluttered like a trapped bird.

"If those traits are the deciding factors, then yes, Harlow definitely has me beat. But he's been around a decade longer than I have. The king rarely allows him to leave the palace walls, claiming he needs one high-ranking Knight in Sciona at all times. I imagine being kept behind the walls doesn't help with his… disposition."

That explained why Harlow hadn't gone into the Mist with Jude a year ago. From the way Jude described it, Harlow didn't have much choice in the matter.

"Was Isiah with you when…" I trailed off, wincing. Now would be the time to ask about his scars and if he'd gotten them in the Mist, but I held my tongue and glanced at my own gloved hands. If anyone understood that some secrets were harder to share than others, it was me.

"No, Isiah and Harlow were the only high-ranking Knights to stay back," Jude said, seeming to understand what I'd been about to ask. I watched the column of his throat as he swallowed hard. "Harlow couldn't run the sanctum alone, and I'm thankful every day he chose Isiah to stay as his second-in-command."

His blood-speckled hands twitched, and he glanced down to them, his brow wrinkling.

Before he could snatch them away again, I reached out and grabbed his hand.

He jolted at the contact, his eyes turning wide. "What are you doing?" he choked out, his breaths uneven.

"What happened here?" I asked, inspecting his fingers while wiping away the dried flakes where I could.

Jude tensed. "Nothing you should concern yourself with."

I shouldn't push but…hells, I *always* pushed.

"Tell me." I averted my gaze, focusing solely on rubbing away the red. He surprised me by allowing it.

When time stretched on and he didn't answer, I garnered the courage and lifted my chin. Jude was staring at *my* hands, at my gloves.

"Tell me why you wear those, and I'll tell you what happened tonight."

The offer hung in the air between us, both a lifeline and an anchor.

If I told him about my past, about what happened that fateful day, he might look at me differently. Or maybe I'd just grown so accustomed to the wicked gossip of the villagers in Cila, all claiming I was some kind of abomination behind the safety of their cupped hands.

A part of me agreed with them.

"I thought so," he said, but there wasn't any bite in his tone, just an easy acceptance, like he understood. "We all have our secrets, Kiara."

My toes curled in my boots at the way he said my name. Soft and slow and deep.

Realizing I still held onto it, I dropped his hand. He brought it to rest beside his other one on his knee.

It was a miracle I could speak at all when I asked, "Tell me a secret, then. One you can part with."

Jude considered, dipping his chin and allowing his disheveled hair to tumble back into his eyes. He didn't look at me as he spoke. "Well, it's not a secret I *should* tell you, but I've broken all the rules as it is." Jude gave me a knowing look before he continued and said, "The king wants the Knights to take the recruits into the Mist. *Soon*."

My heart stopped. "You can't be serious? There's no way any of those boys are ready for that!"

"And *you* are?" A lone raven brow rose in question.

"More so than the rest," I answered without hesitation, lifting my chin.

Jude continued his unnerving assessment, and I suddenly wished for the ability to read minds, especially his.

The commander was not at all how I expected him to be. Cruel? Inhumane? Ruthless? Yes.

But now, and all the other times fate had brought us together, he was almost *too* human. And only with me. That was the question I couldn't seem to find an answer to—what made me so unlike the others?

I didn't think it had anything to do with me being a girl. From the gossip I'd heard, the Knights got plenty of attention, all adored by Sciona's ladies and men for their bravery.

My throat constricted at the thought of Jude with another, but I swallowed down the petty jealousy. He could be with anyone he wanted; I had no claim on him.

That thought didn't help stop the heat from reaching my ears, likely turning them an obscene red. I brushed my hair over them, hiding the evidence.

Jude broke the hush first, his voice turning hard. Grim. "I'm to put together a troop of four recruits," he said, lifting his eyes to me. Thoughts of Jude with another vanished. "There will be three groups sent out, all entering the Mist at various points from the kingdom's borders. The king is hoping to speed up the process. To reunite Asidia with its lost sun. Even if that means sending in helpless recruits in order to do so."

"Why?" What good would poorly trained soldiers do him? Wouldn't it be best to wait until we'd all completed our training?

"Because time is running out. Apparently our food reserves are running out, and we have mere months before nothing is left."

"Time has been running out for years," I argued, subconsciously curving my body toward his, my arm grazing his knee. A bolt of electricity shot through me from the contact. Jude let out a hiss, one so faint I could have imagined it.

"That it has. But the king has been extra…frantic as of late. I imagine he knows more than he lets on," he ground out, his focus lingering on his knee…where I'd touched him. His jaw clenched. "But don't worry, I will only bring a handful of those I believe have the best chance at survival."

His eyes slowly rose to meet mine.

"So you admit it?" I embraced the adrenaline flourishing in my chest. "I am the best recruit." While I hoped for humor to grace my tone, my voice came out all breathy and unrecognizable. I cursed all the gods for it.

"The moment I saw you in that poor excuse for a square—" I opened my mouth to defend my village when his barbed glare shut me up. He continued. "The second you leapt in without hesitation to protect your brother, someone who wouldn't have had a chance in such a fight, I knew. Adam was twice your size, and you didn't care. You didn't stop and think about it. You acted." Jude peered off into the shadows. "There was no fear on your face. Only… hunger."

Hunger for the battle. The adrenaline. The victory.

I gulped, suddenly feeling raw. Vulnerable.

And yet, while I would have bristled at such words and deflected in the past, now my silence admitted what my mouth could not. He was right.

"I recognized something in you that day. And the Knights need someone with that hunger to fight what prowls beyond. Believe me, I would know."

I couldn't hold myself back anymore. I suddenly felt too exposed, and my selfish mind demanded payment in return.

"Will you ever tell me about what happened out there a year ago?" My voice was a whisper of a thing, barely audible to my own ears.

Jude returned that calculating stare to my face, my eyes, my mouth, seeming to inhale each quivering exhale from my lips.

That same rawness I'd felt moments before doubled until each inhale burned.

"One day I might."

A biting disappointment sat heavily upon my chest.

"But," he began, and cool fingers touched my skin, lifting my chin. My rampant pulse quickened at the contact. Never had something as simple as a touch brought about such a chaotic reaction. "What happened to my face took place many, many years before I joined the Knights."

I couldn't look away if I wanted to. I'd barely heard the words he'd spoken when he was touching me. The sensation was akin to the aftermath of a well-fought round in the ring. Addicting in the most devastating way possible.

"You wear your scars well." I spoke without thought. "If anything, they draw me to you." And they did. If only *he* knew the reason why.

Jude abruptly dropped his fingers from my chin, clearing his throat as he placed distance between us.

Why couldn't I simply stop speaking? My admission had broken the comfortable peace that had befallen us.

"I-I should go. As should you."

My chest constricted at the dismissal.

Jude rose to his feet in a single, fluid motion, a blur of black cloth and melancholy silver. Avoiding my eyes entirely, he didn't offer me a hand as I hoisted myself up.

The room lost all of the warmth that had bathed me seconds ago.

"Jude?"

"Yes, recruit?"

Great, we were back to that.

"Thank you for telling me. And for the book." I offered the heavy volume, but his focus strayed to the wall instead, as if the moldy stones were the most fascinating things in the world.

"Yes, well, I figured it would be beneficial. Though you should finish the story." His throat worked as he swallowed hard, the muscles in his shoulders visibly tensing beneath his taut shirt. I wondered what he wasn't saying.

Our easy conversation had turned into something awkward and frigid, and I detested that most of all. Just when I felt like I was getting him to open up to me, he shut down. Walled himself inside whatever fortress guarded his secrets.

"Goodnight, Kiara." Without another furtive glance, Jude bolted from the chamber, his heavy steps thundering across the cracked stones.

"Goodnight," I whispered to his back. My arms encircled his book as though it held the answer to our kingdom's curse, though I knew my protectiveness had everything to do with who it belonged to…

A boy who made my heart thud wildly in his presence. The stone-faced commander with a broken heart, whose past was teeming with dark secrets. And a mystery I was now determined to unravel.

Chapter Sixteen

Jude

A good man is often the one who has known the most evil.

ASIDIAN PROVERB

The next morning, King Cirian sprawled across the arms of his high-backed chair, his too-long limbs splayed leisurely in front of him as if we weren't discussing Asidia's future or possible demise.

The king was arrogant, always had been.

The walls of Cirian's grand war room were painted obsidian, darker than a moonless night. No pictures lined the windowless space, and the only pieces of furniture were the long black table and crimson velvet chairs, all now filled with the kingdom's leading officials and most trusted generals.

It reminded me of the inside of a deep cave—all sharp edges with no discernible way out. Even the air tasted foul, like rotten flesh masked by the floral scent of too many lit candles.

The king had already decided my mission, and only fools argued with a man devoid of reason and gifted with too much power. My appearance here today was, for all purposes, a formality.

I leaned back in my chair, the palest of blue eyes gazing

back at me from the head of the table. They were almost silver in certain lighting, unnatural and unnerving.

But his peculiar eyes and strong jaw were the only visible parts of the king, who wore his usual silver mask, crafted of the finest polished metal and etched with intricate whorls and curving lines. No one had seen him without his mask for decades. The last man who'd dared question it found his head decorating a spike. Put there by me.

"I wonder what it is that's occupying that head of yours, dear commander."

A dozen faces whirled in my direction, and a dozen chairs creaked as the bodies that occupied them shifted.

I could feel invisible flames lick at my skin. How I longed to lunge across the table, to wrap my hands around his neck and squeeze.

"My king." I stood, straining to appear nothing less than calm, indifferent. Loyal. "I am aware you know of my concerns about sending in the young recruits. All I am asking of you is to wait until their training is complete."

"I, too, agree, my king. If time is running out, as you say, we should make sure our final attempt leaves no room for error."

I glanced to Lord Baridin, a once wealthy landowner from the south. He'd pledged his allegiance to Cirian thirty years ago, but since then, his lands had withered in the night—along with his riches.

Cirian shoved out of his chair, his nearly luminescent skin a striking whitish gray in the yellow candlelight. He ignored Baridin entirely as he sauntered my way.

I held my ground, hands clasped behind my back, shoulders tall, as the merciless ruler of Asidia stopped inches from my frame.

He could do his best to intimidate me, but I had long ago ceased to fear this man.

I'd seen enough cruelty in this lifetime to fill a thousand more. A man who no longer feared death did not wither beneath its gaze.

"I thought I made myself very clear, Commander Maddox," the king snapped, cocking his head to the side. My reflection played across the smooth expanse of his mask, my expression stoic and expertly apathetic. If the king only knew what I *truly* thought of him...

"You did, Sire, but this batch of recruits is far from prepared, and I want nothing but the best for your efforts."

Cirian clucked his tongue. "Ah, see, I know you're hardly afraid of a little sacrifice. And we've exhausted the other routes entirely. Soon, the few crops we've been able to harvest will wither away, and our people will have nothing. I'm sure you don't want that."

He flashed a sneer in the direction of his advisor, a slimy man with a protruding gut who quivered beneath his master's penetrating gaze. "Call it intuition. Call it a vision from the gods."

Cirian paused to tilt his head mockingly to the ceiling, aiming for the heavens. "But I've been assured that this is *finally* the right path. That we will find the keys to break the curse out there, our salvation taking the form of three objects that, once united, will bring back the day. And you would do well to not question my judgment. Understood?"

There wasn't any other response I could give but "Yes, Sire."

He didn't elaborate on these mystical objects, the *keys to break the curse*. When Cirian had briefed me earlier, all he'd mentioned was that the gods themselves would aid us in our plight.

But that couldn't be true. The gods didn't care.

"Very well, then." Cirian swiveled in his boots, his long black robes fluttering about his lean frame as he moved back in the direction of his seat. But before he reached it, he grabbed hold of Lord Baridin's graying hair and yanked back. A silver dagger, hidden in the king's sleeves, slipped out and into his gloved hand.

Baridin didn't have a chance to scream as his throat was cut. Blood gushed from the wound, a spray of red wetting the papers he clutched in his still-twitching hands.

Cirian shoved the dying lord onto the table, his head striking the surface with brutal force. Gurgling noises sounded as Baridin bled out beside the refreshments.

The tension in the room became a thing of pain, though I felt hardly anything at all. The sight should have bothered me much more than it did.

"If anyone else wishes to voice their concerns about my plan, now would be the time." Cirian sighed, wiping his bloodied dagger on his long robes.

No one spoke. No one dared breathe.

"Perfect. Now, I am well aware of what needs to be done. And you all should move forward with your instructions." Cirian smiled at his advisors, and the high lords all blanched. Many shook their heads.

I'd yet to settle back into my chair, my muscles taut and on alert.

That could have been you, I thought, my nails digging into the fleshy parts of my palms. *One wrong word, and you're dead.*

I'd carelessly forgotten Cirian's ruthlessness. It was the reason he'd maintained the throne for so long. Many had tried usurping him, and all had failed. He was a man who'd become a monster, and too few were willing to battle a living nightmare.

"Good, then it's settled." King Cirian waved a careless hand in the air, dismissing the room.

It erupted in shuffling footsteps and fluttering papers. The advisors all but ran from the chamber, none willing to give the king an excuse to make them his next victim.

"Commander Maddox," Cirian called, and I halted, halfway

to the doorway and to safety.

I bit back a curse, whirling around. My nails dug into the flesh of my palms, no doubt hard enough to draw blood.

Lord Baridin's body lay halfway on the table, his head face down. A growing pool of red spread across the polished surface, wetting some of the papers left behind. I lifted my eyes.

"Yes, my king?"

"A word, if you will. I have something very important to discuss with you. Something that might clear some things up. Ease your wayward thoughts."

It was only us now in his war chambers, and being this close, this alone, with a man deemed bloodthirsty and heartless had a slick crown of sweat banding across my brow.

I might not fear the man, but his words still held consequences. And not simply for me.

"What is it, Sire?"

The king merely grinned, his canines poking into his full bottom lip. My fists clenched at the sight. Whatever he planned to ask would likely end with more blood on my hands.

I was his chosen weapon to quench his bloodlust.

"I've been given information claiming a girl has been added to your ranks, one hailing from the village of Cila?"

I nodded, my stomach churning. Instantly my mind held one image, a face I'd sworn to keep far from my thoughts. It had proven to be a useless feat.

"I want you to keep a very close eye on that one. Add her to your group, and bring her with you into the Mist. One of my little birds has deemed her rather important to the cause."

"But, Sire—"

"Silence!" he bellowed, losing the playful edge that had lined his words. Carefully, he tilted his head to the lifeless Baridin, as if in warning. "I want her beside you at all times. She might very well help us in our endeavors. Find what we have searched decades for. I am sure that is what you want as well, for our kingdom to be free of the night?" He stepped another inch closer, his breath hot on my cheek.

My brows furrowed. "How would one girl be of any significance?" I tried desperately to sound bored, unaffected by the decree, but the thought of Cirian knowing about Kiara, hoping to somehow *use* her, sent my hackles rising. I loathed how protective I felt.

"That's not for you to worry about, Maddox. But when her use reveals itself to you, I need you to follow through." When I opened my mouth to ask what he meant, Cirian merely shoved a folded piece of parchment into my hands.

"Read it, then burn it," he instructed, tapping a lean finger on my chest. "If everything happens as it should, then you will be rewarded. Richly."

As if I cared at all for riches, for station or promotion. What I desired was the impossible. A dream I'd long ago placed away, nearly forgotten, until that day in Cila's square when Kiara had awakened what I'd believed dead.

"The girl is not qualified," I lied. "She can hardly keep up with the rest of the recruits, and I refuse to send in someone who might hold us back."

King Cirian paused, an eerie calm settling in the too-small room.

My heart was pounding, louder and stronger than during any fight I'd yet to encounter. Never had I spoken so brazenly to the king. I expected him to scold me, to raise his voice and deem me a fool. But instead, he snapped his fingers, his lips curled in sinful triumph.

Seconds later, the double doors to the council room burst open, and three burly bastards, each the size of two men, came barreling in, sick smiles brightening their rugged faces.

"Help remind our beloved commander of his duties," Cirian

ordered, nodding to the men at my back. "And do not stop until he has fully...remembered."

And with that, the king sauntered from the room, two guards closing the doors behind him. I assessed the men before me, who began to circle me like vultures. I saw two options—

Fight back.

Or take it and live another day.

I shut my eyes just as the first punch landed.

Chapter Seventeen

Kiara

I had a dream of Grandmother last night and immediately
thought of you. There was always a bond between the two
of you I never understood. I think I was always envious of
it. You're like her in many ways—stubborn, self-righteous,
and certainly quick to anger. But like her, you attract the
little good in this world, and people—whether they love or
hate you—can't help but be drawn to you. Hells, I think I'm
envious of that as well.

Unmailed letter from Liam Frey to his sister, Kiara Frey,
year 50 of the curse

The morning began like every other one before it.

And that was the problem—Jude didn't make an appearance
during the meetup in the rotunda, and he was noticeably absent
from dinner.

Days passed.

I constantly peered into corridors and alcoves, expecting to
glimpse his shadowy form hiding in the gloom, his broad arms
crossed against his chest as raven hair tumbled into his depthless
eyes. Always observing. Forever guarding.

But he was never there.

He simply vanished like the shadow I likened him to, and not a single Knight spoke of him. As it wasn't a topic I could very well broach, I kept my mouth shut, choosing to keep a vigilant eye out for his scowling face. A face that undid me in more ways than I liked.

On the fourth morning of Jude's absence, Pat, Nic, Jake, and I practiced drills in the rotunda.

Since the trial in the caverns, the four of us had become inseparable. Perhaps our ordeal had bonded us, made us form a ragtag team. But whatever the reason, I was grateful, if begrudgingly so.

On that particularly brisk morning, I'd just instructed Nic on how to complete an exceptionally complex combo. Carter had grimaced at my deviation from his training, but a second later, he was mimicking my motions, grumbling beneath his breath as he tried to perfect the intricate series of motions.

"Not bad," he admitted in that roughened way of his. "You could use some more force behind it, but decent enough." He grabbed at his graying beard, the corner of his eyes crinkling with what I could mistake for amusement.

He moved on to the next group of trainees, ruffling one of the lads' heads before he showed them the new moves. I smiled at the sight.

"Such a suck-up, Ki," Nic said with a smirk.

"Not a suck-up, Nic. It's not my fault Carter took notice of my impeccable form." I batted my lashes playfully. "Maybe if you didn't hesitate before striking, you'd catch his eye too."

Jake snorted, and Nic shot him a warning look.

The boys had just resumed their stances when the hair on the back of my neck tingled, a pleasant rush of air wafting through the dampened strands of my loose braid.

Even as I turned, I knew it was him.

Jude.

I froze where I stood, shocked speechless by the battered mess that was Commander Maddox's face.

Ghastly purple bruises blossomed beneath both eyes, and a nasty cut sliced across his unscarred cheek. The once straight bridge of his nose was crooked and slightly swollen, leading me to believe it had been broken.

But it was the utter lifelessness in his eyes that did me in—a pain so tangible it crashed into my body, ripping the air from my lungs.

A slight gasp accompanied the tremor that worked its way up my spine. My eyes burned with a foreign rage as I rediscovered my voice.

"Commander Maddox!" I yelled across the room, his name tumbling out of my mouth in a flustered rush. "Can I have a word?"

Jude staggered into the light of the sunfires, the soft blaze illuminating each grisly blow he'd been dealt. I envisioned every last one of them, every strike, each bone-shattering punch, and my mouth soured.

He regarded me coldly, both his hands clasped austerely behind his back. Painfully long seconds ticked by, and just when I believed Jude would ignore me, that he'd leave me breathless and questioning, he rigidly jerked his head toward the privacy of the corridor.

He slipped away without a word.

"I'll be right back, guys," I called over my shoulder, not bothering to spare them a glance. They'd likely tease me about the commander again. They certainly hadn't held back since the day he'd carried me to the bath, especially Jake. He was the worst of them.

I barreled into the curving corridor, the pale sunfire sconces providing just enough of a glow so I didn't stumble. A lithe silhouette lingered beneath an empty sconce, Jude's black clothes and hair doing well to camouflage him.

"Ju— Commander," I corrected, closing the gap between us.

His eyes used to flicker in amusement when he spoke with me, but this time, they were as dull as unpolished silver. "Yes, recruit? How can I help you?"

Gods, his tone could cut through stone.

"I-I was wondering," I began, off to a stuttering start, "where you've been all this time? I didn't see you once shadowing Harlow, or at dinner—"

"Where I go is none of your concern, recruit." His jaw ticked, but I noted how his brown eye flared, amber flooding his iris. He crossed his arms against his chest, his breaths uneven and strained.

"I'm sorry, I was just...worried?" I said it like a question, and maybe it was one. I hadn't been entirely truthful as to why I'd sought him out over the last few days. Obviously, something horrific had taken place, or his face wouldn't be painted with bruises and cuts.

My fists clenched, and ice pooled in my belly. I wanted to lash out, wanted to strike something, *anything*. The overwhelming surge of rage should have startled me, but I simply drank it in, swallowing it down like sweet wine.

Jude took a step closer, the torchlight casting macabre shadows beneath his already dark eyes. "Why on earth would you be worried?" he taunted with an acidic bite, his full lips stretched thin. "I am your commander. Not your friend."

The words stung more than I would have liked. Sure, I didn't think we would exchange chocolates and braid one another's hair, but still, I thought we had an understanding. A *unique* relationship. One he didn't share with the others.

Had I been so foolishly wrong?

"My apologies, commander," I ground out, venom wrapped around every syllable. "I will leave you to your duties, then."

Gods, why did I even care? Why had I spent my nights thinking about the well-being of a boy who clearly didn't deserve it? My nostrils flared, and with a look that would have had any man cowering, I turned on my heel, setting off for my friends.

I wasn't prepared for the hand that encircled my wrist, for the shock of those warm fingers wrapping around me, holding me back.

"Kiara."

I turned, my name as coarse as sandpaper coming from his lips.

The hand that secured me pulled, and I allowed it, permitting him to guide me farther into the gloom, farther from prying eyes.

In a whirl of temper, I turned, that familiar rush of icy heat racing down my arms and prickling the tips of my fingers. This man brought out the fire I often failed to smother, stoking the flames until the chaos within could not be contained.

"What do you want, commander?" I asked derisively. "I thought I was dismissed?"

Jude's stare flickered to where his hand grasped mine, a peculiar expression replacing his earlier apathy. I almost relented, nearly softened, but I held firm, meeting him head-on.

When he finally spoke, his voice was lined with gravel, with glass, and with a tinge of what I believed to be bitterness. "That group I told you about?" The one he'd been entrusted to take into the Mist. "We're to set out tomorrow."

"I thought we were departing last week, and then you just disappeared."

"Well." He snaked a hand through his tangled hair, the color taking on a bluish-yellow tint in the light. "I wasn't fond of the idea of sending untrained men into battle. Especially as I know firsthand what lies beyond. But it seems as if I don't have a choice in the matter. Not that I ever did."

The bitterness swelled, stinging my ears. "I relayed my thoughts to my superiors, but they are determined to explore every possible route. For a reason beyond my understanding, it has been decided that three groups of recruits will be led into the cursed lands to seek a cure, without proper training, without time to prepare. Without a damned hope of survival."

It was the starkness of a cutting pain that replaced the burning resentment in his eyes.

"Is that why they…why your face…" I couldn't finish the thought, was unable to form coherent words. But Jude, understanding what I meant, nodded.

My jaw clenched. I wanted to kill the men who'd harmed Jude, who'd made him bleed.

Is this how he'd felt when I'd nearly died in the tunnels? This annoying sense of protectiveness? It made me feel sick in a way I hadn't experienced before.

Black shadows prickled the edges of my vision as my hand rose of its own accord. When my leather-clad fingers made contact with the gruesome gash marring his cheekbone, he flinched. But I didn't pull away.

I expected Jude to shove my hand down and retreat, to put the proper distance befitting those in our positions. But when his unusually scruffy cheek pressed into my hand, both eyes momentarily shutting as he loosed an exhale, my traitorous heart fluttered.

Jude's lids blinked open a heartbeat later, his stare unflinching as his gaze dove into mine and soothed a piece of my soul I'd only recently discovered. He didn't look at me like most people did—not with loathing or indifference, or even doubt.

Jude stared at me like he saw the fighter hidden beneath my skin. The powerful woman I could become. And in the reflection of his eyes, I saw the truest version of myself. Maybe that's why I couldn't look into them for too long.

The stagnant air was sucked from the room, an overwhelming feeling of floating and drowning threatening to weaken my knees. It was a moment captured in a bubble—one that would inevitably burst.

Jude pulled away first, rising to his full height.

Not sure what to say, I shifted nervously on my feet, peering at him from beneath my lashes. What the hells had just happened?

He took a step back, his jaw growing tense once more, the serenity he'd experienced at my touch dispersing into the shadows that pressed at our backs.

"We leave in the morning."

I watched his Adam's apple bob.

"I've selected four recruits to accompany me and two other Knights. The remaining two groups will depart the day after."

I felt myself nod, the words not yet sinking in.

"You're supposed to be on my list."

"I see." The mood was so heavy that I didn't even make a quip about being the best recruit in the bunch. Which was true, but now didn't seem the time to rub that fact in.

Jude's unkempt hair tumbled into his face. He was a mess, and not just physically.

"Are you going to tell me what to expect?" I asked hesitantly.

"We will make camp right before the Mist. There, I will explain everything. It's not safe to do so here." He scanned the empty corridor warily. Perhaps the Knights' sanctum wasn't as secure as I'd been led to believe.

"I see," I repeated, though I didn't understand at all. Not the mission, and certainly not whatever was growing between me and my superior.

Jude lifted his hand as if to touch my cheek, but likely thought better of it, lowering it to his side and balling it into a tight fist. He gave me one final lingering look before abandoning me in the hall.

Tomorrow was the beginning of the end.

Chapter Eighteen

Jude

She is what we've suspected. A little nudging on my part, and the commander will select her all on his own.
No one will be the wiser.

Letter from unknown sender to King Cirian, year 50 of the curse

The recruits were all lined up before Harlow, Carter, and Isiah before I stepped into the rotunda.

Today was the day lives would be changed forever. Today, I would deliver a sentence worse than death.

My stomach was lead as I marched into the center and took my place alongside my men.

Harlow nodded, but Isiah met my eyes and held them, a knowing look passing between us. He silently conveyed everything swirling in my head.

That these boys weren't ready to die.

That fate was cruel and we had no other choice but to follow orders.

I twisted away from my oldest friend. I wouldn't be able to get through today if I stared any longer. Isiah had a gift of worming his way under my skin and *almost* making me forget that I was a servant to the Crown.

The recruits' faces were sober, not one of them daring to speak.

"You must be wondering why you are all gathered here before us." Lieutenant Harlow circled the room like a caged beast, his deep-green eyes sharpening on every lad he passed.

"Today, a small number of you, personally selected by our commander, will be tasked to carry out a dangerous mission. But Commander Maddox has been gracious enough to allow those chosen the option to accept or deny…seeing as you haven't completed your training yet," he added with a grimace.

Harlow hadn't liked that stipulation. Neither had Isiah, who argued that it wasn't wise to go against the king's wishes.

Truthfully, I *shouldn't* be allowing choice, but it was my own way of rebelling against Cirian. I never had that option, and I'd be damned if I sent the recruits into the cursed lands without their consent.

I stepped forward as Harlow fell in line with the other Knights. He shot me a scowl before facing ahead.

"Today, I am asking a select few to journey with me and my men into the Mist," I said, gasps echoing in reply. "You have the choice to turn down this assignment, but just so you know, the king has decreed it vital for the kingdom's safety. You may also know that we lost many Knights on the last mission, and that is why we had to make The Calling mandatory this year for all eligible initiates."

I briefly found Kiara across the room, her rich copper hair glowing beneath the chandelier. At her side were the three boys who followed her everywhere. Patrick, the one with freckles and pale-green eyes, sidled closer, but when he made to reach for her gloved hand, she pulled away. *Interesting*.

I looked away from her, already anticipating the hellfire that would soon rain down on me once she discovered what I'd done.

Or rather, the final decision I'd made.

"When I call your name, please step into the ring." Every one of them straightened, probably holding their breaths. Four names. Four lives lost.

"Nic Danic."

Kiara's attention shot to her new friend, whose skin paled visibly. He recovered quickly enough, squaring his shoulders and striding into the center. He gave me a respectful nod before twisting back to his friends, hands clasped behind his back.

"Jake Carlton." Another of her friends. Jake fell in line next to Nic, the two gazing blankly ahead. Kiara had unknowingly surrounded herself with the best of the lot. Jake excelled at archery and hand-to-hand combat, and Nic was an exceptional swordsman.

"Alec Evans."

Another good soldier, and quick on his feet. I noted how he'd received excellent marks from Harlow, which was impressive in itself.

Four names. Four recruits.

Kiara lifted her chin expectantly, awaiting her turn. She was prepared for me to call her name, to condemn her—

"Patrick Parsons."

She was too stunned to issue a protest, and I watched soundlessly as Patrick ambled into the center of the chamber, his skin a sickly white. He was well versed in lore and botany, both useful attributes for where we were headed. Regardless of his fighting abilities, he'd make a decent addition.

"Commander Maddox!" It appeared as though Kiara had found her voice after all.

"Recruit?" I fixed my face into an expression of indifference. "You have a question?"

She seethed, her hands clenching. "I am just as qualified, if not more so, than the appointed recruits. I would like to take the last recruit's place."

Patrick's face turned a deep crimson, his eyes widening in shock as he urged her to shut her mouth.

"The decision is final," I barked, turning away from her and giving her my back. "However, if the recruits selected would like to decline, now is their chance."

I hadn't been lying when I'd offered them that one small mercy. Sure, turning down this offer would relegate them to the Guard, but at least they'd have a better chance of living.

My heart thundered as Kiara begged them to reconsider, her tone comprised of ice and fury.

No one spoke up. No one answered her pleas.

Secretly, I was thankful. I'd pay for this later though, when the king discovered I'd knowingly disobeyed a direct order, but I'd be too far into the Mist by then to feel his wrath.

Besides, I didn't expect to return back home to Sciona this time. Not breathing, at least.

"Recruits?" I probed, turning to each of them in turn. "Do any of you wish to return to the ranks?"

The recruits steeled their spines and bit their tongues.

"But, commander! You can't possibly expect—"

"Quiet!" The thundering command reverberated throughout the chamber, Kiara's protests freezing on the tip of her tongue.

I cursed all the gods, wishing to wipe away that look on her face. The one that had my insides twisting and my pulse soaring. She hated me. I could see it clearly enough.

Looking away from her, I began conveying orders to the recruits, telling them to head to the stables once they finished packing. Thankfully, Isiah and Carter started rattling off a list of preparations, though deep lines formed across Isiah's forehead, my friend shooting me a curious glance.

Throughout, I felt her stare on my back like a red-hot brand.

Leave, I begged. *Be smart and fucking walk away.*

She didn't. Stubborn woman.

Harlow shouted an order, and those not selected scrambled away to the upper training fields. I didn't move to join them. Not yet. I merely turned, knowing full well what awaited me.

Kiara's stare could cut through metal. With her chin lifted and her eyes clouded with shadows, she looked nothing short of a lethal warrior.

"I told you to leave, recruit," I growled, stepping into her space. Even though I was a good foot taller than her, it still felt like she was looking down on me. It had to be a gift.

"What did I just say?" I hissed, my voice low enough that the others across the room didn't hear. "I told you to leave!"

"And I was told I would be on that list of yours," she answered boldly.

I moved until my chest pressed against hers. "You're wearing on my last nerve, Frey," I snapped, losing what little patience I retained. If she didn't leave now, I'd be forced to make a scene and punish her for disobeying an order from a superior.

"And I simply don't care."

Inhaling a jagged breath at the insolent words, I clenched my fists and swallowed every curse I wanted to release. "You *will* die if you go out there. Don't you understand that?" My voice softened, if only slightly. "This mission of the king's is a fool's errand. A suicide mission. One I've carefully deliberated on and decided not to put you through. Especially when you have the potential to be great."

I'd debated all through the night, and sometime around three in the morning, I'd made a decision. Call it impulsive, but for once in my life, I refused to be a puppet, a pawn. A harbinger of death.

"I'm coming, Jude," she snarled, pressing a finger into my chest. Her eyes turned even darker, narrowing into catlike slits.

"No, you're not coming. I will not be the cause of your death."

"If you think for one moment that I will let them go and die in that cursed fog without me, then you don't know me at all."

I knew her, and that was the problem. Once Kiara had claimed those boys as her own, she would do everything in her power to protect them. Just as she had defended her brother during The Calling.

"Too. Damn. Bad." I bared my teeth in challenge, and a muscle in my jaw feathered.

"You're going to regret that," she threatened, a twisted smile curving her sensuous lips. The certainty of that promise stole my air.

Without bothering to utter one more word, Kiara turned on her heel and bolted, her boots thundering like a storm of wrath and ruin.

I watched every step she took, knowing full well I'd done nothing but poke at the beast lurking within. But my beast matched hers, and we'd only tear one another to pieces in the end.

CHAPTER NINETEEN

KIARA

The time is approaching, and I grow weaker by the day. This
will be my final letter to you, as my previous queries have all
gone unanswered. I worry that your relationship with Cirian
has changed, and I fear your closeness. I pray you have not
forgotten the mission at hand. If we do not succeed,
then Asidia will pay the price.

LETTER FROM AURORA ADAIR TO UNKNOWN RECIPIENT,
YEAR 49 OF THE CURSE

Uncle Micah had taught me many useful things over the
years.

Among them was that anger and fear had no place on the
battlefield. You left those emotions behind you. *Any* emotion
had no place in your mind when facing a mission, a fight.

Thus far, I was utterly failing Micah.

My temper flared, burning brighter than any man-made
flame. It was my greatest weakness—my inability to tame my
fury, to place it inside a box and face the world with clear eyes.

Not when my vision was glazed in red.

He'd all but promised I'd be on that list, and then he'd
turned around and chosen the recruits closest to me? No, I

wouldn't stand for that.

Anger didn't even begin to cover what slithered in my veins.

It was my life in Cila all over again—being told what I could and could not do. If it hadn't been for Uncle Micah and some *particularly* contentious training sessions, I'd have loosed an arrow into the eye of some deserving man back home.

Sure, I understood he was trying to protect me, but Jude should've realized there wouldn't be anything he could do to stop me from going once he'd called those names.

Secretly I suspected he knew this too.

Right after my confrontation with the commander, I'd crept back to the dorms, snagging my only extra set of fresh clothes and a hooded cloak that would provide some warmth against the chill outside these walls. Timepieces were rare—meant only for the wealthy or those in power—but I remembered seeing one of the boys hiding an older model beneath his mattress, and I took that as well.

The next stop was the kitchens, where I loaded up on supplies—and a canteen full of vodka. I'd expected water, but the vodka was a lovely surprise I couldn't turn down.

The mission at hand was simple: I'd stay hidden as my fellow recruits ventured beyond the gates and into the thick of the Pastoria Forest. The trick was to allow them just enough distance to believe they were in the clear before I pursued.

Now, crouching in the unlit corner of the stables, I observed Pat and my friends mounting their prepared steeds, their bags bulging at the seams. They'd been outfitted in leather jackets and coarse black cloaks, their boots replaced with those the Knights wore.

None of them sported the grins I'd gotten to know and memorize over the past few days, and all the good-natured camaraderie was absent.

Ju—Commander Maddox—escorted them through the

wrought-iron gates, riding ahead with his head encased in that menacing steel helmet, the obsidian spikes particularly ominous today. While he didn't wear armor—likely due to the added burden—he was undoubtedly on his way to battle.

The hilt of the jeweled dagger I'd *borrowed* from the training room poked into my side. It would be a good bribe for a greedy stablehand.

"Psst!" I hissed from the shadows, spotting my prey.

The young stablehand's brown eyes rose suspiciously to where I lurked in the dim. He glanced both ways before ambling over, his tawny brow thoroughly furrowed.

"I need a horse that is quick and won't be noticed missing," I barked, not granted the time for a smooth introduction. And sure, it was a tall order, but I prayed the jewels embedded in the dagger would persuade him to take the risk.

The boy gave a derisive scoff, holding back a chuckle. "Get lost." He waved me off, turning to grab a rusted shovel from a hook on the wall. I slid from the shadows.

"So this"—I extracted the polished weapon from its hiding place—"wouldn't interest you, then?" I made sure to twist the blade so that the seductive gleam of the gems caught the light of the torches. Hells, even I would be tempted to accept the offer if our roles were reversed.

As I'd suspected, the stable boy's features brightened in awareness, the sneer he'd worn wiped clean off his gaunt face. "W-where did you get that?"

"Does it matter?" I raised a brow, shrugging. I took a bold step closer. "You either want it or not, and it is well worth the price of a horse. Look at the quality of these sapphires surrounding the ruby." I sounded like some of the traveling merchants that frequented our village every March, pushing their wares onto busy shoppers.

The boy didn't even pretend to think it over.

With a displeased grumble, he relented, shooting me a crude gesture before vanishing into the farthest stall. The smile that lifted the corners of my mouth was triumphant. It had been almost too easy.

My smug grin plummeted upon seeing the horse he'd secured for me.

The chocolate mare had some age on her, that much was apparent. She seemed as ready for a strenuous trek as a three-legged donkey, and that was me being generous. "Are you trying to pull one over on me, boy? That horse has to be older than I am!"

"You want her or not? This is the only mare that will go unnoticed, and it's my only offer." He defiantly crossed his reedy arms at his chest, raising a thin brow as if to ask, 'What are you going to do about it?'

What a cocky little asshole.

"Fine," I growled, snagging the reins before tossing him the sheathed blade. His hands fumbled as he caught it, and he admired it briefly before tucking it beneath his threadbare wool jacket.

"But just so you're warned…"

I paused at his foreboding tone, about to unhook a worn saddle hanging across from the stalls. "Starlight is much feistier than she looks."

I doubted it. The mare looked like she would rear back in fright at the sight of a cockroach. "Thanks for the advice," I sneered, fitting the saddle over her back.

Starlight. Yeah, with a name like that, she would be a real hellion.

"Come on, old broad, let's see what you got."

The mare grunted in reply, shaking her muzzle at me in reproach. "Fine. No need to get sassy with me." I patted her neck, which only seemed to irritate her further. Perhaps the ancient horse had more life in her than I thought.

Grabbing the reins, I led Starlight through the side exit of the courtyard, my hooded head lowered but my steps confident.

You would have thought being the only girl in the heart of the Knights' sanctum would have made me stick out like…well, like the only girl in the Knights' sanctum. But not one of the grumbling stablehands nor any of the scurrying servants paid me any mind.

Maybe the oversized hood of my cloak helped disguise me. Red hair still poked out at the sides, but with my head bent to the packed earth, I might very well pass as one of the many errand boys coming in and out of the palace.

This thought bolstered my conviction, and my shoulders lost some of their rigidness.

When I was beyond the main gates of the palace, a bored soldier in desperate need of coffee having waved me through, I mounted my grumbly horse.

Starlight nickered as I hoisted myself onto her back, settling only when I scolded her in my most reproachful tone. She might be feisty, but she had just met her match.

This early, the neatly paved streets were quiet, and the plentiful torches and lanterns raised above the boulevards cast an eerie glow. With no curious eyes to gawk at me, I lifted my head and took in the skeletal city of gray and black.

"Come on, *Starlight*," I mocked, kicking her flank to urge her forward. Shaking her mane, the tangled black tresses flicking at her sides, she shot ahead, nearly jostling me right out of the worn saddle. "You don't like that name, either, eh, girl?"

I could relate. Kiara wasn't a name I would have chosen for myself.

"Well, if you're nice to me, then perhaps I'll help you out. We can always change it to something more fitting." Like "Thorn"… or "Smart-Ass."

Starlight brought us to the edge of the city of torches and bones, and right before the imposing gates of Sciona. The half-awake guard who signaled me through barely spared me a glance, more worried about who was venturing *into* the capital. I smiled inside.

Past the stone gates and the decaying heads of the king's enemies, I paused at the last flaming torch. The moon itself wouldn't do, as the sky was particularly overcast with leaden clouds. Reaching into the saddlebag, I doused my unlit torch in oil and dipped it into the fluttering blaze, comforted as a warm glow highlighted the mahogany in Starlight's coat.

"All right, girl. Now for the fun part," I whispered into her ear. She snorted in response.

Time to catch up with the commander and my new friends.

I couldn't wait to see the look on Jude's face when I finally caught them.

Gods, it was too damn easy. Or maybe I was just too damn good.

In less than an hour, I'd not only tracked down the assemblage of Knights and recruits, but I'd somehow tamed the beast that was Starlight. Apparently, the mare appreciated a bit of sarcasm and some good old-fashioned head rubs.

Just like Uncle taught me, I maintained a safe distance from my prey, trailing behind the modest group, whose faces were impassive as they likely contemplated what unknown terrors lay in wait. I, too, felt the pressure of foreboding in my chest. The night was fearful, the air too still, the glacial chill punishing. And yet, I could've sworn I heard my name whispered from the trees.

The night could speak all it wished. Didn't mean I was

obliged to listen.

I rolled my shoulders back and did my best to mentally will away the goose bumps dotting my arms. Above my head, the steel clouds framed the moon, which had become tinged with an ominous red hue the farther I journeyed into the Pastoria Forest. At the sight, my goose bumps grew more pronounced, my skin prickling painfully.

The branches sprouting from the charred trunks were all graced with onyx leaves that shimmered as though crusted in diamonds. It was a hauntingly beautiful sight, all those gleaming bits of fractured light, but I knew it merely disguised all the evil that rested among the roots.

Beyond the copse of blackened trees were the trembling lights of the Knights' torches. I maintained my distance, only extinguishing my flame when they slowed for the evening.

Sure enough, Commander Maddox signaled the unit to halt, the recruits dismounting their steeds to unpack. I sighed in relief. I wasn't sure how much time had passed, but my aching limbs thanked him.

Slipping from Starlight, my bones crunching as I struck the hard earth, I led her to a nearby tree, tying her reins around its rugged trunk. She shot me an exasperated look before grazing on the prickly grass.

I could just make out the muffled voices of the others as they shared a quick meal by a hastily constructed fire, Jude's voice absent from the chaotic chorus.

I was well aware I'd have to join them at some point, but prolonging the inevitable, even for one more evening, felt like a safer bet.

Lying on the damp ground, I fashioned my cloak into a makeshift pillow, tilting my gaze toward the stars. While they were always out, the sight of them never ceased to rob my breath.

Liam often teased me, claiming that I belonged in the sky

alongside them, as my head was forever in the clouds.

He wasn't entirely wrong.

There were many restless evenings at home where I'd sneak off and spread a thick woven blanket out beneath the twinkling lights. Sometimes I would bring a mug of Mother's famous hot chocolate, angling my head to watch the fiery gems I could see, but never hold.

I thought I preferred it that way—nothing of beauty and substance should be kept by one person alone.

And in their own way, the stars soothed me more than any dagger or adrenaline-filled fight ever could. They coaxed out a side of me that few had ever seen before—a calm one.

Tonight, the stars were especially radiant, and after the day I'd had, I welcomed the sight. A part of me feared it would be one of the last times I would ever glimpse them, and my heart ached at the melancholy thought.

Sleep must have taken me at some point, because the crunching of a tree branch jerked me awake.

My hand shot to the dagger strapped to my thigh. I knew there were many thieves and rogues that preyed on the vulnerable in this forest. It was near enough to the capital and the surrounding villages to be a temptation to lowlifes looking for easy coin.

Scanning the thicket through narrowed eyes, I searched for signs of life, for anything amiss. The shadows were deeper than before, a thick fog of gray creeping through the underbrush. It hugged the surrounding trees, the air tasting of smoke.

It's just fog, I chastised myself.

This forest was known to play tricks on the mind. It was the reason why most with any semblance of self-preservation steered clear of it.

I was paranoid. After all, I was a fleeing recruit who would be sent to the Patrol if found.

I was a damn *fugitive*, and that was enough to instill fear in the heart of any rational individual.

"Rational" being the key word. I might have toed that line one too many times.

Lowering myself back to the earth, I hesitantly shut my eyes, willing the brimming anxiety to ease. When minutes passed and silence reigned over the stagnant evening air, my weary muscles loosened once again, sleep opening its arms wide to receive me.

I felt the cold metal of the blade before I saw it.

My eyes shot open, lowering to where the sharpened point pressed against the hollow of my throat.

Damn it. I should have listened to my gut.

A deep voice made of pure velvet and ice whispered into the shell of my ear, fiery breath tickling my flesh as the hair on the back of my neck rose in alarm.

"And here I thought you might have actually listened."

Chapter Twenty

Jude

There have been whisperings of a prophecy among my
fellow priestesses. It claims the day will be restored when
the darkness falls for the light. I cannot make sense of these
words, but I do know hope is a powerful thing to have. And
hope rarely comes during times of sense.

FOUND IN THE DIARY OF JUNIPER MARCHANT, SUN PRIESTESS,
YEAR 3 OF THE CURSE

The first word that escaped her lips was a curse. A crude one
at that.

I resisted the urge to smile; I had to remind myself that I
was livid.

"Is that any way to speak in front of your *commander*?" I
still held the blade to her throat, the tip just barely piercing the
skin. A thin line of blood rose to the surface, the coppery scent
wafting to my flaring nostrils.

My thighs rested on either side of her lithe frame, and every
ragged inhale she took had her chest rising to meet mine. My
anger at her being here was quickly being replaced with another
feeling.

Wicked heat curled in my stomach as her breath tickled my

cheeks. My gaze fell, taking in the sight of her face beneath the moon's precious light, memorizing the curve of her full bottom lip, how enticing it looked. I wondered what she'd taste like, if—

"I told you to bring me," she panted. I forced myself to look into her eyes, abandoning her lips. "You knew I'd follow."

I did. Really, I did. Kiara was nothing if not stubborn, a trait I could almost admire. On anyone else, I'd have found it utterly irritating.

"Kiara," I rumbled.

A tremor shook her body, and my palms grew clammy. The hand holding the knife trembled.

"This is my choice, Jude," she whispered. Slowly she brought her hand to my wrist, curling her fingers around it. She made no move to shove me away, to try and free herself. She just held me.

Choice.

King Cirian had never given me a choice. Not in all my years of serving him. Why the hells did she have to use that word?

Kiara took in a deep breath, and the blade at her throat dug deeper. "Do you put blades to all of your recruits' throats? Or am I just special?"

A raspy chuckle left me. I wasn't sure who was more surprised by the sound.

"I think we both know you're not like the other recruits, Kiara." I said the words before I could think better of it. I lost all rational thought around her. Since the beginning, before she'd even known I was her commander, it had been easy to talk with her, but now…

Now, with her *under* me, it was a damned miracle I could form any coherent thought at all.

"I'm flattered, *Jude*," she sneered, though I noted how her voice wavered. "If only I could return the favor."

I smirked as the silver of the blade flashed in the soft moonlight. Without breaking contact or losing my hold on her,

I sheathed the weapon.

I lowered my mouth to her ear, her hair tickling my cheek. "I'd imagine you would rather enjoy that. Perhaps too much."

I had just raised my head when she struck.

Her lips captured mine, the force of her kiss catching me off guard.

I groaned into her mouth, stunned beyond belief, but not disappointed by the turn of events. Kiara let out a breathy sound, and my entire world tilted on its axis.

Gods, her lips were just as soft as I'd imagined, just as plush. Kiara tasted like adventure itself, like a wine I'd happily grow drunk off.

I brought my hand to cup her cheek, the other winding around to the nape of her neck. My fingers fisted her silken hair, gripping the strands and pulling her impossibly close.

A soft sigh escaped her, and I felt her melt into the kiss, into *me*, as her hands traveled to my chest, her fingers clutching the thin fabric of my shirt, her grip unrelenting and desperate.

For a moment we were suspended in time, where the only reality that existed was the sensation of our lips moving as one. Gods, we fit together so perfectly, like we'd been created solely for the other—

This time, when my world tilted, it wasn't because of her kiss. Before I even knew what had happened, I was flung onto my back...into the same position I'd had her in moments before.

Cold steel pressed against my throat.

"Much better, don't you think?" She cocked her head, a daring smile gracing the lips I'd just tasted. I wanted to laugh, to curse, to lift up and kiss her again.

"That wasn't very nice." I *tsk*ed, and she squeezed her thighs against me. The heat in my core grew. Such a devilish deception... though secretly, I wondered if that was all it had been. A lie.

"So easily distracted," she drawled, bringing her face mere

inches from mine. I saw the indecision there, the doubt that had crept into her eyes. The annoying, logical side of me hated that look.

She was *too* close. It was muddling my mind, any cutting remark I could muster dying a swift death on my tongue. And yet, the masochistic part of me wished to see what she was going to do next.

"I didn't want you here for a reason," I finally whispered when the weight of the moment grew too much, the air too thick with her scent. The memory of her lips haunted me. "You may think you're unstoppable, but you have no idea what awaits you out there."

"Why do *you* care so much? You wouldn't treat any other recruit like this. Why me?"

She had every right to ask. It's a question I'd asked myself many times, trying to pinpoint the exact moment things had shifted. Or if they'd always been this way.

"The fight calls to you, Kiara, same as me." The hand holding the blade dropped, the weapon resting at her side. "Most people just survive for themselves. But not you... You don't allow anyone to control you." That's what I envied about her, what I saw whenever I looked into her eyes. Kiara was a wild creature that couldn't be tamed, and I'd been on my leash for far too long. My voice came soft as I said, "In you, I recognized something I long ago believed I'd forgotten. In you, I saw who I used to be."

Free.

"S-so you saw...yourself in me," she stuttered, a rosy blush creeping up her neck. "I mean—"

"I know what you meant," I said, enjoying how that blush turned a deeper shade of red. She might be straddling me, but I was the one undoing her. "And I've cursed picking you every moment of every day."

Because certain lines could never be crossed. Especially by

someone like me.

Kiara flinched. I could feel the confusion radiating off her, could see the battle raging as her heated stare breached my defenses, leaving me exposed.

"Curse me all you want, Jude. But if I'm your reflection, you can't escape me." I was floating and drowning again. A sensation I now associated with her. "And I have a feeling you don't want to…"

My eyes fell to her lips once more, to where the truth had been released.

I didn't deny her words, and my silence drew her closer, her head lowering as if she were equally as bewitched as I. So close, just an inch separating us now.

All I desired was to close the gap and lose myself to the flames she ignited, to burn so deliciously until we were remade, like a blade forged in steel.

Powerful. Kissing Kiara Frey made me feel powerful. Untouchable and—

A branch snapped in the distance, and Kiara jerked away from my lips, shoving off from my chest and to her feet. She moved like smoke on a breeze, fluid and light. I'd just risen to my own feet when the glow of a torch bloomed, pale orange flames highlighting the diamond crystals clinging to every leaf.

"There you are, commander." Isiah's voice reached my ears seconds before he appeared from the corner of my eye. Kiara and I remained frozen, our eyes locked as the unspoken words hovered between us.

"Isiah. I thought I told you to stay at the camp?"

I had the sudden urge to wring his neck.

"You did, but you were gone for a long time. I came to make sure you were all right."

"Everything is fine," I growled, and Isiah chuckled in reply, making my irritation grow. I had no doubt he knew exactly what had transpired, or at least, he had some idea. Twisting to Kiara, I found that blush still heating her cheeks, the sight visible even in the gloom. "I just happened to find a recruit who wouldn't listen to the word 'No.'" She huffed at that. "Apparently, she decided all on her own that she was ready to face the Mist."

"Lovely," Isiah murmured under his breath. "As if we needed another body to look after." He peered over his shoulder. "But maybe she can knock the others out of their stupor. Not one of the bastards has spoken since we left the palace. Especially the one with the freckles. He looks pissed."

At the mention of her friends, Kiara's dark gaze softened.

"I'll bring her to camp. We'll be with you shortly, Isiah."

"You need a light?" he offered, but I shook my head, and without another word, he swiftly retreated into the woods from where he'd come.

Kiara and I were alone once more, but now, we basked in the same darkness that had cast its spell.

I motioned to where Isiah had vanished. "Well, if you insist on dying, you might as well do it with your friends." My tone was biting.

"Why is Patrick here?" she asked, crossing her arms.

"Because his education in lore is valuable. I told you as much."

"Seriously? If a fight broke out, that boy couldn't even throw a decent punch. He'd probably break his hand," she argued back. Her lips thinned, and of course, I thought back to her kiss.

Such a dirty trick—one I wouldn't mind being deceived with again.

I heaved an impatient sigh. "Some strengths do not lie in the physical, recruit."

"So, we're back to 'recruit'? What happened to 'Kiara'? Which, by the way, I hate. Usually my friends call me—"

"Ki. Yes, I'm aware," I interrupted. "But I would hardly call myself your friend." Not after the heat I'd felt between us. I was still burning. Besides, I didn't *want* to be her friend. I wanted—

I didn't know what I wanted. Or maybe I did, and that was the problem.

She scoffed. "I'm not entirely sure you're simply my commander, either." Her hand flew to her mouth as the words tumbled out. "I only mean that I'm not a Knight yet, that's all," she babbled, her quivering voice giving her away. I said nothing of her fumbling, but I couldn't stop a smirk from forming.

"*Whatever* I am, you are Kiara to me," I affirmed, my voice deepening.

Tension built once again, but I didn't allow it to overflow. I marched over to where her mare was tied and took hold of the reins. "Come on, then. Before I send you to the Patrol."

"You've got bigger balls on you than I do." Those were the first words spoken to Kiara the following day.

"Seriously, Jake," Kiara groused, rolling onto her side as she peeled open a sleep-encrusted eye. "While I take immense pleasure in your warmly thought-out compliment, I must say, having you hovering over me is not how I wished to wake. That, and your morning breath could slay a horse. I'll have to keep my horse far away."

By the time we'd snuck into camp, the other recruits were all passed out around the fire, so the surprise of her arrival had had to wait until now. I watched from across the dying flames, pretending to sharpen my blade while studying them all from the corner of my eye.

Jake shoved at Kiara's shoulder before running a hand

through his dark curls, his lips not yet deciding whether to smile or frown. "But really, Ki," he began, lowering his voice. "What *were* you thinking?"

She'd done very little *thinking*. My mind drifted back to when she'd kissed me. Reckless indeed. I absentmindedly brought my hand to my face, about to touch where her lips had met mine, when I caught myself.

It had been nothing. A tactic to disarm me. One that had worked too well.

"Jake, you should know I never follow the rules."

He grunted. "Well, if we run into anything gruesome out there, I'm gonna use you as bait so I can get away."

"You're so chivalrous—"

"Ki!" Two arms flew around her neck, choking off her words. Patrick. "I can't decide whether I want to smack you or hug you," he said, and she smiled up at the lad, not bothering to hide her joy. I growled softly at the sight.

"Patrick, hate to break it to you, but you're currently hugging me."

"Oh." Patrick's grip loosened and his hands fell away. "I can still be angry at you while glad to see you," he said with a frown. Kiara reached out to brush aside a fallen strand of hair from his eyes.

"Is that who I think it is?!" The incredulous voice belonged to Jake's friend, Nic, who scrambled from the ground and over to where Pat and Jake crowded her.

"Afraid so, Nic," she said on a sigh. "As I was telling the boys over here, I couldn't very well let you all go into the Mist by yourselves. You wouldn't last a minute without me."

Nic chortled. "There's the humble girl we all know and love."

"You've known me for like three weeks. Love is such a strong word for a lady of my wistful disposition." She made a show of fanning her face, her eyelashes fluttering.

I nearly chuckled, but I continued swiping the whetstone against my dagger.

"Definitely going to use you as bait." Jake gave her shoulder a good-natured shove. She pretended to fall over from its force, eliciting a few chuckles from the others.

Even Alec smiled from across the fire, his eyes cast to the knife he twirled in his nimble hands. From what I'd learned, he hailed from a village up north, and I hadn't seen him grin at anything besides a sword. It appeared that Kiara was slowly worming her way under his skin as well.

I tracked Isiah and Carter speaking in hushed tones a decent distance away.

Carter had been stationed on the outskirts of the Mist before, but had never gone deep within. He'd been injured last year when the king sent me into the Mist.

A week before our orders came through, he'd saved a recruit from the salendons—just as Kiara had—and the creature managed to break his right leg. Carter never spoke of the incident, and whenever someone asked, he'd say, "Wouldn't want to waste good soldiers."

In truth, I just thought the man had a soft spot for the boys, looking after them like the fathers and mothers they'd been taken from. From the rumors I'd heard about him, Carter once had a child of his own before joining us, but he didn't speak about his past life.

I often wondered what became of his child, but I had the feeling his story ended in heartbreak, like so many others in this wicked kingdom.

I glanced to Carter now, watching nerves spread across his weathered face. He was raising his hands at Isiah, whose face remained neutral and calm.

Isiah understood what they faced. He'd been the one to take care of me after I'd returned, my mind a torn mess. At the time,

I hadn't known what was real and what wasn't. Only he had been able to get me to eat and drink, and at night, he'd slept on a pallet beside my bed. For weeks.

I owed Isiah much more than a life debt.

At the memory, something in me snapped. These recruits shouldn't be laughing and joking around as if this were some game. Were they really so naive not to consider the horrors that awaited them?

I rose abruptly and stormed their way, not stopping until I stood above them. All their chatter ceased.

"Now that you're all caught up, maybe you'll be able to focus on the mission to save your kingdom. I expect you all to take this seriously, and if you don't, I won't bother burying your body when you eventually die out there."

Fear. It was a tactic that had been used on me many times, but now, I found it a necessary tool.

"S-sorry, sir," Patrick stumbled. "We were just happy to see Ki." He jerked his head timidly her way. Kiara gave me a small grin, clearly unaffected by my speech. I glowered.

"Well, hurry and get…reacquainted. We have much to discuss." Turning on a booted heel, I passed a brooding Carter and made my way to where Isiah leaned against a tree, overseeing all of the chaos with a gleam in his gray eyes. In his hands was a steaming cup of coffee.

"I take it they're thrilled," he remarked dryly once I was in hearing distance.

I grunted and settled against the trunk, my shoulder hitting the abrasive black wood.

The forests surrounding the kingdom were covered in them, the black trees, all the deepest shade of onyx. I hadn't been alive when there'd been color in the leaves, but from what the elders claimed, it had been a sight to behold.

I fixed Isiah with a menacing glower before turning back

to the recruits, the weak fire barely lighting their faces. Clouds had washed across the moon, leaving the shadows of the realm to roam freely.

Even I shivered at the thought of the famed shadow beasts, supposedly creatures crafted by the Moon God. Mortals didn't see them coming before arms of night wrapped around them, engulfing them whole, bones and all. I was surprised I hadn't seen any when I'd last been in the Mist. If there was ever a place for them to roam, it'd be there.

Isiah and I watched from the edge of camp as the recruits readied for the day. When Kiara passed us, likely on her way to relieve herself, Isiah waited all of five seconds before hounding me.

"So…" He whistled. "How's *that* going?"

I snorted. "How's what going?"

Isiah rolled his eyes before handing over his cup. I took it, not one to pass up on coffee. "How long have I known you, Maddox?" I didn't answer. "Then you should know better. I might be the silent type, but I still have eyes."

"Then close them."

"Jude," Isiah warned. "You know better than to start something with a recruit. You could have any woman in the palace. As one of Cirian's favorites—"

"As one of his assassins, you mean," I amended.

Isiah ignored that. "What I'm trying to say is, you have to stay away. Not only is it dangerous for you, but it'd be dangerous for *her*."

That stopped the retort I'd planned on delivering.

"I know the king has an interest in her," Isiah said. "I happened upon a letter sent to Harlow, and by 'happened,' I mean I read it before I delivered it to him." I shook my head at his audacity.

"Apparently Cirian asked the lieutenant to keep tabs not

only on her, but on you as well. You need to stay focused, or it'll be your head that decorates the gate next."

"Shit." I ran a hand through my hair. I thought Harlow was a bastard, but the good kind. Had I been wrong? My instincts were typically correct, a trait that had benefited me many times in the past.

"Shit, indeed," Isiah agreed. "I know you hate emotional crap, but I care about you."

I gritted my teeth, unable to look him in the eyes.

"I just don't want to see you hurt. Or worse. You still have time to be your own man, a good one too. But you've got to figure out what's truly important, and Cirian...he's not going to let you go until you complete this mission." Isiah pushed off from the tree and sauntered to the camp, leaving me to ruminate over his words. His *warning*.

Until the world was rid of Cirian, I couldn't become who Isiah thought I could be.

Even though he knew full well what I did for the king, he believed I was meant for more. He didn't know that while I typically waved off his words in the past, I'd secretly collected them like seeds, hoping one day his hopes would take root.

"Gather around!" Isiah bellowed at the recruits from beside the fire.

I groaned as I followed him, taking a seat on a gnarled stump. The others fell into place around the flames, Isiah dropping to the ground at my side.

Since sunfires died out once we hit the cursed lands, we didn't bring any. Whatever magic powered the yellow gems was no match against the Mist.

I shoved another log into the fire, watching as it caught and sputtered.

Kiara took a seat between Patrick and Jake, Nic and Alec beside them. I noted how her dainty face contorted into a scowl when her eyes landed on the cup in my hands.

"Morning, recruits," I said, pausing only to stare each and every one of them down. I eyed Kiara last, lifting the mug to my lips with a shrewd smirk.

She huffed in envy. She had a weakness after all — coffee.

"You know little about the Mist, don't you?" I rested my arms on my knees. "Most know nothing about it other than to stay away. That there are beasts and creatures in the cursed lands who crave human blood."

I took another sip, a rogue breeze wafting the delectable aroma across the fire. Again, I tipped my head in Kiara's direction before I hardened my features and got down to business.

"But what you don't know is that beasts are not the only things you will face out there. There are things much, much worse than claws and teeth."

A few murmurs were silenced by my raised hand. "Yes, there are bears the size of five men, and snakes that can swallow you whole. But the Mist *itself* is just as deadly a foe. The deeper you go, the more dangerous it becomes. At first, you might see a former friend or neighbor, someone who isn't there. It begins as flickers and images that last but a second, gone so fast, you fear you're losing your mind." I snapped my fingers for emphasis.

"But eventually, these visions become more intense." I squeezed my hands into fists to stop their shaking. Even talking about it brought back those horrific final moments when I'd slaughtered my brothers. Bile burned my throat.

"You relive your worst memories. See the ghosts that haunt your dreams. Act out your deepest desires and most depraved wishes. And then, you lose control. There is only the hallucination that becomes your reality. And after a while, you can no longer tell what is true and what is the nightmare."

No one had words. The crackling of the fire was the only

sound besides the roar of blood in my ears.

Broken limbs.

Unseeing eyes.

Bloodied hands.

Grisly images of my former Knights flashed through my head—Ashton's severed and flayed legs, Jeremiah's gutted torso, Will's dripping eye sockets. Obscene amounts of blood decorating torn and shredded skin...

I cleared my throat, digging my nails into my palms until the stinging brought me back to the present. "This is why many of our brothers succumbed to the Mist. Why so many never returned. And because our food reserves are all but gone, and the Dark Winter approaches, time is running out to bring back the sun. Meaning we have no choice but to send out you recruits. You're being tested by the king. An experiment."

"How so?" Kiara blurted out, and I was shocked by the gravity of her voice.

I met her gaze, holding it. "Because never before have we entered from this side of the kingdom. We've made a point to avoid the labyrinth of caves we are headed for now. No one has been foolish enough to explore them."

"Then what changed?" This time I was stunned as Patrick raised his voice. It wavered, but he held firm. "Did he come across new information?"

"Cirian never shares his secrets, claiming he is in tune with the gods themselves." I gritted my teeth, sucking in a forceful inhale. The more likely explanation was that he'd run out of options, and the rebel uprising in the south and north was growing. "Cirian is under the impression there is something divine to be found out there, specifically in the northwest lands. Something sacred that could be used to restore the sun to the skies."

The three keys he spoke of. Cirian said we'd recognize them

the moment we saw them. That they weren't from the mortal plane.

"Even his best advisors warned him against this route, saying we should try the flat lands one more time. Send in our most skilled men all at once. A last attempt to return to *normalcy*," I ground out. "But as usual, Cirian got his way, and settled on a few Knights and recruits."

If the recruits were scandalized by the way I spoke of the king, they didn't show it. In fact, I caught sight of Jake nodding in agreement. He might act the joker, but he had a good head on his shoulders.

"So…now you know why you were sent here, without the proper training you *should* have received. But"—I gripped the mug so hard my knuckles shone white—"just know that I've ventured here before, and I'll do everything in my power to see you back home. I am not prepared to see you all die because of an obsessed king's rantings."

Patrick and Nic let out audible gasps. Alec lifted his blond head for the first time, angling it at me as I openly admonished our feared ruler. One who would surely have my head if these traitorous words reached his ears.

"I no longer care to hold my tongue," I said, answering every unspoken question. "For too long I have remained silent in my protest. And now, I have nothing to lose except the end of our realm if we should fail. *If* we do manage to live, our king will not be my concern."

Silence descended heavily, a thick winter blanket weighing upon all of our shoulders.

It was suffocating.

I could taste the fear in the stagnant air, the alarm racing through the veins of my companions. It coated my insides like sticky char, bubbling up my throat.

I'd said too much, frightened them before they'd even set

foot into the cursed lands.

My plan had been to be truthful, but instead, all I'd done was make everything worse. I opened my mouth, trying to think of something uplifting to say, some bullshit a commander might utter to encourage his men, but nothing but a sputter came out.

All I'd known was fear, and that particular tool wasn't working.

"So, from what I'm gathering, you assembled us here, telling us that we will die in the Mist, and that our attempt to save our kingdom will be futile. And you didn't even bring enough coffee to share with everyone?"

Stunned faces swiveled to Kiara, mouths agape.

Isiah's lips twitched before he let out a riotous laugh, the sound so genuine that, one by one, the others chuckled as well.

"She's right," Jake acquiesced, cocking his head as he stared me down. "You could let us indulge a little before we meet our untimely end."

"You better have some wine then," Nic added, provoking more snickers.

Suddenly the air didn't seem quite as suffocating as it had moments before. Nodding to Kiara, whose lips twitched as she suppressed a smile, I shot her a knowing look. One she returned.

As the other boys began arguing about who would secure the first cup, I caught Kiara's attention once more and mouthed two words.

Thank you.

CHAPTER TWENTY-ONE

KIARA

There are things I find myself needing to warn you of, though I doubt you would heed my caution, as you never have in the past. Whether or not you listen, know this: when you go into the cursed lands, do not send only warriors. Bring scholars, healers, those of strong will and fortitude of mind. They will not only have a better chance of survival, but they will help the Chosen reach the beginning of their destinies.

LETTER FROM AURORA ADAIR TO UNKNOWN RECIPIENT,
YEAR 47 OF THE CURSE

"I told you I could be of some use."

After Jude had been guilted into sharing his stash of coffee with the others, the recruits and the commander's fellow Knights groomed their steeds for the trek ahead. Unable to help myself, I held back, ambling over to where Jude perched in front of the dying flames.

Even the fresh bruises that painted his face made him more striking. More dangerous.

I liked it far too much.

"I suppose that cheeky mouth of yours is good for some things." He smirked, handing over his mug without meeting my eyes. It was half full, and my greedy hands lunged for it.

Bringing the cup to my lips, I swallowed the rest in three gulps, not even savoring it as I should have. With my belly warm and the blessed caffeine coursing through my veins, I regretted nothing.

"Thanks." I handed back the now-empty mug, wiping at my mouth with my sleeve.

Jude stared at it in awe, the flames' glow casting shadows beneath his eyes. "You truly do enjoy your coffee, recruit."

I waved him off with a hand. "It's the best way to get on my good side. My brother would hand me a cup whenever I was in a foul mood. He claimed it was the only way to tame the beast." Liam was always one for dramatics.

Jude scoffed. "I feel for your brother. You must have been a fearsome sibling to have."

"Nah, I was perfect." I grinned wide, waggling my brows. "He would have been incredibly bored in our small village without me. Always had his nose in a book, that boy. Never would have left his bed if I hadn't pulled him out of it."

My smile dipped at the corners. Would I ever see Liam again? I hoped I would, but after Jude's less-than-inspiring speech, I highly doubted it.

"Well, he is lucky to have such a...lively and captivating sister, then."

My smile returned. "Captivating, eh?"

Jude's chin angled down to his lap, but I still caught sight of the twin dimples dotting his cheeks before he quickly wiped them away. His voice lowered as he said, "You're incorrigible, aren't you?"

"Always," I replied, my voice lilting. Bending to my knees, I dropped to his eye level, feeling all sorts of brazen. "But I have a suspicion that's a quality you very much like. Among...other things."

This time, I didn't have the urge to swallow my tongue.

Hells, if we were going to be dead soon, what was the harm in a little flirting? I knew Jude understood the meaning behind my words because he looked anywhere but my lips. When I'd kissed him, I'd just gone for it without thought or hesitation. I could lie and tell myself it had been to catch him unawares and gain the upper hand, but that hadn't been the entire reason.

I'd thought about that kiss well into the early morning hours.

I was so screwed.

"Don't make me regret letting you stay, Kiara." Jude bristled, but I sensed it was a front. There was something different about him today, like he was holding back, trying hard to keep up his walls.

That simply wouldn't do.

"When I save your ass from the Mist, you won't be spewing such blasphemous things, commander."

Jude rolled his eyes, his scars dazzling beneath the moon's caress. I had the urge to reach out and touch them. They reminded me of my own, of the wounds that would never heal. The difference was that he wore his for the world to see.

"I've learned there is much I don't know of the world. Much that I can't explain or control, especially after last year…" He trailed off, jerking his head in the direction we would soon head in. "I've just always hated the unknown."

A muscle in his jaw feathered as he took me in, the intensity of his gaze electrifying my every nerve. "The unknown is dangerous, and not being in control can get you killed."

We certainly weren't only talking about the Mist.

"I don't think life was meant to be lived that way, Jude," I said. "Control is an illusion, something to make us feel grounded and in charge of our destinies."

My hand landed on Jude's knee, and his eyes tracked the movement. "Don't overthink everything. You might be surprised by how much you'd like being out of control. Being alive is chaos, and living in it is half the fun." I saw his throat bob, a question forming on the tip of his tongue as he stared at where my hand rested.

I wasn't a complete fool. I'd heard the rumors of what Jude did for Cirian—what Cirian *made* him do—and I suspected it destroyed him. When was the last time he'd done something for himself? When was the last time he'd truly given in to his own desires?

Before Jude could voice his thoughts and likely deny my words, I said, "I'm going to tend to my horse. Maybe I'll even get another cup of coffee." I lifted to my feet, slowly backing away, indulging him with my most impish of smirks. One I seemed to reserve solely for him.

Jude's lips stretched into a thin line, but his brown eye gleamed with pure gold.

Leaving him and his lingering eyes behind, I scurried off to my mare, who was glaring at me as if to scold.

"Oh hush, Starlight," I chided, petting her mane. "Nothing will come of it, anyway. But a girl's gotta live a little before she kicks the bucket." Starlight nickered and leaned into my touch, savoring the affection I was showing her tangled midnight tresses.

Once she was saddled and packed, I mounted and led her in line with the rest of the Knights, falling in beside Patrick and his snow-white steed. The lucky bastard had procured a fine horse that wasn't as crotchety as mine.

As if she sensed me thinking of her, Starlight shook her thick mane, jerking me roughly up and down in my saddle.

"Did you steal the geriatric horse on purpose?" Patrick snickered, studying Starlight. His head lifted from his lap, those green eyes of his made soft and mellow by the torch Carter carried.

"For your information, I didn't steal her. I bargained for her."

Not entirely a lie.

"Ah, well, whatever you *bargained*, you got duped." Patrick tried to repress his snort and failed. Miserably.

"Starlight here"—I gave her a sturdy pat on the back—"is a fine horse. Any Knight would be lucky to ride her." At my words, Starlight's hooves picked up with a playful determination.

She was growing on me.

Patrick scrubbed a hand over his jaw, his features turning serious. "I wish I could say I'm glad you're here. But I'm not. What you did was careless, Ki."

I bristled. "Again, it was *my* decision. Let it go, Pat." I was growing tired of everyone telling me how naive I'd been coming here. Nothing beyond the borders frightened me. But what *did* worry me was the possibility of Patrick or the others getting hurt without me by their side to protect them. I couldn't lose anything else.

Regret was the harshest of punishments. Not the Mist. And not death. Another life lesson from Uncle Micah.

I'd learned that lesson the hard way on my fourteenth birthday.

Liam had pleaded me for weeks to come with him to the annual village fair. There'd been parades and revelry, and tents selling wares from all across the realm. It was supposed to be a grand spectacle, but being my prickly, antisocial self, I told Liam no. I hadn't wanted to be surrounded by all the people I knew, pretending that their stares didn't bother me, that the way they stole peeks at my gloved hands didn't make me secretly want to hide away and cry.

Liam had begged and begged, but still I'd said no, even though I was his closest friend.

After the accident happened—and my life forever changed—not many had taken it upon themselves to get close to my family. So Liam had ended up venturing into the fair by himself.

He'd had an attack only a week before, but he'd seemed fine—or at least, I'd told myself he was—but truthfully, cowardice was at the heart of my decision.

An hour into the fair, Liam had reportedly gone down, gasping and panting for air, all alone in that crowded square. He'd curled up in a ball as patrons had trampled him, their boots kicking into his ribs. By chance, Mother had taken a break from her stall of linens to walk through the tents, and that's when she'd spotted him.

He'd been so battered and bruised, and his lungs rattled every time he inhaled. Liam had been in bed for the next few weeks afterward, and every time I'd seen his face, shame had filled me.

Knowing how sick he'd been, I should have been there, should have protected him. But no, I had been so fearful of petty gossip that I'd left him. Abandoned him.

I'd learned that day that sometimes we have to give away pieces of ourselves to others we love, even if it hurts at the time. Without sacrificing those parts, nothing new—and possibly wonderful—could grow in their stead.

From then onward, I'd never said no to Liam again—at least to the things that meant something to him. Love was nothing if not sacrifice, and for him, I'd willingly give all of myself.

"You know," Patrick began after many minutes of silence. "You remind me a lot of someone I used to know."

I shook off memories of the past and of Liam. It was far easier than I would've liked.

"A friend?" I asked, winking. I couldn't picture Patrick with a love interest, not that he wasn't attractive, with his strong jaw and surprisingly impressive build given his lack of physical prowess. He was simply shy, sometimes painfully so.

"Something like that," he murmured, his tone turning grim. "She died. Many, many years ago."

My chest constricted as I watched Patrick's face contort with the kind of pain that lay deep below the flesh. "I-I'm so sorry."

"Yeah, me too," he scoffed, swallowing hard. "She was spirited and stubborn, and got into all the trouble she could manage. If it wasn't dangerous, she wouldn't be interested." The corners of his lips turned up at the thought. "I didn't think I started living until I met her, and when she left, nothing was ever the same again."

"What was her name?" I didn't push, but I also wanted to know more about Patrick and his past life before the Knights.

Patrick visibly gulped, his eyes flickering to the side before he answered. "Rosie."

"Rosie. That is a beautiful name."

"And she was beautiful, but where it mattered." He patted his chest. "She may have been reckless, but she never ignored the evil in this world, not if she could do anything about it." Patrick shook his head. "Sometimes it annoyed me, her constant desire to help. I think it was mainly because I didn't want to share her with the rest of the world."

"What happened to her?"

His dreamy smile vanished. "She was the victim of a mugging. On the way to the capital, some thieves attacked, and she was… she was stabbed." I noticed his grip on the reins tightened, his knuckles turning white.

I didn't know what to say.

"Maybe that's why I like you." Patrick twisted my way, his eyes glimmering. "You're just as brave and hardheaded as she was. If not more so. And definitely just as defiant."

"Me? Defiant?" I arched my brows in mock affront, eager to bring back his smile. "Good sir, I am the pinnacle of obedience and respect."

"I'm sorry, did Ki just say she was obedient *and* respectful?" Nic trotted in between us, his long brown hair poking out every which way.

"But of course," I protested, a hand held to my chest. "I would never lie."

"Yeah, right," Jake called on the breeze, just behind us all. I peered over my shoulder, staring him down. His russet skin glowed with amusement, the look on his face challenging me to argue. I didn't.

"Fine, I'm impossible," I relented, swiveling back to the front, my eyes finding Jude. He rode beside Isiah, the pair seeming to be deep in conversation. What I would give to hear their hushed exchange.

"And that's why we *tolerate* you." Nic leaned across his dappled mare to playfully poke at my ribs. "You're certainly never boring."

"Don't poke me unless you want me to cut off that pretty hair of yours while you sleep," I threatened. "And you definitely can't rely on your sparkling personality."

"He brushes it every night!"

"Shut up, Jake!" Nic hissed, absentmindedly tucking a loose strand behind his ears. "My girlfriend loves it, and I gotta keep the girl happy. But you wouldn't know anything about relationships, would you?"

Jake scoffed. "It wouldn't be fair to the world if I settled down with one man. People would get jealous, and I am forever aiming to please."

"Yeah, Jake, I'm sure the boys were just dying to get their hands on you back home. Well, more specifically, their hands around your neck."

Nic snorted, a mischievous glint illuminating his eyes. "She's not wrong, brother. Evan tried to throttle you a week before The Calling. And before him, there was Michael—"

"I'm definitely cutting off your hair," Jake threatened.

"Jealousy doesn't suit you," Nic scoffed, but I noticed how he angled away from Jake. I was sure he'd keep an eye on his friend's blade.

The boys continued to tease and goad one another for the next four hours.

It was an easy conversation, one that didn't include the Mist and the threat of death. It was apparent that they took considerable pleasure in the art of insults, a pastime I found to be immensely entertaining.

Sometimes I would join in on their fun, but mostly I kept my focus trained ahead.

For all my boasting, I was terrified. Not that I regretted my decision to follow Jude and my friends on this suicide mission, but my confidence—which was usually genuine—was now forced. Every smile and eye roll took great effort.

For the first time in my life, I doubted my ability to survive. The Mist wasn't a living entity I could fight with shiny blades and closed fists.

And that was the problem.

I'd been gazing at the back of a certain commander's head, obsessing over my doubts and all things doom, when the man in question turned around. It was as though he'd felt my eyes upon him, his fiery gaze as penetrating as it was raw.

Bringing two fingers to his lips, Jude let out a high-pitched whistle, his onyx steed slowing. Carter and Isiah came to a halt, the rest of us pulling on our reins.

So lost in my own dour thoughts, I hadn't realized where we were.

Looming one hundred or so feet ahead was a monstrous cave, its gaping mouth framed by spindly branches and coal-colored ivy.

The fine hairs on the back of my neck rose in warning, a hint of bile rising in my throat.

We were about to enter the cursed lands—

And there would be no turning back.

CHAPTER TWENTY-TWO

JUDE

Arlo crafted the world with his own two hands. Every bloom, cave, and mountain peak, he fashioned with care, delighting in the simple act of creating. While at times, he is known to be a benevolent god, Arlo does not design anything without purpose—even if that purpose is chaos.

EXCERPT FROM ASIDIAN LORE: A TALE OF THE GODS

My steed's hooves dragged in the dirt, the horse rightfully apprehensive to enter the cave that must have inspired the gates to the underworld.

It was a vacuous pit of nothingness, the slender branches of the trees twining wickedly about its giant maw.

I couldn't say with certainty that once I entered, I would ever return.

Carter relinquished his torch to me.

"Keep your wits about you," I warned the group, kicking into the side of my steed with the heel of my polished boot. The black stallion jerked ahead, fearless in the face of the beckoning emptiness.

My head swam with doubts, but I forced myself to move forward, passing beneath the rocky mouth of the cave.

One after the other, the group followed me into the obscurity, the narrow pathway just wide enough to accommodate one rider at a time. If I balanced on my horse's back, I'd be able to graze the jagged ceiling, which dipped and rose like a midnight wave.

We'd all been born and raised in darkness, but this was an entirely new level of black. Even with the few torches we carried, the voracious shadows ate away at my skin. My resolve.

The air was thick in my lungs, a moldy and putrid stench clogging my nostrils, the smell akin to a decomposing animal. But it was more than the smell and the churning of my stomach that had my hands trembling—

It was what I felt awaken inside my core.

A vicious heat sparked across the expanse of my chest, a flutter of something old and foreign and wholly destructive.

It was gone with a shaky exhale, the familiar icy dread settling back into my veins.

I swallowed the rising bile.

Nerves. It had to be nerves at coming back to this wretched place.

I repeated it over and over again like a twisted mantra. But it was still there—that *feeling*—as we progressed further past the point of no return.

I reached into my pocket and peeked at the silver timepiece Isiah had gifted me two seasons ago, the words *Trust in the Stars* etched into the back. It wasn't too late in the day, which meant we had hours of traveling yet to do. Shivers racked my frame at the thought, as enclosed spaces often sent my pulse hammering.

Knives and blood did nothing to rile me, but trap me in a small space and cold sweat would line my brow.

I wished for a distraction, *any* distraction, but there wasn't much to look at but the vacant darkness ahead. Before the panic could overcome me, I forced myself to inspect the tunnel, focusing on every minuscule detail. Lifting my torch, I took in the roughened walls embracing us, observing them to be a shade of ash and scorched earth, the uneven surface jagged and spiked.

Tipping my head back, I followed the path of the swirling, vein-like designs decorating the ceiling like wilted flowers, the inky hue shimmering a blue-black color as the lights passed beneath. They were dazzling in a ghoulish way, some of the swirls and curving lines bringing to mind the intricate roots of a Midnight Bloom.

I passed the time this way, silently observing and trying not to overthink everything, as Kiara had playfully instructed, when a fork in the path appeared a few hours later.

I raised my hand, indicating the rest to slow.

Two tunnels.

Reaching into my pockets, I retrieved the tattered map Cirian had provided. It was ancient, the ink faded on the page. With care, I unfolded it and brought it inches from the torch I carried in my other hand.

Shit.

Both tunnels led to less-than-ideal routes.

One would take us to a wide river, but the journey beyond it looked easy enough.

However, I wasn't sure how deep the river went, and it would cost us time if we had to abandon our horses. Gods knew I wanted to get in and out as quickly as possible.

We had to make it to the encircled portion of the map, the crude X Cirian had drawn with his feathered pen. I remembered when he'd done it, a wicked smile on his thin lips like he was privy to something I wasn't.

The second option, and the more dangerous of the two, held no wide rivers, but the path included thick underbrush where beasts or enemies alike could easily hide.

"Jude?" Isiah whispered at my back. They were all waiting on me.

"Right." I lifted a gloved finger, pointing in the direction of the smaller of the two passageways, praying to the gods I didn't believe in that I'd been right in my decision. I'd probably just screwed us all.

"Yay," Jake growled derisively from the back of the line, his voice carrying in the tunnel. He seemed about as thrilled as I was about small spaces.

Carter and Isiah trotted behind, both silent and alert. We'd never dared to enter through the caves before. Too much risk of the unknown. Gods forbid we lose our torches, and we'd be lost in there.

The tunnel provided two feet on either side of my steed, an impressive creature I'd never named. Horses died just as often as we did, so what was the point in growing attached?

As the walls seemed to close in on all sides, and the hours passed without any sense of time, my mind faded into a dulled haze. I perceived only the blur of orange and yellow torchlight and the warped designs carved onto the walls.

Another hour and a half passed before the walls of the cave widened. I gripped the reins tight, jerking back. "Slow!"

My heart jumped at the idea of finally getting out of this tunnel, to anywhere that offered even the tiniest bit more room to move. To breathe.

When the passageway opened to reveal a spacious cavern, the sigh I released could be heard by all. Not that I was the only one. Isiah practically groaned with relief. He'd appeared distressed ever since we left the open skies behind us.

The cavern didn't hold my attention for long.

About fifty feet away from the cave's mouth was a tangled mess of bone-white trees sprouting deep-blue leaves flecked with metallic silver. They hung sparingly from each branch, fluttering ominously in the foreign breeze and swirling fog.

"We rest here for the evening," I barked from the front of

the line, steering clear of the open forest. "Tomorrow we set off beyond the cave."

Jumping from my steed, I thrust my shoulders back and briefly twisted toward the languid shadows and open sky.

I had returned. I just wasn't so sure I'd survive the Mist a second time.

"Everyone dismount and water your horses. We have a big day ahead of us tomorrow." Isiah shot me a knowing look before assuming command. He understood well enough where my thoughts had ventured.

The flames of our torches danced across the moistened stones, highlighting the droplets of water that glistened like a million little stars. Those same inky swirls that had painted the cave reached up into the air, touching the top of the ceiling and coiling around the sharp edges.

In a far corner was a bubbling azure pool no larger than a bathtub. It gurgled in welcome, and my throat ached for a sip. I took its presence as a good sign.

"Thank the gods," Jake said on a sigh, his face alight with unbridled joy, even with the Mist mere feet away. Sweat dampened his white linen shirt, the cloth sticking to him like a second skin.

I brought my steed over to the pool to drink and dismounted.

Seconds later, Kiara joined me, her older mare nickering before leaning down to quench her thirst. She muttered the beast's name in reproach, and I swallowed down a snort. By the way Starlight whipped her head angrily in response, I sensed she didn't approve of the name either.

Fixating upon the gurgling pool, I blocked out the chatter of the others as they stretched and attended to their horses. Everyone made a point to ignore the cave's mouth.

"How do you know where we're going?" Kiara asked quietly, mindful to keep her voice down.

I heaved a fatigued sigh, leaving the bubbling water with reluctance and meeting her eyes. "The king gave me the only map in the kingdom detailing these parts. While I wish I could say it was accurate, that is yet to be determined. Supposedly the land had been drawn before the curse."

Kiara nodded. When she grabbed the torch from my grasp, I didn't resist. "I'm sure your arm is tired," she said as she found a slight gap between two jutting rocks nearby. With a grunt and a curse, she maneuvered the torch's crooked grip into the opening. It held.

"So," she began, shoving herself a few inches closer and flashing me a toothy grin. "Was this tunnel on the map? Or did you just choose the most claustrophobic one?"

I glared, not falling for her poor attempt at humor. I shoved my trembling hands into the pockets of my black trousers before she could see.

"I chose the one closest to the details on the map. Again, only time will tell if I was correct." Swiping a hand through my disheveled hair, I ambled across from the pool, selecting a craggy rock to perch upon, my back to the swirling fog. It was far enough away from the others, who were all conversing in hushed tones. Let them find peace with each other. I suspected I wouldn't be a welcome sight.

Of course, the girl I'd told myself I had to avoid trailed after me. Secretly—selfishly—I was thankful. As much as I'd grown accustomed to being alone, I found the idea of *her* company pleasing.

Kiara plopped down beside me, even going so far as to copy my pose, bringing one knee to her chest. We both watched over our exhausted companions.

Isiah's deep voice echoed as he ordered the group to make camp, the recruits scrambling to fulfill the command. He knew what coming back here would mean to me, and I suspected he was doing everything in his power to take away some of the burden. I didn't want a repeat of last year.

"Are you frightened?" Kiara asked quietly.

I surprised myself by answering, "Yes."

She didn't force me to elaborate. I brought my canteen to my lips, many more minutes of nothing passing between us. It was a silence that wasn't necessarily uncomfortable, either. Another reason I didn't mind her company.

Isiah had produced a tattered deck of cards from his sack, and he laid out the worn cards before him and Carter, who motioned for the boys to gather around.

Patrick, Nic, Alec, and Jake eagerly joined them, and a game of poker started. I noticed how Carter shot Nic a small wink before handing over a silver flask. The boy took a sip, grimacing when he realized it wasn't water.

"On a positive note," Kiara said, "I don't have to deal with Harlow anymore. I swear that man hates me more than the curse."

Isiah might have felt the need to read Harlow's mail from the king, but I still trusted him. My instincts were all I had. Even if they were leading me astray as of late.

With the others busy with the game, no one would notice that I scooted closer, leaning over to whisper into the shell of her ear. "If you think he hates you, then you're not nearly as intelligent as I pegged you as."

Kiara shivered—whether from my nearness, or from my words—but she quickly composed herself. "Excuse me. But you've seen the way he looks at me. Like he desires nothing more than to drown me in the Lakes of Candor."

Now *that* would be an awful death, I mused. The lakes were notorious for their frigid waters and the scaled beasts lurking below the surface.

"You're an even worse judge of character than I thought."

This time, when I whispered into her ear, my lips brushed against her warm skin. A full-body shudder racked my frame.

Kiara swallowed audibly, composing herself enough to ask, "Is that why I find myself in *your* company?"

"Perhaps," I said, smirking. "But if you enjoy my company, then you *definitely* can't trust your own mind."

Her head cocked to the side. "I think it's the opposite," she replied cheekily, her voice lilting, turning playful.

"What is?"

"I think it is *you* who enjoys *my* company. And how could anyone blame you?" She sighed dramatically, flinging her loose braid over her shoulder. "It's my charming personality that lures them all in. I simply cannot help it."

A deep chuckle rose from my throat. "Ah yes, that's it. Although, 'charming' might not be the word I would use."

"Prick." She shoved her shoulder into my side, provoking a groan from me.

If only she knew the half of it. I doubt she'd settle on just "prick" alone. "Murderer", "puppet", "bastard"—all applied.

We couldn't be any more different.

Kiara might act as if nothing fazed her, that she felt nothing, but I'd known people who truly were empty inside, and she wasn't one of them. You could tell by the light in her eyes, how they burned like fire, highlighting the gold flecks in her irises.

Maybe that was why I was helpless but to seek her—just as flames greedily sought to set fire to the night.

"How old are you?" she asked, the question catching me off guard.

"Nineteen."

She thrust her shoulder into me again, stunned by my response. "Seriously?! You're only a year older than me! How on earth did you become a commander?"

Lifeless eyes.

Warm blood trickling down my throat.

My brothers pleading—

"Jude?" she pressed. I swallowed hard, focusing on her face as I found my way back from drowning beneath the weight of the past.

"Let's just say I'm good at what I do," I said vaguely, hoping to leave it at that. Of course, she wouldn't let it go.

"And what is it that you do? Because I've yet to see the fearsome commander in action. I've observed Harlow and even Carter during training sessions, but never you, not really. You're always a shadow lurking in the corridors, watching. A ghost, more like. Even when you knocked Adam on his ass in the library, I couldn't see a damned thing."

Her thigh pressed against mine, her inviting heat dispelling the instinct to dodge the question.

I *wanted* to answer. Maybe then she'd see the monster I was. "I'm good at killing the king's enemies." I held her eyes as they widened. To her credit, she didn't recoil. "I'm sure the rumors you've heard of me already paint a pretty accurate picture."

The moment of shock passed quickly, and Kiara raised a single brow. "Don't forget, you're also quite exceptional at shifting most of our conversations toward the horribly bleak. It's actually a skill."

I basically had just admitted that all the rumors of me torturing, maiming, and *killing* were correct. And the weapons with which she chose to respond? Sarcasm and a smile.

"Is that so?"

"Absolutely," she affirmed, nodding emphatically. "You're *nearly* as impressive as I am at turning serious situations around with pure wit and natural charm."

"For such a tiny person, you carry an *obscene* amount of confidence."

She scoffed at my astute assessment.

"I suppose we're lucky we're both here to balance one another out."

That last part slipped out. But it held enough truth that she grinned, the pure genuineness of it devastating me. I dug my nails into the flesh of my palms. The bite of pain did nothing to break her hypnotic hold, so I pressed harder.

I'd killed and tortured men, had their blood paint my face and hands.

I could ignore their desperate begging, turn off my emotions as they screamed for the pain to end. For *me* to end it.

But one spirited girl could send me to my knees.

Kiara didn't seem to notice my struggle. "Together, we make one *almost* stable individual," she replied, repressing a snort.

I wondered what her laughter would sound like if she truly allowed herself to be free. If the weight of this world wasn't so devastating.

That magnetic lure I'd failed to fight pulled us together, and as if an invisible string was tethered between us, we drew closer. Kiara's face hovered but inches before my own, and a burst of adrenaline prickled at my insides, a fiery heat coiling in my stomach.

The rest of the world could go screw itself.

I hardly noticed the others playing their card game, hardly made out their voices.

I forgot about all the reasons I *shouldn't* be talking with her, leaning into her body, allowing my baser desires free rein.

I forgot myself, and therefore, I lost control over my mouth.

"You are what I imagine the sun to be like," I whispered so softly I wasn't sure she could hear the admission. "Fiery. Beautiful. Damning."

She didn't reply, didn't *move*. But her eyes... They fell to my mouth, a rosy blush creeping up her chest and to her neck. The instinct to lean down and taste her heated skin had my hands twitching, my control slipping.

I shouldn't have even said those words, but it was too late, so I hastily added, "Don't have anything to say now, Kiara?"

She shivered as I spoke her name, which came out as a raspy plea.

All the cockiness, the swagger, had been wiped from her features. I had the impulse to close the distance and see if she tasted as I remembered. It had been too brief, that kiss. If anything, it had been a tease of what might happen should we both give in, which was probably why I was acting against Isiah's warning.

I'd never wanted anyone as badly as I did her, and how she looked at me—like I was a *hero*, a man worthy of her respect—had grown addicting. I wanted to drown in that look and never come back up for air.

Kiara's breath tickled my lips. I hadn't realized she'd moved, but she had, and her eyes had darkened—

"Ki!"

She groaned as I jerked away, the grating sound of Patrick's voice stopping us from whatever it was we had been about to do. My heart plummeted into my stomach, the warming sparks dissipating as if they'd been doused in water.

"I-I'm here, Patrick," she called out, her voice wavering and breathy.

I bolted to my feet. "Better check on Isiah," was all I said before vaulting down from the raised rock.

Kiara gave a jerky nod and rose. Her shoulders were stiff and her steps uneven as she walked into the circle of recruits and Knights, a forced grin plastered on her face. She was far too good at faking it, nearly as skilled as myself.

The glances exchanged among the boys weren't lost on me, and more than one of the recruits twisted their heads in my direction.

"Now," she said, studying the card deck, her voice nothing but cool confidence. "Who wants to lose to me first?"

Nic rolled his eyes and Jake elbowed her gently in the side. Alec shook his head as if they were all beneath him, even if I could tell he wanted to join in. But Patrick? He'd turned to me, suspicion marring his face, his lips thinned in distaste.

I'd seen many men glare at me, whether it was right before I slit their throats, or after I delivered the king's threats. But never before had such a look unsettled me as much as his did.

"Patrick!" Kiara shoved his shoulder, and he reluctantly lowered his eyes from mine. I let out a breath through my teeth. "Stop scowling and play," she complained, scooting closer and into his side.

He said something in response, his tone light, but I could still feel the intensity of the warning he'd delivered as if he'd branded it upon my mind.

Stay the hells away.

CHAPTER TWENTY-THREE

KIARA

There have been reports surrounding the northern villages of
Ardain and Rine. Fifteen men and women have gone missing
from their homes near the Pastoria Forest. Only two bodies
have been found, though what little remains of them offers
no insight into the cause of death. The medics I've questioned
have never seen anything quite like this before, and the
decayed and mutilated bodies worry them to no end.

I beg of you to send aid at once.

LETTER FROM RANDALL THORNE OF THE GUARD TO
COMMANDER JUDE MADDOX, YEAR 49 OF THE CURSE

I woke to screams.

A lone torch had been left burning, though it did little to
illuminate the damp cave, let alone the trees belonging to the
Mist on our other side.

I'd fallen asleep beside Patrick hours before, but at some
point my arms had looped around his torso like a tied bow, my
cheek pressed against his warm, broad chest.

"What's going on?" Patrick startled, his entire body shaking
me alert, his voice laden with fatigue and mounting alarm.

"Screams," I rasped, pointing out the obvious. I shoved off

Patrick's chest and bolted to my feet, my friend following suit.

Alec rushed to light the other torches we'd rammed into the various crevices, his face a stoic mask of calm. I shot him a look of thanks and he bestowed me with his signature curt nod, his hand gripping the hilt of his blade.

Jake and Nic dashed to my side, both out of breath, their hair mussed by sleep. The latter stood protectively in front of his friend, his dark eyes alert.

"Where is that coming from?!" I shrieked, confirming that my dagger was in place at my hip.

Isiah and Jude were up and ready for an attack, their weapons out and gleaming in the muted orange-and-amber glow. Outfitted in head-to-toe leather that swathed him like a second skin, his scars flaming and angry across his stormy eye, Jude embodied death itself.

Another shrill screech sliced through the air, the noise originating from deep within the tunnel from where we came. The blood-curdling wails were saturated in unimaginable anguish—so distorted, they hardly sounded human. *If* they were human at all.

"Stay here!" Jude barked over his shoulder, calmly motioning for Isiah to follow as he took off in a sprint, his long legs carrying him toward the sounds of danger.

The commander and his loyal Knight were a whirl of shadows and steel, gone in the blink of an eye.

A minute passed.

"Should we help them?" Alec asked, creeping into the light of one of the torches. He cocked his head toward the screams. They hadn't ceased. In fact, each shriek sounded louder and more tormented than the one before.

"The commander told us we need to stay put," Jake supplied.

"I agree. Whatever the hells is causing that, I want no part of it," Nic agreed, a shiver racking his muscular frame.

Even Patrick nodded.

Only Alec looked conflicted, his shrewd eyes narrowed in on the tunnel Jude and Isiah had stormed through. "We shouldn't just sit here. It isn't right," he muttered beneath his breath. Indecision had his body trembling, and a look that resembled shame turned down the corners of his mouth.

I shifted in place, my heart rate a thunderous drum. What if they needed backup, or what if Jude had been cornered by some beast, or—

A weight settled on my shoulders, Patrick's hand anchoring me and my rampant thoughts. Always at my side when I needed him. "Ki," he warned. "Please don't do what I think you're about to do. You need to stay safe. *Please*."

Patrick's pleading broke my heart, but my mind had already been made up thirty seconds ago.

I was never crafted to sit and *wait*. To huddle in fear and wrap my arms about myself as others fought the monsters that thrived in the dark.

I wouldn't have been able to stop myself if I tried.

Without warning, I shook off Patrick's hold, disregarding Jake's begging and Nic's shouting of "Don't you dare, Ki!"

Without a shred of hesitation, I raced gracefully across the uneven rocks, trailing after the distant light of Jude's torch, the glow shrinking the farther they advanced.

I didn't think as I bolted, didn't consider what I ran toward. There was only instinct and a desperate need to act.

To slay the darkness itself.

Amid the screeches, I could make out my friends still yelling my name, pleading with me to come back, but as usual, I wasn't great at following the rules. Or listening.

Not when Ju—*people* might be in trouble.

My grip stiffened on my dagger's handle as fear, apprehension, and adrenaline pushed me forward and into the narrow tunnel.

I was reminded of when Micah had praised me, right after I'd attempted to save the travelers who'd been set upon by those thieves. He'd been proud that I'd rushed into the fight, even if he later chastised my failure. His scolding hadn't mattered. It was one of the rare times I'd earned his genuine approval, and I had done so by following my instincts.

Now, my instincts were luring me into the heart of danger once more.

As the light from Jude's torch grew brighter, my steps became quicker. I barreled down the tapered path, and my breath caught when Jude and Isiah finally popped into view—

Right next to Carter…whose wails filled the tunnel.

Shit. I hadn't even realized the older Knight was missing.

My legs pumped until I was but ten feet away, and my mouth fell open when I saw what was making Carter cry out in torment.

Spiders.

Hundreds and hundreds of spiders flew across his clothes and exposed ashen skin, swirling like an onyx noose about his thick neck. Their black bodies glowed from within, chilling red and white threads radiating from their spindly legs.

And they were biting Carter. *Eating* him.

Devouring him alive.

Jude and Isiah waved their torches back and forth, endeavoring to frighten the ravenous creatures away, but the flames only seemed to excite them more.

Carter feebly reached out, one foot stumbling over the other as he tumbled to the dusty earth. All he could manage to do was hoarsely scream for help. For someone to save him as his body failed him.

"They're poisonous!" Jude bellowed, his injured eye shining an almost milky white.

I'd never seen spiders look like that before. The poisonous ones I could identify didn't *glow*.

"What do we *do*?" My voice didn't sound like my own. It was shrill and filled with glass shards. My fingertips started to buzz beneath the leather of my gloves, a prickling sensation that coursed up and down my arms. For a moment, darkness edged in on all sides, and a coldness unlike anything I'd ever known chilled my blood.

Jude twisted to me, an irate look gracing his severe features as he unexpectedly lunged, the broad palms of his hands roughly colliding with my shoulders. "You need to leave. NOW!" he roared, inadvertently pushing me to the ground in his attempt to usher me away.

I crashed onto the packed earth with a resounding thud, my attention drawn to the atrocity taking place in front of me. I couldn't look away.

And I would have given *anything* to have been able to.

Carter's shaved head was covered in black legs and moving bodies, his brawny form thrashing back and forth across the packed dirt. I might have screamed myself as I helplessly watched him curl into a ball, his arms and legs contorting. Shriveling.

Shrinking.

Blood flowed across the packed dirt, the red appearing nearly black. The insects wove around his face, biting mercilessly into chunks of flesh as he wailed.

No one was doing anything to help him! He was dying a horrible and painful death, and my commander wasn't doing a damn thing.

The prickling in my fingers grew, as did the shadows, the black wisps of midnight gliding across my eyes, turning the dimly lit tunnel impossibly dark. Yet I could make out Carter, could hear his pitiful begging.

"He's gone!" Jude growled, reading my look of violent outrage. "One bite would kill him, and he's been bitten over a hundred times."

But he still screamed, still fought. Crying through the sheer agony of being eaten alive.

If Carter was already past saving, he needed to be put out of his misery. I might not have known him well, but I couldn't sit back and *watch*.

My hand shot to my belt, and before I could think about it, I sent my dagger sailing through the air—

Straight through Carter's right eye.

The shrieks instantly ceased, his flayed and mutilated body going motionless. I choked on an inhale, a biting shiver running down the length of my spine.

Carter was dead.

And I'd just killed him.

Jude lowered his gaze to me for only the briefest of seconds, a flicker of sorrow darkening his brown eye to an impossible black.

Before the spiders could finish their meal, Jude's torch landed on his fellow Knight's lifeless shell, his black clothing catching the flames before the rest of the fire scorched him.

It wasn't the sight of the spiders feasting on his mutilated body that propelled me to twist over and retch, but rather, the smell of burning flesh. Burning *hair*.

I heaved my earlier meal of nuts and granola, my hands fisting the dirt as I emptied my stomach. The smell suffocated me. The ash and smoke and Carter's phantom wails—

Two powerful arms reached around my waist, hauling me up and away. Away from the charred Knight who had given his life to his kingdom. Who'd died in the worst way imaginable.

My head pressed against a broad chest, and an arm slipped around my waist, supporting me in case my knees gave way. I knew I was moving, but the putrid smell still clogged my nostrils, and my mind replayed the last few minutes over and over again until it was all that I could see.

My rational side argued that Carter had already been gone. That I'd saved him from more misery. But I wasn't thinking rationally.

I'd never *killed* before.

Above the smoldering fumes and singed human flesh, I smelled a hint of pine and musk as my nose nuzzled into Jude's shirt.

Patrick's voice sounded from far away, joined by Nic's and Jake's.

Suddenly, there were more hands touching me, rubbing at my skin. Comforting words were murmured into my hair, words I didn't catch. The blanket of night that had cloaked my vision began to wane, as did the stinging in my fingertips as reality settled in and robbed all else.

I *killed* someone.

I kept repeating the words and I couldn't stop. I understood that I'd have to kill eventually if I ever became a true Knight, but...doing it? That was an entirely different story.

Somewhere behind me, I heard shouts to light the torches. Another voice demanding something called nightshade.

But the only thing I could feel were those firm arms holding me, clutching me securely. And all I could hear was that deep, velvety voice telling me that everything was going to be all right—

Though I didn't believe a single word.

Chapter Twenty-Four

Jude

Danger lurks on the outskirts of the Mist. Travelers claim to have seen bears the size of five men and wolves with red eyes and razor-sharp claws. The worst, they claimed, were the spiders. Their venom, like acid, burns through the skin, and one bite causes the victim unimaginable pain. There is no cure.

Letter from Admiral Jarkon to King Cirian, year 7 of the curse

Kiara stared off in the direction of the cave where Carter had met his end.

An hour had come and gone, and still I couldn't seem to shake her from her stupor.

The first thing I'd done was to lead her away from prying eyes. Isiah's gaze lingered on us for a second too long before he nodded his understanding and barked orders for the recruits to settle within the curve of the torches, far from the Mist's entrance.

He had talked to them, trying to ease their fears. He'd probably shared a story from his youth, one of religion and of the gods he so revered. Stories I never believed. The most powerful of the gods were useless, and even the minor deities had rarely shown their faces since Raina's disappearance. They deserved none of my reverence.

Carter was dead, and faith was the furthest thing from my mind. He'd been a decent man, and the fact that I wasn't broken in two was a testament to my coarseness. Death had become my truth.

I shook thoughts of my own callousness aside and shifted to where the recruits were huddled around Patrick, who spoke animatedly about his understanding of nightshade. The boy knew more than most about the deadly poison. He'd produced a sack of it and handed it to Isiah as a precaution, should more spiders appear. Apparently they feared the scent. I'd noticed all the texts Patrick had kept beneath his cot back at the sanctum, and I was grateful I had—his knowledge might save us.

"Kiara?" I tried again, hating that vacant look on her face. There was no spark, no *anything*. Just a shell. I'd brought her to where we'd sat earlier, far from the light.

She needed time to process. But that emptiness…

Carefully, I wound my arms around her waist and hauled her into my lap, hoping my warmth might jolt her out of her daze. Gently, I positioned her to where her head rested against my chest, her ear above my heart. She didn't respond.

"You're all right," I murmured in her ear, rocking us back and forth. I'd never comforted another, so I wasn't sure if I was doing it properly. I felt foolish even trying, my movements awkward.

I began to take one of her gloved hands in mine when she flinched. She instantly jerked away and took her hand with her. Whenever I so much as looked at her hands, she tended to shut down.

Slowly, so very slowly, she drew back, just enough to peer into my eyes. I wanted to thank all the gods I hated when I saw recognition shine within them.

"W-what happened?" she croaked, and fighting my urge to pull her closer, to clutch her tighter, I loosened my hold enough for her to sit up.

"The spiders have been dealt with," I said, not sure what else to say.

"I killed him." Her voice was small, not like the girl I knew who spoke with unwavering conviction and a grating amount of confidence.

I shook my head. "You saved him from more pain. He was already gone. Bitten by hundreds of them. You did what I would have done myself."

Kiara shivered, her gaze once more following back to the tunnel. "But they're gone? The spiders?"

"Yes," I assured. "The fire wiped out most of them, but the nightshade Patrick possessed acted like an acidic poison, killing the lingering few. They're all dead."

Her nod was stiffer than my body. "Where are the others?" she asked, scanning the cavern. She relaxed slightly when she found them attempting sleep once more. Though I doubted they'd managed to even shut their eyes.

"You did what you had to do," I murmured into her ear again, knowing my words meant shit. "The first kill is always the hardest."

The first life you took marked you, branded you in ways you'd never recover from.

After mine, I'd had no one to talk to about it—how the blood had stained my hands, how my dreams had been filled with his dying breaths.

Isiah had tried to coax answers from me a year later, but by then, it had been too late. There would be no washing my hands or my thoughts of that kill.

"I should have known I'd have to do that at some point," she said, turning her piercing stare to me. Water lined her lower lids, but she didn't allow those tears to fall. Kiara was stubborn, even in her grief.

"I felt like this after my first kill." My throat constricted the second after I spoke.

I shouldn't be discussing this with her, but the way her brow creased and her eyes shone with water was a torture unlike anything I'd ever known. I just wanted it to go away.

"I was thirteen," I continued.

Kiara went rigid in my arms, concern marring her delicate features.

"My father...he wasn't a good man. He was a criminal who trained me from a young age to fight. To be useful to him and his band of rogues." I swallowed down my hatred, my searing hot loathing for the man who'd given me life.

"One day, my father told me we were going to attack a carriage off the main road leading to the capital. I had been a part of a few assaults before, so I expected it to be some courtier or wealthy merchant. I was wrong."

I lifted my head to the rocky ceiling, avoiding her eyes. The worry in them made my skin itch.

"This particular carriage was guarded by fifteen or so trained soldiers. A few of my father's men were struck down immediately. My father, on the other hand, was caught in a fierce scuffle with a giant of a soldier. I'd been too frightened at the time to fully recognize the royal tunics the guards wore, but I understood that my father was on the losing end of the fight.

"The guard flipped him onto his back, and when he raised a silver blade high in the air, set to bring it down into his heart, I just reacted. Before my mind could catch up, I'd flung my dagger into the back of the man's head. The soldier died instantly, his body falling onto my father, who was drenched in his blood."

Kiara's hand reached out to grasp mine, squeezing. I glanced down to where we connected, my jaw twitching. There was no hesitation this time when she curved her fingers around mine.

"What happened then?" she asked in a shaky whisper.

I pulled my hand back. The look of hurt that crossed her face stung.

"Then the carriage door opened, and a masked man stepped out. I remember he wore the finest clothes I'd ever seen, his mask a pure silver that gleamed beneath the moonlight. He was stately and robust and carried himself as though he were above it all. It wasn't until later that I realized why he held himself in such a way. That man was the king."

She gasped. "King Cirian?!"

I nodded. "My father was subdued easily enough by one of his guards, held on his knees in the dirt. The king approached me, assessing me with each step he took. I thought he'd kill me on the spot, but then he handed me a jeweled dagger from his belt, a shining ruby on the hilt. He told me I had two choices. That I could either die alongside my father and his men, or…or I could execute him and live."

Her mouth fell open. She likely wondered what type of man would make a *child* choose between killing their own blood or living. Cirian enjoyed his games, and I'd been just another toy for him to play with that day.

"As you can see, I am before you now." I chuckled, the sound coming out strangled and pained. Now I just wanted to drop the entire conversation. Regret tore through me at even bringing it up.

"But what happened after? Where did you go?" she pressed, and it took everything in me not to shove her away. Every nerve became electrified, painful. I wanted to run and not look back at her sympathetic face. It tore me to pieces.

"The king was impressed with me," I ground out, my nostrils flaring. "He was impressed with the way I didn't hesitate to take his blade and stab my father in the heart, and he decided he could use someone like me. One who didn't shy away from violence. I was with the Guard for the next year, and shortly after, the Knights recruited me."

"Do you regret what you did?" Kiara asked, toying with the hem of one of her gloves.

Gods, I wanted to know what they concealed, but she'd tell me when she was ready. *If* she ever was.

"No, I regretted nothing," I replied curtly, without pause. "My father was a wicked man. A man who took great joy in using his fists and exploiting his only child for his own gains. There wasn't a drop of love inside of him. Not for me, at least."

"But he was still your father—"

"He was no father of mine," I interjected. "A man who treats his kin like that is not a man at all. The world became a better place after he was gone. Though I can't blame you for not understanding," I grumbled, feeling as if her concern had shifted to judgment, just like everyone else's.

"I don't condemn you for what you did." She held my stare, the conviction in her tone shocking me. "You did what you had to in order to survive. And at the end of the day, that's all that matters."

"I highly doubt that," I growled, my upper lip twitching. "Most of my fellow Knights look at me in disgust for slaying my own father. I cannot fathom how you could not feel revulsion as well."

Her hand seized mine once more, this time her grip unrelenting. "I thought you knew me better than that," she argued, bringing her other hand to cup the side of my face.

I stiffened at the contact.

"I haven't known you for long, this is true, but I also know a decent man when I see him. And there are not many in this world. But"—she paused, her fingers tracing the lines of my jaw, her touch featherlight—"you *are* a decent man, no matter what you've done in your past. And I trust you."

I scanned the details of her face, seeking a hint of a lie. I detected none.

Perhaps that was why I couldn't help myself when I brought our entwined hands to my lips, planting a warm kiss on the back of her hand. Her lips parted, her eyes growing clouded once more.

"I wish you'd never followed me here, Kiara." Our hands dropped into my lap, although I didn't release her this time.

"I wish you'd never come…because now I might have to watch you die. And *that*, I would regret for the rest of my days. However many I have left."

K iara snored softly below me, the muscles in her face loose and relaxed.

Last night, she'd eventually fallen asleep against me, and I'd shifted her into my lap and moved her head back to where it had rested right above my heart. My fingers had shaken when I allowed them to trail down her cheek, her smoothness like silk.

After she'd heard the darkest tale of my sordid past, she hadn't looked at me as if I were a monster, a killer. The understanding in her golden eyes had somehow been worse. It had taken every ounce of willpower to lift her into my arms and bring her back to the others. It wouldn't do for them to see her nestled against my chest when the new day approached. I had placed her satchel beneath her head and brought a threadbare blanket up to her chin. I lingered over her far longer than necessary.

Now, hours later, I loomed over her once more, itching to feel her in my hold and recreate the sensation she'd brought up the night before.

I could've sworn the God of Devotion had cursed me, for I had the idiotic urge to reach out and brush aside a wayward strand of silken copper hair that had fallen across her eye. I wanted to run the back of my hand across her cheek, waking her gently with a soft touch. A kiss to her brow.

No.

These thoughts had to cease.

I never should have added her to the ranks. And while she'd been the obvious choice, my decision went much deeper than that.

Gods above, I knew if I gave in and allowed myself one selfish moment, it would surely be the ruin of me.

And possibly the damnation of her soul.

"Time to get up, Kiara," I whispered, lowering to my knees. When she didn't stir, I gently shook her shoulder, my teeth grinding together as I did so. Touching her weakened my resolve, and gods knew, it was already a flimsy lie as it was.

"Can I get five more minutes?" she grumbled.

I almost laughed. "Not looking forward to today, are we?"

Kiara peeled open her eyes, not looking amused in the least. "You haven't even told us what we're looking for. How am I supposed to be thrilled to risk my life when I don't even know why I'm doing it?"

I considered her words, knowing full well how vague I'd been about the mission. That had been done purposely. The king wanted mindless grunts, not soldiers with opinions of their own.

"Oh, just tell me," she groused, lifting herself onto an elbow. Her usually braided hair was undone and loose, and she tossed it over a shoulder. "We've already passed that point in our relationship."

Gods, she was brazen. "I seem to have forgotten how cheeky that mouth is." Her ensuing glare had me heaving a sigh, relenting. "Fine. But you're not going to like it."

"When have I liked *anything* since joining the Knights? And by *joining*, I mean being *forced* to give my life to a power-hungry king and an unsolvable curse. If I recall, that was actually your fault—"

"Fair enough," I hastily cut her off, rocking back on my boots. "We weren't told what *it* looks like, but—" I shot her a scowl when she opened her mouth to protest. She closed it. "We know there are three pieces. Three objects that Cirian believes once belonged to the Goddess of the Sun. If we reunite all three, then we break the curse. That's all Cirian would relinquish, at least."

"Lovely," she snapped. "Another thrilling mystery to solve."

I remembered she said her brother used to wake her with coffee some mornings, so I decided to employ my peace offering then. I could relate. I wasn't a morning person either.

"Would you be happy to hear I had just enough coffee left over for you to have a cup?"

She shot up. I held her interest now.

"You better not be toying with me now, commander," she threatened, her hair sticking out every which way.

My gaze flicked down to the fallen tresses before lifting back to her hopeful eyes. "What would you do if I were?"

"If this is your attempt at being funny, then you don't know who you're messing with."

I couldn't stop my grin from forming, and I really should have. "I wouldn't dare dream of it, Kiara." Stretching out a hand behind me, I produced a tin mug.

Her eyes grew comically large at the sight of the steaming offering.

"Gimme," she demanded like an imprudent child.

I chuckled as her fingers wrapped around the handle, jerking the cup away from me before I could change my mind. She immediately took a few mouthfuls and sighed contentedly.

"This is how I wish to be awoken every morning."

"Well, seeing as I smuggled this last cup to you before the others could see, you may have to do without for the rest of our journey."

She paused mid-sip and said, "You giving me your last cup is basically like you proclaiming your love for me."

Every muscle in my body stiffened at that. I leaned back on my heels, putting some distance between us. I had to focus.

"I wouldn't go that far," I said uncomfortably. "And about the other evening…"

Kiara gripped the mug hard, her breath audibly catching.

The other evening, when I'd held her in my arms and told her my darkest secret.

When I'd crossed yet another line.

"I know what you're about to say, so I'll spare you the trouble," she said before I could get a word out. "It's fine, really. We should keep things…professional."

"You're right," I forced out. "I just don't want either of us to lose focus." *I don't want to see you killed.*

Kiara fixed a fake smile on her face, the sight of it causing my left eye to twitch. "It's a good idea. The others were probably getting jealous."

I lifted a brow, and she continued with a wave of her hand. "You know, seeing as I was your obvious favorite and all."

"So cocky." I shook my head, some of the tension leaving my shoulders. "It's a wonder you can walk with that inflated ego of yours."

"And it's a miracle you can walk at all with that giant chip on your shoulder."

My mouth gaped. This girl was going to be the death of me.

Clearing my throat, I said, "Well, neither of us will be walking if you get caught with the last cup. The others would probably murder you for it." I shoved off from the ground with a grunt.

"Yes, sir." She saluted, my heart pounding when she bestowed me with one last lingering look. There was so much inside those mysterious eyes of hers, but even though I couldn't name the emotion they contained, I *felt* it.

When I approached Isiah across the camp, he gave me an approving nod, though a crease had formed between his brows. "Time to get going," he said before making his way to the still-sleeping bodies sprawled around the torches.

"Wake up, lads!" he shouted, making the boys groan. Alec shot him a dirty look. "Time is of the essence." He lightly kicked Nic's still form. The boy was evidently able to sleep through anything.

Kiara downed her cup before hiding it away in her bag. I looked away the second her head shifted in my direction.

Some time later, when we'd all packed and readied to mount our steeds, I found Patrick approaching Kiara, his shoulders drooped with apprehension.

He liked her, that much was clear, and gods above, I hated that.

"Sleep all right?" Patrick asked.

She chuckled, the sound like bells. "As best as could be expected, given that we slept on rocks. I miss that poor excuse of a cot back at the palace right about now."

"Same." Patrick's eyes warily scanned the shadowed tree line.

I pretended to be busy with fixing my saddlebags in place. My steed nickered as if he knew what a fool I'd turned into.

"Nervous?" Kiara inquired softly, lowering her voice.

"Obviously," he snorted. "I'm terrified."

"Me too. But I have your back."

She would too. That was why she'd snuck away from the sanctum to come here in the first place. To protect them.

Either that, or she had a death wish.

"And you better have mine!" Jake called out as he lunged

into her shoulder, causing her to stagger a few steps to the side.

"You're too energized in the morning," she grumbled, but Jake merely smiled.

"Better than being cranky. But as I was saying, we all have each other's backs out there. Especially Ki," he clarified, grabbing on to her shoulder. "You better protect us all." Patrick managed a chuckle as Jake ruffled her already disheveled hair. "Ohhh, and I like this look. You should let your hair down more often."

She should. Kiara looked—

No. None of that.

"But it would be easier to kill you if it were out of my face," she replied, her smile turning sickly sweet.

"This one over here"—Jake jerked his thumb at Kiara—"always with the jokes." He slung an arm around her shoulders, tugging her into his lanky frame.

I bit down my growl, deciding it was the perfect time to interrupt.

"Recruits!" I thundered, unable to wipe the scowl from my face as I took in Jake, his arm still slung casually over Kiara's shoulders.

"We stick close together out there. No one wanders off alone. If you must relieve yourself, you bring someone with you," I said, my voice hard and unforgiving. "If you fall behind, we all fall behind. There are things in this place that even I do not know of. We fight by each other's sides. That is the only way we will make it out alive."

Kiara glowered when I shot Jake another glare, but his arm dropped from her body, the lad taking a generous step back.

"Now get mounted up. And remember, you should *never* be alone out there. The Mist loves to play tricks on the mind, and you need someone to watch over you." I'd told them of the hallucinations earlier, that they might see things that weren't there. People that had long passed or monsters that haunted dreams.

The recruits sobered as they mounted and brought their horses to the mouth of the cave. I positioned myself at the front, Isiah at my side. We hadn't spoken about Carter, not yet. As a rule, we only talked about the dead once we weren't in danger of death ourselves.

Unable to help myself, I stole a glance behind me.

The boys' eyes were all brimming with fear, but when I took in Kiara, perched like a warrior queen atop her mare, none filled her stare. She looked…excited.

That expression would be wiped off her face soon enough.

With a *tsk* of my tongue, my steed shot out from the cave's mouth, the rest of the recruits falling into line behind me.

And as the rocky ceiling gave way to open charcoal skies, exposing us to the cursed haze, I felt a slight tremble rack my body.

And I knew this time would be different, worse than before.

This time, I felt like I had something to lose.

Chapter Twenty-Five

Kiara

The few survivors of the Mist assert that the use of torches isn't as needed in the cursed lands. That the moon shines bright enough to light your way. Although, they also claim that they felt watched, that the brightness of the sky gave them no place to hide when the shadows crept upon them.

Camille Ashton, Asidian historian,
year 45 of the curse

The moon was bigger here—nearly double the size it appeared within the kingdom's borders.

There wasn't an explanation for it, and I didn't have the energy to care. Not as it hovered in the overcast skies like a king on a throne of ash. Though, for the first time in my life, I didn't need a flaming torch in order to see. That was a plus in my book.

While the ice-blue wisps of fog coated the ground like a thick batch of fresh snow, they only rose to brush Starlight's underbelly. As with all good things, I had a nagging suspicion that would soon change.

But it didn't mean I couldn't appreciate it now.

It *was* stunning, in an eerily macabre way. Like a graveyard full of skeletal trees and electrifying blue. So far, the Mist had the quality of a dream realm—all the shades of ethereal white and blue in stark contrast to the anxious group of dark-clothed mortals that rode through it.

Still, I couldn't shake the sense of being watched. I half expected a shadow beast to appear, to unfurl itself from the branches and wrap around us like we were prey, sucking the flesh from our bones and swallowing our screams. I shivered at the thought.

For the first time, I desired the night to whisper into my ear. To offer reassurance…or a sweet lie. Either would do. Anything was better than the eerie hush that had fallen.

Patrick rode soundlessly to my left, his suspicious eyes scanning the reedy trees and their slender branches for signs of danger. We had yet to see another living soul in this realm of nightmares and chilling reality.

Not one bird sang, and not a single forest creature scurried across the brush to catch its next meal. Even the gods' spies, the notorious starwings, kept away, the lack of their constant twittering leaving the air too quiet. Maybe the gods didn't want to see what occurred beyond the borders either, or maybe they were just as frightened by what they'd find.

Ahead of us rode Alec, the first in line after Isiah and Jude.

A soldier through and through, he scanned the trees, his hand resting on the hilt of his blade.

As usual, Jake and Nic lagged behind everyone else, leaning over their steeds to whisper conspiratorially to one another, the two friends anything but stealthy.

Jake took a twisted pleasure in teasing Nic about absolutely anything and everything, especially if it pertained to his silken hair, tresses that I was envious of myself. I had to admit, the tall jokester was growing on me.

I understood that the friends were working to take their minds off our current surroundings, and I couldn't fault them;

the cursed lands weren't what I expected. There was this sense that we'd entered a fairytale realm, but like most of Asidia's legends, the monsters always appeared when the hero least expected it. And won.

Asidia needed to work on its lore. We were seriously grim people.

"We've been traveling for over an hour, and I've yet to see a single animal. It's not normal," Patrick warned in a low murmur. He rubbed at the back of his neck, suspicion causing his shoulders to visibly tense.

I snorted. "Nothing about this is *normal*, dear Patrick. If you haven't noticed, we are well into the Mist already. It rises every couple of hours." Indeed, the fog was now resting just above Starlight's belly.

Patrick grumbled something I couldn't make out, casting his attention to the moon. He stared upon its surface, swallowing thickly.

"You never told me you knew so much about herbs and poisons." I shot him a curious glance. Maybe Jake and Nic were right, and a little distraction couldn't hurt. "You might say you're lucky to have me here with you, but after what I saw in the tunnels, it seems to be the other way around."

He blushed, and his shoulders lifted at the compliment, his eyes sparkling in the obscurity. "I wouldn't say that. I just enjoy reading." His lips twitched. "Especially when all of the world's secrets are splayed across the pages for anyone to see. I could never count on people, but books...they don't lie or betray you."

He had a point there.

"What's your favorite—"

Thunderous howls exploded from every direction, the forest quivering as the sounds wafted through the brittle blue leaves.

I might've thought them to belong to wolves, but they were much deeper, shaking my bones. Or maybe my teeth were just rattling with fear.

"What was that?" Patrick jerked in his saddle, his fingers twitching for his dagger. "That wasn't like any wolf I've ever heard."

He read my mind. "No, it sounds larger." Much larger.

I surveyed the trees, looking for any flash of movement or the glinting of yellow eyes.

There was nothing. Not even the branches shook or a wind blustered.

"Stop!" Jude's order seemed to echo as it made its way to my ears. The sound was distorted, broken up into multiple pieces.

Starlight whinnied in alarm as I yanked on the reins, her long legs trotting wildly in place. She was restless standing still, agitated. Not that she wasn't *always* agitated with me, but this was different. Like she was trying to warn me of some threat I couldn't see.

"Be on your guard!" Jude boomed, his voice still coming at me in waves of varying tenors. "Isiah, take up the rear!"

Isiah whirled past me as he raced to the back of the line, his form flickering like a candle in the wind. Like he wasn't solid at all. I swore he shone a brilliant silver.

I blinked, squeezing my eyes tightly shut. Maybe there was dust or dirt stuck in them and my eyesight was being affected? I rubbed at them until black spots prickled my vision.

Another loud cry split the air, the vibrations tingling my goose-pimpled flesh.

Whatever that thing was, it was huge. And *loud*.

The cold metal of my hilt bit into my hand, adrenaline searing my insides as I prepared for the unknown. A part of me pulsated with a sick, perverse excitement, wondering what foreign creature would emerge from the viscous haze.

"Ki," Patrick hissed between his teeth. A peculiar look sharpened his eyes, ones that were no longer soft and serene.

They'd taken on a feral edge. "I think I see it." He raised a lone finger to the trees.

My breath caught as I followed where he indicated, landing on a mass of vibrant cobalt shrubbery below a silver-flecked white tree. It was an exact copy of the trees that encircled it, nothing out of the ordinary given our location.

I was scrutinizing each branch and crinkled leaf—trying desperately to understand what he'd motioned to—when a coppery taste landed on the tip of my tongue like a fallen snowflake. Licking my lips only made the jarring tang of metal intensify. It reminded me of blood.

"D-do you taste that?" I asked Patrick, my voice quivering. "Metal."

I called out his name once more, but Patrick didn't answer. He was too consumed by whatever it was I couldn't see in the trees.

"Patrick?" I tried again, blinking rapidly as I saw double of my friend. The two Patricks swayed back and forth before meeting in the middle, one never quite rejoining the other. Panic simmered in my blood, turning my skin ice cold.

"Patrick!"

Nothing. He didn't seem to hear me at all.

He was made of stone and unmoved by my pleas. Leaning back in my saddle, I aimed my attention at Jake and Nic, who were utterly mesmerized by whatever Patrick claimed to have seen. They were staring at that same damned tree, the one that matched all the others.

What the living hells is going on?

"Jake! Nic!" I waved my hands back and forth, desperately seeking their attention. Any trace of calm left me, and my limbs tingled.

Doing my best to ignore how my gloved hands itched, how the hair on the back of my neck rose in alarm, I nudged Starlight over to a frozen Alec, whose face was just as lifeless as the others.

What were they seeing that I wasn't? There was nothing there. Definitely not a beast substantial enough to have made those chilling screeches.

Everyone had lost their grip on reality.

I kept urging Starlight forward until I was beside Jude, whose head was lowered toward his lap, rasps of unsettled breaths racking his chest. The whites of his knuckles shone in the eerie glow of the moon, his fingers wrapped securely around the reins.

Blue-black hair hung limply before his closed eyes, his neck bent sharply as his breathing accelerated. I could practically taste the fear he exhaled with every shuddering breath, his weakening control over himself as he clenched his jaw, hints of red flushing his cheeks.

"Jude," I whispered, the commander's form doubling as my compromised vision distorted him further. "What's happening?" I was being affected too, just not as badly as the others from the looks of it.

"Jude!" This time I didn't bother to whisper, giant wolves and monsters be damned.

Still, he did not open his eyes and seek me, although his lips quivered as he silently murmured beneath his breath. Was that a prayer? Or a curse?

Inching Starlight closer, I made a bold grab for his hand, wrapping my gloved one around his. "Jude, look at me," I begged, my voice taking on a note of desperation. I couldn't do this alone.

Jude's throat worked hard as he swallowed, his hand twitching where mine rested. "Please open your eyes. Everyone is f-frozen. Looking at some tree." Peering over my shoulder, I found them all in the exact position I'd left them in, though this time, the tree in question appeared tinged in a deep cobalt blue, tiny black veins running the length of its coarse wood.

Shit.

I rubbed at my eyes, but the color only grew more vivid, more inviting, the veins pulsating rhythmically. My hands started to shake, and that itching worsened.

My fingers were pure ice, the cold painful. I flexed them, trying to regain the sensation I was losing. It didn't work.

Tearing myself from the ever-changing tree, I tightened my hold on Jude's hand, the bruising force causing his lids to cautiously flutter open. Now wasn't the time to be gentle.

"Kiara?" he whispered, the crease between his brows deepening.

"Yes! Now please look at me." I was outright pleading with him now.

"I-I can't," he began, his grip crushing my bones. "If I open my eyes, I'll see it too."

"See what?" I beseeched. "There is nothing here!"

Jude rapidly shook his head, his eyes squeezed tighter than before. "This is what happened last time. They all started to see things. Beasts. People. Things that weren't there. And then…" He trailed off, scrunching his face as though in physical pain. "They killed each other. And then themselves. And I"—he choked on his words—"I finished the rest."

Black smoke swirled around the edges of my sight. I wasn't afraid of Jude because of what he'd done. I was pissed he carried that guilt. If what he'd said was true, then whatever was coming for us planned to use our minds against us.

That damned coppery taste coated my tongue, overwhelming in its intensity. It was getting worse with each passing second. I heard the other boys start to talk, all motioning and pointing frantically.

"Jude." I leaned over and shook him. "When you and your men encountered this before, did you taste something? Metal or blood, perhaps?"

Refusing to open his eyes, Jude considered my query, or I hoped he did.

After too many pounding heartbeats, he finally answered me, his voice low and haunted. "I-I remember a strange aroma, a scent. One that smelled of copper, but not in my mouth. I thought it was just the Mist, another odd effect. And then anarchy ensued and…" He broke off, lost in a nightmarish past.

I'd never seen him lose himself like this.

"It's all right," I soothed, rubbing his hand. While my vision remained unfocused and my hands burned from ice, I didn't have the overwhelming urge to do anything not within my control.

"Jude," I tried again, this time softening my voice. I could be the strong one today, for the both of us. "Is it better if you close your eyes?" He nodded, the movement so subtle I wasn't sure if I caught it. "All right, then I need you to keep doing that. From what you said, the scent, that aroma you smelled in the air, eventually went away. Maybe we just have to wait it out." For all I knew it would linger here forever, or the hallucinations weren't a side effect of the foul breeze at all. But it was the only hope I had.

"I need to get the others to—"

"There!" Nic's cry rattled my ears, his voice sharp and unrecognizable. Gone was the sarcastic and playful boy I was only beginning to get to know. To befriend. "It's right there, don't you see it! As large as four wolves put together!"

There was no wolf, only the scent of metal and bone trees.

"Keep your eyes closed, Jude," I bellowed, right before whisking Starlight back down the line of stoic recruits, back over to Nic.

"It's there! Can't you see?" he cried, beating his hand against his chest in frustration. "We need to kill it before it kills us! Why are we just sitting here?"

"Nic, you need to calm down, please! Close your eyes!" I shouted, leaning over my anxious mare and reaching for one of Nic's flailing hands. He resisted me.

I cursed my blurred sight as I missed and Nic flung out a fist—one that landed with surprising force against my rib cage. With a yelp, I was tossed from my saddle, landing on my backside with a bruising thud. I scrambled to my trembling limbs before the pale blue fog could envelop me.

"I see it too!" Jake screeched, his voice like nails on glass.

My feet planted in the soft earth, and I gazed in horror as every face sprang to life, panic contorting their features as they shouted for action against an invisible enemy. Their movements were jerky and clumsy like they were being controlled by some grand puppeteer.

Jake had jumped from his steed first, his polished sword raised high in the air as if going into battle. "What are we waiting for? Go!" he urged, motioning forward with the tip of the lethal blade. "Now!"

More boots landed upon the dirt, everyone besides Jude dismounting their steeds and setting off for that blasted tree.

"Wait!" I shrieked, waving my hands. "You need to close your eyes! There's nothing there!"

They didn't listen.

"It's in the air, screwing with your vision. With your sense of reality! It will pass, but we need to ride it out. Close your eyes!" I implored, breathless. Never had I felt as helpless as I did now, watching powerlessly as my friends raced away, their weapons drawn and battle cries on their lips.

Patrick was roaring right alongside a wrathful Nic. The kindhearted boy I knew was nowhere in sight as he waved his weapon high and lurched ahead.

"Kiara!" Jude called from his horse. His mismatched eyes were open but glazed, though I didn't mistake how he narrowed them into slits, determined to overpower the sickly influence of the fog.

My mouth gaped as he swung a leg over his steed, instantly bolting off in a blurred sprint. "No!" I heard him shout, his long limbs struggling to catch up to the boys he was sworn to protect. "Close your eyes! Fight it!"

I cursed as I took off in a dash behind Jude, my legs nowhere near as quick as his. But I had to reach him. Had to stop them all from committing whatever heinous actions the Mist coaxed them into.

As I sprinted the distance to the tree, the others having just arrived beneath its curving branches, I quickly thought of what I could do to stop them. If I *could* do anything at all at this point. Maybe it was already too late.

When I approached, Nic was shouting, his words filled with uncharacteristic venom. "You!" He pointed to Alec, the black of his pupils flaring. "You scared it off!"

Alec sneered, his lips curling back against his teeth as he growled. "What are you talking about, you heavy-footed oaf? You're the one who screamed like some prepubescent youngling, and now it'll come back and kill us in our sleep!" He waved a hand in the air, motioning to the deadened forest.

None of what they were spewing made sense. Wisps of darkened clouds limned their dilated pupils, the *wrongness* of their gazes both otherworldly and chilling.

"Great. Now you two are fighting. You all just *love* to find anything and everything to bicker about. You're just vile, petty children. I cannot believe I am being subjected to this pathetic lot." My mouth fell as Patrick joined in the quarrel.

This was going to get out of hand. Fast.

Sputtering a curse that would have my mother fainting, I darted to Jude's side and grabbed hold of his muscled biceps. His gaze flashed to me, his brown eye flickering with contempt.

But it was the other eye, the one swirling with snow and frost, that unsettled me, had me eager to step back.

He looked at me as though I were a stranger, and when my fingers tightened around him, Jude reacted. In a motion too quick for me to comprehend, he grabbed at my gloved right hand, his grip harsh.

"Get away from me," he seethed. With a grunt, he kicked my stomach with his boot, knocking the air from my lungs. My balance was lost, but the grip he had on my glove didn't waver.

It slipped off...

The blue of my scars shimmered in the dense shroud of white, iridescent onyx threads gleaming from the vein-like wounds. I hissed, clutching it to my chest, trying to hide what I'd kept from the world for over a decade.

Jude didn't stop his assault. His right eye blazed with fire, and he moved—gods, he moved so quickly. His looming form was on mine in the time it took me to blink, and instinctively, I brought my ungloved hand to his chest, trying to shove him off, to stop him from killing me.

"You're poison," he murmured, fighting to hold me down. I stayed strong, moving my other hand to block him from crushing me. "Vile, vile darkness. Poison."

Tears prickled behind my eyes, hot and angry ones.

How many times had I ignored the whispers of Cila's villagers? They'd look at my little hands, clutched in my parents', and balk, making the sign of the Sun Goddess across their chests. They thought I was evil, touched by the cursed lands.

"It's me!" I cried, my scarred hand flying to Jude's neck, to his cheek. The sight of my hand made me sick, the reminder of the accident causing black shadows to swarm my vision. Jude stilled, froze so suddenly that I jerked, my back digging into the rocky ground.

With my hand on his cheek, he ceased his assault, his eyes

clearing, growing sharper. For a moment, he leaned into my palm as if it were a lifeline, but then horror twisted his features.

"K-Kiara?" He reared back, his mouth falling open, those wide eyes searching me for injuries—ones he might've caused.

The Mist had released him.

"It's all right," I whispered, climbing to my feet. Shock rippled down my spine, rendering me a mess of wobbly knees and trembling breaths. Without my glove, he'd know, he'd see.

His stare shifted to my hand.

I was going to be sick, was going to—

A thud sounded, a body landing on the ground as it was shoved by a livid Nic, his hair flowing wildly around his determined face like some sort of demonic halo. "I told you to stay away from me!" Thick beads of sweat dripped profusely down his forehead. "Stay back!" he warned Alec as his fellow recruit inched closer, a blade at the ready.

"Dammit!" Without time to hesitate, I snatched Jude's hand and dragged him over to where Alec lurked, ready to lunge at Nic and deliver a deadly blow. My bare fingers intertwined with his, and I swore a jolt of electricity shot between us.

Before Alec could act on whatever sordid intentions swirled about his tainted thoughts, I released Jude and took hold of Alec's arm, using all of my waning force to swing him around to face me.

Alec's wide green eyes held that same fierce animosity as Nic's did. As all of theirs did.

"Alec. It's the Mist!" I shouted loud enough for everyone to hear. The muscles in the arm beneath my hand grew less tense. "It's the Mist making you think these things."

His murky eyes flashed as he took me in, a blink of recognition dawning on his roughened features. I hardly noticed how my scarred hand moved to touch the exposed skin of his chest.

I pleaded, "Stay with me," over and over again until I felt his muscles gradually relax, his body swaying unsteadily on his feet.

"Ki?"

I nodded. Just as with Jude, his eyes were softening, the pupils returning to their normal size. "I— I don't know what—"

"It's okay," I rushed to say, glancing to where Patrick and Jake were facing off, circling one another like dueling predators.

Jake darted from the left, barreling into Patrick. Isiah lingered off to the side, motionless, eyes closed, a statue of calm. Though that had to be a lie, as his lips were moving frantically, likely uttering some misbegotten prayer beneath his breath. He didn't appear to be a threat.

Releasing both a stunned Jude and Alec, I shot out like an arrow, my sights set on Patrick. I had to get him away from Jake, who could slaughter him with ease.

Diving into the pearly abyss, I tumbled along with the fighting pair, Patrick somehow scrambling atop Jake's chest, his glinting blade poised directly over his friend's beating heart. He'd never moved so quickly in training, and his skilled movements surprised me.

"NO!" I grabbed the hand holding the dagger. It took considerable effort to hold his hand steady as I spoke. "You need to let go, Patrick. This is some sort of trick the Mist plays on you."

Turning brothers against one another. Killing them.

I pinched his chin with my exposed fingers, the black in my scars seeming to glow in the low light. Patrick's pale eyes brightened, his hand trembling as his fingers relaxed their hold. The dagger tumbled to the dirt, lost in the pool of white.

Before Jake could attack, I swiveled to him, grasping his hand and clutching it tightly.

"What— What did I do?" Jake stumbled back, jerking away from me as he fell to his knees. "I-I wanted to kill—"

"It wasn't you," I interrupted, already hoisting myself up, shoving my hand deep into my pocket, hoping to hide the evidence of my truth. Thankfully, he was too dazed by his own actions to notice.

They would have no doubt murdered one another until only one man stood. Jude had been right; the Mist itself was our enemy.

"Can't you all see? It's inside of us! It wants us to let it out. Only then can we be free of the sickness!"

Nic. I'd forgotten about him.

"We need to cut it out!" Nic screeched wildly, his head swiveling back and forth among the stunned recruits. "It's the only way!"

Nic lifted his blade to his throat.

Without hesitation, I bolted for Nic, my new friend just fifteen feet away. All the blood rushed to my ears, drowning out the cries of protest, the others shouting for him to put down the blade.

"Nic!" Jake screamed, his voice hoarse. "Stop!"

I was nearly on him now. All I had to do was reach out and—

With one swift motion, Nic sliced through the thin skin of his throat, blood instantly bubbling to the surface.

"NO!" I howled, grasping his arms as he collapsed to his knees, his youthful eyes full of terror as fresh blood gushed from his fatal wound. He choked on it, a sickening gurgling sound escaping his red lips.

Within seconds, the noise stopped, and Nic was no longer choking on his blood.

He was dead.

CHAPTER TWENTY-SIX

JUDE

The mind can be the sharpest weapon one possesses, but it can also be the blade that delivers the fatal blow.

ASIDIAN PROVERB

It was quiet for a long time after Nic sliced open his own throat.

The winds were changing, taking the cursed poison with them—whatever it was that had caused such chaos to ensue. A poison that had compelled a young boy to kill himself in the most gruesome of ways.

Jake was the first to react, rushing to cradle his dead friend in his lap. Tears cascaded down his golden cheeks, sobs racking his lithe frame as he wailed. As he mourned for his friend.

I stopped breathing, my limbs weighted down by the realization of what I'd just witnessed. What *I* had failed to stop. Again.

Kiara moved quickly as she reached for her discarded glove, sliding it on while the others were distracted. Her entire body trembled, and I wanted to reach out, to hold her in my arms.

But her scars…

I'd finally seen what she concealed, and… There were

no words. I had never seen anything like them before, and gods knew I had seen every manner of injury over the years. They'd been *black*, veiny, tinges of blue whispering among the glimmering onyx. My throat constricted as I peeled my eyes from her.

Kiara had hidden herself from me out of fear of my reaction, but while shocked by the revelation, I didn't feel repulsed, only curious.

Jake continued to rock Nic in his arms, his tears splattering upon his friend's open wound. Kiara rushed away from the group, leaning over to heave up the meager contents of her stomach.

I was beside her in a heartbeat, winding my fingers through her hair and holding the strands away from her face, mustering whatever soothing words I could find and whispering them in her ear. I couldn't help it, and thoughts of maintaining my distance vanished entirely. Someone had killed themselves before our very eyes, and pushing her away would just be cruel.

The moment she'd gotten everything out of her system, she took off, marching to where Starlight and the other horses rested. She grabbed at her canteen, unscrewing the cap and chugging the cool water.

Starlight protested beside her, waving her head back and forth as she kicked out her front legs.

"Shhh, girl. It's all right," she whispered, leaning her head against the mare's neck.

She settled at Kiara's touch, allowing Kiara to hold her as a lone tear escaped down her cheek, dripping onto Starlight's velvety coat.

"Kiara."

She jerked at the sound of her name.

I spoke it again, and her body tensed when I wound my arms around her, holding onto her waist as my chest pressed into her back. "This was why I didn't want you to come."

No one should bear witness to this.

I rubbed soft circles onto her back, resting my chin atop her hair. She let out a soft whimpering sound before giving in to the sensation of being held.

I could tell it was new to her as well, the touching. Given how she barely touched the others—unless it was a playful jab or a punch to the face during training—she hadn't displayed intimacy with anyone else. Not like she did with me.

It made me relax, knowing that we both were unaccustomed to this, to embracing.

I only wished to ease her fears, to silently let her know that I'd seen her secret and that it didn't bother me. She, of all people, should have known that.

After many minutes passed, I angled my head, pressing my cheek against her red hair. "This is what it does. The curse. But I can't understand how you weren't affected. All I know is that you seemed to stop it from getting worse. Before all of us killed one another. You saved us."

She winced at my words, but I merely tightened my grip around her waist.

"You killed your brothers," she said softly.

My breath hitched. I'd almost entirely forgotten I'd confessed my dark truth. "And I regret what I've done every single day. Every moment of my existence."

"It wasn't *you*, though. Even Patrick wanted to kill Jake. He almost did." Twisting in my arms, she slanted her chin to meet me head on, her features turning hard. I despised the inches between us. "You say you wished I'd never come here, but if what you believe is true, that I somehow broke the Mist's hold, then I'm right where I should be."

Raising her chin, she sniffed back the tears aching to be released. I noted her fists clenched at her sides, the leather of her gloves straining. I wouldn't speak of that, not now and not with the others. They might not have noticed in all the chaos, and I refused to push her.

My hand trembled as it made its way to her cheek, my own rules to drive her away forgotten. They seemed so trivial now that we'd almost died.

"You're magnificent, Kiara," I murmured. "All of you." I stared at her fists, at her right hand. She tracked the movement.

"Don't go all sappy on me now, commander." She sniffled, attempting a half smile, even as she shoved her hand into her pocket.

Still, it felt like acceptance, like she knew what I'd seen and that I hadn't turned away.

I moved closer, and at this point I was nearly flush against her. Kiara's hands instinctively went to rest on my hips.

"I'm sorry if I hurt you," I said, shame eating at me as I remembered how I kicked her.

She blew out a breath. "You didn't hurt me. My uncle trained me to make sure that no punch or kick or weapon could wound me, not where it matters."

Her eyes shone, the clouds within them dispersing. I understood exactly what she meant. "Either way, I *am* sorry." Gods, was I sorry, even if I'd been but a puppet, my strings pulled by some invisible master.

"I told you, Jude," she said, casting a crestfallen look to where her friends surrounded Nic's body, Patrick holding Jake in a tight hug. "It's this place; it's the poison in the air that's at fault. *You* would never hurt me."

I wouldn't. But I had hurt others.

"I've taken more lives than I ever wish to count. You have no idea what I've done—"

"All I care about is what you do now," she said, steeling her spine.

Gone was the raw vulnerability, the trembling girl who'd melted in my embrace. Still, she was unable to stop her lower lip from quivering, and I lifted my arm, brushing my thumb across the fullness of her mouth. I wasn't thinking straight, my eyes fixated on the soft skin I caressed.

Kiara sucked in a strangled breath, turning to where Nic's lifeless body lay surrounded by his friends. It jolted me back to my damned senses, and I dropped my hand and released her entirely. Nic had died, and here I was thinking about how I wanted to hold her.

I had known I was a twisted bastard, but that shocked even me.

"We should check on the others, then make camp and bury Nic," I forced out, hating myself and the coldness of my tone.

Her face contorted with grief. "He didn't deserve that," she murmured. "Nic had a whole life ahead of him, and he was so damned witty and smart and so *not* funny that he actually *was* funny."

Kiara's throat worked as she swallowed her tears. "He was my friend." The last part she said in a whisper, eyes downcast so I couldn't see.

"He didn't deserve it." There was nothing else I could think of to say.

Isiah and I had lost so many of our brothers that it had become normal. We grieved behind closed doors and spoke to no one of our sorrows. Kiara hadn't yet been infected with our apathy. I didn't want her to be.

Just when I thought this world to be cruel, it went ahead and proved it could get so much worse. And now I had to dig a hole for a boy who would never see the sun we fought to restore.

Chapter Twenty-Seven

Kiara

*I miss your stubborn face more and more as the days progress.
I find it ironic that only after you left me did I realize just how
much I needed you. I think you've always claimed you were
hard to love, but really, you just saw the best in
everyone else and the worst in yourself.*

Unmailed letter from Liam Frey to his sister, Kiara Frey,
year 50 of the curse

We buried Nic beneath the brittle blue and white branches of the tree where he'd taken his life.

Jude dropped to his knees as we all watched, the commander's head bent to the gray soil as his hands began to claw at the dirt. Mud and blood stained his long fingers, the earth trapped beneath his nails. But he didn't stop his methodical movements, and one by one, the others followed. I, too, started to dig.

Jake remained frozen on the dewy ground, his lean arms wrapped around Nic, his blue eyes a shade of steel and hopelessness.

It took an hour before the hole was deep enough, every recruit coated in the dust of the earth. When the time came for Jake to release his friend, it took both Jude and Isiah to pry him off Nic's lifeless body.

I held back the lingering nausea as Nic's eyes were closed with the back of Jude's hand, my friend's skin the color of snow on the coldest day of winter.

Jake didn't cry. He was in a state of shock as I wound my arm around his shoulder and led him to where the others circled the grave, their backs ramrod straight, their hands clasped behind them in a demonstration of respect.

Jude and Isiah swaddled Nic in ripped linen before lowering him to the bottom of the shallow grave, dirt and fallen leaves sullying the ivory cloth. The recruits somberly filled the hole as I enfolded Jake in my arms, clutching him tightly.

Only when the last grain fell did Jake shed a lone tear—then he cried no more.

The commander tucked his helmet under his arm, his focus trained on the obsidian metal. With the others watching, Jude stepped up to the freshly packed soil and dropped to a knee. Shutting his eyes, he spoke, his voice too low for me to hear. When the last silent word fell, he opened his eyes and placed his infamous spiked helmet—the mask he'd donned whenever he played the role of death—upon the earth.

Jude stood, rigidly backing away, though his attention never strayed from his offering.

I tried to catch his gaze, but he swiftly turned on a heel and marched toward the horses. Away from us all.

The weight of the moment wasn't lost on me.

Jake continued to stare into space, glassy-eyed and numb, throughout the remaining hours of the day. Even when we settled around the campfire later, sharing dried meat and fruits packed from the palace, he simply sat beside me, a specter, an empty shell.

Nic's absence was heavily felt.

There were no clever comments or playful jabs. No

boisterous laughter or shrewd smiles. My chest ached whenever I thought about my handsome and sarcastic friend—because that's what he'd become, a friend who would have stayed at my side until the bitter end.

Nic and Jake and Patrick had all taken me under their wings back at the sanctum, and when the loneliness had threatened to swallow me, they would appear like a wish made real, ruffling my hair and teasing me endlessly until the void in my heart was filled.

I felt like the biggest failure for letting Nic down.

That evening, instead of curling up beside Patrick, I covered Jake's body with my own, dragging his quivering frame flush against my chest. There were no words I could utter that would ease his pain, no apology that would bring Nic back. But I could do *this*. Hold him.

In the past, I'd believed that I'd never been fond of touching because it felt too intimate, allowing people the opportunity to get close enough to weaken me. To break me. But the truth was, I'd been broken a long time ago. It was the fractured pieces of myself I didn't trust with others. Until now.

Until we'd all stepped into the Mist and were united by something greater than fear.

Jude passed by once, his stare lingering where my body met Jake's.

As we connected, an undecipherable look flashed across his eyes, a muscle in his jaw tensing. Was he imagining my hand? The gruesome scars that tainted my skin? It was selfish to think of such things then, but I couldn't help it.

Never had I felt so exposed, and my heart skipped several beats when he broke eye contact, striding away with heavy steps. He slept on the other side of our camp that night, as far away from me as he could manage.

When my eyes fluttered open after a restless sleep, my skin

was cold, and my arms were empty.

Rising from my spot beside the dying fire, the rest of the camp only just waking, I made my way to the tree where Nic would remain forever.

It made me sick that we'd buried him here, where he'd succumbed to the Mist and its will, but we hadn't had a choice.

"Jake." I placed a gloved hand on his shoulder when I found him before the tree.

He was on his knees, eyes cast to where the gravel and fog hid the body of our fallen recruit. Jake flinched when I took a spot beside him, my knee touching his.

"I don't know how to carry on without him." Jake's raw voice broke. "We've been inseparable since we were five years old. Friends. Brothers."

I kept quiet, allowing him to release the grief that threatened to wreck him.

"My parents were never really a big part of my life. Whenever my dad spent all our money on ale or lost it all on cards, Nic would sneak me over some bread or leftover dinner from his house. That was the first way he kept me alive." Jake swiped at an escaped tear, sniffling.

"And the second way?" I asked, massaging Jake's shoulders as he cried. The physical ache in my chest throbbed.

Lowering a reverent hand flat upon the earth, Jake answered, "The second way he kept me alive was showing me that I wasn't alone. That while I didn't have much, I did have someone who cared about me. Someone who would mourn me if I died." Jake scoffed. "I sound like such a damned sap."

I vehemently shook my head.

"I may not have known him as well as I would have liked," I began hesitantly, gently twisting his head to face me. "But it sounds like he loved you dearly. And not many of us are lucky to have that kind of unbreakable bond." I swallowed the lump that always appeared when I thought of Liam. "Nic would have wanted you to continue on. To live your life and honor him by simply remembering all the good that he was."

And he had been good. Funny and sarcastic and all kinds of warm. I felt as if someone had cut off a limb, like our little ragtag group had lost something vital—a piece of our united heart. It would never beat the same.

Jake squeezed his eyes, jerking his head out of my grasp.

"It's also normal to grieve, Jake. To feel this pain." I tilted my chin, snuggling close so my shoulder rested against his chest. "You, Nic, and Patrick were there for me when no one else looked my way. You became my friends." The lump in my throat grew. "But you are not alone. Not anymore. I know I am not the same. Nowhere near what Nic was to you. But I promise you this… From here on out, you are *my* friend, *my* brother. My family."

It stunned me how easily the words came out. And how much I truly meant them.

In Jake, I had a brother. Two more in Patrick and Alec. It was now us against the curse of a goddess. Us against the demise of our kingdom. And we would either triumph together or die together, and that bound us.

A fresh wave of tears trickled from his swollen eyes, disappearing one by one into the swirling haze as the moon vanished behind a shroud of clouds.

I was just about to leave Jake to his grief, to allow him to mourn in peace, when a hand fell heavily on mine, stopping me.

"And you, Kiara Frey, are my friend. My sister. My family." Jake's fingers crushed my own, an unspoken promise passing between us. Briefly, he glanced to the hand he held, and he nodded. I didn't ask if he knew what lay beneath, if he'd seen my scars. I found it didn't really matter.

So I sat there, right beside him with our hands entwined.

I didn't have the delusion that this would be our last burial.

We'd lose more friends, but that time had yet to pass. And right now, I was grateful to find myself in the company of someone I was honored to call my brother.

The next day went by just like the first.

We trekked through the Mist, the blue-tinged fog now up to my mid-calves. No one spoke unless absolutely necessary. When dinner was ready and the fire roaring, we ate silently and settled in for the night. There were no stories told beside the fire.

Again, I draped myself around Jake like a human blanket, Patrick curled up on my other side. This time, Jude didn't deign to glance my way. He had made a point to steer clear of me.

By the new day, none of us felt rested, but we continued on, Jude guiding us with the scrap of a map the king had gifted him.

A part of me wanted to ask Jude if I could see it, to get a better sense of where we were headed, but like all the others, I'd misplaced my spirit and lost my resolve.

The third day after Nic was killed, when we were well and deep into the land of no return, I began to feel a profound unease. It crept across my skin like a million tiny insects, stinging my flesh.

This sense of disquiet worsened as the day progressed, the once red ring around the moon gradually turning a hue of sickly yellow. It did nothing to alleviate my anxiety.

I couldn't help but feel like something was coming.

What that thing was, I hadn't the faintest idea, but we'd gone days without a new incident, and that screamed that it was only a matter of time before our luck ran out.

Starlight was just as agitated and restless as I, the old mare's ears flicking in warning. I shushed her and comforted her as best as I could, but she would not settle.

The deeper we traveled, the more the brittle underbrush gave way to razor-sharp reeds the color of cinder and ash. They sliced at the white trunks with every gust of wind, swishing in the air like honed knives.

I was so lost in the shifting scenery that I barely heard the telltale whoosh of an arrow.

"Ki!" Patrick screeched, forcing my head to twist just before the sharpened tip would've pierced my skull.

Starlight reared back on her hind legs as I jerked on her reins, the mare letting out a distraught whinny.

"Attack!" Jude thundered from the front of the line.

I glimpsed a flash of steel as he unsheathed his sword, and then there was the pounding of his steed's hooves. Quick as the arrow that had nearly ended me, Jude materialized at my side, the commander wildly scanning the tree line for the source of the attack.

My heart hammered behind my ribs, and I wasn't sure if I was breathing at all. If I'd been an inch to the right, I would have been dead. Buried beneath the Mist and the gray soil that covered these cursed lands.

Time slowed to a crawl as we all searched the obscurity, anxiously awaiting the next arrow to fly. Waiting for the bedlam to unfold.

We didn't have to wait long.

Another whooshing sound echoed before the second arrow struck a target.

Isiah.

He slumped over his steed, an arrow piercing his shoulder. His horse whinnied beneath him, the panicked animal bucking his rider off before galloping into the copse of trees.

Arrows fell across us like a wave of silver, the moon's glow shining on the gleaming metal tips as they descended. Foolishly, I looked up, covering my head with my hands, knowing that without a shield, I was helpless.

"It's coming from our left!" Jude dismounted his horse, his lean frame vanishing as the fog swallowed him up.

Following his lead, I dismounted Starlight, Patrick at my heels. We stuck out like sore thumbs on our steeds, and we had a better chance of survival if we used the Mist and its unnatural cover to our advantage.

While I sprinted, keenly picking up on Jude's heavy steps, I heard more boots hit the ground.

Who could possibly be attacking us?

No one survived out here—the king made that quite clear to any who thought to try their luck beyond the kingdom's borders. We'd been led to believe it was a realm occupied only by beasts and monsters.

Judging by the arrows that had been aimed at our heads, that hardly seemed the case. They were nocked and released, and my breath caught when a startled whinny rang out into the gloom. I stopped dead in my tracks.

Starlight.

One of the damned arrows had struck her in her belly, blood already dripping from the fresh wound. I began to backtrack, a cry of rage lodged in my throat, when a hand encircled mine.

"Kiara!" Jude's voice penetrated the haze, the sound of my name on his lips a growl. "We have to go. Now!"

My heart fell further into my stomach as Starlight collapsed, nothing but a blur of red-stained hair. Her cries of pain tore through me, had my hackles rising and wisps of darkness clouding my vision. I couldn't just leave her here, I had to—

"Kiara!" Jude snapped, yanking me so hard I went flying into the solid muscle of his chest. "You can't save her," he whispered, understanding lacing the cutting words.

I swallowed down my rage, the black spots receding enough for me to focus on him. It took everything in me not to bolt.

"Who's attacking us? I thought no human could survive?" I asked as Jude's hand gripped my arms, his mismatched eyes wide and full of confusion.

"There shouldn't be anyone. Last time I was here, we never came across another living soul."

That didn't make me feel any better. "We need to—"

The flicker of a sword cut me off, the gleaming metal emerging from nowhere. Before I had the chance to alert Jude, he'd already spun around on his heel—

Bringing his blade directly down upon his attacker's head.

Black liquid oozed from the man's skull, his face masked by a crudely wound cloth. The scream died in my throat, my adrenaline surging as I watched Jude jerk his blade free from bone.

It happened so quickly, Jude a flash of vengeful lightning.

"Get ready! There are more." He held his blade out before him, swiveling protectively in front of me as I stared open-mouthed at the black blood streaming around the man's lifeless gray eyes.

"Kiara, focus!" Jude bellowed, shaking me from my daze.

Regaining my balance and swallowing my suffocating fury, I brought my dagger before me, angling my back against Jude's as we awaited the next assault.

For a moment, instinct kicked in, my mind going back to all the exercises Micah made me perform back home.

Stand this way. No, not like that. Don't drop your guard! His commands looped around and around in my head, and I fixed my form, preparing for the inevitable onslaught.

This time, three masked men charged toward us, their hooded forms seeming to have manifested from the Mist itself.

With a roar, I bent my body and swerved just as the one

closest to me lifted a crudely fashioned blade. Through gritted teeth, I hissed as I spun, raising my dagger before cleaving it into the man's meaty back, the sound of squishing flesh making its way to my ears.

Yanking the blade free, I didn't hesitate to strike again, right between his ribs.

My attacker wailed and collapsed to his knees, black blood trickling from his wounds. To be safe, I stabbed him a third time and kicked him to the ground.

One could never be too safe.

Jude was grunting behind me, fighting two men at once. He dodged every attack, moving like a wraith dancing in a nightmare. His leg shot out and sent one of them flying several feet back, allowing Jude a fraction of a heartbeat to twist and drive his sword deep into the belly of the second man.

By the time the first attacker righted himself, a battle cry on his exposed, chapped lips, Jude was ready for him, swinging his blade and slicing cleanly into the man's neck—

The man's head rolled off his stout shoulders a moment later, his mouth gaping as viscous black ooze spilled free.

Jude's breathing was even and calm, his sword raised and eager for the next contender. The fluid way he moved was inhuman, skilled in ways I could only dream to be. The way he swung his blade with ease and sensed the moves of his foes was extraordinary.

Jude was magnificent.

I didn't even have the chance to respond when a gray silhouette lunged our way, but Jude effortlessly drove the tip of his sword into the heart of our masked enemy. The man never stood a chance.

Two more silhouettes approached, and two more men fell, their bodies practically hitting the ground at the same time. Wiping his brow, Jude turned to face me, a hard look contorting his sharp features—a look without emotion or thought. Soulless.

"We need to find the others!" I rasped out, my pathetic dagger raised. I would have to petition Jude for a better weapon once we got out of this mess.

Nodding, Jude's fingers seized my hand, holding firmly as he navigated through the thick blue fog. Only when we heard the grunts of a fight did we slow, following the guttural noises until we came across a wounded Isiah and a pair of masked attackers.

By the looks of it, Isiah had not only taken an arrow to the shoulder, but he'd been stabbed in the chest, crimson blood pooling from his injuries. But his wounds weren't enough to slow him. Driving down his sword with a roar, Isiah slashed through the meaty flesh of his foe.

The other attacker, the stockier of the two, lunged, aiming to propel his crude blade into Isiah's heart. But he never made it that far. Jude cleaved his head clean off his shoulders in the time it took me to exhale.

Grabbing hold of Isiah, Jude made quick work of scanning his friend's injuries as Isiah groaned, his icy-gray eyes fluttering as he fought to stay conscious.

"Help me lift him!" Jude brushed his hand through Isiah's hair, black blood and dirt coating the strands. Hoisting one of Isiah's arms over my shoulder, Jude doing the same, we struggled through the suffocating white, our ears straining for the voices of our friends. For anything at all.

We heard nothing.

"We need to get him to safety," Jude ground out between his teeth, heaving most of the weight onto his shoulder so I didn't have to carry it. "I need to stop the bleeding."

Before he bled out. Before we lost another soul to this suicide mission.

There were no more sounds as we stumbled through the fog and trees. Not even the cries of the dying or injured.

And that's what terrified me the most.

I prayed that we weren't the only ones left alive. That Alec, Patrick, and Jake had been lucky enough to locate shelter.

But for now, we were on our own, and I shocked myself when I silently prayed to the lost Goddess of the Sun, begging for her to spare my new friends.

Foolish.

Raina had long ago ceased to listen.

We were all alone.

Chapter Twenty-Eight

Jude

"Do not trust your eyes. Do not trust anything."
Those were Commander Maddox's first words after returning
from the cursed lands.

LETTER FROM RANDALL THORNE OF THE GUARD TO
LIEUTENANT HARLOW, YEAR 49 OF THE CURSE

Isiah couldn't hold on much longer if we didn't tend to his wounds. Crimson dripped with every step into the forest of eternal night, the Knight losing precious minutes.

He couldn't die. Not like this.

All I could think about were the hundreds of times he'd tended to my wounds over the years, every time I'd come sneaking back into the sanctum after a particularly awful mission. Now it was my turn to make sure he was all right and—

"We need to stop, now," Kiara urged, gently shrugging Isiah's weight from her shoulder. We lowered him beneath an ivory trunk, both of us grimacing as feral sounds climbed from Isiah's throat. They made my heart falter and my eyes burn.

"Hold on, brother." I wiped away the sweat coating my fellow Knight's brow. My *friend's* brow. "Let me see what we're working with here." Ripping his shirt in two, I located the grisly puncture, a cascade of red pumping from the hole in Isiah's chest. "We've both been through worse, old man."

We'd been shredded and practically torn to bits during riots Cirian had sent us to squash. Hells, we both had been stabbed before, shot full of arrows. One look at our bodies would paint a gruesome picture. *This is nothing*, I told myself. *Just an arrow. Just a stab wound.*

I felt Kiara's heavy gaze upon me, and when I lifted my head, pity and uncertainty greeted me. She didn't think Isiah would make it. I abruptly stood, shrugging off my weapons and soiled leather jacket.

"What are you doing?" she asked when I started to take off my long-sleeved shirt.

"We need to apply pressure." Whipping off the thick linen shirt, left in nothing but a thin cotton undershirt, I dropped to my knees, wadding the material as I pushed it against the gushing wound.

Kiara's eyes flickered to mine again, wild and full of helplessness. Already, Isiah's blood drenched my shirt.

"Once we stop the bleeding, we need to cauterize the wound." I continued to talk, but Kiara didn't move, let alone speak.

"Jude." She placed a hand on my shoulder. I ignored her, my hands desperately thrusting into my oldest friend's chest.

"We just need to stop it…" Too much blood. The bastards had struck something vital.

"Jude," she tried again, giving me a firm squeeze.

I kept working, my breathing hard and uneven.

Isiah bringing me coffee in the morning after missions.

Ruffling my hair and darting out of the way before I could smack him.

Him telling me to "stop brooding and smile for once."

Memories flashed across my mind and my chest squeezed. I felt like I was drowning, weights tied to my ankles, the surface too far away.

Kiara kept repeating my name, kept shaking me, but I just pushed on Isiah's unmoving chest, hissing his name in anger.

He couldn't leave me. Not like my father. Not like my mother.

He was the only family I had left.

A cold breeze gusted, seeming to wrap itself up around me and hold tight. It soothed the sweat on my brow, and instead of the red rage covering my vision, pacifying shadows washed away the color of loss.

I looked up.

"Jude, he's gone," Kiara whispered, and that mollifying breeze caressed my bare skin. "I'm so, so sorry." Her fingers enfolded around my wrist, her gloves stained with Isiah's blood.

"He's been through worse than this!" I growled, my teeth bared. "He's going to be fine!"

She was against me now, her other hand snaking around my waist. "Jude, p-please," she begged, and that damned crack in her voice did me in.

Eventually, I lifted my eyes from what remained of my friend, harsh realization dawning on me like a crashing wave during a storm.

Isiah was gone, and in his place, an empty ache took up residence in my chest.

My friend. My brother.

I should've smiled more, laughed with him more, put aside my stubbornness and gone on every adventure he'd tried to entice me with.

The man had loved me like his kin, and instead of embracing such a gift, I'd turned my cheek, too fearful of what might happen should I let him in. And, gods, I should've had the damned courage to let him in.

"I'm so sorry," Kiara murmured again and again, as if she

didn't know what else to say.

I tumbled back, thrusting my arms out behind me as the swirls of white enveloped me.

The hoarse curse I released echoed in the darkness, and I clenched the packed soil between my fingers, knowing it was wet with Isiah's blood.

Kiara wasted no time closing the distance, flinging her arms around my neck and pushing me roughly to her chest. I struggled but she didn't relent, and eventually I gave in.

I let it all go. Not the tears that threatened to fall, or the screams of fury I wished to release. But surrounded by her heat, I fell into the void that housed all of my loss, my pain...my joy. A closed-off place that was too vivid, too intense.

Still I drifted, down, down, down. And still she held me.

She murmured in my ear, telling me everything would be all right, her hands in my hair, smoothing down the bloodied strands.

For a moment I was a child again, my left eye dripping red all over the carpet as my father screamed. But back then, I'd had no one to hold me.

Eventually, I pulled back.

I looked down at Isiah, hating how his eyes would never open again. Hating how his steadying presence was suddenly gone.

"We need to bury him," I said, the mask of the Hand of Death falling back into place. It should've frightened me how easy it was to put it on.

I searched the swirling plumes, hunting for danger and the men who'd assaulted us. I had no idea how long we'd been here or how long Kiara had allowed me to mourn.

"Jude," she began softly. "We can't stay. We need to go on and find shelter."

It was nearing the end of the day. Add on the hours and

hours of riding, and we were long past due our rest.

Not that I believed I'd get much of that tonight.

I opened my mouth, ready to protest and insist we give my brother a proper burial, but when my eyes locked on hers, I stopped.

"Should we try to search for our horses? The others?" She spoke barely above a whisper.

Retrieving my jacket from where I'd tossed it, I reached into the pockets, revealing an old but finely crafted silver compass, along with the wrinkled map.

The compass had apparently belonged to my mother, a single claw etched onto its back. For years I had no idea what the symbol meant, but when I found out, I wished I'd never learned its meaning. Isiah had glowered at the compass with distaste, arguing that I should've sold it for a few coins, but I'd kept it as a reminder. People were never who you thought they were. Even your parents.

"We go northwest." I avoided Kiara's question about the others, knowing she wasn't going to like my answer. I clipped the lid of the compass shut, sliding it into my trousers and trying to ignore the way my white undershirt clung to my body, the fabric a macabre splattering of savage red and black.

Against my will, I shifted my gaze to Isiah. His eyes didn't flutter, nor did he move an inch. I must've been delirious, because for one second, I swore his chest lifted ever so slightly.

But no matter how much I wished it, when I blinked, he remained still.

Kiara crouched beside him, and I wondered if we shared the same hallucination. But before she touched his pallid skin, she jerked her hand away, dropping it defeatedly at her side.

Bile rose in my throat. A part of me wanted to curse everything and abandon the mission, the recruits, even Kiara. But I knew Isiah wouldn't want that.

You still have time to be your own man, a good one, too. His words from days ago echoed.

He was already a good man.

I, on the other hand? I was about to leave my friend's body in this wretched place.

Good men didn't do that.

Slipping into the leather jacket, doing my best to avoid looking at Isiah again, I jerked my head into the abyss. "Let's go, Kiara." Before I physically wouldn't be able to move.

She hesitated, looking between me and Isiah, a question poised on the tip of her tongue, but I didn't wait for her to ask it. I couldn't stay here another damned second.

Her footsteps sounded shortly after, hurrying to catch up to me as I all but ran into the fog. "Jude, wait. How are we going to find the others?" she asked once she'd reached me.

I gazed into the ice-blue beyond. Thank the gods the moon shone brighter in these parts, as we no longer had torches at the ready. Not that it would be a problem—those of us born into the darkness knew how to craft our own light, should we need it.

"We aren't. We leave them."

She stopped in her tracks. "What do you mean, 'We leave them'?"

I didn't meet her eyes. I was physically unable to. "We can't find them in such conditions." I motioned around to the fog. We could see but five feet in front of us.

"But we can't just leave them!" she protested, knowing full well it was a useless argument. If we tried to retrace our steps, we would lose precious time and possibly our lives. Especially since we were no longer alone out here.

"We have to," I asserted, taking a sharp inhale. A furrow formed between her eyes, and I could have sworn her irises turned a shade darker. "If there was another way, I would take it. All we can hope is that they found each other. When all this is done, then we can go back and find them."

Her nostrils flared, and the shadows in her eyes grew stormy.

"We have a mission, Kiara. And if we do not succeed, then it will be more than just your friends you will lose."

She straightened her shoulders, her chin raised defiantly. I could all but taste the rage and hurt rolling off of her in waves.

"There's no time to argue with me," I said, cutting her off before she could open her mouth. "If we don't hurry and find the three pieces, then you won't even be able to save yourself."

I gave her my back, ending the conversation.

Kiara didn't understand what was at stake.

Cirian might be a ruthless bastard, but he'd always been hellbent on us reaching the mysterious X and securing the cure. The note he'd given me that day in his council chambers burned a hole in my jacket pocket.

Two sentences had been scribbled on it, two sentences that had had bile rising whenever I'd thought about them.

I should have tossed it into the fire right after I read the words, but something had stopped me. I had a feeling it was due to the girl who currently seethed at my back.

Hells, even if we succeeded, I'd lose her. She just didn't know it yet.

We must have walked about an hour before we came upon a massive tree that had fallen across a dip in the land.

It provided just enough room for the two of us to huddle beneath its coarse trunk, though my head still grazed the top. At least it would provide some semblance of shelter, and we needed the sleep.

I settled as far from Kiara as possible. Her fury at persisting without the others continued to radiate off of her, but at the moment all I could think about was my fallen brother. Isiah's face wouldn't leave my thoughts, no matter how hard I pushed it away. I couldn't erase him like I'd done all the other Knights who'd been brutally slain. What kind of person that made me, I wasn't sure.

"He was a respectable man," I found myself whispering, the words slipping out before I could take them back. Kiara perked up as my gravelly voice pierced the silence that had befallen us. "He was my first friend. And he deserved a far better death than that."

I cleared my throat when she remained silent, fixing my features into stone and peering out into the thicket.

A moment later, she closed the distance I'd put between us and pressed her cheek against my leather-clad shoulder. We melded together, my heat seeping through her trousers and jacket. I dropped my head on top of hers, the act too easy.

We were torn apart and broken, even if our bodies remained whole. I'd stared death in its eyes and found nothing but emptiness and cutting loss. It pierced me like shattered glass.

"Try to sleep, Kiara," I murmured, my arm winding around her waist. The hand at her back began to rub soothing circles, and soon her chest rose and fell evenly, sleep ushering her into its folds. I wasn't sure what possessed me, but I took her hand in mine and brought it to rest on my heart.

The last thing I remembered was placing a kiss on the back of it, and whispering her name and a prayer.

I woke covered in warmth and softness.

Sometime during her slumber, Kiara had managed to wind both arms around my torso, her hands fisting the back of my shirt. She was practically straddling me, using me as a pillow.

But she wasn't the only one who had changed positions.

My stubbled cheek pressed against her smooth temple, my nose nuzzling her hair, my arms wrapped snugly around her waist.

I went completely still.

Kiara began to shift in place, mumbling beneath her breath.

Inwardly, I cursed. My change in breathing must've roused her, because she was awake now, the uneven rise of her chest giving her away. Still she didn't move, and neither did I.

This was the closest we had ever been, and while I couldn't get Isiah's lifeless body out of my thoughts, the pressure of her embrace told me she needed the contact. I did too.

Her hair, which was an unruly mess of tangled red tresses, tickled my chin, and I brought my hand up to smooth the wild strands. A tremor worked through her body as I ran my fingers through her hair, the move probably surprising her. Hells, it surprised me how easy it was. How utterly *normal*.

When I tucked a few loose pieces behind her ear, her head angled upward. Our eyes connected, and a bolt of fire shot into my chest.

"Are you all right?" I asked, my voice hoarse and roughened by sleep. I dropped my hand from her hair, clearing my throat.

"I'm alive," she murmured. "Did you sleep well?"

"I think I got a few hours in," I said. Great. Now we were making awkward small talk. And I had yet to move.

"You make a decent pillow," she attempted to joke, and the barest hint of a smile graced my lips. "Although you're a little lumpy, but I managed." She poked at the muscles in my stomach as if to prove her point.

I scoffed. "You make for a decent heater."

She bestowed me with a timid smile, one that told me she knew I was far from fine. My brother was dead, gone forever. That heat in my belly intensified.

"We really should get going."

"We should," she agreed, not moving.

"Kiara," I pressed, a lone finger tracing the side of her cheek. "Thank you for…" I paused, trying to find the proper word. I couldn't think of anything that didn't sound clichéd or empty. "Being there for me," I finished clumsily.

"Of course," she said, her eyes still upon me, vibrant and fierce. "I'm always here. Even if you want to talk about it. About him."

Talking about Isiah wouldn't help. Maybe one day, when our lives weren't on the line, but now I had to keep my thoughts clear, if only to get through this mission. "Not today," was all I said, my body tensing as I prepared to stand.

"Wait!"

I froze, one arm still encircling her waist.

Reaching into her trouser pocket, she retrieved a golden pin. The Knights' emblem.

"He would have wanted you to have this," she whispered, angling herself so she could fasten it to my leather collar. The gold pin rested right below my matching one. Her hand fell across the emblems, my chest barely moving as I watched her fingers work.

She'd taken Isiah's pin knowing I'd want a piece of him. Something to remember him by. My heart squeezed.

I should have said thank you, or something else that relayed my gratitude, but my mouth didn't work. Kiara dipped her chin as if she understood everything I couldn't say, and at that simple nod, a wall fractured within me. If I didn't move soon, I risked cracking altogether.

With a final, lingering glance, I released her waist and gently nudged her forward. She followed my lead and stood, though she did so awkwardly.

Suddenly I was cold all over, and not just because I didn't have a body pressed against mine.

CHAPTER TWENTY-NINE

KIARA

*Raina is often said to have possessed beauty such as the world
has never seen. There have been few lucky enough to have
been blessed by her presence, but they all claim the same
thing—her eyes glowed a brilliant gold, a devastating eruption
of light that blinded them and brought them to their knees.*

CAMILLE ASHTON, ASIDIAN HISTORIAN,
YEAR 40 OF THE CURSE

We spent the following evening out in the open.

Alec, Patrick, Jake. Alec, Patrick, Jake. I couldn't stop
thinking about them. Were they safe? Were they angry with me?

Were they alive?

I matched every footfall to the rhythm of their names
bouncing around in my head. *Alec, Patrick, Jake.*

It felt as though we were walking in circles. If I didn't see
another white tree with blue leaves ever again, I would die in
peace.

I griped about this for the majority of the morning as my
empty stomach grumbled in violent protest.

We passed some black berries a while back, but neither
of us wanted to risk getting poisoned by a *berry*, of all things.

Wild men oozing black blood? Sure. A hallucination-producing breeze? I could understand.

But a damn berry? No way was I going down like that.

Jude indulged my hunger-induced whining, occasionally sprinkling in an "uh-huh" or "I see" now and again. I didn't think he was listening.

When I questioned his navigating abilities, he raised his dark brows in affront, awarding me an icy look that stopped me dead in my tracks. He then proceeded to enlighten me on his expertise in that particular area—how he was *such* a skilled hunter and tracker—and this was when I inserted my own "uh-huhs" and "I sees."

Ever determined to make his point, Jude flipped open his silver compass, pointing to the creased map as he explained we were to go northwest. Apparently, the king believed the keys were located in a valley quaintly named Nightshade's Cradle.

It was during that first full day when I heard the glorious sounds of a bubbling stream.

"Thank the gods." Jude exhaled sharply, his relief matching my own.

Our canteens had run out of water last night. Coming across this stream was pure luck.

Relying solely on our hearing, Jude and I padded through the thicket, nearly tumbling face-first into the stream before we realized it was in front of us. My boot splashed into the flowing waters, and I yelped, stumbling back.

"Graceful." Jude repressed his smirk, but his eyes danced with laughter. Like the two sides of him, his eyes were portals into his soul. On one hand, he could be thoughtful and kind, warm. On the other, he could slay his enemies in seconds, a mask of death adorning his handsome features like he was born to wear it.

"Don't push me, or I'll toss you in," I threatened, but I wasn't as strong as Jude, because a smile curved my lips.

"Promises, promises," he taunted, dropping to his knees with a groan. Cupping the water in both palms, he brought it to his lips to drink. He gave a growl of approval.

I wasn't as refined as my commander. Lacking both dignity and grace, I let out a squeal of joy, collapsed to my knees, and proceeded to dunk my entire face into the stream.

It was divine.

Gods, I even shook my head beneath the chilled water, letting out a bubbling scream. I didn't care that Jude shot me a peculiar look as I flipped my hair back, my face deliciously soaked and my parched lips painted in crystal droplets. I felt like a new woman.

"What?" I scoffed, unscrewing my canteen before submerging it into the depths. "Don't tell me you didn't want to do the very same."

Jude just shook his head, but a wry smile tugged at his lips. "You just say and do whatever you want, don't you?"

"Life is too damn depressing not to find joy anywhere you can. I learned that the hard way in Cila." I swiped at my hair, allowing the residual water to slick back the coppery strands. "And as far as speaking my mind"—I paused to raise a brow—"why waste precious time with word games when we don't have all that much left?"

Jude lifted his gaze, a mischievous sparkle in his brown eye. Without warning, he dove right into the water, his face and shoulders fully submerged.

I smiled, my grin turning into riotous laughter when he surfaced for air, shaking his black strands like a wet dog.

He beamed, a full and genuine smile making a rare appearance. "All right, yes. That was surprisingly needed. Perhaps you're right. About *some* things," he clarified.

"See? Live a little, commander."

That impish look of his returned, and even his scars seemed to shimmer. I noticed how in the Mist, the raised bumps appeared more intense, the faint red turning a deeper maroon.

I hadn't taken off my gloves since Jude had inadvertently yanked the left one off during the attack. While I found his scars intriguing, beautiful even, mine hardly could compare. They were dark and ugly and reminded me of the prickly underbrush we trudged through. They reminded me of the Mist.

Before I could even process what he intended, Jude sent a cascade of water flying through the air, the chilled water splashing across my cheeks.

I sputtered, blinking away the falling droplets clinging to the tips of my lashes. Thoughts of my own scars vanished, and I shot him an incredulous look.

"Did you just splash me?"

I was a complete disaster right about now, but I couldn't care less. Not as the most indecent dimples appeared on either side of his mouth. My heart thumped in my ears.

"I'm going to kill you," I vowed.

Jude only smiled more. I wasn't sure what was more surprising—that Jude possessed a playful side, or that he was sharing it with me.

Flattening my hand and skimming the top of the water, I returned the favor, giggling like a fool as it soaked his devilish face. His grin never faltered.

Jude snorted. "That went right up my nose." He ran long fingers through his black hair, pushing it out of his eyes. Of course, he managed to look even more handsome, whereas I likely resembled a drowned rat.

His eyes locked on mine, his throat bobbing. All the playful teasing was wiped away, replaced by a scorching look that prompted a prickling warmth to pool in my belly. My gaze briefly fell to his mouth.

"Payback, dear commander," I taunted, covering up the fact that he'd disarmed me with a single stare. And here I'd thought only weapons and fists could destroy me.

A slight breeze picked up, playing with his dark locks, the pieces flying into eyes that turned cloudy and fiery all at the same time. I needed to look away, to fracture the spell Jude had placed on me.

I was Kiara Frey, and I could kick ass like it was my job, yet here I stood, rendered immobile by this enigmatic commander.

"Kiara," Jude whispered, my name like a song on his full lips. He leaned closer—close enough that I could feel his breath tickle the tip of my nose. My lips parted on their own, inhaling the air that left his body in short, quivering pants. Time itself stood still, as did my heart. "There's something I should tell you—"

But he never got to finish his thought.

A branch crunched in the distance, and Jude jerked back, rising to his full height. He brought his index finger to his lips, the muscles in his neck tightening.

On unsteady limbs, I rose, searching all of the brittle white for what I prayed to be a rather large rabbit. Or—however naive the thought—maybe it was Alec, Patrick, and Jake finally catching up with us.

Naturally, it was neither.

CHAPTER THIRTY

KIARA

Some of the sun priestesses believe that while Raina has left our realm, her magic remains, for how else would crops and trees grow? If there is still life, there is hope.

EXCERPT FROM ASIDIAN LORE: A TALE OF THE GODS

A cluster of masked men catapulted from across the narrow stream, jagged spears fashioned from white trees in their gloved hands. They roared as they advanced, not caring that their voices echoed.

Another attack.

Jude cursed, his eyes meeting my widened stare. "Get ready!"

My dagger had been in my hand the moment he'd stood.

But I didn't go on the offensive just yet. No, I waited until one of the burly bastards lunged at me, releasing a screech of war from his gray, chapped lips. The feral sound shook my bones, but it didn't slow me.

At the last second, I sidestepped him, watching with a sick glee as he stumbled over his feet, not having expected to swipe empty air. He wouldn't be surprised next time.

For the brief moment my opponent was incapacitated, I twisted to seek Jude. While I could barely make him out, I could have sworn I saw three of the masked men teaming up to take him down.

I cursed and ducked beneath a flailing arm, digging my blade up and through the thick padding of my attacker's coat, directly between his ribs.

With a wail, he fell, clutching at his side. But he didn't stay down for long.

Jumping to his feet, his side coated in that peculiar black ooze, the masked man lifted his spear, aiming right for my heart. Using my many grueling years of training, I shifted to the right, missing the spear by a mere inch.

Twisting around, I spun on my heels, angling myself until I was at his back, my arms flying around his neck as my sharpened blade slashed through the thin skin of his throat. Micah didn't say I was faster than the wind without reason.

This time, the man didn't rise.

I never got the chance to catch my breath.

There was a flash of silver and a guttural roar—and then a searing pain shot across my upper arm. I whirled around. The man looked just like his fallen brother, whose blood currently pooled from his wound, his lifeless eyes open. But this new foe didn't spare his companion a glance, not as he raised his weapon to strike me again.

Ignoring the stinging that radiated from the shallow cut, I pounced and grabbed the sides of his face before proceeding to headbutt him with a sickening crunch. When he staggered back, disoriented from my unexpected assault, I roared, thrusting my bloodied dagger up into his jaw. Blood instantly gushed from his mouth, a bubbling stream of black.

My head throbbed something fierce, but the fight was far from over. Swiping a hand across my sweaty brow, I reeled around, finding Jude.

I didn't allow myself a moment of joy when I saw that he

was still alive, two of the three men lying dead at his feet. There would be more coming, and my fingers tightened on the hilt of my blade.

I swallowed hard as three more shadows seemed to materialize out of thin air, steel specters that began to dance around Jude like the vultures they were.

How many are there?

I was about to race over to his aid when a solid body of pure rock sent me sailing several feet through the air. I sputtered as I flew, the wind whipping at my face as my pulse skyrocketed.

I landed on my side with a groan, my ribs aching and bruised. My hands fisted the dirt, my teeth grinding against the pain that seared across my torso. With a hiss, I scrambled to my feet, ready to—

A fist collided with my jaw, the impact causing me to see stars.

Whoever this one was, he enjoyed using his fists. And he would pay for the bruises that would inevitably mar my skin. I wasn't vain, but I didn't enjoy looking like a fresh kill.

A snarl ripped free from my throat as I stumbled back a step, putting distance between me and my latest foe. Although he was more lithe than the rest, I'd kill him like I had his friends. No one came after me and my...friend...and could expect to leave with all their body parts intact.

A yelp from my left distracted me as Jude cried out in pain.

Instinctively, my head spun in his direction, my heart plummeting. If anyone hurt him, I'd rip their damn throats out. *Slowly.* But in the split second I glanced away, my attacker was at *my* throat, a blade pressed to my neck. I cursed myself as the metal dug deeper.

My stomach dropped, a steel band winding mercilessly around my chest, every breath drawn out and forced.

This was it. I was going to die.

A lesser woman might have shut her eyes and met her death in soothing darkness. But not me. I stared at the masked man, his eyes an icy shade of blue-gray. They were wide and determined, the haunting black of his pupils nearly eclipsing his irises.

Jude cried out again, a deep groan that penetrated all the darkest parts of my soul. If I did nothing, he would surely die. Traitorous tears welled, fighting to be freed.

All of this had been for naught. Jude had been right when he'd said it was a suicide mission. And now we were both going to die, and I would never…I'd never do all the things I wanted to do with my life.

With death looming, I suddenly realized that a few of those things involved Jude.

Images of a life I'd never have whirled past my open eyes.

A life of adventure and freedom, with secret smiles and intimate evenings nestled beside a fire. I envisioned a partner who embraced me in my darkest moments and fought my demons just as I battled theirs. I coveted a love so profound, so realm-shattering, that my home became their arms and the music in my ears belonged to the beating of their hearts.

For some reason, Jude called to all of my shadows; the parts of my soul I'd shown him without me even realizing it. And I wanted more. More time to see what *else* I could feel.

Time slowed, the clashing of swords ceasing as blood rushed to my ears. There was a ringing sound, shrill and eerie, and it punctured my skin as it clawed at my insides like an angry creature with teeth.

Then, I smelled home in the air.

CHAPTER THIRTY-ONE

KIARA

Courage is unlocking the door to your cage and taking flight.
True bravery is burning the cage to the ground.

ASIDIAN PROVERB

Cila.

The subtle scent of spice and smoke.

Jude called out my name, his voice muffled as blood rushed to my ears, a cold wind whipping at my cheeks.

The man attacking me let out a choked grunt. His eyes watered and oozed pus as he shrieked, the viscous liquid drenching the cloth swathing his features. That bitter wind carrying traces of home continued to whistle in my ears, but it didn't hurt me, not in the way it viciously struck my opponent, who let out a feral roar as though it burned him alive.

Swirls of onyx streamed from around me, slithering across the underbrush and reaching for my opponent. Just before they could grab him, he dropped his knife, his stare widening as he took in the sight of the advancing darkness rising around me.

I staggered back when he shifted away, my breaths coming out raspy and uneven. I nearly stabbed Jude when he suddenly appeared at my side, his hand encircling my arm to move me protectively behind him.

The attacker stumbled, guttural noises leaving his lips. It was a husky and thick language I didn't recognize—if it was a language at all. Clutching at his throat, fear shining in his eyes, he cautiously took a few tentative steps away.

My mouth parted as I gulped in air, my fingers gripping my blade, waiting for him to lunge. But he did no such thing.

He fled, bolting into the trees without a glance behind him. The whispering shadows trailed after, until all that remained was a dense layer of white.

"Are you all right?" Jude asked.

I lifted my head and met his gaze head-on, my pulse thudding like a drum in my ears. His left eye shone in the darkness, a beacon of fury that sent shivers down my spine. "What the hells was that?"

I didn't answer. I couldn't.

His fingers were digging into my skin, his jaw taut with bone-chilling rage. I didn't recognize him.

"It has to be similar to that breeze from the first day," Jude said. "Making us see things that aren't there. But either way, we need to get out of here before—"

Boots pounded the ground as more masked men rushed toward us.

Jude shoved me out of the way and lifted his sword before him. I tumbled onto my back, out of the reach of the men with death haunting their eyes.

Jude drove his blade through a broad chest with sickening ease before twisting to face another opponent. I watched as eight of them swarmed him on all sides, circling him like ravenous predators, their crude weapons glinting in the white light as they sought to land a killing blow.

As skilled a warrior as he was, there was no way Jude could fend off eight men, especially these beasts. They had the upper hand, and I had the nagging suspicion they wouldn't stop until their blades were slick with red.

I shoved to my feet, crying out Jude's name like a tormented prayer. He answered my call, raising his head as he locked his sight on me, sweat dripping down the sides of his face, a superficial cut marring his cheek.

While his attention remained on me, another figure whirled like a reckless breeze from the corner of my eye, a dagger rising—

An earsplitting scream pierced the veil as the blade sliced through Jude's leather jacket.

I realized the scream had come from me.

The brutes leisurely circled, snarling as Jude grew unsteady, weary after a full day without food and proper rest. He wouldn't be able to last much longer.

In the span of an enraged heartbeat, I lost all sense of sanity.

There was the ash and the clouds of cold blue.

And then there was a vengeful darkness.

A foreign wind jolted my body, sending my frame bowing back at an unnatural angle. I felt ice shatter through me, an electrical current blasting from the very core of my being.

I was drowning in the night, ripped apart from the inside out.

Ash coated my mouth, and the stench of rotten skin clogged my nostrils. My lids drooped and shut, and electricity detonated from everywhere and nowhere at once, sending me to my knees with a scream.

Agonized shrieks saturated the air, haunting and full of the kind of pain no person—friend or foe—ever deserved to experience. They crippled me, the screeches ungodly and depraved, and my body bent forward abruptly, curving in on itself.

Gritting my teeth, I forced my heavy lids open, tilting my eyes up from the ground to the scene of death I expected to find. But that same perverse breeze that had saved me earlier whooshed past my ears, parting the fog. The trees swayed and cracked, the rotten wood splintering down the middle and shattering like glass, the shards blown in every direction.

But that wasn't the only disturbing sight.

The men—our attackers—clawed at their faces, their eyes. Gut-wrenching screams reverberated and shook the forest, muffled only by the ravishing wind.

They were dying, slowly. So very slowly.

My taut body relaxed, the unexplained hold on me loosening its unholy grip. And amid the tormented shouts and bursts of black shadows and fiery electricity, I saw the commander rising from the ashes.

Nearly unscathed.

He walked through the charred remains, the Mist gradually washing across the woods, engulfing the world in white once more.

Jude looked like a vengeful angel above me, his left eye aglow. My head lolled to the side, and soon, all thoughts were lost to the screams of the dying.

Chapter Thirty-Two

Kiara

I plead with you to come and take your son. When I look
into his eyes, I feel nothing but coldness. It unnerves me.
Something isn't right with that boy.

Letter from Jack Maddox to unknown recipient,
year 38 of the curse

My dreams spun a tale of magic.

I was in my room back home, a thick white coverlet
tossed over my head, my toes swathed in my favorite fuzzy socks
Mother knitted me last winter. There was no aching or bruising
weighing down my body, which currently felt like it was made
of cotton instead of bones.

A whisper of a breeze grazed the soft linen shielding me,
the air tasting of freshly baked pies and nostalgia. My eyelids
fluttered open as the wind whistled a melancholy tune that
gingerly hinted at hope and rebirth.

Answering its bittersweet call with a grin, I flung the covers
from my face, eager to discover its source.

Light.

It struck me like a punch to the gut—rich, dazzling rays of
light traversing across every inch of my bedroom. I blinked at

the harshness of it, convinced my eyes were playing tricks on me.

But no otherworldly shadows took shape upon the walls, and not a single torch or melting candle was lit. There was just that spectacular light painting the room like a thousand brushstrokes of gold. It touched my skin and coated it in pure warmth, the hair framing my face glinting as rays kissed each strand.

This had to be the afterlife and I was dead, or I was dreaming the most wonderful dream.

With my luck, it wasn't a dream.

Even knowing I was likely bleeding out somewhere in the real world, I swung my feet to the floor and raced across my sparse room to the open window overlooking the street. That same sugary breeze teased my unbraided hair, which whipped about my face, the strands vibrant in this unreal glow.

Just beyond the thin pane of glass, I beheld a world of vivid color. I might've stopped breathing altogether.

It was the most heavenly place I'd ever seen. And it was the village I'd known for all of my eighteen years. The same ashen stones and pale brick buildings lined a neatly paved street, but now, they shone like crushed diamonds.

Villagers passed by my window, smiles adorning their faces, their pearly teeth almost too white and brilliant. My mouth gaped as the light touched their hair—glossy raven tresses shimmered, and blond hair turned to gold. And their eyes…they twinkled with gems of varying tints and intensities.

Magic.

That was the only reasonable explanation. That, and I reminded myself I was most certainly dead.

Realistically, my luck had to run out at some point.

I lifted my eyes to the clearest blue sky, not a single star visible among all that color. A few fluffy clouds littered its canvas, moving leisurely across the great expanse of space.

And then I saw it—as the clouds sailed ahead, they revealed the most exquisite of sights yet.

Blinding. Stunning. Unreal.

The all-consuming globe in the sky emptied my head of all thoughts. I saw and thought and breathed only the shimmering rays stemming from the impossible orb, which both excited and terrified me all at once.

The sun. It had to be the sun.

"Magnificent, isn't it?"

I spun around, stumbling as I did so. I would recognize that melodic sound anywhere.

"Grandmother?" I whispered, my voice coming out all airy and breathless.

She was just as I remembered her—long red hair streaked in gray, bright amber eyes, and a curving mouth that hinted at a joke that only she knew.

"I've missed you, child." She tilted her chin, carefully assessing me from head to toe. It had only been a year since she'd passed, but it seemed a tragic eternity.

My legs carried me until I was enveloped in her frail arms, my cheek resting on her shoulder. Bits of her wispy straight hair tickled my nose, the color identical to mine.

"Gods, I wish you were still here." I inhaled her scent of Midnight Blooms and dulcet sugar. Of freshly baked pies. That was what I'd smelled on that otherworldly breeze.

My grandmother.

An alarming thought struck me. "Am I truly dead?" I rasped, pulling away to read her eyes. Ones filled with the kind of wisdom I doubted I'd ever attain.

"No, you're not dead, silly girl." Grandmother tutted, shaking her head. Her hands settled at my back, rubbing soothing circles there.

"Then why am I here?" I motioned to the window. To what

could only be the lost sun. Nothing made sense.

The last thing I remembered was…

Jude. The Mist. The masked men attacking us.

The shadows and the stinging electricity in the air.

Grandmother gave me a strained smile, one that didn't reach her eyes. "You're a smart girl." Her weathered hand cupped my cheek. "You know I can't just *tell* you the reason. Where's the fun in that?"

There was the grandmother I knew and loved. "I'm kind of on a time limit here." Especially if this was a dream after all. "Can't you help out your favorite grandchild?" My mouth gave a slight pout as I widened my eyes. It was a look that always won her over. I never messed with the tried and true.

But not even my doe eyes did the trick. Instead, Grandmother let loose a roar of a laugh, the type that was contagious. I wanted to join her and curse her calmness at the same time.

"Grandmother! This isn't funny!" I cocked my head, memorizing her face—every wrinkle of a life well lived.

"No, it's not." She sighed, her features losing their softness. "I suppose I've just missed you, my fearless girl. Missed that spark in those eyes." She tapped my wrinkling nose. "But you're right. This is far from a joyous moment."

My grip on her tightened. I was afraid she would float away.

"Tell me," I demanded, my chin jutting out. "What do I need to know? Are the keys even out here, the ones that will save us?" Or was it yet another rumor, a lie? A hundred questions popped up, but for once, I shoved them down, studying my grandmother's face as a solemn expression weighed down her features.

"All I can tell you is that this"—she tilted her face toward the window, to the sun just beyond our reach—"is what could await you, should you succeed."

"At finding the keys," I groused, my jaw tensing. Back to

business, it seemed. "So they *are* out here."

"The tool to save us does lie in the cursed lands." She looked like she wanted to say more, but she sucked in a sharp breath and averted her eyes.

It was obvious she was holding something back, and I'd long ago grown tired of vague answers. "Can you at least tell me what any of it means? Why Raina left? Why the king—"

Grandmother held up a single finger, silencing me. "Patience was never one of your virtues."

"And that's one of the *many* reasons you love me," I retorted, growing more irritated by the second. Hells, if I was in some dreamlike world, having a conversation with my dead grandmother, you'd think I'd come out of it knowing more than I did before.

"Fine," she said with her trademark huff. "I can say that—"

A deep rumbling shook the house, the floorboards beneath our feet groaning and trembling. Grandmother's gaze widened as her movements turned frantic.

I swore I heard my name being called from somewhere in the distance.

"Kiara, listen to me." She gripped my shoulders, surprisingly strong for a woman her age. "You need to finish reading the book. You'll find the answers you're looking for inside."

Book? What book?

The only book I'd been reading had been... Realization dawned on me. *The book Jude gave me.*

"And please be careful around the commander. History always has a way of repeating itself, no matter how hard we try to rewrite the story."

"Jude?" Why should I be careful around him?

My vision swam with shards of dusted sunshine and onyx ash, my grandmother's gentle face growing fuzzy.

"What's happening?" I shouted, desperate for this moment

to last a bit longer. To spend just another minute with her.

"You're waking up, Kiara," she answered, her voice not sounding like her own. It lilted at the end in clashing discord. "Gods, I should have told you years ago. I was hoping to find another way, but I ran out of time."

Told me what? I wanted to ask, but my voice didn't work.

Her mouth continued to move though I couldn't make out the words, a wrecking thunder shaking this dream world. One that was slowly being razed.

Just beyond the window, my village shattered and crumbled, bricks dropping from the skies as people vanished from sight, leaving nothing but plumes of black smoke where they'd stood.

The dream and my grandmother faded away.

"Kiara."

Black and gray blinded me, the sun from my dreams a distant memory.

"Kiara." A voice wafted from above, growing more urgent. Desperate.

"Wake up, dammit!"

"Kiara, if you wake up right this second, I'll tell you about my scars. I'll tell you anything you want to know! I'll give you all my secrets."

Jude.

"I know you want to know. I can always see the questions in your eyes." A choked growl rumbled in his chest. "Just wake up and open that cheeky mouth of yours. Insult me! Just say *something*," he added with an uncharacteristic whine.

Maybe it was that final plea or how my heart ached at his tangible anguish, but my heavy lids fluttered open.

A blurry face hovered over me, pale skin framed by night-black strands. He was so close that his warm breath tickled my lips, my nose inhaling his scent of smoke and pine.

That familiar warmth spread in my belly, the same heat that was growing more and more prevalent in his presence.

"All I had to do was nearly die for you to offer me answers?" I finally rasped, my throat hoarse and raw. It felt like I'd swallowed a torch.

"Thank the gods!" Jude's arms wrapped forcefully around my frame, his calloused hands moving to cradle my head. His unusually warm touch burned my skin on contact, and he winced as I let out a slight hiss. He removed his hands with a nearly imperceptible scowl, but I saw his reaction well enough.

"You weren't breathing for a good two minutes!" A sudden fierceness graced his tone, underscored only by the bitterness of fear.

"Don't worry," I murmured, attempting to sit up. My head spun. "I'm not that easy to kill."

Jude didn't find me at all amusing. Sweat dripped from his forehead, dampening his unkempt hair. It hung across his scarred eye, masking some of the sinister clouds trapped inside.

"You're the most infuriating person I've ever met." His jaw ticked, all the concern he'd radiated abruptly transforming into exasperation.

"You must not have met a lot of people then," I retorted, moving to my elbows.

Plumes of ivory pirouetted around us, my vision gradually growing less blurred. The dream world and my grandmother were far behind me, and now, the moon and its greedy shadows reigned once more.

I peered around the clearing, expecting to see the bodies of the masked men, but I found none. Only piles of ash.

A wave of sudden nausea nearly sent me doubling over,

and the last thing I wanted to do was vomit on the handsome commander.

"You promised me something," I ground out, swallowing the rising bile.

Jude cocked his head, his stormy eye sinister as he bored into my soul. He knew exactly what I meant. While I should have been more consumed with what had just happened—between the attack and my sunshine-filled dream—my mouth had a mind of its own.

"Seriously? That's the answer you want?" Jude fumed, his teeth bared. "You practically *died*. You dropped to the ground just as those shadows devoured them. Whatever the hells they were." He ran a hand through his hair. "And *that's* your first priority?"

"Yep." I popped the *p*. "Do tell me more of these murderous shadows, though. It all sounds quite thrilling." While everything was hazy and blurry at the edges, I did recall some of what happened. But even that was more of a *feeling*, slippery around the edges. I wasn't ready to process what had happened during the attack, let alone talk about it.

"This is no time for jokes," Jude scolded, leaning back on his knees. "I've never seen anything like that before and you were..." His gaze flickered to the broken trees. "You were frozen and so pale. Kiara, you weren't *breathing*."

What does a *somewhat* rational person say to that? Add in the visible exasperation painting his skin a red hue, and I couldn't muster a single coherent word. But I knew his anger wasn't directed at me.

Instead, I picked myself up from the dirt, ignoring Jude's outstretched hand. I stretched my legs, still off-kilter, as Jude watched from a respectable distance. I could sense he wanted to close the gap between us, his eyes wild as his hands restlessly formed into fists at his sides.

Jude.

My grandmother's words came back to me in a rush.

"And please be careful around the commander. History always has a way of repeating itself, no matter how hard we try to rewrite the story."

Whatever that meant.

But Jude was...Jude. I'd trusted him thus far, and I was still alive. Why had she told me to be wary of him?

"What's wrong?"

I flinched, Jude seeming to materialize at my side. "Nothing." An obvious lie. "I'm just overwhelmed," I added when he raised a skeptical brow, the moon casting a generous glow on his face. Was it my imagination, or were his scars even darker than before?

"Tell me," he pressed. "I know you're hiding something from me."

"I told you nothing is wrong. I'm fine. I'm alive, right? That's all that matters."

There was *so* much wrong. So much I couldn't explain.

"You're pale." Jude tenderly placed a hand to my forehead as if I had a temperature. While his touch remained warm, it didn't burn as badly as before.

An unreadable look flashed across his face. "We need to get out of here. More will come." He scanned the woods with clenched teeth. "And you need to rest after…"

After I'd supposedly died? Yes, I could easily agree it was time to move on.

Jude hesitantly turned his back to me, his steps unhurried as he waited for me to follow. I knew this wasn't the end to our conversation, but we had to find shelter before we dove into that mess.

As I took my first cautious step, I felt a noticeable weight pressing against my ribs.

It wasn't the profound unease stemming from my dream—or what had come before—but something physical. Heavy.

Reaching into my coat pocket, I curled my fingers around aged leather and worn pages. I didn't need to see it in order to know exactly what it was. I released the tome as if it had scorched my skin.

Jude's book.

The last time I'd seen it had been when I'd packed it in my bag and left the palace with Starlight. My throat constricted at the memory of her bleeding out on the ground, her pained whinnying echoing. I blinked away her image and focused on the tome currently weighing down my jacket.

"You need to finish reading the book. You'll find the answers you're looking for inside."

And now, it had mysteriously found its way back to me.

It could only be magic.

I wondered how I could find truth in something that belonged to the man I supposedly couldn't trust. I mean, he'd *given* it to me.

My legs worked hard to catch up to Jude, who made a strained effort to take the pace easy. From the corner of my eye, I caught him stealing glimpses from beneath his hair, yet he didn't speak. For some reason, those glances held a different type of fear, one that wasn't a result of masked men and ungodly mist.

Even if I didn't wish to learn them, whatever answers I sought had to be within those pages. And as soon as Jude fell asleep this evening, I'd find them.

It was time to figure out what the hells was going on.

Chapter Thirty-Three

Jude

I am beginning to see why you are concerned about him. As he grows, the boy loses more and more of his humanity every day. I pray the damage can be undone.

Letter to Aurora Adair from unknown recipient,
year 44 of the curse

One of the bastards had sliced my shoulder. Deep, but not too deep. Just far enough for it to be a pain in the ass. But there were much bigger things to consider than some insignificant wound.

I'd almost lost control. Nearly allowed the rage to take over entirely. And Kiara would've borne witness to the monster I kept locked away. She had likely seen too much as it was. In the future, it might escape, but for now, I wanted to bask in her admiration just a little while longer. To revel in the warmth that shone in her eyes whenever she took me in.

But my time was running out.

Before, the thought of dying hadn't frightened me. I'd been prepared for death's welcoming embrace since I first took my oath. Life had never been kind; not that I was going to sit there and whine about it, but cruelty had a way of burrowing into your soul and making a home. For people like me, death would be a relief.

But now?

Things had changed.

Because of *her*.

It had been less than an hour since the *attack*. I didn't know how to describe what had happened back there in the clearing. That river of darkness had flooded through the trees and consumed our enemies, turning them to ash, sweeping them away in an icy breeze.

It all left me on edge, my hand placed on my dagger, almost eager to pull it from its sheath. There'd always be the next kill, the next enemy. I didn't wish the same future for Kiara.

The girl I hadn't been able to stop thinking about was shockingly quiet at my side.

While I'd convinced myself her incessant speech was grating, I found I missed it.

Suddenly, the quiet I usually craved had my stomach churning. Sneaking a peek at her from the corner of my good eye, I found a similarly perplexed expression weighing down the corners of her lips. Her upturned nose wrinkled slightly, her eyes creased at the sides. She was deep in thought. A dangerous thing to be, I knew well.

Her rich red hair shimmered in the moon's glow, each strand capturing a bit of its mystic magic, and those amber eyes of hers ensnared the night, the golden flecks twinkling like the distant stars overhead. She was equal parts light and darkness.

Light.

I'd lied when I compared her to the sun. When I said I'd *imagined* she was what it was like to glimpse the sun. Every year on the exact same day—what had once been the longest day of the year—I'd fall asleep and dream of a shattering orb of light high in the sky.

It was a sweet torture to see its beauty and never feel its warmth. Sometimes I would envision a meadow, orange and yellow flowers sweeping across tall green grass. Other times, the sun would show itself to me between the peaks of snowy mountains, rising like a phoenix. The image I saw the most was a marble temple of the purest white, golden rays cascading across its slick surface like spilled water, a barren field at its feet.

But whatever false world I'd conjured would vanish the second I awoke.

The next days would be full of nightmares—of the Mist and sliced throats and wailing screams. But once a year, I'd find that sweet peace.

Whether I wished it or not, Kiara had slowly become that peace for me. That dream of light.

I suppressed a groan when my boot hooked beneath an upturned root, barely catching my balance before I ate dirt. It was unlike me to be so clumsy. I didn't acquire my illustrious reputation by tripping over fallen branches.

Unfortunately for me, Kiara was perceptive.

She cursed, halting abruptly, and forcing me to do the same.

"Your shoulder!" she exclaimed, realization widening her eyes. "I saw one of them slice you."

And my leg and my arm, I added silently. But those were just simple flesh wounds. Kiara's eyes flashed with concern. My heart beat faster.

"I'll be fine," I promised, turning away. "It isn't deep."

Kiara was having none of that.

"Stop being a tough guy and let me take a look." She put both hands on her hips, cocking them out in a way that likely wasn't meant to be provocative but was. I ground my teeth.

"A tough guy, eh?" I chided. "You say that like you don't know who I am."

"I know you well enough. And you're stubborn and prideful,"

she snapped, her biting tone shocking me. If she knew about the innocent blood that covered my hands, she wouldn't want anything to do with me.

"Here." Kiara grabbed the collar of my shirt, giving it a tug. "Let me look, you big brute."

My lips curled. "Is that any way to speak to your commander?" It was laughable since we were never just commander and recruit. That was as obvious to me as the scars on my face.

Great. I remembered I'd promised her the story behind them. A story I wasn't keen on retelling.

When she wouldn't wake—wouldn't *breathe*—I'd lost all sense of composure and begun erratically shouting promises. In my delirious state, I'd even prayed to the absent gods.

"Yeah, yeah, yeah." She rolled her eyes, a dimple popping up on her left cheek. She had the most distracting smirk.

With all the care in the world, she helped me slip out of my torn leather jacket, tossing it to the side before gently pulling up the sleeve of my undershirt, which was still covered in my brother's blood.

I didn't want to think about Isiah. His death cut me more than I let on.

"It stopped bleeding," she whispered, her attention gliding across the expanse of exposed skin. "Must not have been as deep as I thought," she mused, absently sucking at her lower lip. I held back a groan at the sight.

This damned woman.

"But it needs to be cleaned and properly looked at to make sure it doesn't get infected. And the cut on your leg," she added, her eyes falling to my trousers.

Making a hasty grab for my jacket, I eased it back on, hating that she saw me in such a feeble state. I was exceptionally effective at what I did, but with little food and rest, even I couldn't fight off eight men at once.

Her fingers played at the collar of my shirt, her head cocked to the side as she traced my skin with bright eyes. Her gloved touch sent a current zapping straight across my hardened heart, shocking it to life.

I cleared my throat, the nearness of her too much. "We need to continue and find shelter," I bit out, an uncharacteristic pang of fear slicing through me. Whatever was happening with Kiara and me, it was changing. Morphing into something more. I'd always *seen* her, and she was dangerously close to seeing me. All of me.

She felt it too, that pull.

I hated it. Fought it. *Failed* to fight it.

Just like the sun that only visited me in my dreams, Kiara was addictive.

Forging ahead, my steps leaden, we made it another hour into the Mist—hopefully in the correct direction. That damn map was older than my great-grandfather, whoever he was.

I didn't know much about my family, and when I'd asked my father about my mother, he'd told me she was just some girl from the village brothel who'd dropped me off on his doorstep when I'd been two months old.

It wasn't until I'd grown up that I'd realized the story of my mother was a lie.

"I think I see something!" Kiara's face lit up in the most luminous of ways, her full lips slightly parted, a rosy hue on her cheeks. Even her unusual eyes seemed to glow from within. They were a whole shade lighter than usual, actually.

Focus.

How on earth could she see anything at all in this blasted blue fog?

I couldn't wait to get out of it. I despised not being in control, not being able to spot an attacker until they were nearly upon me. Getting caught off guard *twice* wasn't anything to be proud of.

Kiara bolted into the obscurity, forcing me to grunt out a curse and stumble after her.

"Up here!" she shouted, her hair flowing behind her in a tangled red blur. She was like a sprite, a forest nymph, and I wanted to catch her. Steal some of that wonder, that spirit. Not to keep forever, but maybe just to borrow some of her magic.

Kiara let out a breathy gasp, stopping so abruptly that I collided with her back with a *thump*. Her feet lurched forward at the impact, but before she could fall, I wound my arms around her waist, holding her steady.

"Sorry," I mumbled, my mouth at her ear. Soft hair tickled my jaw, each strand shining like a burning flame.

Kiara jerked in my embrace, her breathing growing heavy, slower. "Thanks," she rasped, her hands lowering to rest on my arms. Even through the leather, I felt the shock of her caress.

A minute passed, and neither of us moved.

If anything, my hands tightened. My restraint was loosening. Fast.

"Jude," she breathed, her voice a whisper of a thing.

My head dropped so I could inhale the scent clinging to her hair, my nose tracing the shell of her ear. Kiara smelled like pure wildfire and open forest, and I greedily committed it to memory. She let out a barely audible hiss.

But still she didn't move.

Right now, I wasn't the logical, unfeeling commander I'd been molded to be. Before I could second-guess myself, I flipped her around in my arms, a startled gasp leaving her lips. Lips I couldn't stop staring at like a starving man.

She noted where my eyes fell, her tongue peeking out to wet them. I wanted to taste her again more than I wanted anything. That kiss in the Pastoria Forest wasn't nearly enough. I wanted more, so much more. Never in all my life had a woman affected me in such an intense way. Kiara was strong, witty, fearless, and impossibly stubborn.

She was an enigma.

I leaned closer, just an inch. She was so short I had to crane my neck, her petite frame trembling as I closed in. Hungry. Desperate for just a taste of the fiery sunshine she reminded me of. A brightness in a world of night.

But then my gaze shifted upward, away from those delectable lips—

Kiara stared up at me with wide, innocent eyes. Trusting eyes.

Trust I didn't deserve.

My hands fell, releasing her.

I could've sworn a look of hurt crossed her features, but I ignored it. I had to.

Not once had I questioned my actions in the past, but ever since she'd come barreling into my life, I'd been tasting shame and bitter remorse. I wasn't what a woman like her deserved. Not some scarred, heartless monster.

With the moment thoroughly broken, Kiara stumbled back a step. "I-I saw something, right before you, uh, bumped into me." She jerked her head behind her, an uncharacteristic nervousness lining her words. "I'll show you."

I gave a curt nod, my jaw tensing painfully. "Let's go."

Spinning around, Kiara took cautious steps into the eddying fog, keeping her gaze ahead, looking anywhere *but* at me. I saw how she wobbled. How her hands formed loose fists at her sides.

I affected her, maybe just as much as she affected me. It was a disaster waiting to happen. I was about to open my mouth and ask what she thought she'd seen when all the air left my lungs.

Kiara cursed. A foul curse that would have brought a smile to my lips if disbelief hadn't rendered me speechless.

A clearing.

But not just any clearing. There was no fog, no bone trees

with brittle blue leaves.

No. It was a paradise.

"What the fu..." Kiara trailed off, her lips parted as her mouth curved into a wide *O*.

The brightest colors I'd ever seen—lush greens, vibrant reds, playful yellows—fell across the earth like a painted masterpiece. Better than that. Because it was *real*.

Only in my sunshine dreams had I seen such light.

It wasn't as bright as those dreams, but the clearing brimming with plants and flowers of varying colors was *glowing*.

"Beautiful," Kiara said, taking in all the foreign splendor.

Instinctively, I reached for the folded map, bringing it before my eyes. There was nothing on it but more trees where the clearing should have been.

"This isn't on the map," I said, my voice harder than stone despite how my stomach fluttered.

"Screw your map." Kiara let loose a lighthearted giggle, bounding fearlessly into the clearing, her fingers trailing across the blooms as she went. I admired that about her—that reckless bravery.

"Wait!" I shouted, the paranoid part of me on edge. There had to be a catch.

But Kiara didn't listen, twirling like a child among the flowers and greenery, a luminous smile adding to the radiating light enfolding us in its embrace.

I bounded after her—my cheeky sprite— straight into a clearing that was nothing short of impossible.

Chapter Thirty-Four

Kiara

Cerys, the God of Devotion, is often described as nothing more than a dulcet whisper in the night, striking at a time when the mind is at its most malleable. Cerys, a magnificent entity of pure, indescribable beauty and warmth, bestows their blessings upon the luckiest of mortals. A shame, because most of those Cerys visits do not even realize they've been given the greatest gift known to mankind.

Excerpt from Asidian Lore: A Tale of the Gods

Holy gods. Had Jude been about to kiss me?

This was the singular thought that consumed me as I ran through a meadow crafted by magic and hopeful dreams. Instead of noting every lush plant and diamond-encrusted red rose or purple-and-glistening-yellow bud, I replayed the last minute on an infinite loop.

I still thought about the too-brief kiss we'd shared when I'd worked to distract him and gain the upper hand. Never had I experienced such fire in a single brush of lips, such intensity. I wondered what it might feel like should we give in and completely let go.

There were so many other things to think about *besides*

wondering if Jude had been about to kiss me. Mainly the inescapable panic that hadn't left me since the forest attack. Since I'd lost consciousness.

Snap out of it, Ki, you're in a fantastical garden from a damn fairy tale.

Still, it was difficult to wrap my head around such a place existing in a world of nightmares. Even the stones glistened like tiny trapped raindrops.

Unreal.

All of it.

The sea of colorful blooms and emerald leaves gave way to a mighty oak, its dense branches towering over a quarter of the clearing. A small bubbling stream ran through it, the waters clear and welcoming. And not a hint of white or blue haze, though it still surrounded the glade like an unwelcome hug. I felt like I was in one of the snow globes sold in Cila's marketplace, the ones Mother never let me buy.

"This is incredible." Jude moved to stand at my side, his shoulder pressing against mine, his eyes tapering into a squint while he adjusted to the brightness.

Ever since I'd stopped breathing, the commander had been sticking to me like glue. Not that it was necessarily a bad thing.

In truth, I'd *wanted* him to kiss me earlier. And not as a ploy.

"Kiara?"

"Huh?" I lifted my chin to Jude, whose face scrunched with confusion. Even uncertainty looked good on him. Damn him.

"I said your name three times."

Oh.

"Sorry, I was a little distracted." I waved a hand around our surroundings to make my point. "If you haven't noticed, this is a little mind-boggling." *And I was thinking about you and your pretty lips.*

"Then why are you blushing?" Jude's lips quirked, seeming

to read my traitorous thoughts. Whatever he was seeing on my face pleased him.

"I am not blushing," I protested. Even to my own ears, it sounded weak. "It's just chilly, and I have very sensitive skin." Not a lie.

"Uh-huh." His smirk grew impish.

Who was this man, and what had he done with my resigned commander?

Maybe the Mist was to blame yet again.

"There is no way we *aren't* spending the evening here." Bounding to the mighty oak, I rose onto my tiptoes and plucked a leaf from a low branch. Tiny veins shot out from the stem, crinkling the thin membrane. The color was so green. So vibrant and rich.

"I wonder…" Jude murmured, rubbing at his growing scruff. "This shouldn't be here. Not in this place."

And he was right.

There had to be an explanation for why a paradise flourished in the Mist. Paranoia prickled at my chest as ice dripped into my veins. The logical thing would be to ignore the beauty and focus on reality. Uncle Micah had often told me that things were never as they appeared. That sometimes even the most beautiful things could be poisonous. I supposed that applied to people as well.

"You're right," I asserted. Jude's brow lifted. He was clearly stunned at my easy acceptance. "Let's investigate some more."

Jude let out a whistle. "And here I thought I was going to get scolded for being too cynical. Not that I'm complaining," he added, with a whisper-soft chuckle. The sound went straight to my core.

I cleared my throat. "All right, let's split up and see what we can find. There has to be something out of the ordinary." I paused mid-step. "Aside from *everything* here, that is."

Jude gave me a curt nod, spinning around and ambling off to the left, leaving me to explore the right side of the clearing. It wasn't a large area, perhaps a little over two hundred feet. A space filled with heavenly, effulgent light.

As if an artist had dipped his brush in pots of pale yellow and gold and coated every leaf and bloom and blade of grass. And because this place was real—or as real as anything beyond the borders—I found myself tilting my head to the sky and spinning around and around.

The dense clouds overhead were kept away, as though this place was untouchable by even the deadliest of curses. When I settled, having spun myself silly, I dizzily staggered over to a patch of the brightest blue blossoms.

Five heart-shaped petals burst from wide, buttery centers, flecks of silver scattered amid the blue like glitter. When I lowered my head to inhale the heady floral scent, a distinct crunch sounded behind me, and my hand whipped to my dagger.

I was a whirl of red hair as I twisted around, my dagger sailing skillfully through the air—

Only to pierce a ball of gray fur.

A rabbit.

"I think I just caught dinner!" I shouted over my shoulder to Jude, my stomach applauding my efforts with a growl.

Boots pounded, and the commander appeared at my side in an instant, a flustered hue of pink on his cheeks.

"What's wrong with you?" I studied him from his boots to the crown of his mussed hair, a thin sheen of sweat coating his brow.

"Nothing." His right eye twitched. "I just heard you scream."

Instantly, my smile blossomed into something wicked. "Aww." I bopped his nose, much to his chagrin. He scowled. "You were worried about me, and now you're all flustered."

"Quiet." Jude bit into the side of his cheek. "I'm in charge of recruits' safety, that's all."

A wave of guilt and sadness hit me upon hearing Jude mention the recruits. *Alec, Patrick, Jake.* They would have loved this. Here I was in the middle of this sumptuous, lush wonder in the middle of the Mist, and my friends were—

No. Don't think like that. They're okay. They have to be.

I couldn't voice my thoughts to Jude and break this spell, however brief. He deserved this moment of playfulness, of happiness, after everything he'd been through.

My friends were fine and likely attempting to follow our earlier path to meet us. I refused to believe otherwise.

I focused on Jude and his stern expression. "I'm sure that's all it is." I clasped my hands behind my back and adopted my most innocent of expressions. The doe eyes were out in full force.

Jude grumbled something beneath his breath, swiping a hand through his blue-black hair. It stuck up at awkward angles, oil and dirt coating the strands.

"Man, do you need a bath," I remarked, lifting my hand to run my fingers through it without thought. The moment I touched his silken, albeit filthy, hair, I jerked my hand away, forcing it to my side. Jude bit extra hard on his cheek to keep his smile at bay, but a roguish gleam ignited his brown eye.

"Gross," I snorted, as I wiped my hand on my trousers, covering up the fact that I'd just run my damn fingers through his hair. Thankfully, he put me out of my misery.

"The same could be said about you." His eyes narrowed into teasing slits as he took in my grimy clothes and smudged cheeks. He wasn't wrong.

In reply I winked and said, "How about you cook up the rabbit I so graciously caught for us, and after, we can take turns making use of that stream?"

Just looking at the crystal-clear water tempted me to run headfirst into its shallow depths. I didn't even care if it was freezing. Smelling like body odor and dried blood was not something I particularly enjoyed.

Jude visibly stiffened at my words, but he awarded me his signature nod, the one he gave me whenever he didn't care to speak. I often wondered what he was thinking when he resorted to those.

"Fine." Jude bent down and snagged the limp creature, jerking out my dagger before flipping it deftly in his hands and handing it over. "I'll start a fire, since you so *graciously* killed this poor animal."

"Eh, he never stood a chance." I'd been the reason my family's table had never been empty when the fields were barren. What few creatures I found in the woods I caught, my aim a thing of beauty.

"Oh, and if you don't tend to that shoulder and bandage it, you'll face my wrath," I warned.

He grunted. "Fine. But your 'wrath' isn't as terrifying as you think."

Before I could retort, Jude sauntered out of sight, presumably to clean his wound and search for firewood. With his absence, curiosity settled into me.

The book.

It still weighed heavily against my chest, its presence eating away at me. Now would be an ideal opportunity to delve in, if only for a few pages while Jude was cooking. Who knew if I'd get the chance this evening like I'd originally planned? Exhaustion was already calling me, so the time would have to be now.

And holy hells, did I have the perfect lighting, like my dream with Grandmother but muted.

After peering over my shoulder and finding Jude busy picking up kindling, I wandered around the trunk of the mighty oak at the center of the glen and rested my back against the coarse bark. Reaching into my jacket, I pulled out the tome, propping it against my bent knees.

Here goes nothing, Grandmother. I glanced to the sky as if she were peering down at me, watching all my blunders.

She'd said the answers would be in here.

Suddenly, my chest constricted. For some reason, I wondered if I even wanted to know the truth. Knowledge had a way of altering one's world, and sometimes not in a good way.

Yep. I still want to know.

Shaking my head with a quivering exhale, I flipped open the pages with haste.

The last chapter I'd read was about Raina falling in love with a mortal man, one she'd gifted with immortality. But when the goddess couldn't remain with him during the day, when the people had needed her light, her lover had become greedy.

Returning to where I'd left off, I continued reading…

Forever young, Raina's once mortal lover shone with dewy youth and innocence, but his heart was anything but. The man who had fallen for the sun was no longer content with only having her when night fell. He craved his newfound influence and Raina, but jealousy crept its way into his foul heart.

He wished for power himself.

If he could steal the essence the Earth God, Arlo, had gifted her, the man could free his love from her shackles and then consume the divinity she hardly seemed to appreciate.

So, when the goddess busied herself with her duties, he journeyed to Arlo's temple near the capital, pleading for the god's help. Having been bitter for decades and envying the people's love for the luminous Sun Goddess, Arlo appeared before him, offering knowledge that would prove useful to his plan.

Raina's lover would have to extract her gift—the light within her soul that burned eternal. It required a dagger crafted of pure moonshine, found in the center of a meadow nearly impossible for any human to find.

Arlo sliced open his palm, allowing his blood to drop onto a single black bloom in the ephemeral meadow of color. An onyx dagger capable of cutting an immortal's flesh rose from the roots, and the god bestowed his gift on Raina's lover. All he had to do was pierce her heart, and her power would be his. She wouldn't die, but she *would* become mortal.

But the man, so eager in his pursuit to have everything, made a fatal mistake.

What he didn't realize was that when he unbound his lover's power, he would have no control over where her essence went.

So, on the following evening, as Raina descended from the heavens on a cloud of silk, her lover waited with the dagger behind his back. The goddess, having no clue as to what he'd planned, raced into his arms. Just as their bodies met, a bolt of pain seared across her chest—her love had driven the moonshine dagger into her heart.

With wide eyes, she gasped, pleading for an answer as to why he would betray her so. But the mortal simply drove the blade in deeper, watching the devastation line her amber eyes in silver, the pieces of her holy soul split into three.

As if just realizing what he had done, the man quickly grabbed at one of the bursts of light before it could drift into the night. As his hand enclosed around the orb, as the ray of pure sunshine seeped into his skin, his black heart absorbed a fragment of the woman he'd claimed to love.

The second piece shot out across the realm before he could capture it. The ray would travel across the realm until it found a host of its own—an unsuspecting mortal destined to be born on what had been the longest day of the year.

But the final piece, the greatest fragment of her power, refused to leave the Sun Goddess. And while she held onto her last remaining light, her heart broke with betrayal. Even with a drop of her magic left, the dagger had rendered her all but mortal.

The man proclaimed his feelings for her, desperately attempting to convince the fallen goddess that this was better. That he could feel her inside his soul, and that, in that way, they would never be apart.

But it was too late.

Raina, with the last drop of her gifts, vanished into the darkness that soon plagued the kingdom.

From that moment on, the sun never did rise again, and the kingdom of Asidia and its peoples were cursed to live beneath an infinite moon, the realm surrounded by a poisonous mist.

The trees turned black, flowers wilted, and the earth shriveled, Arlo unable to mend what he'd helped break. The early days were the harshest, but the people pushed on, forced to survive without their beloved goddess watching over them.

Try as he might, Raina's traitorous lover could not expose the goddess, the woman he'd shattered. He spent the rest of his days obsessed, searching a midnight kingdom so he could reunite with Raina and convince her of his affection, for he had realized too late the error of his ways.

The years passed, and there was no sign of the goddess.

But because of his deception, the man was relegated to a life of immortal loneliness and infatuation. He would spend his long days scouring the kingdom for what he had broken, although he would never see the Sun Goddess again.

Somewhere, out in a world of eternal night, a woman who once ruled in the heavens had made a human life of her own, far away from the man who had stolen her power and shattered her beating heart.

However, many years later, rumors spread she'd made a family of her own, and that a child was born, one whom Raina kept hidden—her precious gift, and the owner of what remained of her melancholy heart.

"What are you doing?"

I slammed the book shut.

"Reading," I croaked, finding Jude watching me closely.

He glanced at the thick green cover, recognition brightening his scowl. "That's the one I gave you, eh? I'm surprised you have that on you instead of an extra dagger."

Thoughts of Raina and her traitorous lover vanished.

"I figured I'd get bored," I lied. He didn't need to know how I'd gotten my hands back on the book. "You can be rather serious, you know, so I brought some fun reading to lighten the mood." Scrunching up my face, I mimicked his signature grimace. Jude raised a brow in reply, but his lips curled upward and the crease between his eyes smoothed.

The clearing and its supernatural lighting gave Jude's alabaster skin a golden glow, his scars lightening to a faded red. No shadows painted his lower lids, and he appeared…happy?

I'd never seen the genuine emotion on his face, so I couldn't be positive, but the way he gazed upon me now, his eyes softening and a grin taking shape, it just might be joy.

"I'm surprised you didn't hear me coming. Our meal hadn't been so fortunate." Jude closed the distance and plopped down right next to me, not even attempting to place an inch between us.

My thigh aligned with his as he rocked his knee back and forth. "I wish we could just stay here," he admitted after a minute of peaceful quiet.

"You and me both." We had all we needed right here in this glen to survive. No Mist, no heartless king—and there was *light*.

Jude surprised me with his next words. "Can we pretend, just for now, that we are? That we aren't leaving here and that there's no timeline or threat of the world ending?" He said the last part with a sarcastic lilt, but beneath the playfulness lay a cruel truth. Jude believed we would never make it out of the cursed lands alive.

Without thinking, I grabbed his hand, my fingers weaving between his. "I think we agree on something, commander." My head lolled to the side as I took him in. He did the same, his long hair tumbling across his temples.

As logic and thought had clearly been thrown out the window, I lifted my free hand, the one not wrapped up in his, and grazed the raised lines of his scars. Beneath the leather of my glove, my fingers tingled.

Jude flinched, but he didn't pull away. Taking that as an invitation, I grew bold, tracing the scars and learning their story with my fingertips, a sense of raw grief flowing into my chest.

"I was six when it happened."

My fingers ceased their soothing movements.

"I'll never forget the day my own father blinded me."

CHAPTER THIRTY-FIVE

JUDE

Shadow beasts roamed the world for centuries before Raina supposedly wiped them away with her light. They are an abomination, a failed experiment on behalf of the Moon God. Supposedly after she'd slain them all, his wrath shook the world, and he hid from the skies for three months. When he returned, his light was never as bright nor as inviting.

EXCERPT FROM ASIDIAN LORE: A TALE OF THE GODS

Kiara hissed out a breath, stunned.

I imagined she hadn't thought my father was a good man based on the story I'd told her in the cavern, but she likely hadn't expected him to be the reason behind my injury.

I released her hand only so that I could bring mine to my face and cover her fingers, which rested right over my scars. I leaned into her touch and shut my eyes.

"My father barely raised me growing up. He would toss me to whatever woman he was with, and then go off and steal from the wealthy. But when I grew bigger, beyond a babe that could be held and controlled, he decided he no longer wanted me."

Memories flashed across my mind, of the drunken rages he'd fly into, of the women he hurt. I'd been too young to stop him at the time. I regretted not being strong enough.

"One day, Father and his crew had botched a job. They'd nearly been caught by the guards when they attempted to rob a transport of the king's gold. I remember coming up to his side, trying to ask if he was all right, but he shoved me to the ground and snagged a bottle of liquor. Foolishly, I rose and tried again, wanting to make him happy, for him to let me hug him."

My throat grew impossibly tight. I'd never shared this, not even with Isiah. "But when I reached for him that second time, he slammed the glass bottle across my face. I screamed, clawing at myself, at the shard of glass that had embedded itself in my left eye."

He'd blinded me right then and there, the broken bottle leaving those two jagged scars running across my eye. Kiara pressed her fingers deeper into my cheek, my lids still shut. I couldn't look at her when I spoke of the next part. The blinding hadn't been the worst of it.

"Afterward, when I lay bleeding on the floor, shaking and frightened, he'd grabbed my hair, pulled me across the mildewed planks of our home, and tossed me out in the cold. I don't remember much, but I managed to crawl on my hands and knees through the dirt and fallen snow. I must've passed out, because the next time I awoke, I was in a strange bed, one of our neighbors having taken pity on me. She told me I'd been found facedown in the mud and grime, left outside in the freezing winter air for hours.

"Not only had the glass blinded me, but the wound had gotten infected. Our neighbor wasn't a healer, but she claimed I would've been a lost cause if she hadn't found me in time. Dead from hypothermia first, most likely."

I felt Kiara shift closer to me, pressing her body against mine. I squeezed my lids tighter.

"As she couldn't afford to feed me much longer, she was

forced to return me to my father a week later. He took one look at me, spit, and said, 'Now he's crippled and dimwitted,' before lugging me inside and slamming the door in our neighbor's face. He never apologized, and he never spoke of it again."

"Gods, Jude," Kiara whispered, anger deepening her voice.

I paused, pulling away from her touch to scan the paradise at our feet. Her hand dropped to my knee, where she gripped me gently.

"It wasn't until I hid away in the bath that I unwound the linen from my face and saw the monster I'd become."

Her hand tightened on my knee. "Don't ever say that again," she scolded, her tone turning severe. "They're only scars. They don't make you into a monster. Your father was the monster."

My gaze dropped to her hands, to the gloves that concealed her own scars.

"If they're only scars, then why—"

"Why do I hide mine?" she asked, her entire body tensing. "I knew you would ask."

"I haven't pushed you once." Even though I'd wanted to.

Now it was her turn to look away. She was silent for many minutes, her brows furrowed as if a million thoughts filled her head. When she removed her hand from my knee, I believed the conversation was over and done with, but then...then she started to pull off the leather, finger by finger.

She did so slowly, her chest moving and falling rapidly. I could only imagine what she was going through, her fear at being exposed. Biting my tongue, I waited as she went at her own pace, until the first glove fell to the soft earth.

Holy gods.

I'd thought I remembered her scars from that first day in the Mist, but I'd forgotten just how deep and unusual they were. The eerie blue-and-black color, the shape of the wounds, like tiny veins spreading to graze her wrists.

"I know. They're hideous," she said as she yanked off the other glove. Her head lowered in shame, and I couldn't allow that.

I grasped her chin between my fingers and turned her head. What I saw in her gaze hurt more than any dagger.

"That day in the bathing suite, when you saw my face," I began, leaning closer. "I've never had someone look at me like that, like you were awed by me, enthralled by the ugliness marring me."

She opened her mouth to speak, but I shook my head.

"I had never felt seen before, Kiara, not like that. You looked past what others mocked, what they feared, and you *smiled*."

"It's different, you don't understand." She sighed, wetness lining her eyes. "It was *how* I got these injuries that marked me as an outcast. People looked at me as though I were evil. Some tainted creature who…" She sniffled, twisting out of my grasp.

I didn't care how the hells she got the odd scars, how she'd been irrevocably marked.

"You wear your scars well," I said, echoing the words she'd once told me. "If anything, they draw me to you."

Her head gradually rose, a beautiful kind of wonder painting her stunning features. Carefully, I lifted one of her hands to my mouth, pressing a kiss upon each finger, each twisting mark. She trembled in my hold, but I continued, my lips expressing what words failed to.

Before I could make my way to the inside of her wrist, Kiara thrust her fingers into my hair and yanked me close, our noses brushing. She inhaled my every exhale, and I breathed in her trust, her fears, her doubts.

And then I lowered my mouth to hers and captured her lips.

CHAPTER THIRTY-SIX

KIARA

The heart is the wickedest of beasts,
for it can never be tamed.

ASIDIAN PROVERB

There was nothing gentle about the way Jude kissed me. How he commanded my breath and inhaled my sanity, exhaling something wicked and wonderful in its place.

He tasted of possibility and hope and everything I never knew I could become addicted to—an intoxicating combination that set delicious adrenaline surging across every inch of my flesh as he devoured me, his lips moving wildly and without control.

I still trembled from when he'd gently brought my hands to his mouth and kissed away years and years of humiliation and disgrace. Treating me—my scars and all—as if I were something wonderful to behold. Something precious.

Jude nibbled on my lower lip, sucking it between his teeth, and something feral awakened inside me. My bare fingers were in his hair, running through the black strands and tugging, holding him just the way I wanted as I pressed him closer. I shouldn't be surprised I was trying to assume command.

Jude let out a growl and wrapped a hand around the nape of my neck, his fingers winding through my hair as he, too, fought for control. Of course we would battle, even while we kissed. His hands were everywhere, my own seeking out his warmth, sliding beneath his shirt and gliding up the hard planes of his stomach.

We both craved the fight, and in each other, we found the perfect partner.

Touching him without my gloves, without my armor, felt better than anything I could have ever imagined. My fingers tingled as I brought my hands to his hair and fisted the strands, and suddenly, I was filled with such raw *freedom*.

Jude let out a strangled groan when I prodded at the seam of his lips, my tongue slipping inside to explore. The noises that left him became my favorite sounds. They were animalistic, primal, and needy.

His tongue danced with mine, swirling deliciously before giving my lips more attention. As he sucked my bottom lip between his teeth, a bolt of lightning struck my core, and even Jude tensed, like he was hit by the same shock of electricity.

Light dazzled behind my closed lids, a sun of my own making igniting my world. And as tingles raced down my spine and my heart thundered wildly, I gave in to the consuming chaos that was kissing Commander Jude Maddox.

When he eventually pulled away, albeit reluctantly, I was a panting mess.

"Kiara," he breathed reverently, bringing the tip of his nose to mine, our foreheads pressed against one another. "I— That was…"

"We should have been doing that this whole time," I cut him off, my chest rising and falling unevenly. I must have had the widest of grins plastered across my face.

If I had known Jude could kiss like it was his job, then I would have been all over him a lot sooner. It took everything in me now not to jump him and start all over again.

We'd shared our secrets, and even if I hadn't told him the story behind the accident that had marred me for life, I vowed one day I would.

Jude chuckled, his body pressing against mine as he wound an arm around my waist. With a swift pull, I landed in his lap, his arms hugging me to his chest as he burrowed his nose in my hair. Every inch of him was hard, solid muscle—a deadly killer.

And I'd never felt more at ease.

"We need to do that again."

Jude's chest shook with laughter, and he rubbed his stubbled jaw against my heated cheeks. The scruff tickled my skin in the best possible way.

"I think we found another thing we can agree on." His arms tightened. "Maybe *after* we get you a proper meal first."

Being the mood killer that it was, my stomach let out a thunderous grumble. "Fine," I relented, not entirely pleased, but willing to accept the compromise. I probably needed to calm myself down. My body still tingled, and my lips were perfectly swollen.

"Jude?"

"Yes, recruit?" I felt him smile against my skin.

"Thank you for sharing your story with me," I said softly. "And thank you for…" I couldn't say the words, but I didn't need to.

Jude stilled for a moment, and then he reached for my hand. He placed it on his heart. "Never thank me for that, Kiara," he rasped. A mischievous glint entered his right eye. "Not when there are other things I'd prefer you thank me for."

I gently jabbed him in the ribs. "Commander!" I said in mock disbelief. "And here I thought your ego was already large enough."

His lips lifted, and he shifted his hips suggestively.

Immediately, heat rose from my neck and to my cheeks.

"Are you sure you're talking about my ego, recruit?"

I shot him a look. "Who are you, and what have you done with my brooding commander?" A man whose smile never had reached his eyes until recently.

"You've thoroughly ruined him."

"Good," I said, suddenly feeling breathless. "I like you ruined for me."

I didn't need to tell him he'd done the same to me. He already knew.

Jude carefully scooped me up in his arms and stood, holding me like I weighed nothing. Like he didn't have a damned injured shoulder to worry about.

Instinctively, I wound my hands around his neck, my eyes locking with his as he carried me to where the rabbit cooked over the fire. But while my stomach growled and begged for food, I was captivated by the way in which he returned my stare.

That look triggered my heart to flutter all over again. Something about this man sparked me to life, made me feel like I was struck by lightning and dipped in flames.

Never breaking contact, Jude set me gently on my feet, his broad hands still holding onto my waist. "Your throne." He nodded toward a polished boulder directly before the flickering orange and yellow flames. I rolled my eyes but ambled over to my seat, my knees wobbling.

Jude hesitantly looked away, but not before I saw the shy smile that flourished upon his lips.

You and me both, I thought, feeling happier than I had in years. So completely happy that it frightened me.

Jude understood me. I couldn't describe it to someone, should they ask, but that didn't matter. *I* felt it. How our beating hearts could speak to each other in a language only we seemed to know.

Every time he looked at me, even on that fateful day in my village, he saw a woman who wanted to fight, to become something greater than anyone could imagine. All of our jagged pieces might not have fit together perfectly, but what a beautiful, disastrous mosaic we made.

I watched him work, slicing up the rabbit and preparing our meal, all the while heartbroken over the childhood he'd endured.

Jude had opened up to me, exposing a side of himself I doubted many, if any, had seen. And that, *that* was the reason I knew without a doubt that I could trust him with my own secrets, regardless of what my grandmother had warned.

Sometimes people were wrong.

"It might be a little overcooked, but I never claimed to be a chef." A chunk of meat on a stick waved beneath my nose, and I startled, having been thoroughly lost in thought.

"After not eating for so long, this is going to be the best meal I've ever had." Snatching the stick, I thrust the rabbit into my mouth with little to no finesse. Jude would have to deal with my poor manners.

All he did was chuckle, digging into his meal, although he ate his like a refined human being. The rabbit was gone within minutes, and my stomach thanked me as the food weighed heavy in my belly.

Without a word, Jude handed me his canteen, which he must have filled up at some point from the stream. "Thanks." I grinned, unscrewing the lid to chug half the contents.

With dehydration and hunger no longer a concern, I decided it was time to scrub the grime from my flesh.

"I'm going to wash up."

Jude's eyes popped up from his rabbit, flickering back to the flames a heartbeat later. "I'll be right here." He kept his gaze lowered, a slight tinge of pink on the fearsome Knight's cheeks. I was feeling generous, as I likely was blushing myself, so I let it slide.

Once I'd made my way to the stream, I peeled off my soiled garments with a groan. I already felt naked without the protection of my gloves. I'd left them beside the fire, beside Jude, and my fingers curled as I inspected the flowing blue-black lines.

I twisted the wrist of my left hand, the one Jude had kissed so reverently.

No one had ever taken the time to look upon my scars before, but when Jude had so lovingly inspected them, I'd finally allowed myself to do the same. The deep hues shimmered, and for just a moment, I saw the haunting beauty in them.

A smile tugged at my lips, unbidden, and I stole a curious glance over my shoulder, finding Jude in the same position I'd left him in, his eyes glued to the fire.

With a shake of my head, I splashed into the lukewarm stream, a squeal escaping my lips. My bare feet touched the bottom, polished rocks tickling my toes, a floral scent mixed with what smelled like heavenly sugar coating the water.

Dipping my head beneath the surface, I went about my task, meticulously scrubbing my skin clean of dried blood and muddy streaks, the water seeming to wash away my sins. Perhaps The Water God had magicked it himself.

"You have *got* to take a dip," I insisted when I returned to Jude and the fire. The warmth radiated across every inch of my skin, and I sighed dramatically before plopping down before it. I slid my bare hands into my trouser pockets, not quite ready for full exposure just yet. "Whatever's in there, it has to be imbued with magic."

Indeed, even in my filthy clothes, I still felt squeaky-clean. "Go on," I urged, tilting my head, "enjoy yourself."

The corners of his lips quirked, and without any more prodding, Jude bolted to his feet and raced off, leaving me alone.

While sorely tempted, I kept my eyes lowered, snagging

Jude's creased map instead. The weathered page was worn with age and use, but thankfully still legible. I rubbed at the bottom corner, my thumb brushing over what appeared to be a single eight-pointed star, the ink smeared and faded. There were no other ornamental designs, the land drawn out simply and without excessive detail. After careful perusal, I took a stab at our location—it all looked the same to me—though the glen we were settled in was not on the map.

A crudely fashioned *X* was marked about ten miles north. That had to be where we were headed. A bolt of excitement lifted my spirits, and the idea of actually fulfilling this mission and *not* dying sounded marvelous.

"We're almost there." I flinched at Jude's voice.

Tilting my head up from the weathered parchment, I drank in the commander as he placed his blood-spattered shirt beside the fire to dry.

He was a sight to behold, stunning enough to drive away any more thoughts of death.

With his dark hair slicked back from his face, I itched to run my fingers through the mess of glistening locks. Jude's wide shoulders and the rippling muscles of his abdomen were on full display, droplets of water glancing across every ridge and dip. I greedily inhaled the divine sight.

"We should reach whatever lies at the *X* no later than early afternoon. Or sooner, if the map is correct."

"You have a good swim?" I said, unable to focus on the damned mission. I prayed he was ignorant as to the direction my eyes strayed. At least he'd done as I'd instructed. His shoulder was carefully bandaged with fresh linen. I'd have to keep an eye on it for infection.

Jude shook his head. "I'm not a piece of meat, recruit," he scolded playfully.

He caught me. No longer making a point to hide it, I leisurely perused him from head to toe, arching my brows and whistling.

"You're incorrigible." He sighed, still beaming.

I was about to tell him what he meant to say was "perfect," or even "enchanting," when I recalled the time I'd run into him at the bath.

"Your tattoo," I blurted, and Jude's face scrunched in confusion. "What does it mean? The three interwoven circles?"

Jude gave me his powerful back, displaying the three perfectly rounded circles inked into his abused and marked skin. Tiny whorls decorated the insides of every loop, the intricate designs reminding me of flowing vines.

Or of my scars.

But that couldn't be right.

After a moment, he shrugged his broad shoulders and eased closer to the fire. "I got it when I was younger," he admitted, seemingly mesmerized by the dancing flames. "I kept drawing that symbol as a kid. I had notebooks filled with it."

"That's...odd." I had expected them to have some greater meaning.

"Yeah, well, it means nothing, really. A few Knights and I got tattoos after our oaths. This was what I chose." He shrugged again, his many silvery scars glistening in the soft blaze. They lined his arms and torso, some raised, others faint. I wanted to know the story behind every single one.

"You think we'd be lucky enough to find all the keys in one place?" I mused, changing topics. Jude had fallen into his own thoughts at the mention of the tattoo, delving somewhere I couldn't reach him. I scoured the map, searching for any other intricate markings.

Jude scooted beside me on the boulder, his leg resting against mine. "There's only one *X*. But I'd be a hopeful fool to assume all three keys are in one place. That would be too easy, and I hardly count us as lucky. We've encountered more danger than I expected, mainly the masked inhabitants."

His nose wrinkled. "I wonder if the king knows of their presence. If he sent us this direction knowing what we'd face. Their blood was black, for gods' sake, and they certainly didn't appear entirely...human."

Not in the way they moved or how their skin shone gray. Jude was right. Something about them was different...*disturbing*.

"If he did know, he kept them a secret for a reason," I mused. If Asidia learned of their existence, I imagined the people might try and venture into the lands by themselves, perhaps believing there was a chance at survival. And a way out of our kingdom.

"That man has more secrets than truths," Jude grumbled.

I ran my hand over his, not grasping it, but simply letting my weight settle. "No more talk of Cirian," I pushed, sensing his ire. "I, for one, am still pretending that we live here, and that there is no suicide mission or curse to contend with. We made a deal, remember?"

"Ahh, yes. Likely a horrible deal I never should have made." My heart fell, but then he added, "And one I don't regret."

Jude snuggled in close, tentatively snaking his hand around my waist. It was new, the touching, but since we'd kissed, it was like Jude couldn't resist anymore. I rested my head on his uninjured shoulder, a yawn breaking free.

In this ethereal place made of dreams, we could just...*be*.

Jude stroked a hand through my damp hair, absentmindedly playing with the strands. "Such a rare color," he remarked, almost to himself.

Silence ensued for some time, but then he finally said, "It's beautiful. Unique, like you."

I snorted. "Such a poet, commander."

Jude rolled his eyes. "Come on, heathen, let's get some rest before I change my mind and show you all the ways I'd like to keep you up." His words were like a sensual promise, and I might've ceased breathing. Just the thought of what he insinuated had my heart racing in the most delicious way.

Jude lifted to his feet and offered me his hand, a sly grin brightening his features as if he knew just how much he'd affected me. Those blasted tingles raced across my palm as I placed my hand in his.

"But before we sleep…"

Jude's hand grabbed at the nape of my neck, yanking me to his lips.

He kissed me like he might never do so again, like tomorrow we'd wake and everything would go back to normal; he would be my vexingly responsible superior, and I his insubordinate recruit.

I dug my fingers into his bare skin, my nails likely leaving marks, but my eagerness seemed to excite him further, and his tongue darted into my mouth, tasting me.

Fire blossomed as I moved my hands to his chest, the pads of my fingers trailing down and across the rippling lines of his stomach. I could feel every dip and indented scar, his body a map I wished to learn.

"Gods, even your touch holds such power over me," he murmured against my lips. "You have no idea how you've thoroughly destroyed me, do you, Kiara?"

I didn't have a chance to reply as the grip on the back of my neck tightened, his fingers holding me in place as he devoured me. His free hand traveled to my waist, my back, and then he was cupping my chest.

I cursed the fabric separating us.

Smiling against his mouth, I leaned into his touch, craving him in a way that was physically painful. We were both burning alive, our wandering hands everywhere at once. And yet it wasn't enough. I wanted all of him, to *touch* all of him.

"Dammit, Kiara." He groaned when he pulled back, allowing us both a chance to catch our breath. "You taste better than I imagined. And I've imagined you so very much."

The blush that painted my cheeks burned in its intensity.

"I could spend hours tasting you. Kissing you." His lips touched mine, soft and sweet. "I know we shouldn't be doing this, but—"

"Shut up, Jude," I cut him off. "Will you get out of that stubborn head of yours for just one second?"

"You're calling *me* stubborn?"

"More so than me," I replied, heaving a sigh before resting my head against his chest. His heartbeat raced beneath my ear.

"We really do need to sleep before we do something we shouldn't."

I lifted my head, peering up at him. "I'm not as naive as you believe me to be, dear commander." It took considerable effort to force out the next words. "Although, I begrudgingly agree. We should probably get some sleep."

But gods, did my body disagree.

"Come on, recruit." Jude guided me to the fire, his eyes never once leaving me. They were molten fire, pools of searing desperation. "At least let me hold you."

I shuddered at the low timbre of his voice. Yes, I could certainly allow that.

When we were curled up on our sides, the flames dancing before us, all the adrenaline I'd felt dissipated, replaced with a heady exhaustion. While Jude maintained an inch of space between our bodies, his broad hand rested on the exposed skin of my hip. Without warning, I pushed back against his chest, snuggling in close.

Jude flinched, but his arm around me tightened.

Eventually, I drifted into a deep slumber, the crackling fire and Jude's even breathing lulling me to sleep.

Whatever dreams I might have that evening, they wouldn't compare to my reality. And that frightened me the most.

When I'd asked Grandmother about the sun when I was a young girl, all she'd told me was, "You cannot covet what you do not know." And now that I'd tasted but a hint of happiness, I feared I would miss it when it was inevitably taken from me.

Chapter Thirty-Seven

Jude

Maliah, Goddess of Revenge and Redemption, is a fickle
master. She often acts with spite, causing chaos and war
simply to watch the ensuing bedlam. Not much is known
about Maliah, but there have been reports of her many lovers,
both men and women, whom she gifts with acts of vengeance
on their behalf. Perhaps this is why many seek her favor,
hoping they might catch her eye and be rewarded in return.

Excerpt from Asidian Lore: A Tale of the Gods

For the second time in as many days, I woke up with Kiara's
body pressed against mine.

Sometime during her sleep she'd rolled over, her small body
draped across my torso like a warm blanket. Her head rested
against my chest, right above my enlivened heart, and one lean
leg was tossed carelessly across both of mine. Her tiny hand
grasped a fistful of my thin undershirt, pinning me in place.

This certainly was a pleasant way to start the day.

I was her personal pillow, *again*. And I didn't mind in the
least.

Peering down my nose, careful not to disturb her rest, I took
in the sight of her—of the long sweeping lashes that dusted her

rosy cheeks and the slightly parted lips that sent a different kind of heat spreading like wildfire across my chest.

My goddess of war was so very docile in her sleep.

I couldn't remember a time when I hadn't dreamed of the sun or the dark shadows that eventually stole it away. And I knew my peaceful sleep was due to the stunning creature in my arms—one crafted of both strength and ethereal lightness. She chased my demons away.

"Mmmm." Kiara shifted in my arms, and instinctively, they tightened.

Her bare fingers curled and tugged me against her chest as if, even in her sleep, she fought to keep me impossibly close.

I glanced down at her hands, recalling the sheer terror that had filled her eyes when she'd shown me her secret. I'd been honored—"honored" being too small a word—that she trusted me. It felt like that pull between us had finally snapped, and now we were irrevocably tied together.

How could I push her away now? I'd be a bastard if I did. Isiah would've frowned at me and called me an idiot, but...but Isiah wasn't here. When was the last time peace had fallen over me and a sense of safety had warmed my chest? Never. That was the cold truth of it.

Kiara twitched, her lashes fluttering as a chilled wind swept across her cheeks. Sleep had lost its hold.

"Morning," I murmured into her copper hair, my nose inhaling her distinct scent—an exquisite aroma of the open woods and some foreign bloom. Kiara angled her head, peering up at me with those striking amber eyes. Eyes familiar to me in a way I couldn't describe.

"Morning, commander." She stretched, arching her back and raising her arms like a kitten. "You still make a fine pillow," she said.

"And you still make an excellent heater." My lips curled.

"Although, you do snore like a bear." A lie, but it got the reaction I was aiming for.

One moment she was nestled in my arms, pliant and content, and the next, she was straddling me, her hands resting on either side of my head, her fists in the soft dirt.

"Say that again, and I'll slit your throat in your sleep," she threatened, her tone saturated with mischief. She loved the challenge as much as I loved the fight.

"I only speak the truth," I cooed, goading her further. Poking her beast was becoming my new favorite hobby.

"Well, I—"

Kiara's full lips froze. Whatever she'd planned to threaten died on her tongue, and her eyes turned shrewd as she scanned the forest.

Following her gaze, I, too, startled. "Where the hells are we?"

Apparently, our sleeping positions were not the only things to shift overnight. The magical glen we'd drifted off in? Yeah, that was nowhere to be seen.

We were back in the Mist, in the silvery-white forest smothered with blue leaves. Wisps of fog drifted by.

Scrambling off me, her hand reaching for her dagger, Kiara surveyed the area, alert and ready for an attack. I'd been so lost in her I hadn't even realized the change. That alone should have been a warning that I was in danger.

"I knew it was too good to last." I sighed, hoisting myself to my feet and grabbing my discarded shirt. Thankfully it was dry, and I shrugged it on before slipping into my jacket.

It wasn't shocking that we'd fallen asleep in one place only to wake in another. Not in this cursed place. It was a shame, though, for the glen held its own kind of enchantment, and a hint of…remembrance. Like a memory that was all hazy at the edges whenever I thought too hard on it.

"Lovely," Kiara grumbled, sheathing her dagger. Her

attention never left the trees. "Where do you think we are?"

"Probably in the same place, minus the glowing paradise."

Kiara didn't look too convinced.

"If anything, it was the *garden* that moved, not us," I added. At least, I assumed that to be the case—but assumptions could, I knew, be dangerous. "Let's head out and see what we can find."

It was time to leave anyway. While the glen had been a pleasant reprieve, like a dream, reality couldn't be ignored.

Kiara nodded, cracking her knuckles, her nose wrinkling as it so often did before a fight. The fierceness that overtook her features painted her as the warrior goddess I'd likened her to—

An otherworldly creature composed of lethal beauty.

She might be a petite thing, but I felt fairly confident with her at my side. Over the last few weeks, I'd witnessed her fight, and she could put many of my trained Knights to shame. If we ever got out of here alive, she would make a fine addition to them.

Instantly, my chest constricted. If we ever got out alive, and things went back to how they were—

Knights swore an oath to the kingdom. Not to each other.

This budding *thing* of ours would have to stop. Even if I didn't want it to anymore.

A large part of me seethed at the idea, but it would have to be done—once a Knight, death was the only escape. If the king caught us, if he found out what she meant to me...

Cirian wouldn't give up his most prized assassin, and if he learned how much I cared for her, he'd use her to further control me. The idea of the king threatening her made me murderous, and I pictured his throat opening beneath my blade. The image had an oddly calming effect. Maybe I'd make it a reality.

Yesterday had been so easy. I'd never told a living soul the truth of my scars, not even Isiah. My fingers traced the golden pin on my jacket. I was grateful Kiara had taken it off his body.

I'd been too pissed at the time to think of it myself.

The band around my chest grew painfully taut, stealing my air, my focus.

"Ready?" Kiara questioned, eager to get out of here. She was back to business, the gleam in her eyes dimmed to an ember.

I nodded, trailing behind as she took the lead, her steps heavy from sleep.

While the blue fog was still abundant, it wasn't nearly as thick as before. That was either a good sign, or a very, *very* bad one.

Ever since I'd emerged from the Mist last year, not only a trained killer, but a traitor to my brothers, my thoughts continuously ventured back to this place.

Isiah often compared my left eye to the Mist, and in a way, he was right. When I gazed upon a person, I saw two sides of them—one solid, and the other a shadow. With both eyes open, I could see them clearly enough, although they were surrounded by wisps of white and the lightest blue.

It had taken me years to get used to my sight, but after a while, the bluish-tinged haze actually helped me in battle. I could sense my opponents' moves, how the air shifted and flowed right before they went in for an attack. In that way, my injury aided me.

But no one else knew that. To let on to your strengths was to grant your opponent the upper hand. It was better to let them believe I was a scarred beast, a quiet killer with a useless eye.

Not that I pitied myself or my appearance—not now, at least—but when people proclaim you to be one thing your whole life, you begin to believe them. And yet the wild girl before me only stared up at me in wonder.

I couldn't help but think our scars spoke to each other as well. Bonded us. It had taken restraint not to pry and ask her about her accident, but I resisted the temptation, content that she'd finally removed her gloves and showed me all of her.

To me, she was the most beautiful thing I'd ever beheld, and her wounds only made her that much more alluring.

We must have walked for two hours straight, the silence easy and comfortable, as it always had been between us.

The Mist continued to thin out, and I kept my dagger within reach, the blade ready to spill blood. Before we'd settled down in the clearing yesterday, the fog had been dense enough that I could only see five or six feet in front of me. Now I could stare off into a distance of fifteen feet or more, perhaps even farther.

One would assume it would grow thicker the deeper we ventured, which was why my instincts were screaming that something was off. While there was no discernible danger, my rapid heartbeat told me otherwise.

The moonlight helped ease my fears, and I tilted my head to the sky. I noted that the moon appeared bigger than before, which was mind-boggling in itself, for it was already unnaturally large. Today, blue tinted its glow, a soft shade that reminded me of the lakes of the southern lands.

After another five minutes, Kiara halted, her sudden stop causing me to jerk back in surprise.

"What is it?" I whispered, peering over her shoulder as I took a step back.

She didn't need to answer.

Kiara had almost stumbled right off a cliff, the rocky edge but a few feet ahead. And at the base of that cliff lay a ramshackle village. Opaque spirals of white and gray wound about tents and wandering villagers, their feet shrouded entirely by the fog. It was thicker than the blue haze we'd journeyed through, as if no color dared to touch the foulness of the village and its inhabitants.

"It's them," she hissed between her teeth.

I knew who she spoke of—the masked men. Bending into

a crouch, she examined the torchlit village and its many torn and ragged cloth tents. Everything was in shades of slate and ivory, not a trace of color to be found. And from the looks of it, I'd speculate there to be no more than forty people living there.

"What do we do?" Kiara's breaths came out ragged. Her dagger was at her side.

I thought on that. We only had one option, really. "We go around them."

The two of us combined wouldn't be anywhere near enough to take down a whole horde of masked fighters. They weren't as well trained as Knights, but they were still skilled. I surmised that you would have to be a decent enough fighter to live out here.

Kiara gave a jerk of her head. "Fine, but I want to wait a second before we go on."

"Why?" The longer we sat here twiddling our thumbs, the greater were our chances of exposure.

"Just…I don't know," she huffed. "I have a feeling." Great. A *feeling*. Those were never good.

"We don't have the time, Kiara," I groused, the inner commander in me rearing his head. I'd allowed her actions to slide too many times, and with our safety—*her* safety—in question, I had to toughen up.

"*You* can leave. I'm staying here." Kiara met my penetrating stare head-on, never flinching beneath my icy gaze.

Gods, this woman.

"I am still your commander," I ground out, my patience wearing thin. "We shouldn't risk an entire kingdom full of lives just to satiate your *feeling*."

"Then I guess I'm disobeying a direct order." A hand went to her hip, a feral gleam lighting her determined eyes.

She was challenging me.

"Kiara…" I warned, my tone turning low. "While things

between us might be blurred"—I grimaced, knowing full well it was my fault—"we still have a mission." I should never have crossed that line to begin with, even though we'd been dancing around it for weeks.

"Blurred?" she scoffed, her free hand clenching into a fist. "Blurred?" she echoed, and I didn't like the sound of that. Taking a mighty step forward, the tips of her boots bumping against mine, she raised her head. "The lines didn't seem so *blurry* yesterday when you had your tongue down my throat."

"That's not what—"

"And besides"—she interrupted, her hand shoving against my chest—"why would you listen to me? The person who saved your ass that first day when you couldn't even open your eyes? Hmmm?" Her voice rose with her swelling ire. Kiara's temper burned bright, and once sparked, it could easily catch flame.

I grasped both of her arms. "We will stay *five* minutes. That is my only compromise. And you should think yourself lucky I'm even allowing that."

Kiara shook me off her, shooting daggers into my skull with her eyes before lowering herself into a crouching position behind a patch of thick black reeds. I watched the back of her head a moment longer, knowing full well I'd given in to her demands. I was getting soft, and that was a weakness I couldn't afford.

But now that I'd gotten a taste of her, I craved more. Kiara's lips on mine brought air back into lungs that hadn't taken a full breath in years.

Grumbling, I assumed a similar position, landing on my knees and crouching behind the tall charcoal reeds. If any of my soldiers saw me giving in to a recruit, I'd be the laughingstock of the brotherhood.

Kiara didn't look back at me, not even to glower. She fixed her eyes on the village below, watching every movement like a hawk.

There were around twenty tents along with a few firepits, and I suspected everything here could be easily packed up and moved if need be. I spotted both men and women, but no trace of a child.

"I can practically feel you fuming from here," Kiara hissed, deigning to glance over her shoulder. Her hair whipped about her face in a foul breeze. I prayed it was coming from the smoldering fires below and wasn't another hallucination-inducing wind.

"I'm being safe, and you know that. You're just being difficult," I dared to add. "Believe it or not, I kind of like you *alive*."

I tacked that last part on knowing she couldn't say anything snappy in response. I hid my smile as she growled, flipping her head back to the village. "Another minute, and I promise we'll leave," was all she said, so low I could hardly make it out.

I'd won one round, at least.

Five minutes passed, and then, "Wait." She held up a lone finger. My eyes sharpened. "There."

Before I glimpsed whatever had captured her attention, a scream shook the humble village, the shrill sound piercing my eardrums.

Shoving Kiara into the thicket, making sure the onyx reeds shielded her, I pressed her body into the hard soil. I could feel her breathing go ragged beneath my arm, which was curled protectively about her torso.

"Shhh," I soothed, or tried to. It probably came out as a harsh growl, but at this moment I didn't very much care. Beside me, Kiara froze, her chest going frighteningly still.

Forcing my attention away, I squinted into the dark, noting a group of masked men clutching torches. There were about ten of them, five on each side of what appeared to be...

No.

It couldn't be. How had they managed to round them up in the fog? Unless they had somehow found one another after the attack.

Kiara gasped as Patrick and Jake came into view, followed by Alec.

A soft hiss escaped from between Kiara's teeth, the muscles in her back seizing.

I secured my arm around her body, partly to reassure her and partly to make sure she didn't go bolting to the rescue like a fool.

She would, too—run down this paltry cliff and toss herself in harm's way. All because she couldn't bear to see her friends tortured and killed. Still, I wouldn't let her throw her life away, even if she despised me for it afterward.

All the boys had their hands tied before them as they were kicked and prodded forward through the zig-zagging tents, the villagers grunting and making incoherent noises as they passed. Whatever language these people spoke, it was not one I knew.

Jake wasn't as collected as his friends, his long legs tripping over rocks and debris, his bright blue eyes wide enough to shine through the darkness to where we hid atop the rocky hill.

"We need to get them."

There it was.

"Wait," I murmured, holding firm. I could sense Kiara's limbs itching to move. That wasn't going to happen. Something about these people was off in a way I couldn't put my finger on.

The rotten air grew stronger as the villagers howled in delight, some snapping their jaws and clawing in the recruits' direction. Their movements were animalistic in nature, as if they couldn't control their limbs.

I wished they would take off those damned masks.

"We can't just stand by and wait for them to do gods knows what to them," Kiara snapped with a fierce bite.

Enough.

My features were sharp and deadly when I twisted to her, the unyielding facade I wore for my inferiors securely in place.

"We will not make a single move. Not yet. And not until I say so." I enunciated every word, an assault of dismissal.

Undeterred, Kiara wrinkled her nose, her eyes darkening. "You do not tell me what to do. Not anymore." The breeze turned frigid, and my skin prickled from the sudden cold.

I flinched. "We just went over this, Kiara. What part of 'I don't want you to die' do you not understand? You *will* die if you go in there unprepared. And your friends will die because of your recklessness and your innate need to act first and think later. I won't be around to bury all your bodies."

Kiara ground her teeth, battling with her need to act and ultimately conceding to my logic. When moments passed and she remained in position, I nearly sighed with relief.

If I wasn't harsh, she wouldn't listen. A healthy dose of fear was required, or she would get herself killed. And the thought of her dead, of her body lifeless and cold, brought a whole new wave of emotion crashing into my chest.

I loathed it. Caring for someone was how you got yourself killed.

The group of recruits was led around the many derelict shelters and then thrust into a circular area constructed of stone and cracked white—

Bones.

Maybe there wouldn't be as much time to plan as I'd thought.

A man wearing a thick black coat that billowed out behind him entered the ring, and the recruits were all kicked down to their knees by the guards. Patrick lifted his head, staring boldly into the masked man's eyes at the center of it all. Again, his bravery was surprising.

"Who are you?!"

That was Jake, shouting and desperate. He lost his balance and tumbled onto his side, only to be hauled back into position by one of the guards.

The man cloaked in black, the clear leader of these feral people, raised his gloved hands to the heavens, to the moon glowing brightly above. I held my breath as I awaited his next move, looking for any indication of how this day would end.

If there wasn't enough time to save them, then I would have to drag Kiara out of here kicking and screaming. My hands twitched on her back, readying themselves for action.

Slowly, the man began to remove his cloth mask, the linen falling to the ground at his feet. In that moment, I knew blood was sure to be spilled today.

His skin was as gray as the reeds we crouched behind, chunks of his flesh missing and other patches blackened by decay. But that wasn't what had me reaching for my blade.

No. It was the long, sharp teeth that protruded from a gaping mouth devoid of lips.

He unhinged his jaw, releasing a spine-chilling howl that was most certainly not human. The rest joined in, a chorus of beasts and death.

I knew what was about to happen—

And it wouldn't end well for the recruits.

Chapter Thirty-Eight

Kiara

The cursed lands are said to be protected by creatures neither
human nor animal. Few have seen them and lived to tell the
tale, but it is often wondered if they're there to safeguard the
cure to Asidia's plight. Or if they're simply the result
of the Mist's poison.

Excerpt from Asidian Lore: A Tale of the Gods

Even at a distance, I could see the fangs.
Patrick nearly tumbled to his side as the ringleader
removed the cloth masking his grotesque features. Features
that weren't human. The fangs jutted out from his gums like a
hundred ivory daggers, the tips falling to the dip of his chin. Had
he any lips, they would have been sliced and bloody.

As his jaw unhinged and contorted, widening to a degree
that should have been impossible, I knew what was in store for
my fellow recruits.

I felt an arm tighten around my torso.

Jude.

I'd almost completely forgotten about him in my panic.
Peering over my shoulder, I noted that he, too, was wide-eyed
and full of healthy fear, and the emotions he usually hid so well

were now on clear display.

Coming from him, that wasn't a good sign.

While my body burned to move, to do anything at all besides stay hidden like a coward, my limbs simply wouldn't work.

The men and women of the village stomped closer, forming a line around the circle and their undead leader. One by one, the villagers removed the cloths covering their faces, the dusty rags dropping to the ground and swept away by the vile wind. It reeked of rotten flesh and mold—how I imagined Death himself to smell.

We needed to do something. *Now*.

"Jude," I hissed, alarm distorting my voice. "What do we do?"

I hadn't the faintest idea of how to stop these things. They weren't human—or at least, not anymore. Their flesh was decayed and *missing* in some places. One of the men appeared to be lacking half of his face, ivory bone poking out beneath a flap of what used to be skin.

Jude had yet to speak. I shook him, his solid frame not budging an inch. "Jude!" I whisper-hissed, my heart racing, my blood icy. "Talk to me!"

The commander's face was frozen, apathetic, and calculating.

"Jude—"

"We wait," he cut me off. "There is no other option I can see that doesn't end with us right alongside them."

My head swiveled back to my friends, my nails digging into the dirt. I wanted to scream, to slice some throats, to do *something*. But Jude was right, and I despised that even more.

The snarling and hissing ceased.

As did my heartbeat.

Raising his spindly hands to the sky, his steel eyes cast to the overly bright moon, the leader took a step in the direction of my friends. Lined up in a straight row, they quivered beneath the beast's glare. Jake was close to losing his mind entirely, his mouth going slack and beads of sweat coating his forehead. I could see him trembling from the top of the hill.

The leader sauntered over to Patrick, who refused to lower his head. I was proud of him at that moment, knowing full well how terrified I would be if I were in a similar position. But Patrick showed no fear, his stocky frame still and his curly head raised.

I held my breath as the leader placed a gloved hand atop Patrick's head.

I'd burn them all to the ground if—

The leader snarled in what sounded like disgust before releasing him with a shove, moving on. I sighed in relief, but that was short-lived.

The next in line was Jake, who shook violently as the beast clutched his head. I heard distant whimpers, ones I knew emerged from the deepest parts of my new friend. The desire to wrap him in my arms consumed me. Yet, just as he had done with Patrick, the leader freed Jake—though not as venomously—and turned to Alec.

He was just as defiant as Patrick, just as stoic. Alec allowed the beast to touch his forehead and didn't flinch when those lean fingers gripped his blond strands.

While he'd been raised by the ruthless people of the north, Alec didn't possess their hardened hearts. He'd known monsters existed, and gods knew what he'd endured while living among the warriors of the Rine.

And now, his throat bobbed as he met the gaze of one of the most gruesome monsters I'd ever seen. He lifted his head, almost daring the beast to attack, his green eyes narrowed in challenge.

My stomach churned. The leader was pausing, holding onto Alec far longer than the others...

I stopped breathing entirely as another howl escaped the

creature's sharp mouth, his hundreds of overlapping teeth glistening in the moonlight.

No.

I wasn't given a second to react, not as the other beasts howled and shrieked. Not as the leader unhinged his jaw farther and pierced his jagged teeth through Alec's flesh. I didn't move as blood gushed from his neck, a silent cry trapped on his lips.

His green eyes flashed silver as he was torn apart, his muscles and skin shredded like ribbons. Still he never released that scream, didn't give the beast the satisfaction. His clenched fists were the only sign of his agony, his knuckles so white I could see them from where we hid.

Jude's grip was unrelenting as he held me in place. He thought I was going to run down there and try to stop this, but what he didn't know was that I physically couldn't move, even if I wanted to. And gods, how I wanted to.

I wanted Alec to call me his friend. I wanted that time to learn about him and his life, and I wanted him to know that he wasn't alone. Not anymore.

But I would never get the chance now. And he'd never forge his own path.

I was helpless as I witnessed the beast grip Alec's neck, drinking his fill and draining his body. The other masked men grunted and shouted their approval, taking small steps closer to their leader.

Alec was barely hanging on, his handsome face contorting in unimaginable pain. My hands tingled, and I curled them into tight fists, my jaw clenched so hard I feared it would shatter. When the creature released my friend's throat and raised his head toward the moon, a wave of nausea struck me.

The leader, that *thing*, held Alec's vocal cords between his teeth.

Alec's lifeless body tumbled to the dirt, his unseeing eyes

cast to the heavens, to the stars that watched his demise.

I might as well have been the one down there, my throat ripped to pieces, my heart stilled forever. Again, I had failed, and never before had I felt this useless and unworthy. Ice filled me, the cold overwhelming. All I saw was Alec, discarded on the ground like rubbish.

Yelps sounded as the rest of the monsters descended upon the fallen boy, the leader stepping back to allow his brethren to feast on the remains. A horde of them lunged at Alec, their teeth flashing, their steel eyes full of hunger.

I lost track of my friend entirely, his body covered by whirling limbs and glinting teeth. The bile that rose in my throat burned, the heat painful against the icy cold flooding my veins.

Jude and I watched it all. We stayed rooted even as the other recruits were led away, taken back to gods knew where. But we were unable to pull away from the grisly sight of Alec's murder. His *sacrifice*.

I ached in places I didn't know existed.

These *things* were creatures of the Mist. Cursed and far more monstrous than anything I could have imagined. My blood boiled as the last of Alec disappeared into the mouth of a petite female, one of his eyes dangling from the lips of a man missing his nose.

I refused to sit here and watch as the others were eaten and tortured. I'd rather die myself *trying* to save them than simply watch from above—a coward.

Uncle Micah would have told me to run, that saving them was pointless and a waste of time. He was a harsh man who rarely showed kindness, least of all to me. But he'd taught me how to defend myself, all so that I could have a chance to survive this world.

"When a battle seems lost, Kiara, you retreat," he'd told me one day as we'd trained, thick pellets of rain pounding into my skin, my eyes, my hair. Micah had thrust forward, prepared to deliver a blow to my ribs, when I'd shifted at the last second, veering right. "As much as it might pain you, sometimes withdrawing from a fight will help you win the war."

I had growled at him, out of breath and on the verge of collapse. He'd pushed me hard those last couple of months, like he'd been attempting to cram years of training into just a few short weeks. "I'll never retreat," I'd snarled, wind whipping at my hair. "No one can break me." Because that's what retreat felt like — giving up all that I was.

Uncle had stilled, and I'd begrudgingly lowered my fists. "Then you will die a pointless death, Kiara," he'd said, his cold eyes hard and lined with fury and disappointment. "And all of this will mean nothing."

Looking down at the village, where Alec had been shredded to pieces, I thought on that particular memory, a day months before I'd been recruited.

Micah had punished me for my insolence later, and I'd all but crawled home, bruises dotting my arms and legs, aching from the ensuing hits to my body. I'd never claimed he was a compassionate man, my uncle, but I respected him.

He might want me to retreat, but all of Micah's harsh training, all of his brutal lessons, had only strengthened my resolve to never give in.

I met Jude's eyes, and a knowing look passed between us.

"I hope you have a plan, commander," I ground out between my teeth, my wrath flourishing as adrenaline coursed through my veins and swirled about my blackened heart.

Jude's left brow twitched. "I assume you do?"

"We're going to kill them all."

Or die trying.

Chapter Thirty-Nine

Jude

While awaiting your aid, I came across a young woman named Cael. She grasped my arm and said she saw the creatures that stole her neighbors away. She claimed they wore thick cloaks and masks that covered their faces. But she also told me that she caught sight of one of the brutes when his mask slipped. And she said, with certainty, that these things were not human. They were pure evil.

Letter from Randall Thorne of the Guard to unknown recipient, year 49 of the curse

A plan of this magnitude was no simple thing to work out. It required all evening and the following morning to prepare, Kiara and I both finding very little sleep.

Logic once again argued against her, with her plan to save her friends.

I was so close to telling her no, prepared to have her curse my name. I would have taken every slur, every blow, because her hating me would have been better than the alternative; Kiara being killed at the hands of these monsters.

Then I looked into her eyes. Nothing I could say or do would change her mind, and if I prevented her from going after her friends, not only would she hate me, but *I* would hate myself as a result.

In my years under the king's service, I hadn't questioned his cruel demands, knowing that if I did, I would face a fate worse than death. Kiara would have questioned it, though. No matter what Cirian might have demanded from her, she'd stubbornly follow the code of morals I knew to be ingrained in her very spirit.

Besides, if it had been Isiah down there, I wouldn't have even thought about it. Which was why I told her we would strike the next day and try to save the remaining recruits. I didn't need to tell her that the odds weren't in our favor.

The following morning, Kiara woke in my arms, her fists clutching my shirt for dear life. I suspected she knew I was awake, but we remained entangled in one another, relishing these final moments.

I'd spent all my life waking alone, but after three days of having her sleep beside me, her head resting peacefully on my chest while her hair tickled my cheeks, I couldn't imagine waking up any other way. For the moment, I didn't allow myself to think about the future or how this would only be temporary. Just as I had in the glen, I pretended.

Some time passed before I forced my arms to loosen, drawing away from her lush curves. She let out a soft sigh in response, tilting her head my direction. I knew determination would fill her eyes soon enough, but now, only wonder danced across the splashes of gold, her irises alight with hope and a kind of quiet affection I'd never known.

My heart swelled. No one had ever looked at me in such a way, and I wanted to bottle it up and steal it forever.

"You ready?" I asked, my pulse thundering beneath my jacket, right below my and Isiah's pins. We'd gone over the plan five times last night, but I still needed to hear her words.

"As ready as I'll ever be to face a bunch of half-dead beasts with a thousand teeth," she said, sitting up and rising to her feet. She brushed dirt from her trousers, avoiding my eyes.

"Kiara," I growled, not amused by her sarcasm. I closed the distance and grasped her chin between my fingers. "If anything goes wrong, if we can't save them—"

"Nothing will go wrong," she cut me off, placing a gloved finger against my lips. She'd put her gloves back on last night, and I didn't argue; they were her armor. "We've gone over this a hundred times, and I trust you."

I searched her gaze for a lie, an ounce of hesitation. There was none. Just…faith.

A heavy sigh shuddered through me, but before I could overthink things, namely the foreign emotion swirling in my chest, Kiara rose on the tips of her toes and placed a gentle kiss on the twin scars branding the left side of my face. I startled, my heart hammering and fear pulsating through my veins.

If Kiara noticed, she didn't stop. She continued her slow exploring, lightly moving upward to gift me a final kiss above my brow.

"I've grown rather fond of you, commander," she said against my skin. "So don't you dare die." Kiara began to turn, but I grabbed her wrist and flung her around, my lips finding hers as if they were always meant to be there.

Grasping both sides of my face, Kiara met my lips with equal hunger. I tasted all the things she hid from the world, devouring her truths with every inhale. We were different in so many ways, but when we connected, *truly* connected, everything that separated us was just one more thing to find beauty in.

I'd all but forgotten our mission when Kiara finally pulled away, her hands lingering on my cheeks like she loathed letting go.

She shot me a fierce glare that sent fire into my core. I loved this side of her. Watching her morph from the soft girl waking in my arms to the powerful fighter standing before me now certainly didn't help settle my racing pulse.

"Let's go save your friends," I said on a rasp, still enraptured by her.

Kiara brushed my arm as she passed me, adding over her shoulder, "They could be your friends too, Jude. If only you let them."

I didn't reply, but I felt invisible stones shift within me, the walls I'd erected long ago growing weak from Kiara's weapon of hope.

It was only a matter of time before they all crumbled.

The masked men—masked *creatures*—were about to change their scouts.

Every three hours, two beasts were sent to walk the perimeter of the camp. We'd waited until the camp fell into a lull and most slept. Just like this time yesterday, they dispatched half the usual guards, seemingly unafraid of an attack at such a quiet hour.

This was our chance.

Cloaked in my stained tunic and trousers, my back pressed against the trunk of a tree, I readied my blade. My fingers twitched on the handle, the serrated dagger raised to my chest, begging to be used. How many lives had I ended with this dagger alone? It had been crafted by the peoples of the Rine Mountains—Alec's people—the metal they mined supposedly blessed by Maliah, Goddess of Revenge and Redemption herself.

I couldn't make out Kiara anywhere, but I sensed her nearby. She all but dissolved into the night when she slipped away and to her post. Stealthy, lethal, and gorgeous. The most dangerous of combinations.

Leaves crunched in the distance.

The patrol approached.

My breath caught, and my body tensed, going as still as the Lakes of Candor. The twisted side of me enjoyed this part the most; the seconds before the kill, when anticipation heated my blood and sent a thrill of adrenaline down my spine.

A branch snapped loudly, accompanied by an animalistic grunt. The masked men made no attempt to hide themselves— and why would they? They were the apex predators out here... or, at least, I hoped so. My fingers constricted around the handle.

Any second now...

When the breeze shifted, just as the scent of rotten flesh clogged my nostrils, I whirled into action.

The advancing guard never saw me coming.

My blade was pressed to his throat before he could make a sound of alarm, my dagger slicing through the thin, grayish skin of his neck. Blood gushed from his gaping wound, the color an unnatural and inky black as it dripped into the fog swirling about our feet.

The creature gurgled, clutching at his throat, his depthless eyes wide. Before his knees bent and he tumbled to the dirt, a squelching sound came from my left.

Kiara. She must've taken her guard down.

The man I'd slaughtered was dead the instant his decayed face slumped forward, his body accepted into the embrace of the Mist.

It was difficult to remind myself he wasn't a man, not really. I'd seen what they concealed beneath their cloths, and if ever there were monsters, it was them. Wiping my blade on my trousers, my nose wrinkling at the foul stench, I scoured the obscurity for Kiara.

I only had to wait a minute.

"Well, that was fun." She materialized before my eyes, cleaning her dagger on her soiled undershirt, which was now slick with black.

"Your definition of fun worries me," I said, even as my own pulse raced with wicked delight. But that had been the easy part of our plan. It was what followed that would be tricky.

I nodded pointedly to the fallen body at my feet. Knowing the next step was necessary, Kiara grimaced before bending to remove the masked man's garments and face wrappings. I spotted the leg of the guard she'd slain in the distance and did the same, her man not nearly as well-preserved as the one I'd brought down.

The stench grew so rank that my stomach heaved in warning, but I swallowed it down.

It was nearly as bad as the time Cirian had made me torture a man for a week straight, cutting off various body parts until he'd revealed the names of a group of lords planning to stage a coup. He'd been covered in so much vomit and feces and piss by the time I was done with him that he'd smelled like death long before his heart had stopped beating.

It scared me, sometimes, the memories that lived within me.

Shifting the body to the side, I carefully undid his cloak, cringing as dried flakes of flesh clung to my fingertips. In minutes, his clothing was off and his mask had been successfully removed. I began the gruesome work of dressing.

I smelled Kiara before I saw her. A moss-green cloak smelling of decay swathed her small frame, the hem coated in what appeared to be either dirt or blood. I'd only just finished donning my own tattered garments when I noticed the face cloth laying in a tangled heap in the palm of her hands. She hesitated to put it on.

"Let me." I sidled next to her, seizing the vile material. My chest pressed against her back as I slid the cloth over her lips and wrapped it around her nose and forehead. It was thin enough so she could breathe, but her nerves must have gotten the best of her because she sucked frantically at the fabric.

"You'll get used to it. Just try to take slow, even breaths." I tied off the back, knotting it behind her head.

Kiara spun around, only her eyes visible, which reminded me—

"If you get cornered, don't let them see your eyes." She nodded. Among all the gray, her bright amber irises would get her killed. My own peculiar eyes would get *me* killed.

This was it.

I stepped into her space and began securing the hood over her head, hiding all that luminous red. "I've lived with my brother's blood on my hands," I whispered, tucking a loose strand behind her ear. "I won't let you do the same."

Kiara's stare turned fierce, even as she gently placed a gloved hand on my cheek.

"But you need to run if anything goes south," I said, sharpening my tone. "I don't care if we don't get them out. You run, you hear me?"

Begrudgingly, she nodded, but I knew she was lying. Kiara wouldn't run, especially from her friends. Or from me, I realized, my stomach twisting into knots. She let her hand fall, though I could still feel her warmth long after.

Kiara was a ghost as she slipped into the trees. One moment she was beside me—touching me, gazing deeply into my eyes—and the next she was gone, an illusion carried on a breeze. I could've sworn the shadows trailed at her heels like loyal hounds, swallowing up her frame and turning her into the night itself.

I waited one more second before I darted along the tree line, my feet swift and sure. In these moments, during a mission, my brain shut down and an eerie sort of peace drove away the crushing weight of reality. There was only here and now and the end goal.

As always, the end goal would be my blade sliding across a throat.

When I was in position, just on the outskirts of the northern side of the village, I took a deep breath and slipped beyond the safety of the woods, keeping my head down, the hood covering my eyes.

A woman wearing a torn dress that had been ripped to her upper thighs trudged by me, snapping her teeth in the air, snarling at nothing. Perhaps she smelled the freshness of my blood. It would explain how they'd been able to find us in the woods. Thankfully, my clothes reeked of decay, and I hoped it would be enough to conceal the truth. Slowing my pace, I tried to adopt the masked people's walk, their rigid and unnatural movements.

They fed off blood and muscle, and when they'd slaughtered Alec, I noticed how wide their eyes had gone as his warm, fresh blood filled them. They were both alive and dead, creatures poisoned by the cursed lands, desperate to quench their thirst.

And yet, at the same time, they weren't just mindless animals; they fought and moved with skill when they cornered their prey. That made them beyond dangerous.

I reached a tent, the biggest one in the village, eyeing what appeared to be human finger bones tied to the flaps. They clinked in the breeze, sounding almost welcoming. Two guards were positioned before its entrance, unspeaking as they stared off into space. It had to belong to the leader.

Creeping around the back, I noted a torch on the other side. All I had to do was knock it over, start a fire, and cause a distraction while Kiara got the boys out.

But when I grabbed the wooden handle from its stand and lit the tent, I didn't expect a dozen masked men to come barreling toward me at once.

The flame had barely caught when the first one thrust his blade at my chest.

CHAPTER FORTY

KIARA

When Raina fell from the skies forever, the God of the Moon
rejoiced. Raina had once taken away his beloved creations, his
shadow beasts, and he smiled at her ruin, believing, perhaps,
that it was his turn to rule the mortals' hearts.

EXCERPT FROM ASIDIAN LORE: A TALE OF THE GODS

Cracking my knuckles and concentrating on *not*
hyperventilating, I glided into the shadows.

For once, I cursed the luminous moon overhead, feeling
exposed, even in my disguise. Stealing through the thicket, I
made my way to the southwest side of the camp, crouching in
the slim reeds that lined the clearing as I awaited Jude's signal.

With every gust of wind, prickly branches tickled my back
and arms, the forest alive and restless. I felt like I was being
watched, as if the trees retained eyes. For all I knew, they very
well did.

The minutes passed at an unbearably sluggish pace, the men
and women of the village unaware of the two outsiders about to
breach their defenses as they went about their business.

Come on, Jude, I pleaded, my throat constricting. *Where
are you?*

He should have sent the signal minutes ago.

I'd just begun to hyperventilate again when a single shout sounded in the gloom.

It had to be Jude.

Angling my head, I hoisted my body from the frozen ground, peering past the icy blue fog across the clearing. Burning orange light flickered on the northern side, a hairbreadth beyond the edge of the tents.

The signal.

When the first scream was joined by a chorus of shrill cries, I bolted.

The recruits had been brought to an ashen-colored tent in the center of the settlement, a lone scrap of white fabric tied to the flap. Yesterday, Jude and I had noted that there were always a handful of guards posted outside, but we prayed that the fire would be enough to lure them away. I doubted that would be the case.

I sprinted head-on into the village of torn and mismatched linens and dusty bones, lowering my head and avoiding the horde of scrambling bodies. The masked creatures scurried to where Jude had set the fire, spears and other crude weapons in hand.

I wouldn't have much time once they figured out there wasn't an attack, that the fire was a mere distraction. My leg muscles burned as I forged ahead, the white tent less than thirty feet away.

Two of the creatures stood at the tent's entrance, likely debating whether or not they should abandon their post. They growled and whipped their heads to the spreading flames, tentative to make a decision.

As I predicted, they remained in place.

Jude promised he'd meet me once the flames caught, but I didn't have time to waste, and neither did my friends.

I was a vengeful storm as my dagger slid into my grasp, a blur of ash and steel as I lunged upon the first guard, angling my sharpened blade up and through his jaw. His pointed teeth sheared the thin linen around his mouth, the ends glistening in the dim.

I yanked the blade free just as the other guard swiveled to attack.

After years of training with Micah, I expected his ensuing dive, predicted how he would instinctively throw himself upon me, which was why I tumbled to the ground and fell into a graceful roll. I was on my feet again and spinning before he whirled around, a hand reaching for his crude blade.

With a muffled growl, I lifted my dagger, setting my sights on my decaying opponent. I raised my arm, sending the weapon soaring through the air before he blinked.

The blade penetrated his skull, a sickening crack echoing in my ears.

Killing had gotten frighteningly easier the deeper I'd gone into the Mist.

The giant of a man tumbled to his knees and fell flat on his face, driving the blade deeper into his own brain. Panting, I reached into the churning fog and twisted the creature's head, yanking violently on the hilt of my dagger. When it didn't easily release, I ground my boot on his skull, using it as leverage to free my weapon.

Hurry!

Sweat drenched the fabric covering my forehead, the brisk wind sending tingles across my damp skin. I grunted as I tightened my fingers on the blade, determined not to let my friends down.

With a final heave, his skull split open, and my blade finally came free.

Thank the gods. Now on to the boys.

Hurling the tent flap open—my weapon at the ready should there be more guards—I prepared to strike. Instead of more enemies, I saw two bodies huddled on their knees with their hands tied. They shivered at the sight of me, Jake rocking back and forth as I approached him, my blade raised.

"It's just me!" I shouted, lifting my hands as Jake tried to scramble away. My voice came out muffled, but it was recognizable.

His brows furrowed as understanding took hold. "K-Kiara?"

"Yes, you idiot." I sliced through his bindings. "Did you think I'd leave your sorry asses behind?"

"I knew you'd come!" Patrick beamed, the usual light in his eyes dolefully dimmed. "I told him you wouldn't leave us." He glared at Jake, reprimanding him for his doubts.

My heart warmed as I cut Patrick's ropes next. "Of course not, Pat." I ruffled his hair, and he narrowed his eyes.

"We don't have much time, so I need you to keep up and follow me. If you fall behind, I won't be able to come back for you." I knew they were weak, exhausted, and beyond frightened, but they needed to run, and run fast.

They nodded as a unit, Jake still trembling.

"Then let's get the hells out of here!"

Patrick seized my hand as I turned, holding tight when I barreled past the tent's flap and into the wintry darkness. Jake followed at my heels, eager not to become this evening's next meal.

"Hurry!" I shouted over my shoulder, guiding them to the tree line. To safety. To where Jude better be waiting. I'd kill him if he somehow got ambushed. If he was injured or—

I halted my steps, the boys stumbling into my back.

At first I thought it was just the fog playing tricks on my mind, that the shadows before us were trees—

But I'd been wrong.

Taking shape at the tree line—directly where we were headed—were ten or more silhouettes.

And they were barreling directly toward us.

"We are so screwed."

"Not helping, Jake," I snapped, frantically racking my brain for a genius way out of this mess.

"We could throw Jake at them as a distraction. His body will take them longer to consume," Patrick joked, though it sounded half-hearted.

"Shut it, Pat," Jake groused. "Or I might just use that plan on you."

"Children!" I snapped. "Not the time."

The creatures weren't stopping. We had less than a minute before they overran us entirely.

"We can't fight them all!" Patrick was heaving, gulping in air as his hand tightened around mine.

Pulling down my mask, I swiveled around and faced them. "You all need to run north. That's where Jude and I planned to meet should we get separated. We marked a tree with only bone-white leaves on its branches. It's huge, you can't miss it." You *could* miss it, but I needed them to hurry before we all perished.

"You're coming too, right?" Jake hesitated, eyeing me suspiciously.

"Yes! Now, go!" I barked, scaring them into submission.

"What are we waiting for, then?" Patrick yanked on my hand. Jake began scrambling north, along the path free of the masked creatures.

I tugged my arm away, shoving Patrick behind me. "Listen. If you don't want to die, then you'll run. I'll hold them off and follow. I promise."

"No! I can't leave—"

"If you don't leave now, then *I* will die trying to defend you!" It was harsh, but it was true.

I would probably *still* die, but I could buy the boys some time. "Go!" I screeched, shoving at his chest hard enough to knock the air from his lungs. A flicker of ire and some unnamed emotion shone across Patrick's irises.

"I'm not going to leave your side." He stood his ground, staring at me as if I were his whole world. "I need you, Ki. Don't you understand what you've become to me?"

I ground my teeth. His gaze was fierce and filled with emotion, and I had a nagging suspicion he was insinuating that he cared for me in a way I could never return.

"If you don't go right this instant, I'll never forgive you, you hear me? Even if we do manage to make it out alive, I'll still resent you for putting me at risk."

The hurt morphed into a tangible alarm, his feet shifting indecisively.

"Go, Patrick! *Please*. I can't lose anyone else."

Gods. I envisioned my brother before me now rather than Patrick, begging me not to leave him. Maybe I'd put that burden on Patrick by comparing him to Liam, but regardless, I couldn't watch as these creatures killed him.

The muscles in his jaw tensed. "Fine. But you better stay alive." He started to back away, glaring at me to further his point; that he hated every step he took to safety but knew I'd accept nothing else.

Twisting on his heel, he darted after Jake, glancing over his shoulder once before vanishing around the tents. That last, lingering look nearly sent me to my knees. I wasn't sure what to do with myself now that I had others relying on me. *Caring* for me.

I heaved a sigh of relief. At least he would be safe. I'd make sure of that.

"Come on, now," I taunted into the dim, shoving down thoughts of Jude, Patrick, and Jake. They couldn't help me now.

"Let's see you try to take a bite out of me!"

A chorus of growls and shrieks rang in my ears, the noise like a siren call of death. Uncle Micah hovered like a phantom in my head, his presence always with me, much like the moon above my head.

"Retreat, Kiara," he'd say in that no-nonsense way of his. *"Know when you can't win."*

I likely *couldn't* win. But the ten creatures hurtling toward me at once were too near, and I'd already made my stand.

This was it. I peered to the sky one last time, praying not to the lost goddess, but to my grandmother, asking her to forgive me for failing. For dying.

I supposed I'd see her soon enough.

Chapter Forty-One

Jude

*I heard you blinded our son. Next time you dare touch him,
perhaps it is you who shall lose an eye.*

**Letter from unknown sender to Jack Maddox,
year 37 of the curse**

A few of the bastards got away and alerted the others.
Swarms of masked creatures fell around me like an
ominous shroud. I had my sword ready, but it wouldn't be
enough, not with the fifteen or so monsters all eager to tear out
my throat and make a meal out of me.

I swore, twisting out of the way at the last second before a
blade sank into my gut. I was already covered in small cuts and
scrapes, having brought down five of them. Now I'd be lucky
if I didn't lose my other eye before they eventually ended me.

Something shifted from my right, and I spun, thrusting my
blade between a pair of ribs. Yanking on the hilt, I twisted to my
left, slicing my weapon cleanly across a throat.

Two down. Thirteen to go.

As one, they inched forward, ridding me of any hope of
escape. If they all lunged at once—

A scream filled the air, and the hair on the back of my neck rose. *Kiara.* She let out another shout, sending a dose of white-hot rage into my blood. If they hurt her…

I jabbed forward the second I noticed the air ripple in my blinded eye, taking out a monster who thought he could sneak up on me from behind. Flesh squelched as I turned the blade and gutted him until he exhaled his final, wheezing breath.

Kiara shrieked again, and this time, more than my chest warmed; my entire body became a living and breathing beacon of wrath, every inch of my flesh prickling with ire.

I sliced the throat of another faceless enemy. He went down without a fight.

I couldn't stay here, not when she was likely bleeding out or…shit, I could barely think of her dying. The mere thought fanned the flames within until all I could hold onto was the carnage of the battle. The only thing that had ever made sense.

I couldn't think straight, could hardly move; there was only her face in the night, *her* eyes glowing with affection. I refused to let that die, that warmth that I knew was meant just for me.

Call it selfish—and perhaps it was—but I couldn't allow that to happen, because if I lost her, there was no chance I'd ever recover. Kiara was my tether to the world, a beautiful, fearless, disastrous reminder of what could be possible.

I screamed, though it didn't sound like me.

Then I exploded.

The noise that came bubbling up my throat was guttural and primal. Every inch of me buzzed and a white light pulsated, blinding me to all else.

It could've been seconds or hours, but when it eventually dimmed, so did the intense warmth flooding my veins.

I hadn't realized my eyes had shut until I opened them.

Bodies surrounded me. Men writhed in agony as burnt orange and red flames licked at their clothes, their skin, their cold eyes. I stumbled back, my own body overheated, exhausted, and full of adrenaline.

What just happened? Or more importantly, *what* had saved me? It didn't feel evil, that source of light, seeing as it had left me unscathed.

Dazed, I fumbled a step toward the sound of Kiara's cries, my body aching everywhere, that blasted heat burning my throat with every breath. I fought, thinking of her once more, shoving aside flailing bodies alight with fire.

Rounding a cluster of tents, I saw her...in the arms of the enemy.

I took a step, about to unleash the monster I was, when something hard and jagged struck my skull. Black spots clouded my sight, but I never tore my eyes away from her, not even as I heard footsteps behind me and the *whoosh* of a blade being freed from a sheath.

Kiara screamed a final time, right before my lids shuttered closed.

I awaited the cold edge of the blade, but it never came. Instead, I heard a voice, though I couldn't place it with how my reality bled into nightmarish chaos.

"Shit. He *is* the other one," the voice said, cursing softly.

I heard footsteps pound the earth, and then darkness swallowed me up.

Chapter Forty-Two

Kiara

She is too wild and too untamed. I fear that after the attack,
there is not much I can do for her. She is touched by so much
darkness, and I do not have faith in the prophecy you sun
priests whisper about. Truth be told, she's likely a lost cause.
As is our world.

Letter from Micah to unknown recipient,
year 46 of the curse

The first creature lunged, the frayed cloth around his face
exposing his jagged rows of teeth.

I dove to the left, eliciting a snarl from the beast, the noise
feral. He leaped for me again, and when he was close enough,
I leaned back and shoved out my leg, sending him tumbling to
the dirt with a hiss.

There wasn't time to focus on him, not when another one of
the bastards came at me from the right, a serrated blade in hand.
He swiped at my neck and face, missing my cheek by a mere
inch. Another swing and miss, and I used the opening to thrust
my shoulder into his chest, aiming to knock him off-balance.
Unfortunately, my size was not enough to take the behemoth
down.

I reared back as his blade swooshed by my left eye this time, his aim improving. For a bloodthirsty creature who might or might not be dead, he moved with vexing ease. Cursing, I dropped to the ground and rolled out of the way. I was on my feet and twisting to strike when a searing twinge shot across my arm. He'd nicked me.

Without looking, I knew the wound wasn't too deep, but it still hurt like a bitch.

He might have gotten in a good blow, but now he had well and truly pissed me off. Feigning left, I turned at the last second and swung, wedging my dagger through his bulky coat and puncturing his ribs. A howl escaped his mouth as he fell.

I'd just yanked my blade free as another attack came at me from behind.

I felt the pain before I even saw him take a step, the white-hot stinging stealing my breath as a blade lodged in the muscle of my shoulder. I screamed as I jerked it free, blood drenching my black tunic. I'd never been stabbed before, and I could now officially say I wasn't keen on reliving the experience.

Something foreign began to wake, something I'd long ago buried on the outskirts of the Pastoria Forest. My chest tingled as I charged the nimble beast, my limbs coursing with icy adrenaline.

Leaping into the air, my dagger positioned above my head, I brought down the blade with a growl, piercing the creature's skull. My skin crawled and prickled, the air in my lungs charged with that familiar spark, and a coldness crept down my body, sentient wisps of black dancing at my feet for the second time in my life.

The first time happened mere days ago when I'd been cornered and on the cusp of having my throat sliced clean open. The darkness that had always thrived inside of me had rushed to the surface and reacted. The shadows had saved my life.

Then, I'd lied to Jude, too afraid of exposing the truth.

I knew exactly what had happened when the masked creatures burst into ash.

I had happened.

Arms of midnight, reaching for me, holding me down to feast. Jagged teeth attached to a face devoid of eyes, only black pits in their place. And then it—the creature that had attacked me—clawed at my tiny hands, which were covering my face and throat protectively.

I'll never forget the pain. How the shadow beast had dug its talons into my skin. While I'd been a child, weak and hardly able to defend myself, I managed to fight, to hold on and withstand the shrieking monster's blows.

That's when the light had come.

Gold had radiated from my chest, shooting out like a flare, causing the creature to shrink away in alarm and scurry into the trees with a hiss. The light had dimmed when footsteps approached, my father having heard my screams from the village. He'd taken one look at me and slunk back, his mouth agape, fear creasing his brow.

The damage had already been done, my hands torn and shredded. The marks of the shadow beast forever on my skin.

Ten years, and I'd never forget Father's face.

I jolted back to the present when the next beast attacked, my limbs acting of their own accord, driven by some foreign instinct. I whirled around, my red hair whipping in the breeze as I sliced open the creature's throat. Its blood spilled before I had the chance to exhale.

Onyx clouds encircled me as I moved, the darkness spilling free.

As much as I despised what I'd become, *who* I was, the shadows I'd suppressed would be my salvation, and I tore off my gloves with a fierce growl.

Only monsters could defeat monsters.

I shook out my arm, readying for the next foe. The tingling sensations sliding up my arms and around my torso didn't dissipate, and the shadows at my feet never wavered. A sigh shuddered through me, relief loosening my muscles.

While he'd seen my scars and hadn't run, for Jude to know that *I* had controlled the shadows that had turned our enemies to dust was too much. It would be the final barrier crashing down, and if he didn't like what he saw, if he didn't like *me*, then I wasn't sure my heart could take it.

Now, as my unholy power slithered and writhed within me, I didn't have Jude or the others to hold me back. They wouldn't bear witness to the evil that I was.

I felt free.

So I unleashed every ounce of the darkness I'd bottled up, images of that fateful day ten years ago flooding into my mind.

Narrowing my eyes to size up the nearest enemy, I noted how sluggishly the remaining creatures were moving. As though wading through molasses, they inched closer, silent screams ripping through their gaping mouths. Either time had slowed, or I had become faster.

I felt different from the last time I used my powers in the Mist, when my chaotic emotions ruled. Then, my powers had snuck up on me, bursting forth without my control.

This time, I welcomed them.

Accepted them as a part of me.

I snarled, my faithful shadows rising to graze my fingertips.

Rushing toward a creature on my right, I sliced cleanly through the decayed skin of his throat, slaughtering him like the one before. He was still falling, his hands clutching at the gaping wound, when I chose my next victim, delivering an identical blow. All the while, a frigid breeze seemed to carry my feet forward, into the fight, and to the creatures threatening those I loved.

Sweat seeped through every pore as I killed and slew without mercy. Less than five seconds later, I'd brought three more down, my dagger dripping with the blood of the felled.

There was nothing but black and noiseless screams, my limbs relentless as I gracefully moved between bodies like I was exchanging dance partners.

Two left.

Gods, the cold. It caused my teeth to chatter and my knees to tremble, but I was too damn close to stop and give in to the agony and crumble.

Propelled on that frozen wind of vengeance, I swept the legs out from under the second-to-last beast. As he began to fall, his lethargic eyes widening, I pierced his chest and kicked out my leg, driving him into the ground. The creature's body plowed through the soil and earth, the force of my supernatural kick, aided by a wave of shadows, burying him in the bloodstained dirt.

So much power…and all at once.

The sensation of such brute strength surged, the coldness inside my chest nearly unbearable at this point. It was beginning to ache, to sting. With a yelp, I clutched at my pounding heart, my entire body drenched in the blood of my enemies.

I realized with sheer terror that time had started to speed up again, to resume its natural pace.

Whatever power had taken hold of me was waning.

I tumbled to my knees as my vision blurred, black dots

dancing before my eyes. I couldn't retain the force of it any longer, and my human body was shattering beneath the pressure.

A figure approached, the final creature but feet away… And yet, I couldn't move. I was too weak, too drained by a wicked magic I'd never dared to practice.

Micah had made sure of that.

"Don't give in to its perverse whispers, child," he'd told me after he arrived in our village, days following the attack in the forest. Mother and Father had merely exchanged worried glances while Grandmother had clutched at her throat, her scarred thumb rubbing anxious circles. I'd never met the man before, but Mother claimed he was her older brother and here to help me. "Don't resort to the dark when you could hold the very sun in your hands."

He'd been wrong. The darkness was the only reason I'd made it this far, allowing my friends time to flee. Giving Jude a chance to escape…and to find the key to ending the curse once and for all.

The creature's scuffed boots filled my vision. They were as black as a moonless sky, human bones decorating the sides. My hands fisted the dirt as I peered up beneath my lashes, greeting the face of my demise. When my eyes met the steel ones of the masked leader, the one who'd devoured Alec right in front of me, I flinched.

Of course I'd have to face him.

My shoulders slumped as the creature let out a chilling cackle, the sound penetrating my pores, digging its way through flesh and bone. A skeletal hand snatched my tunic, yanking me from the ground, holding my body in midair as I went limp. A pathetic squeal escaped before I could swallow it down.

All of his teeth were on display, no cloth in sight. This close, I could spot flecks of dried blood tipping the pointed ends—the remains of my fallen brother.

I struggled to free myself from his viselike grip, my legs kicking feebly in the air. But I was grievously weakened, no match against the leader's abnormal strength.

I held his lifeless eyes, refusing to bend, just as Alec had refused to cower before he'd met his end. My defiance seemed to excite the beast, who unhinged his jaw, his sharpened teeth inches away from my skin. Lowering his hooded head, he let out one final howl at the moon, right before he sank his teeth deep into my throat.

I might have screamed—I probably did—but all I could hear was the blood rushing into my ears, my pounding heartbeat hammering in my skull.

Taking his time, enjoying himself, the leader drank from me, warmth spreading down my neck and staining the dried earth. My world spun as I lifted to the expanse of black, my eyes consuming the soothing glow of the moon. The final thing I would ever see.

Just as my eyes fluttered shut, as my body began to lose all sensation of life, the familiar rush of frozen wind whooshed past my ears.

I was falling.

Plummeting into swirls of black.

I clawed at the air as I sought purchase, for anything to hold me to this world. My body collided painfully with the earth, my bones groaning as my full weight landed on my arm.

The leader whirled toward me, my blood trickling from his gaping mouth. He started to cough and sputter, his stomach hurling up the blood he'd stolen from me.

A violent convulsion shook the creature's mighty frame, his chest spasming as he let out an agonizing screech.

Claws of smoke curled around his form, winding up and around until they gripped his throat, choking off his scream. Vein-like lines of onyx—much like my own scars—started to spread, first climbing from his chest to his neck, then snaking around the column of his throat to his ears, his cheeks, and across the uneven bridge of his nose.

The leader flailed as the ink spread, steam rising from the fresh wounds and filling the air with the pungent stench of rot. I should have gotten up and run, but I was rendered immobile by the scene playing out before me. And the strangest part of it all? I didn't feel fear, not like I should.

What slithered into my blood and set my heart pounding was akin to *delight*.

"Kiara!"

My name sounded from far away.

"Kiara! I'm coming!" The voice floated to my ears like a long-forgotten memory.

Muscled forearms enveloped me in an earthy aroma, constricting around my body as they lifted me up. Greedily, I breathed it in, relishing the calm that overtook me. The familiarity. I knew that scent. That voice.

"I'm here, Kiara," he rasped into my hair. A quiver racked the body holding me. "I'm sorry I was late."

There was wetness on my cheeks, but I could barely feel it. I must have been crying. I might be hallucinating, but I welcomed the lie.

My eyes returned to the silhouette of the leader, now a motionless heap on the ground.

With the adrenaline leaving me, and reality returning in a sickening rush, the rage I'd felt turned to numbness. I wanted the monsters to die for what they'd done to Isiah and Alec, but what I'd done in return only made me feel empty and hollow.

What did I just lose of myself?

Another tear fell, its heat at odds with the coldness of my cheek. It slowly glided down to my chin, and I sucked in my first true breath of air since giving myself over to a darker nature.

Maybe Cila's villagers had been right; I was a monster.

Yet the moment the droplet—the evidence of my shame and regret—hit the ground, a single spark of silver ignited and bloomed where the masked man's heart should have been, and then a searing light of marigold yellow and burnt orange detonated. I squeezed my eyes shut as the arms around me tightened.

Wind raged against my raw skin, a rush of energy blasting across the clearing. It was so very different from the coldness of my shadows, and yet it felt just as familiar.

When the winds settled and the blinding light dimmed ever so slightly, I peeled open a heavy eye, a faint gasp leaving my lips at the sight before me.

The night was aflame.

As was the leader of the masked creatures.

The last thing I saw before the serene darkness took me was the creature burning as the world exploded in passionate gold.

CHAPTER FORTY-THREE

JUDE

I will not come for our son. He is exactly where he is meant to be. Trust me in this, and do not write me again.

Letter from unknown sender to Jack Maddox,
year 38 of the curse

I came back to consciousness and stumbled into the clearing where I'd heard Kiara scream. It was no surprise that I was too late.

Charred bodies filled the field, the smell causing me to lift a hand to my nose, sputtering coughs escaping my parted fingers.

Everywhere I looked, lifeless heaps sizzled and burned, a few still snarling helplessly. Maybe the otherworldly entity that had helped me earlier had also aided Kiara.

As I thought of her, I spotted movement just ahead, a head of red hair shining in the moon's light. But she wasn't alone—my girl was currently being whisked away by a hooded man taller than any human I'd ever seen.

I might not have been able to see clearly, but that hardly mattered. I jumped into action, staggering across the field and after the hooded man carrying her in his arms. The ring around the moon shifted once more, the blue morphing to a pale yellow, but it provided enough light to see, and I shot through the bone-white trees after her.

All I could think about was that man taking her somewhere and hurting her. He wasn't a recruit, and he certainly didn't move like one of the masked creatures.

I faltered as I made my way through the prickly brush, my head pounding. I was certain there'd be a bump the size of a grapefruit, and judging by the stickiness coating my cheek, whoever had attacked me had broken skin.

Cursing the spineless prick who'd knocked me out, I sprinted, Kiara's safety propelling my exhausted limbs. I could sleep later, once I knew she was safe. Safe with *me*.

The massive tree with only white and silver leaves was coming up fast. Any second now, I'd be at our meeting spot, and if she wasn't there, I'd burn the world down and—

I jerked to a stop, not believing what was right before me.

Underneath the sanctuary of the tree lay Kiara, wrapped in clean blankets, her face impossibly free of cuts and bruises. Patrick and Jake hovered over her, the former lovingly tucking her hair back from her face. Her eyes were closed.

Panic swelled in my chest, and a fire raged. Every inch of me trembled, each step bringing me closer to learning if she lived or died. I didn't think I so much as breathed.

"Kiara," I finally called out, ignoring the startled faces of Patrick and Jake. I shoved them aside, scooping her small body into my arms. The boys already knew I didn't treat Kiara like the rest of them; they understood that something had occurred between us. Which was why when I brought my brow to rest against hers, no one spoke a word. Jake even moved back, allowing me more room.

"What happened?" I ground out between my teeth once I felt her steady pulse. It was slow but strong.

"She… She told us to go," Jake supplied from beside me. "I

thought she was right on our heels, but when I turned back, I was alone." He cursed and ran his hand through his hair. "I'm such a coward. I should've made sure she followed."

"We left her." Patrick's voice carried the shame I hoped he felt deep in his bones.

Jake was right; they were cowards for abandoning her. If she had died, I feared what I would've done to them as a result.

A throat cleared, bringing me back from my murderous thoughts. "What, uh, what happened to you?" Jake asked.

I didn't need to look at his face to know he referred to the warm blood slicking my brow, my cheek. My temples throbbed, an unbearable headache sending stabbing pain across my eyes, but it wasn't anything I couldn't handle.

"Someone attacked me," I replied, my calloused fingers brushing against Kiara's smooth cheeks. I drew back enough to stare at her perfection. She was everything I wasn't, and I almost felt bad for holding her in my stained hands.

Patrick cursed. "One of the monsters?" he asked, his voice quaking. His entire body gave a violent shudder.

I shook my head, finally deigning to look their way. "I don't think so," I said. "I heard a voice right after, but I can't remember what they said." I scrunched my brow, trying to recall those few words, but they slipped out of reach. I probably had a concussion.

"I'm glad you're all right." Jake patted my arm, but when I shot him a glare, he quickly retracted his hand. "Fine, no touching," he muttered under his breath.

"We all got lucky. And we're lucky to have you," Patrick added, dipping his chin to me in a sign of respect. I noted how stiff his movements were.

"No, you're lucky she's all right," I snarled, and both boys flinched. Good. They seemed to have forgotten who stood before them.

"I failed another friend. I was so terrified that when she told me to run, I just...did," Jake whispered, glancing to his muddied boots. After what had happened to Nic, he should have known better, but being angry at the lad wouldn't change anything.

"Who brought her here?" I asked. My fingers dug into the blankets swathing Kiara.

"We didn't see him," Patrick said. "We were waiting here for you both, when there was a flash of blue light, and then, she just was...*there*. Not a cut or scrape in sight." He motioned to the girl I held, and a soft whimper left her lips. She tossed her head to the side, but then she settled against my chest, as if seeking me out, even in her sleep. Something dangerous tugged at my heart.

"It doesn't make sense," Jake mused, saying what I, too, thought. "If it wasn't one of us, then who saved her? I know the king sent out three different groups, so maybe..."

Maybe it had been another Knight? But that didn't make sense either. They'd all entered the Mist in different locations.

"If it had been a Knight, then he wouldn't have fled, and it doesn't explain the light you claim to have seen."

"So...yay mysterious savior?" Jake shrugged, a brow arching. I refrained from rolling my eyes.

"Either way, she's alive," Patrick cut in, his attention focused only on Kiara. The intensity that swirled in the depths of his eyes had me tightening my grip. He lifted his gaze to me then, his expression quickly shifting to anger. "You say you were attacked, but you're the Hand of Death. I find it hard to believe you were taken off guard like that." Suspicion crept into his voice, which had turned cutting.

He didn't trust *me*.

I wanted to ask why *he* had left if he cared so much about her safety, but I refrained, holding onto my temper by a thread. Patrick continued, seeming to read my thoughts anyway. "You failed her, same as us, so maybe wipe that look off your face. You're no better."

I'd never heard him speak above a whisper. Around Kiara, he always appeared levelheaded, albeit shy. Though he was fiercely protective of her, just as she was of him.

"Patrick," Jake warned, shifting to his friend. "It's none of our faults. Lay off."

But he didn't.

"No." Patrick shot to his feet, pointing an accusatory finger my way. "He only cares about the mission. Finding the keys." He motioned to Kiara again. "She will always come second to him, don't you see?"

Jake had the decency to lower his head, but he didn't utter a reply.

"We aren't naive, commander." Patrick shook his head in disgust. "We all saw how the two of you interacted, and while we might have teased her occasionally, we were good enough friends to not interfere."

His chest puffed out, his fists curling at his sides, and I blinked at the muscles I'd never noticed before.

"I won't hold my tongue anymore, not if you hurt her and make promises you can't keep. She matters to me, Maddox. More than you could ever know."

I almost dropped Kiara in my lap. His words cut through me, striking the intended target in my chest.

"You'll never be good enough," Patrick murmured right before slipping back, aiming for the other side of the clearing, presumably to cool down. He faced the trees, hands shoved deep into his pockets, giving me his back—and his dismissal.

Silence fell, and only the soft breaths escaping Kiara's parted lips could be heard.

"He doesn't mean that," Jake whispered sometime later. I'd lost myself in the rise and fall of her chest. "Patrick cares about her a lot, and he's protective."

There was no doubt that what Patrick felt for her went

beyond friendship, and I didn't blame him, not when I…

No. I couldn't think like that. If I got her out of here alive, maybe I'd allow myself to indulge in such thoughts, but not now. Patrick had been right—I'd failed her when I'd lowered my walls.

My oath to the Knights. Hadn't I thought about the very same things only a day ago?

Back in Sciona, Kiara and I could never be…*us*.

Just as I placed her back on the earth, her eyes opened.

"J-Jude?" she rasped, her voice hoarse. She gazed at me as if I were her savior, not the only reason she was here in the Mist and nearly dead.

"Ki!" Jake was beside her in an instant, his shoulder bumping mine. I bit back my growl.

"Jake? You made it." She gave a soft smile, hope a dazzling shade of gold in her eyes.

"I'm right here, Ki," Jake said. "Shhh. It's all right now. You're safe."

Patrick abandoned his sulking and raced over, nearly shoving me aside to get to her. He gripped her hand. I noticed how her jaw clenched at the contact.

"W-what happened?" Her brows knit in thought. "The last thing I remember is the leader falling and…dying." I knew she held something back by the way her gaze hesitantly slid to mine.

"You, ummm… Someone brought you here. To us," Patrick said.

"Jude?" she croaked, giving me her full attention. "I felt arms. They felt safe."

She thought I'd saved her. More disgust and shame filled me.

Jake shook his head. "No, not Jude, Ki. Someone else."

"Who was it, then?" Her head swiveled among us. "I can't remember a face, everything's so fuzzy right now."

"Well, that's the thing," her friend began, his blue eyes piercing the gloom. "We're not entirely sure who it was. There was a flash of a man and then you were simply *here*."

She started to try and sit up when I reacted. "Kiara." I lightly placed my hand on her shoulder. "You need to lie down for a bit. Rest."

She smiled at me, and my world shattered.

I couldn't handle that look—I didn't deserve it. Bolting to my feet, I backed up, away from her, away from Jake and Patrick. Confusion marred her features.

"Where are you going?" she called out, straining her neck. "Jude!"

But I didn't respond. I needed to center myself and put distance between us before I got us all killed.

She continued to call my name, and every time, my heart fractured that much more.

I couldn't think clearly when she was around, and that weakened me, putting her at risk. And I would never let her down again. Even if my chest tightened painfully at the thought, it was for her own good, and whether or not it cleaved me in two, I would keep my distance until we got out of this cursed place.

I realized I'd do anything for her, even if it meant hurting myself in the meantime.

Chapter Forty-Four

Kiara

The Gods grow powerful with the prayers of mortals. Every wish and token bestowed on them grants them strength, and perhaps that was why Raina had been one of the mightiest deities ever known. It could be argued that the other gods had grown jealous, and some even celebrated her fall.

Excerpt from Asidian Lore: A Tale of the Gods

Before my weak heart could ache at Jude's absence, Patrick shoved into my line of sight, his green eyes creased with concern. And a tinge of something else.

"I'm here, Ki," he cooed, wiping the sweat from my brow and smoothing the hair back from my face. "I won't leave you. Ever again."

My skin burned where his hand caressed. Whereas Jude's touch soothed, Patrick's scalded.

"Water. Please."

Patrick nodded at my feeble request. Diving into his jacket, he retrieved his canteen and cradled the back of my head as he brought the spout to my lips. "Drink," he whispered, his lips grazing my ear.

The water seared my throat as it went down, but I thanked

him afterward, licking at my chapped lips. "Why were you all arguing?" I thought I'd heard raised voices as I came to. Accusations of some sort. Jake eased to my other side, my two friends sandwiching me between them. It was Jake who answered my question.

"Patrick was just concerned for you, that's all." He glanced at Pat, who stared off, anywhere but at me. "We're all just overwhelmed."

"I shouldn't have said all those things to him," Patrick muttered, mainly to himself. "But what I regret more is leaving you. I abandoned you, and I was a coward."

I bolted upright, a throbbing ache pulsating down my limbs. I vividly remembered taking off my gloves, and yet cool leather swathed my hands and fingers, causing me to doubt my own memory. Tingles radiated from each fingertip, and while the details of the fight remained shrouded, I could practically feel the viscous, black blood that had covered me. I shuddered. There was a limit to what someone could handle, and focusing on the wickedness living inside me was not at the top of my list.

"Don't you dare say that, Pat," I snapped, my hand reaching out to grasp his chin. I held his stare as I said, "I couldn't have lived with myself if I didn't get you *both*" — I shot a look at Jake — "to safety. It would have haunted me for the rest of my days."

And it was true. Somewhere along the way, these boys had become my brothers. And I fought for my family. Patrick gave a somber nod, not entirely believing my impassioned words.

A part of me wondered what they'd think if they knew the monster I was.

My hands twitched at my side as I contemplated taking off my gloves and exposing my secrets once and for all. Instead of being brave, I curled them into fists.

I glanced to the trees, to where Jude vanished. He'd be back;

he had to. We had yet to make it to the *X*, after all. Still, his absence stung.

As if reading my thoughts, Jake said, "Someone attacked him, Ki. That's why Jude was late, and why he didn't help you. I think he couldn't stomach letting you down, and that's why he left to cool off." He jerked his chin toward the trees, his deep-golden skin a shade paler.

I softened instantly. *See*, I told myself, *he didn't leave you. He never would.*

Focusing on Patrick, I asked, "I still don't understand who dropped me off here?" Those arms, that familiar voice—

"Like we said, it was a flash, a trick of the dark, and then… then you were simply here, nestled in a fresh blanket and cleaned up. Not a drop of blood in sight." Patrick scrubbed a dirty hand across his face, clearly just as lost as I felt.

My hand flew to where the monster had bitten me, stunned when I was met with only smooth skin. No puncture wounds. Nothing.

"We didn't understand it either," Patrick added. "Can't say I'm not grateful, though." His eyes flickered to my throat, and he let loose a relieved sigh. For a moment I tensed, wondering how he seemed to know where the creature had attacked me, but when I recalled he'd been present for Alec's execution, I relaxed. The monster had gone straight for Alec's throat.

While the major injuries had magically healed, my muscles ached and throbbed, my bones groaning with each breath. Then again, from the flickers of memory I retained, I'd been…

I'd been a living and breathing nightmare, so I supposed that had to take a toll on the body. Needing to do something with my hands, I took another sip from the canteen, ash still coating my tongue.

"Get some rest. After you're better, we'll head to the *X*. The sooner the better." Patrick ran a heated finger down my cheek, and I involuntarily flinched.

His green eyes sharpened at the movement, and he opened his mouth but promptly shut it; whatever he wanted to say could obviously wait.

"We'll be right here if you need us, Ki," Jake promised, bestowing me with a tender smile brimming with adoration. Love. "And I promise I won't take off into a sprint at the first sign of danger this time."

I shook my head and gave him my best attempt at a smile, but he was right, I *was* tired. What good would I be to them if I could barely lift my head?

Unconsciousness claimed me a minute later, sleep's pull too strong for me to resist. And just as I let go of the real world, about to greet the realm of dreams, an ethereal face flickered before my shut eyes. Though it didn't belong to Jude or Grandmother.

I saw the face of the man I'd known most of my life—

The face of the man who'd saved me.

Copper.

I smelled copper. Metal.

Blood.

My eyes snapped open.

"Jake, Patrick, get over here!" I shouted, jumping to my feet. The world wobbled precariously as a blurred image clouded my thoughts. Something I couldn't seem to hold onto tightly enough before it floated away.

I shook my head. With the promise of that foul wind and the horrors it could inflict on us, I couldn't focus on whose face I might or might not have seen. I'd survived this far, and the battle wouldn't pause for me to gain my footing.

My friends were at my side in an instant, hands on their daggers and eyes alert for danger. "Do not panic, but I think the wind that brought the hallucinations is back," I hissed, reaching for my own blade.

Ha. As if *not* panicking was at all possible.

Jake's blue eyes turned dark. His best friend had killed himself as a result of that venomous breeze, and no doubt the memory of it hovered at the forefront of his thoughts.

"Last time, you snapped us out of it, Ki." Patrick grabbed my other hand, positioning himself in front of me. His eyes retained an unfamiliar edge to them, but his touch was gentle. "We just need to ride it out. You seem to be immune."

"We stay by her side," Jake agreed, his voice raw with emotion. "We'll surround Ki and hold on to one another."

Internally I swore. The last time I'd saved them my gloves had been off, and...

They didn't remember. Only Jude had been cognizant enough to recall the wounds painting my hands. But if my touch had been the reason I'd saved them—

My scars. I'd been touched by a shadow beast, a creature of the night. Maybe my tainted skin had been the reason I could withstand the Mist's influence.

"What's wrong?" Jake asked, panic causing his voice to waver. "Ki?"

I sucked in a deep breath, noting the scent of copper growing closer, becoming more powerful. There were two choices, and neither of them ended well for me.

"I'm going to remove my gloves, and when I do, I don't want to hear any questions." I eyed them both. Jake opened his mouth, but I narrowed my gaze into slits. "No questions. I just need... I need you to trust me."

And not be afraid of me and run for the damned hills.

It was a risk, showing them, exposing myself, but I couldn't allow my doubts to play a role in their demise. If they hurt themselves like Nic had, I'd never recover. Screw what Uncle Micah had said, telling me to hide no matter the consequences. He wasn't here, and he sure as shit wasn't going to save us.

I was.

The *monster* was.

I didn't look at them as I peeled the leather from my fingers, the cool air kissing my bare flesh. The black scars shimmered beneath the moon, the traces of blue glimmering like fallen stars. Patrick gasped. Jake hissed. I ceased to breathe.

"Ki..." Patrick murmured, and I could feel his eyes burning into my skin. There was fear in his voice, genuine fear. But there was no time for that.

I lifted my head at the same time as I grabbed them, forcing my fingers through theirs. Jake flinched, but to his credit, he didn't jerk away. Patrick gritted his teeth, eyeing where we touched, a thousand and one emotions swirling across his irises. I blinked back tears as I beheld the disgust in his stare. Disgust that had never crossed Jude's face.

I cursed the commander for storming off. If anything happened to him while under the Mist's influence, I'd... Well, I didn't know what I'd do anymore. What horrors I was *capable* of when it came to him. All I could do now was hope he'd wandered far enough away from the path of the poisonous winds.

"Just hold on and let it pass," I whispered, staring at my boots, willing to bare myself but not willing to hold their eyes. I added a quiet, "Trust me."

Gods, I prayed they would listen. They could recoil in disgust later, once that coppery breeze left.

It was chillingly silent as our breaths filled the void of sound, the overpowering scent riding the winds. I could taste the blood on the tip of my tongue.

"Is it working?" Patrick asked with a quivering breath.

"Well, you aren't trying to kill me this time," Jake muttered. "So that's an improvement already." My chest squeezed when Jake tightened his grip on me, even if his palms were slick with sweat.

Freak. Monster. Witch.

I'd been called all three and much more. Even though I wore my gloves after the attack, the so-called "accident," the townspeople of Cila all knew the truth, and no one wanted to be friends with someone who'd literally been touched by a creature of evil.

"You know I'm gonna ask later, Ki, but for now, I sure as shit am not letting go." Jake nudged into my side, his signature teasing acting as a balm.

"I—" Patrick paused, and I dared a peek at him. He tried to mask his fear, but I saw it all the same. My first friend. Afraid of me.

"It's all right," I said to him, faking a smile. "They're atrocious."

The winds shifted east, and the metallic taste lessened a fraction.

Patrick shook his head. "It's not that, it's just a shock, that's all. I've heard rumors and read accounts, but those touched by the shadow beasts never lived long enough to tell the tale. I thought it was some quirk, the gloves. We all have our armor." Patrick shrugged his shoulders. "I just thought the gloves were yours."

They *were* my armor. Just not in the way he'd imagined them to be.

"Again, I'm just…confused." He lingered on my hands once more, swallowing thickly. "Though please know that this changes nothing. I know what lies within your heart is pure and golden, and a few scars can't change that."

Thankfully Jake switched topics. "Anyone seen our brooding commander?"

"We all saw him leave," Patrick said. "But even as pissed as he was, he should've stayed. We need him." I'd never heard Patrick speak so sternly. I swore the temperature dropped ten degrees.

"What *exactly* did you tell him?" I asked, still clutching both their hands. The danger hadn't left us yet.

He sighed. "You and him are close. One day, and maybe one day soon, he's going to hurt you, and I can't stand to watch that happen. We all know who he belongs to."

I didn't like that one bit, that word "belong." Jude shouldn't belong to anyone but himself.

Or me, I thought selfishly.

Still, his absence worried me. If he were out there alone, gods knew what he faced, especially if the hallucinations began. Maybe we'd have a miraculous stroke of luck and Jude would be spared.

I prepared to open my mouth and scream his name, hoping it would reach him beyond the trees, when a flare ignited the night.

And it wasn't fire.

Chapter Forty-Five

Jude

There is a boy I wish to acquire. They say he has mismatched
eyes and scars slanting across one cheek. Find out where he
will be a week from today. My spies have told me he holds
immense value. I plan on seeing what he is capable of.

Letter from King Cirian to Lieutenant Harlow,
year 36 of the curse

I'd walked farther out than I should have.

The camp was at least half a mile away, and Kiara and my
recruits were alone, sitting ducks waiting for an attack. I forced
myself to stop and turn, aiming back the way I'd come.

Always protect your brothers.

It was the first rule in our code. I'd already done a good job
at screwing up every other decree in our sacred book, which was
why I started to pick up my pace and enter into a sprint.

Somewhere in the distance, I made out the telltale sound of
hoofbeats pounding the earth.

Slowing to a halt, I eased into a crouch behind a dense patch
of reeds. Lifting my dagger, I waited, the horse's steady gallop
growing louder.

Leaves rustled at my back, and I spun—

Coming face-to-face with Kiara's mare. Starlight.

I dropped my arm and sheathed my blade, letting loose a relieved breath, although her presence should have been impossible, considering the last time I'd seen her.

Starlight nickered as she trotted over, her belly free of the arrow's puncture wound, her coat silken and smooth as if she'd never been injured at all. Disbelieving, I froze, my pulse racing as I looked at her, *truly* looked, for the first time.

Something tugged at my thoughts, like a long-lost memory shoved into a dark, locked box. The mare stood before me, as still as a statue…suddenly reminding me of the marble fountain back at the palace. The one depicting Thea, Raina's legendary mare.

Neither of us moved; neither breathed. It was like the creature waited for me to make the first move. So I did, approaching her slowly, fearful of her racing away should I make a sudden movement.

The horse just narrowed her eyes, the recognition in them appearing far too human. My fingers trembled slightly as I ran them through her thick black mane, which looked much healthier than before. Gods, everything about her seemed healthier and more youthful.

Starlight lowered her head and nuzzled my cheek without hesitation, her hot breath coming out in impatient puffs.

"Where did you come from, girl? And how the hells are you still alive?" I asked, drawing away to inspect her. In place of an answer, she merely tossed her head to her still saddled back. The invitation was clear enough.

"I won't say no to a ride."

I grabbed the pommel and slipped my foot through the stirrup before hoisting myself into the saddle. I'd find the others quicker this way, and—

Light flared behind my eyes. It was so crushingly bright that

I fell across the mare's back, gripping her mane tightly. A shout rent the night. Probably mine.

For seconds, or maybe even minutes, I drowned in that light, barely holding onto the horse as I struggled for air. It was everywhere all at once, and I wasn't afforded a single coherent thought.

Rather, I was gifted images.

They raced across my mind, most too quick to grasp, but a few I snatched, tucking them away.

The sun, bright in the sky, the world cast in a golden glow.

Two lovers on a mountainside, professing their love.

Them meeting at midnight. A blade glinting beneath the moon.

Orbs of light dancing into the heavens, followed by a scream of heartbreak.

The otherworldly light rippled around me as I clutched Starlight, its radiance dissipating and allowing me to suck in a shaking inhale. Soon, the shadows of the world crept up and engulfed the remaining rays, and the now-familiar fog rose.

I sat up in the saddle, my pulse racing.

I didn't know how to describe what had just occurred, but I knew it wasn't some hallucination. Whatever I'd seen had been a gift given to me by the gods themselves; a warning.

And if what those images had shown me was real—as I knew it was—then I had to warn Kiara. Now.

CHAPTER FORTY-SIX

KIARA

I do not fear death. I fear what I leave behind. There is
so much Kiara doesn't yet know. I should tell her, explain
what she is, but I want her to live just a little while longer in
ignorant bliss. The moment she uncovers the truth, her life will
end...and I fear it is all my doing.

LETTER FROM AURORA ADAIR TO UNKNOWN RECIPIENT,
YEAR 48 OF THE CURSE

Another curse fell from my lips. Jude needed to be here,
with me, where I could protect him from himself.

"Don't even think about breaking contact, Ki. Jude will find
us soon," Jake asserted, tugging on my hand. His voice was firm
and resolute, his vibrant blue eyes swimming with determination.
Nic's death had been a warning—one he would heed.

The metal in the air clogged my nostrils, the scent sweeping
across the campsite. If the boys noticed, they didn't point it out.
It appeared my tainted touch worked.

I steadied my body and shut down my mind, relying on
Uncle Micah's training.

Uncle Micah.

I swayed on my feet, the missing piece of my memory

rushing to the surface. The man who'd rescued me. Those safe, *familiar* arms. Micah's weathered face hovering above my own like a dream. When the scent of copper had woken me, his face had been a blur, a hallucination I refused to accept was real. But now there was no denying the clarity of his features as they played out across my mind.

Maybe the wind affected me after all. It was impossible that Micah was here, in the Mist.

A snarl ripped the air, and thoughts of Micah vanished like dust.

I slowly turned my head. "Shit," I hissed, following up that swear word with a few more colorful ones. My knees, which were already trembling, almost gave out entirely.

Nic.

Or at least a version of him, hovered before us in the clearing.

His skin, which had been pale before, was now the same color as the masked creatures'. The gaping wound on his neck — where he'd brought his own blade across his throat — had turned black and rotten, and as he stepped closer, I noted that his movements were rigid and ungainly. Nothing like those of the nimble warrior I'd gotten to know.

"N-Nic?" Jake sobbed. His friend's name was all he could manage. I tightened my grip on his hand in warning. No one knew quite how to react.

The creature wearing Nic's face snarled again, low and deep in his throat. It was inhuman, wrong. By this time, I was sure my fingers were bruising Jake's hand as I kept him in place.

"Look at his clothing," Patrick said sadly. Indeed, pieces of shredded linen clung to his tall frame; the remnants of the cloths Jude and Isiah had buried him in. Further proof that the boy we all knew was gone.

"It's not him, Jake," I whispered, even though I suspected he wasn't listening. He was too focused on Nic, on his oldest and most loyal friend. His brother.

Tears fell from Jake's eyes, who was no longer able to contain his grief. He started to pull on my hand, desperately trying to break free and run across the small clearing.

"Jake, no!" I snapped, forcing bite into my tone. The copper in the air was almost gone, but I worried about the lingering effects. Then again, the creature might attack, and holding hands wouldn't save us from his teeth.

"Let go of me!" Jake thundered, and Patrick tightened his own grip as our friend thrashed. Jake's golden cheeks were slicked with wetness, his eyes full of hope. "It's you. It's really you." He kicked out at me, lost to his delirium. "I knew you'd find me again. You always did."

My heart broke, shattered, and fell into the white clouds at our feet like broken glass.

"That isn't him," I repeated, but it didn't matter. Jake managed to break free from me and Patrick, and he was bolting across the ground toward the undead Nic before I could reach out.

The creature smiled, his teeth yellowed, the gaps crusted with what looked like blood. Nic turned his glassy eyes to me.

Before Jake could throw his arms around him, Nic thrust his hand out, sending him flying through the air and onto his back. Only the top of Jake's head remained visible. He didn't move from where he lay, likely stunned beyond all belief.

Nic ambled my way, much like a predator. The sides of his mouth curled up further, revealing sharp, pointed canines. Red coated them.

"Ki," Patrick warned, still grasping me.

"Pat, I see it." *It*, not him. I had to keep reminding myself of that fact. His body wasn't old enough to have decayed to the same extent as those of the other masked men, but there wasn't a question that he wasn't alive.

My blade was in my hand and flying through the air in the span of a blink.

Nic shifted at the last second, the tip of my dagger missing him by less than an inch.

"Shit." Patrick finally released me, stepping back. "We need to get out of here."

Jake hadn't moved from where he'd been tossed, but I felt his hurt from across the distance. I'd become so attuned to my friends that his heartache felt like my own. And in a way, it was. When Nic had died, I'd finally permitted myself to love Patrick and Jake. I'd realized how quickly life could be stolen.

I reached for Patrick and yanked him to me, snatching his blade from his sheath before he could protest. I knew he had an extra blade at his ankle should he need to protect himself, and I'd not lose one more second. Neither would Jake. Patrick. Jude.

We'd live to see another day.

I'd raised the weapon high into the air, preparing to lunge at Nic, to kill him for the second time, when a flicker of recognition sharpened his eyes.

Against my will, I paused…

And that pause was my damnation. As quickly as it had appeared, that spark in his eyes vanished, and Nic dove, his teeth elongating into fine points aimed directly at me. At my throat.

There wasn't time to shift out of the way.

We toppled to the ground, Nic's body like a brick wall as he landed on top of me. He snapped his teeth, his jaw unhinging, and his jagged fingernails dug painfully into my skin.

"Nic!" Jake screamed from somewhere in the distance. "Fight this!"

He still held out hope that his friend was trapped somewhere in that shell of a body.

I couldn't blame him; I'd probably feel the same way.

Sometimes in order not to break, we saw only what we wanted. What we *needed*.

Patrick yelled and cursed, trying his best to pull Nic off me, but it was no use. Pat's dagger was pinned at my side, along with my arms. Still I bucked and kicked, but Nic lowered his head, undeterred, as he aimed for my throat.

Jake continued to call out to the monster atop me, though I barely registered much of anything, and my shadows were too stunned to make an appearance.

One moment of hesitation will get you killed. Micah's old warning repeated in my head. Of course his voice would be the last one I ever heard.

Nic reared back and brought his teeth to my neck, the pointed canines poised above my artery—

He jerked, just as black blood oozed from his right eye. It dripped onto my face as he slumped forward, a choked noise bubbling from his throat.

I blinked, stunned to see the pointed end of a blade peeking through an eye that was once a warm shade of honey. Patrick appeared and shoved Nic to the side, off me, just as a final rush of air left his undead body.

Jake stood above me, his hands bloodied and dripping wet with that rotten black. He lifted his gaze from his unmoving friend and met my eyes. The light blue in them darkened, and his shoulders drooped before his knees gave out beneath him.

"Jake," I whispered, unable to feel anything at all. He'd… *killed* for me. Chosen me.

I managed to crawl to him, to wrap my arms around his neck. He didn't embrace me as I clutched him, my gloveless fingers digging into his back. My chest shook as I let loose sobs of my own, tears streaming down my face, overwhelmed by both grief and love.

Jake's tears melded with my own, pattering to the ground

like rain. He didn't hold me back, but he leaned into my chest and rested his head atop my hair.

I felt Patrick's presence looming above, but he didn't touch us or provide comfort of his own. Maybe he stayed back, allowing us time for ourselves. When Jake pulled away first, his gaze was just as clouded as before, but he took my face between his hands.

"Family," he said. One word. But a word that spoke thousands more.

Hesitantly, I lifted my scarred hands to his face. This time, he didn't flinch at the sight of them. He leaned *into* my touch.

"Family," I echoed, wishing I could swallow his heartache for my own, that I could take away the torment that would surely follow him for the rest of his days.

Until then, I'd fight for him, just as he had for me.

When I looked around us, searching for Patrick, wanting to tell him how much he'd come to mean to me as well, I saw nothing but shadows and white trees.

Jake cursed, swiping at his eyes. He, too, scanned the woods.

Patrick was gone.

CHAPTER FORTY-SEVEN

JUDE

The mortal who deceived Raina disappeared the night he
betrayed her. There are no records of him, his name wiped
entirely from record. Some say he was handsome, others say
he was grotesque and fearsome. The only commonality the
rumors share is the color of his eyes.

CAMILLE ASHTON, ASIDIAN HISTORIAN,
YEAR 40 OF THE CURSE

They weren't at the camp, not where I'd left them when I'd
stormed off into the woods. I dropped from Starlight's back
to inspect the chaos of footprints. There had been a scuffle of
some sort. A fight.

I was too late.

Someone could've hurt her, and at the thought, heat swept
through my blood, and my skin burned with fury.

Starlight grew agitated behind me, her hooves pounding the
dirt, her head swaying back and forth as if to tell me to hurry. As
if I already didn't suspect that the worst was yet to come.

Mounting the anxious mare, I eyed the faint tracks, all
leading north. The footprints were spaced far apart, which
meant they'd been in a rush, possibly running from an enemy.

It also meant I had no time to waste.

I nudged Starlight forward with the heels of my boots, taking off into the night. I could have sworn the trees shone as I passed, the blue and silver leaves shifting colors, turning into a muted green. Even the fog seemed to part for me. I was burning from the inside out and too lost in my own head to care.

I had to get to her. I had to get to Kiara before the man who'd fooled us all finished the job he'd started decades ago.

Chapter Forty-Eight

Kiara

Our old friend died today, and my heart is broken. Perhaps Juniper's death has weakened my resolve for our sacred mission, but I implore you to seek another way. Her final words to me were, "Look to Fortuna." I'm not sure what the city of gambling and sin has to do with this, but as one of the Elder Knights, you have access where I do not.

Letter from Aurora Adair to unknown recipient, year 46 of the curse

Jake and I had taken off into the woods.

We screamed Patrick's name while racing through the underbrush, sharp reeds and fallen branches tearing into our clothes. Bleeding and out of breath, we pressed on, cupping our hands to our lips and calling out to our friend.

No one answered.

A wave of clammy cold washed over my face, and a band of sweat soon formed around my brow like a crown.

Jake, as though sensing my unease, slid his bloodied hand into mine. I had forgotten to put my gloves back on, but he didn't hesitate. And he hadn't hesitated when he'd driven that blade into his friend's skull. I squeezed him back.

At least now we knew how the masked creatures came to be; they were raised from the dead. All of those who perished in the cursed lands became monsters.

I shivered, thinking of Isiah. I didn't think I'd have the heart to tell Jude.

With Patrick's life on the line, Jake and I ran through the trees, shoving aside the swinging ivory branches reaching out like claws. We ran until our chests heaved and our exhales were nothing but wheezing pants.

So much had been lost already, and we couldn't lose Patrick. Whatever had taken him hadn't left a trail of blood, so he might still be alive. Again, my hope refused to be killed.

"Ki." Jake pulled me to a halt. "We're running in circles."

"We know where Jude planned to go." To the mysterious *X*. "Maybe Patrick knew to flee that direction." Or he'd been taken by a monster and was lying in a pool of his own blood.

My fingertips buzzed, and ice skittered down my spine. My very own monster yearned to be let free, yet something held it back.

"We should find Jude first," Jake rasped, out of breath. "Together we can look for Pat. Jude's been here before and survived, and he has that map the king gave him."

Jude might have stormed off into the woods to clear his head, but I suspected he would've returned. He might be a Knight first and foremost, and dedicated to the mission, but deep down, I knew he wouldn't just *leave*.

"What do we do, Ki?" Both of Jake's hands clasped my arms, his head angled as he questioned my tear-lined eyes.

What *do* we do?

"Ki?" Jake pushed, shaking me.

I heaved a sigh. I might not want this—to make this *call*— but I was being forced to.

"Maddox would return to where we camped first, and if he discovered we weren't there, he'd head to the *X*." I tried to put myself in his shoes, thinking of what he would do upon finding us gone. "He would hope we'd have the brains to meet him should we be separated."

And Patrick... He was alone out here. He'd hardly been able to defend himself back at the sanctum. Deep down, I suspected he'd been acting oddly as of late, and he had slowly begun to stare at me as if I held more importance for him than a mere friend. Had I unknowingly pushed him away as a result? Was he hurt, angry with me for how I felt for the commander?

I wanted to crumble, to fall to the earth and shed a million tears—tears that currently prickled my eyes with every blink, begging to be freed. My first friend, the one I'd promised I would always protect.

I couldn't breathe.

"Then we need to hurry." Jake let go of me, and something akin to determination lifted his shoulders. I wanted to tell him I was so damned sorry he'd had to kill his friend. Even if it hadn't been *Nic* anymore, it had still borne his face. But I couldn't do that. We had to move.

The night tilted and blurred, those blasted tears pushing to be released. But not one more drop fell.

"Let's go then," I ground out, my tone full of steel. "We march ahead."

To the *X*—

And all the other unknowns that could easily wreck me.

We'd been walking for an hour.

Jake didn't ask for a break, and I didn't stop to allow us one. From what I remembered of the map, we had to follow the brightest star. We'd been close already, so I speculated we would arrive within the next half hour.

Jake remained by my side, his long legs keeping pace. The moon shone down on his russet skin, morbid shadows skimming his lower lids.

The farther we walked, the less dense the blue-tinged fog became. That was something to be thankful for—we could finally see where we were headed. Not that I believed for one second that the Mist's influence had been diminished. Uncle always said that danger liked to hide in plain sight.

It was twenty or so minutes later, when we'd both passed the point of exhaustion, that the ground softened.

The gleaming silver in the leaves grew less apparent, and a subtle green tinge painted the bark. I couldn't help but twist my head and take in the jade hue, which was so unlike anything I'd seen outside that magical glen Jude and I had stumbled across.

But the world was changing, color slowly seeping into the chasm of white and dull blue. Jake plucked a leaf, holding it to his eye for inspection. He muttered a low curse.

It couldn't be much farther.

I brought my hand out behind me. "Wait," I murmured, shutting my eyes and giving over to my instincts. There was a... buzzing sound. Whatever it was, it beckoned, calling out into the gloom and seeking me like a tender memory.

Jake went stock-still. "What do you hear—"

The trees shook, so violently and forcefully that the fragile leaves attached to the branches flitted down to the forest floor. The ground rocked beneath my boots, and I braced myself, hands on either side of me for balance, my knife clutched securely.

Jake hissed as ivory roots erupted from the soil, rising into the misty air and slithering out to reach us. Grabbing hold of him, I spun us around, preparing to bolt in the opposite direction.

We weren't afforded the chance.

More vines and roots and branches came to life, weaving

through the brittle underbrush, some knitting together, creating an unyielding wall. Or a cage.

I shrank in on myself, my hands aching, ice numbing everything but innate fear. The forest fought to trap us, our growing cage making escape all but impossible as it rose into the air, the intricate braiding solid and impenetrable.

Hisses saturated the air, and Jake and I swiveled around, searching for their source.

Hazy silhouettes materialized from the other side of the gloom, behind the wooden cage. They floated, humanoid in appearance, though their faces were blank, featureless. Only pale, white-blue light emanated from them, from where their eyes should have been.

Jake lifted his dagger as if that would do much of anything. He pressed his back against mine, his sweat seeping into my shirt. We were well and truly screwed.

The floating creatures merely rested where they were, their too-long arms drifting at their sides, their soft blue gowns whipping at their bare feet in a supernatural breeze I didn't feel.

Against my will, dark shadows coiled at my fingers like extensions of myself. I could feel the kiss of the air they touched, could scent the divinity around us.

This wasn't *only* the Mist playing tricks.

"Kiara." My name seemed to come from all directions. It was deep and familiar, and I knew instantly who spoke.

The man who had rescued me.

"Come out and show yourself," I growled, my fear sinking, replaced by my shadows and the adrenaline they gifted.

A bone-chilling chuckle rattled the leaves, and then, "Always so impatient."

Jake, likely too stunned to speak, merely snatched my free hand.

"I thought I was imagining it, you know," I began with false calm. "But you were real. Your arms. Your voice. What I couldn't understand is *how*. How you were here."

The spectral forms wavered in and out of focus, their blue and white lights sputtering. Another silhouette appeared, this one shrouded in black, though it did little to mask his sheer size. He stood not ten feet away, a cape billowing behind him.

Micah always did have a flair for the dramatic.

"I never tried to hide myself from you," he said, stepping closer. The moon highlighted his weathered and wise face, the graying beard, the steel eyes brightened with sapphire blue. "You simply never asked the right questions."

"You *know* him?" Jake hissed. His body trembled.

"I thought I did," I whispered back, not sure whether I wanted to fall to my knees or bolt for the cage and tear it to pieces. "That's who rescued me." Right after the masked leader had drunk from me, choking on my tainted blood like poison.

I thought I'd made it all up—or maybe I didn't want to remember. My life already felt like a lie, and Micah had been a constant, however merciless he'd been growing up. Nevertheless, here he stood—or *hovered*.

"Everything I've done has been to help you, Kiara. *Everything*." He growled the word, a line forming between his brows. "Whether you believe it or not, I crafted you into the warrior you are today. You've always been special, but after you were attacked in the woods, after you became...what you are...I had to intervene."

My upper lip threatened to curl back. "Who are you, really?" I asked. He definitely wasn't my uncle. That was a damned fact.

Micah sighed. "Aurora. She...prayed for my help, and I answered."

My brows scrunched. "Aurora? What does my grandmother have to do with all of this?" I waved my hand around the Mist, to the figures cloaked in blue light. They had yet to move. "Why pretend to be my uncle? Why train me to fight?"

Now my eyes prickled and burned. I wasn't sure if I could keep my promise to myself to hold back my tears. The years of lies were a betrayal that pierced too deep.

"Aurora gave her life to a cause, a vital one." Micah cocked his head, assessing me in that typical, calculated way of his. I knew him so well, and yet, I didn't know him at all. "She'd suspected what resided inside of you ever since you were born, and after you survived the shadow beast's attack, it was confirmed."

He wanted me to ask. To beg and plead for scraps of information. I didn't.

"So stubborn," Micah chided after some moments had passed. "I suppose I always did like that best about you." He waved a hand, and the shining figures and their light scattered.

I stepped up to the cage, every nerve electrified.

"Did you do this?" I asked, searching the twining wood for a weak spot. There was none.

He raised a shoulder. "Only so I could warn you without you trying to kill me. Or hurting yourself as you *failed* to kill me."

"Who are you?" I asked again, my teeth nearly bared. "Tell me. No more lies, *Uncle*." Gods, I was sick of them.

He didn't pause for long.

"Aurora Adair was a sun priestess."

My heart thundered in my ears as he spoke.

"She devoted her life to Raina at a young age, but years after the goddess's disappearance, Aurora chose love and family instead of prayer." Micah scoffed. "That was until *you* were born on the longest night of the year, shaking the earth as you emerged from your mother's womb. When Aurora held you, when you placed your tiny hand in hers, she claimed your touch branded her."

Grandmother's scar on her thumb. She'd always refused to tell me how she'd gotten it.

"I don't understand." Truer words had never been spoken.

"You burned her with a divine heat. A power that could only belong to one goddess," Micah explained. "She knew then what you possessed. A little bit of Raina's magic. She kept it to herself until the attack in the woods, fear prompting her to journey to my temple a week later, begging for help.

"The second I saw the mark from above, I fell, materializing before her. While Raina and I may not have gotten along well in the past, I was one of the only gods Aurora could ask, and one of the few who might deign to help. So she implored me for aid, and I gave it to her." He rubbed at his bearded chin, his brow crinkling as if in confusion. "I believe you humans may say my actions were borne of guilt."

My knees wobbled. I was going to fall. Pass out. Throw up.

If my grandmother went to *him* for help, then that meant...

Shit. Uncle Micah was more than a mere liar. He was a *god*.

"Why act as if you were family? Why the charade?" Out of all the secrets, that's the one that tugged at my heart. I should've asked a thousand other questions.

Jake touched my back, and I flinched. I'd forgotten he was there.

"I made the mistake of giving in to my jealousy fifty years ago. It was I who gave her lover the Godslayer blade that would split Raina's magic, and I've regretted my actions every moment since."

Something akin to shame—if a god could feel shame—clouded his glacial eyes. "I decided I would train you, personally, and make sure you were ready for the battle ahead."

His gaze flicked to my exposed hands. "I didn't want you to know about the darkness within you," he said, reading my thoughts. "If you gave in and used your unnatural powers, I feared it would overtake you, as it eventually does all shadow beasts. But you were made for bigger things, and I had to make sure you remained pure, and that you survived long enough to meet him." Jake's fingers dug painfully into my shoulder as we awaited Micah's next words.

"Who is *him*?" Jake asked, his voice a quivering whisper.

Micah smiled, a sad smile that felt more grim than hopeful. "You've already met the man who was born to hold all three pieces of Raina's power and take his place in the heavens."

He glanced over his shoulder. "He'll be here shortly, though I fear I cannot intervene any more than I have. I've done more than I should have as it is, and the rest, I will leave to you. It's going to be a long fight, and you have powerful enemies who want nothing more than to stop you from succeeding."

His form began to glimmer and shudder, but before he faded into the Mist, he spoke.

"My true name is Arlo, God of Earth and Soil, and you, Kiara Frey, born on the longest night of the year, contain one of three pieces of the lost Sun Goddess."

My shadows furled at my fingers, slipping past the cage and reaching for a man who claimed to be a *god*.

Arlo dipped his chin. "*You* are one of the keys."

CHAPTER FORTY-NINE

JUDE

There isn't much known about Raina's mortal life. It is said that she married and had a child, but none have been officially recorded. She did well to hide her identity and that of her descendants. Although, one historian claims Raina had a daughter, her hair the color of midnight and her eyes the deepest honey.

EXCERPT FROM ASIDIAN LORE: A TALE OF THE GODS

The horse seemed to have a decent idea where she was going. Or rather, she sure as shit didn't let me lead her.

Starlight galloped through the dense fog, not once stumbling or slowing. She was an arrow in the night, her deep-chocolate coat warm against all the cold white trees we passed, her strong limbs a blur.

"Slow down," I yelled, yanking on her reins, hardly able to keep upright in the saddle. But she didn't listen. If anything, she increased her pace, whinnying at me as if in warning.

I swore, gripping tightly to the pommel, my body bouncing wildly as we flew. Ten minutes passed before the stubborn mare reduced her speed to a trot, and I squinted into the gloom, expecting masked men or monsters or some unknown enemy to jump out at me and end my life.

Nothing leaped out and grabbed me, and I heard only the wind whistling through the trees. But then—

A voice. One I'd know anywhere.

I pushed into Starlight's sides, urging her forward to where that sharp, strong voice rose with frightening resolve.

Kiara.

It was her, and she was speaking, which meant she was alive, which meant…

The mare halted. When she wouldn't move another inch, I dismounted, wasting no time in sprinting to Kiara. When the clouds dispersed, and I could see more than ten feet in front of me, I snatched my dagger.

Roots and branches and other parts of the forest had grown high, tangling together to form a cage. Trapped within were Kiara and Jake, their mouths open and eyes wide.

"Where did he go?" Jake yelled, head swiveling around the enclosure.

"Who?" I asked, only looking at Kiara, making sure she was unharmed and whole. A growl left me when I noticed the dried blood on her face, and I grabbed the damned wooden bars with my bare hands, trying to yank apart the vines and branches.

She simply stared ahead, lost in thought, her usually sharp features soft and uncertain. What had happened here? Gods, she didn't even look at me.

I grunted with the effort, but eventually, I managed to tear a decent hole in the cage. Reaching inside, I seized her hand. I'd never seen doubt mar her so terribly.

"Kiara," I whispered, gently taking her scarred hand in mine. The blue hue of her hands, which had once been masked by the inky black, seemed to shimmer as our fingers entwined. Coldness seeped into my skin where she held me, but I pulled her to the opening I'd made.

"Please come out." We could talk about why she was in a wooden cage in a moment, but right then, I had the overwhelming need to hold her. Even briefly. I would have to let go, I knew, but seeing her so small and frightened did something strange to my heart. It thumped against my ribs, painful and feral, like a cornered animal.

Kiara allowed me to help her through the gap, and Jake followed after, his blue eyes dark and full of panic. I didn't give a damn if Jake saw me wrap my arms around her and tug her close. Not that he appeared at all surprised.

"Can someone please explain to me what happened?" I asked, studying the enclosure. Jake's gaze shifted to Kiara, who proceeded to glance down between our bodies. I had yet to release her. "Look at me," I commanded, lifting her chin.

Kiara swallowed hard enough for me to track the movement. When her bright, nearly yellow eyes found mine, they were brimming with a different kind of grief.

"My uncle," she whispered, so low I hardly heard her. "Or *not* my uncle, I mean. He was here."

"Your uncle?"

Kiara nodded, shaking me off. My arms fell to my sides, itching to return to where they belonged. I held back as she paced.

"He was never my uncle," she snapped. "And my grandmother, she lied to me my entire life."

Kiara's face became a contorted mess of emotion. "Everything I have ever known has been a cruel lie." She lifted her injured hands, laughing mockingly. "I'm a fucking *key*, Jude." I took a cautious step, but she hissed in warning. "He said he was Arlo, God of Earth and Soil. A *god*."

She gave me her back and resumed her pacing.

Jake's eyes darted between us, looking just as confused as I felt. But then he lingered on me as if examining me for the first time.

"I'm one of the three keys," Kiara repeated, stilling in place before spinning around. "He—*Arlo*—said I was, that I have a piece of Raina in my soul, and that my grandmother was a damned sun priestess. Like one of the old sun priestesses devoted to Raina before the curse." She laughed at the last part as though *that* were the most absurd thing she'd said.

"I'm a monster with a piece of a god," she cackled, lifting up her hands, twisting them for us to see.

A monster? I had no clue what she meant. And if she was one of the keys, then why were we sent here? Cirian's map burned a hole in my pocket. If I wasn't mistaken, we should be at, or near, the marked *X*.

"Kiara, we will figure this out." I damned the consequences and took a brazen step. "We just need a moment to talk—"

"You don't get it," she whispered. "I was attacked by a *shadow beast*. That's how I got my damned scars. And I don't know how that affects any of this. If it taints the magic I apparently possess. Magic that doesn't even belong to me."

I froze. Her scars… A shadow beast had attacked her. How she even managed to survive in the first place was a miracle.

I squared my shoulders. It didn't matter what happened ten years ago. What mattered was keeping her safe now.

Lightning struck nearby, the force of it causing my knees to wobble.

Another bolt hit in the same spot, about fifty feet east. Jake sidled to her, his arms hovering protectively before her. I didn't think he was aware of how he safeguarded Kiara with his own body.

"What now?" I groaned, not in the mood for more games. I needed a second to process what Kiara had revealed. Her uncle was a god? Her grandmother some old sun priestess? And the part about her being a key? There was more to the story.

And I'd *finally* learned the secret behind her scars.

I'd been gone all of a couple hours and all hells had broken loose.

"Ki!"

Her name was called from afar, the familiar voice causing the hair on my arms to raise. I grabbed my dagger and patted my thigh, assuring myself my second blade was securely strapped in place.

Patrick called for her again, and before I could reach for her to stop her from making a huge mistake, she bolted. Shadows trailed after, cloaking her from sight, wisps of blue glittering like gems in the chaos of onyx.

Kiara didn't stop as I continued to scream her name, trying to tell her the truth about her friend. As fast as I was, she ran faster, carried by whatever supernatural magic she'd summoned. Who knew what she could do, touched by the dark power of a shadow beast? *And* with a key inside her...

I hurtled forward, slowing when I reached a wide clearing bursting with soft lilac and blue Midnight Blooms.

Patrick stood in the very center, his arms outstretched in welcome, a smile on his boyish face. Kiara ran to him, returning his smile, his name on her lips. She flung her arms around his neck, squeezing him tight.

I started to run again, shouting at her to get back, away from Patrick, but it didn't matter.

Patrick reached into his jacket and plunged a dagger into her chest.

Chapter Fifty

Kiara

A man visited our temple. He was young, handsome, and undeniably arrogant. He asked me if a woman possessing brilliant red hair had ever visited us. I lied, of course, but I have a feeling he will be back. There was something lurking behind those pale-green eyes of his. I hesitate to use the word "evil", but it is the only word I can use to describe what I felt.

Found in the diary of Juniper Marchant, Sun Priestess, year 30 of the curse

"P-Patrick?"

My voice wasn't my own. It was a rasp of a thing, a choked hiss. Pain radiated from my chest, searing stabs of blistering lightning. I couldn't take in a breath, and blackness swept across my eyes, muting an already dark world.

"Oh, *Ki*," Patrick said, his voice not sounding the same. It was severe and biting. *Cruel.* "I've been waiting for this moment for a very long time."

He twisted the knife, and I gasped.

"W-why—" I staggered back, peering between our bodies to the dagger currently embedded in my chest, inches below my heart. My eyes went back to him.

Patrick...smiled.

"All this time I thought *you* were the only one I needed, but really, I needed him too. The *true* descendant of the Sun Goddess." He scoffed, the sound bitter. "For decades, I followed that insipid sun priestess, a favorite of Raina's, around the realm. Apparently, it was your precious Aurora who aided my dearest love when she fell. When she became a worthless human."

Patrick swallowed thickly, briefly squeezing his eyes as if in regret. "If she had simply *waited* before fleeing, I would have made sure she stayed immortal, ruling at my side. But instead, she chose not to trust me, chose to think the worst before I even had time to explain."

The blade was yanked from my chest and in his hand before I could register the pain. Blood bubbled up in my throat, and I sputtered, spitting red on the ground. Behind me, I heard Jude shouting, anguish tainting his voice.

But all I could focus on was the boy in front of me.

Who wasn't really a boy at all.

"Y-you're the mortal man she fell in love with." It wasn't a question. Patrick was the man who'd cut her to pieces. Who'd cursed us all to darkness.

The flickers of sorrow vanished from his features. "Yes, Raina did love me. But it wasn't enough. For either of us. She was content with me always being below her, never her equal. It ruined us."

There was no trace of the person I'd gotten to know all these weeks. The friend who'd *protected* me. Taken me under his wing. The boy who'd taught me how to open myself up and allow another in. I'd fallen for his lies without much of a fight, all because he'd reminded me of Liam. Maybe that had been his plan the entire time.

Raina's traitorous lover. He'd impaled her with a blade

gifted to him by Arlo in the hopes of stealing her magic for himself. He could argue he did it for love all he wanted, but his words would ring hollow.

Love was acceptance, and Patrick had never accepted Raina for what she was. No, he coveted her, turning her into the object of his envy.

A wave of dizziness had me swaying, and Patrick watched with an emotionless expression as I tumbled to the ground, gasping for air.

Gods, I felt cold, and it wasn't the kind of cold that came when I used my shadows. No—this was the coldness of death.

"Step away from her!" Jude snarled from behind me. I felt hands grasp me, moving up and down my arms, inspecting my wound.

I couldn't feel much of anything other than his warmth. Wherever he touched, heat singed my skin, chasing away that persistent chill. Why was he so warm? It hurt, his touch, even as I welcomed it.

"Jude," I whispered, blood filling my mouth, making it hard to speak. Peering through my lashes, I found his stare on Patrick, his mismatched eyes changing, shifting into something new. He inhaled sharply, his rage causing his body to tremble, and when he opened his eyes once more, they were molten. *Literally* filled with glowing fire and scorching wrath.

I blinked at the impending darkness, Jude and his fiery eyes coming in and out of focus. I'd lose consciousness soon, and then…

Then I would well and truly die.

Before my lids closed, I noticed Jude give a subtle jerk of his head. It would have gone unnoticed by anyone else, but I'd become too aware of him, of his every move and every breath.

Steps pounded like muted drums, and then Jake spoke, his tone dripping acid. "You were supposed to be my friend," he seethed. I couldn't see him, but I felt his temper swell. "Why betray us?"

My eyes were fully closed now, and the sweet pull of nothingness called out to me. It would be so easy to slip away, to give in and finally find peace.

"Stay with me," Jude's voice hissed above my ear.

Jake was still talking, screaming at Patrick. I didn't hear Patrick's reply, but they were arguing.

I understood then that Jake was working to distract him.

Fingers pressed against my bloodied flesh, and that warmth I felt crawled across my gaping wound like spreading flames eating away at cloth. It consumed me in an instant, the agony not permitting me to scream.

Jude gripped me harshly, his fingers biting into my skin. Managing to peel open my lids, I glimpsed his determined stare, his injured eye a bright orb of liquid gold, his other filled with a dusky yellow.

"You're not leaving me, Kiara," he commanded, nostrils flaring. "I won't allow it." He let out a reverberating growl, more animal than man. "You say you're a monster"—he dug deeper into the wound, and tears streaked my cheeks—"but a monster didn't rescue me, didn't make me believe in hope again."

A strangled noise sounded from deep in my throat. Something was happening to me, my body quivering and burning and full of magic.

"*You* saved me. Kiara Frey. You are the only light I will vow to protect."

I shattered then, gold flashing behind my eyes, a buzzing working its way from my toes to the crown of my head. And all the while, Jude held me, telling me to hold on, demanding I not leave him here alone.

I clung on to those words, to his pleas. They held me to this plane as I burned alive.

He wasn't strong enough to endure what happened next.

One moment I was in Jude's arms, and the next, I detonated, the force of power leaving my body sending me tumbling around and around across the gray soil. Dirt got into my mouth, my eyes, my nose. My limbs were so battered, I barely felt the impact. But my chest…that hurt in ways I didn't know was possible. Jaw clenched in determination, I thrust up and onto my elbows, lifting my head and searching for the Knight who had thoroughly given me his heart.

"How predictable," Patrick grumbled, moving to a curled-up figure ten feet away. Jude groaned, shifting onto his side, feebly reaching for his dagger.

I turned my head, finding Jake sprawled on the ground where he'd confronted Patrick, his eyes closed. I wasn't sure he breathed.

"You've played the martyr before, haven't you, commander? But did you ever wonder what it would be like to play a different role? One where you weren't an afterthought. A side note."

I screamed when Patrick kicked Jude's side, his boot digging into the commander's ribs.

"You used the precious time Jake afforded you to help *her* when you could've come for me and ended this once and for all."

He tutted, disappointed. "I'm surprised the prophecy those sun priestesses always whine about hasn't worked. You're both vessels for Raina's light, both drawn to one another. If anyone could've made that inane prophecy come true, it would've been you."

I didn't know much of the lore, and I scrambled to understand his meaning.

But all thoughts of the mysterious prophecy were wiped away when Patrick grasped Jude's hair, yanking his head up. He held a blade in his hand, and he swiped it across the uninjured side of Jude's face. A river of red slid down Jude's cheek, his new wound deep.

"Hmmm. Now it'll match," Patrick said darkly. "If you *were* to live, I'd say this new scar would be a reminder to put yourself first for once."

He dropped Jude without care and turned to the soil, bending to his knees. Holding out his hand, he sliced across his palm, adding more blood to the mix. "This clearing, before the curse, was sacred, blessed by Arlo himself. It's the mysterious *X* you've been searching for, and we are the keys." He gestured to me and Jude. "You, me, and *him*." He snarled out the word. "Only when I feed the soil with the blood of all three can I bring forth the Godslayer." He rolled his eyes as if he'd made a silly mistake. "Or, in this case, the weapon I'll use to create a god."

I gritted my teeth, crawling over to where Jude lay motionless. From the corner of my eye, I saw Patrick plunge the bloodied weapon into the ground beside a patch of flourishing Midnight Blooms, his face lighting up as his plan slowly came to fruition. How long he must've waited for this moment of pain.

I'd just made it over to Jude's side and turned back to Raina's former lover when black roots sprouted from the earth, three Midnight Blooms growing around the hilt of an onyx dagger.

Patrick's twisted smile grew, and he pulled the weapon from the earth.

It wasn't the same weapon he'd used to stab me, nor was it the one he'd used to slice Jude's face. That one had been dull and silver. This one was monstrous.

The intricate hilt was fashioned of gleaming vines, pointed thorns poking out at the sides and below the handle. The blade itself was sheer black metal, decorated with glowing white symbols I didn't recognize.

"Finally," Patrick sighed, twisting it from side to side. "Now

I can do this properly. And this time, there's no one standing in my way to claim what I worked so hard for. Love truly is overvalued."

I gently prodded Jude's shoulder as Patrick rose and started to stride over, but the commander remained unmoving. He let out a raspy groan, my name on his lips.

"You need to get up," I breathed, clumsily rising. I peered down to my chest, expecting blood to be seeping from the stab wound, but through the shredded linen of my shirt, I saw only dry, raised skin, the gash seemingly stitched together and healed. I gasped, turning down to Jude.

Patrick was beaming, full of triumph.

"Jude probably didn't even know what he was doing," he mused, slowing five feet away. "All those years and he never used his gift, the magic inside of him."

Patrick shook his head. "Only with you did he use it. And he used it fruitlessly. I merely needed you alive long enough to get to this place, to retrieve what is rightfully mine. The enchantment requires fresh blood, after all."

Patrick lifted the blade. "At least now you can die together like the foolish heroes from lore." He advanced, the Godslayer in his hand, a slight glow illuminating his skin. "It's funny, because I always sensed the third piece nearby, wherever you were. Initially, I thought it had to be a recruit." His stare briefly landed on Jake, who released a soft groan. I thanked the gods he lived. "While I had my suspicions about the commander, it wasn't until the village attack that I knew for certain. Right after he burned those vile beasts alive."

So Patrick was the one who'd attacked Jude.

I grimaced, hating myself more for allowing him beyond my walls and trusting him. Patrick had hurt Jude, had planned on killing him before he discovered he was of use. If I'd only looked beyond his exterior, I might've seen the clues—how he'd tried to turn me against the commander. The moments when his tone would become hard and cutting. The story of "Rosie," the woman he supposedly cared for.

He was a master manipulator, and I'd made it far too easy for him to accomplish his goal.

A blur of limbs rammed into Patrick's side, knocking him down with a roar.

Jake.

He rose to his feet, a nasty bruise on his cheek, one eye already swelling shut. He lurched back from the traitor, the immortal lover of the Sun Goddess, and he spit on his face.

"That was for Nic," he said. If Patrick hadn't cursed them all, Nic would still be alive. So many others would still be alive.

Patrick swiped at his cheek, the thick glob of spit smearing the dirt painting him. Overhead, the moon shone brighter, as if it wished to see the fight unfolding clearly. I noted how red seeped around it in a bloodied ring.

I clutched at Jude, trying to haul him up and to his feet. He groaned, but he rose with me, leaning against me for support. Whatever he'd done for me had weakened him. His body burned, his heat seeping through my shirt and causing my own flesh to tingle uncomfortably.

"That wasn't smart," Patrick growled at Jake, though his smirk hadn't yet fallen. "I've wanted to kill you for weeks now, and you've just given me an excuse."

Jake screeched as Patrick lifted a hand and clenched his fingers into a fist, his eyes aglow with foreign magic. Tendrils of steam and sparks of fire whispered around Jake's body, and my friend slumped to the ground once more, curling into a ball as he writhed in agony.

Patrick had decades on us, years of practicing his magic. Jude only just discovered that part of himself, and healing me had nearly destroyed him.

"You were my friend," I screamed, stealing Patrick's attention away from Jake.

He dropped his arm, and Jake shook from the aftereffects of Patrick's magic—or of his *stolen* magic.

"We all cared about you." Tears dripped from my eyes and into the murky depths of the Mist. "I would've given my life to protect you."

"You're giving me your life anyway," Patrick said coldly.

Jude lifted his head. "I will tear you limb from limb if you hurt her—"

"Yes, yes," Patrick cut him off. "You can threaten me if it makes you feel better, but it won't change the ending. Though I'll kill you first and carve out Raina's magic *before* I kill her. It's much harder to watch someone you care for bleeding out. Believe me, I'd know."

And yet he'd stab Raina all over again. He only regretted failing.

The arm slung around my shoulders scorched my shirt, and the smell of burning cloth clogged my nostrils. When I hissed, Jude jerked away, realizing what he'd inadvertently done. He didn't go far, though.

What Patrick had said, about Jude being Raina's mortal descendant? I didn't understand it. But the way his eyes had glowed, how hot his skin felt... Hells, how he'd *healed* me, it all made some sort of screwed-up sense.

"It's three against one, Patrick," Jude spit out, the fearsome mask of the commander sliding back into place, despite his exhaustion. "I like those odds."

Patrick cocked his head, and a chill went down my spine. "Who said it was only me?"

CHAPTER FIFTY-ONE

JUDE

Lorian, God of Beasts and Prey, is more creature than man.
He roams the woods like a lone wolf, searching for a pack,
for a soul that matches his own. In all his many years, he has
never come across an equal, and therefore,
he continues his search.

EXCERPT FROM ASIDIAN LORE: A TALE OF THE GODS

Blood-curdling howls pierced the air, the pounding of feet
nearing from the distance.

"When you're as old as I am, you never come unprepared."
Patrick waved to the tree line. "I'll make sure your deaths are
quick. Especially yours, Kiara."

He shot her a pointed look, and I stepped in front of her.

"I actually enjoyed some of my time with you. I wasn't lying
when I said you reminded me of someone I used to know. You're
more like Raina than you might think, and maybe that's why
your death may hurt more than I expected."

She lifted her chin, that defiance I loved about her a beacon
in the night.

"When *I* kill you, it'll be slow," she vowed, shadows hissing
at her fingertips. Her lower lip quivered as if repressing all the

emotion she'd bottled up. Patrick and the other recruits had become her family, and from what she'd told me of her village, how its people had spurned her after the accident, she wasn't used to having friends. This had cut her deep.

I had no doubt she *would* kill him, but Patrick, as the famed traitor of the realm, still retained a piece of Raina's magic; the third piece. He'd just displayed a hint of what he could do when he'd attacked Jake, who was only now climbing to his feet. His skin had turned a harsh red, a few bubbling blisters dotting his cheeks and neck.

Kiara would have to carve out Patrick's stolen magic very carefully. But where would it go afterward? According to my mother's book of lore that I'd lent Kiara, Raina's power had split into three parts—the three *keys*—that had vanished so quickly Patrick had only had time to seize one.

I cursed myself, feeling guilty for not seeing through his shy, helpless act. There had been times when I'd thought I'd see a glimmer of an edge in his eyes, though I'd foolishly suspected it had to do with Kiara and me getting closer. I'd thought it to be petty jealousy.

Maybe, in some twisted way, it had been.

The branches of the nearest trees cracked and splintered, and a great roar rattled the Mist. Even Patrick lifted his head and gazed to the woods, a grim smile curving his mouth.

Emerging from the north were three wolf-like creatures, all standing well over five feet. Their bodies were masked almost entirely by the darkness, though thick fur tufted from their lethal forms, the color of pure, fresh snow. And while I couldn't see all of their features, their glowing red eyes shone clear enough.

Kiara righted herself, adopting a fighting position.

Jake, who hardly looked able to stand, let alone ready for battle, ambled to her other side, his hands shaking as he lifted his weapon.

I'd seen the loyalty in his character from day one. It had been one of the reasons I'd chosen him for this mission, in addition to his exceptional combat skills. Loyalty was a greater commodity than brute force or skill. Tonight had proven that.

Before the wolves pounced, a man materialized before them, the pelt of a black bear draped across his broad shoulders. Tangled, ash-white hair fell below his chin, his eyes glowing a predatory yellow. He walked before the beasts, and they followed like hounds after their master. With the brawn of a bear and the smooth advancement of a coiling serpent, he led the devilish creatures into the center of the field, his eyes trained on Patrick. It wasn't a kind look, or one borne of respect. He stared at Patrick as if he, too, wished to slice his throat.

"Thank you for joining us, Lorian," Patrick said, bowing his head. "I figured it was past time I call in my favor."

Lorian, God of Beasts and Prey.

My pulse thrummed against my neck. One look at him said it all, from the way he appeared more animal than man to the shining yellow eyes. He wasn't human, and a dormant part of me stood at attention, recognizing his devastating might.

The god grunted, tilting his head to the side as if assessing his next victim. "I'd hardly call this a favor," he growled, his shoulders hunched and his upper lip curled.

Patrick turned to Kiara, whispering, "I may have promised him something for his aid. He's been weakened, something precious stolen from him. I merely gifted him the information needed to right that wrong." He shook his head in a mockery of concern. "But that tale is for another day."

I hadn't the faintest idea of what they spoke. Either way, Lorian being here and on Patrick's side wouldn't bode well for us.

The exhaustion I'd felt earlier slowly receded, and a quick look at Kiara told me she'd regained some energy as well. As screwed-up as it was, pride filled me. I'd done that. *Healed* her.

All I could recall was that fire inside me, my mind screaming into a void of bright light, begging for her to be saved. Electricity had shot through me then, right from my chest to my fingers, which had been pressed against her wound. I'd been too focused on her face to notice the injury stitching itself up. If she had died... I couldn't help but feel as if I would have joined her. We were tied together, and not simply because of what Patrick insinuated. It was greater than divinity, than magic. What I felt for her was infinite.

"Have fun, Lorian," Patrick murmured, waving an idle hand as he stepped to the side. "Hopefully, once this is all over, we can form our own alliance for the dark days ahead. Just remember to save the killing blows for me."

That's right. He needed to be close when the pieces of Raina's power were released.

I was going to kill him. *Slowly.*

But before I could make my move, the wolves dashed into the clearing, tearing at the ground with their clawed feet, their mouths open as frothy spittle flew.

"You got a plan, right?" Jake asked, bumping into Kiara.

She worked her way in front of her friend. "Aim for the heart or head, Jake. That's the plan."

"Solid," he grumbled, even as he raised his weapon.

The first wolf lunged, aiming for Kiara. She was a whirl of limbs as she shoved Jake to the ground, far away from the creature. Before she, too, could move to the side and lift her weapon, the wolf's paws knocked her down. My pulse raced as it brought its claws up in the air, ready to slice her chest, her throat, her face.

Kiara rolled to the side at the last second, and the wolf slashed across the soil, sending dirt and debris soaring.

The next wolf dove for me, but I was ready.

Isiah had gifted me the blade in my hand, and while simple, it had been crafted by the people of Rine, Alec's kin from the north. When it sliced through the air, it whistled, a song of promise.

The creature shifted back, but I'd nicked him, a superficial cut, one that had his hackles rising.

Somewhere nearby, I heard an irritated scoff. Patrick, likely sitting back and enjoying Lorian doing his dirty work. He didn't appear keen on getting his hands dirty.

Jake cursed as his wolf parted the fog and pounced, but he managed to duck and roll. I sent a prayer to Maliah, Goddess of Revenge and Redemption, hoping she'd aid him, but for now, I had to focus on my own battle.

The wolf came at me again, this time going right for the throat. Pain lanced down my neck while I shoved myself to the ground, and thick warmth slid down to my collarbones. I swallowed hard. While not enough to kill me, it hurt like a bitch.

Between that and the cut Patrick had inflicted, I'd be lucky to have a patch of skin not bleeding by the end of this.

Jumping to my feet, I waited until the animal was a few feet away before I moved. When it lunged, I vaulted onto its back, digging my fingers into its pristine white hide.

It howled, attempting to buck me off, but I held on, knowing that if I died, Kiara and Jake would be by themselves. That thought strengthened my hold, and that same heat I'd felt when healing Kiara resurfaced in a sickening rush.

My entire body became a living and breathing flame.

Around me, the Mist lightened, and when my gaze landed on Lorian's, a stunned expression marred his rugged features.

With the fire in my veins and an unbreakable purpose swelling in my heart, I twisted down and thrust Isiah's blade into the wolf's head with a roar. Lorian's beast thrashed up and then jerked violently before dropping to the ground, taking me with it. I shifted out of the way, rolling so I wasn't pinned beneath hundreds of pounds of muscle and fur.

When I stilled, I stole a peek at Kiara, who had a nasty cut across her right arm. She'd gotten in a blow of her own, her wolf's hide matted with red. Not a lethal wound.

She smiled as it kicked at the dirt with one paw, preparing to pounce. Shadows swirled along her frame, darkening when she lifted her hands, one gripping her blade. The other, however, she opened, aimed directly at the beast.

"Kiara!" I shouted, just as the wolf soared. It knocked her onto her back, but she didn't drop her grin. If anything, it flourished.

I bounded over, about to drive my dagger into his side, when pure night shot out of her.

Tendrils of it blasted from her body, wrapping around the wolf's thick neck. Her teeth were gritted in determination, her eyes narrowed on her kill.

The wolf's head snapped off its body.

It didn't even have time to cry out as her shadows devoured it, as they spun around its fallen head. Only when they ceased, flying back into her body, did I see what remained of the wolf.

Ash.

For a heartbeat, Kiara's smile turned wicked, her eyes dimming, but then they cleared, and her smile dropped as she turned to Jake, concern causing her brow to wrinkle. But I'd seen it; how she seemed to radiate the darkness itself and all of the nightmares it concealed. I should have been afraid—and maybe, in truth, I was—but the emotion at the forefront was pure relief.

Kiara had ripped off her mask, finally allowing the world to see the two sides of herself: the light and the dark. Such a creature shouldn't exist, but there she stood, proof of the impossible.

"Jake!" She jumped up and raced to her friend, who had managed to get himself halfway across the clearing of Midnight Blooms. He was barely holding his wolf back.

As she went to help Jake, I turned my sights on Patrick and a god. I had faith that she'd best the wolf. Again, pride overwhelmed me; how lucky I was to have her on my side.

Lorian bared his teeth as we killed his creatures, but his focus locked on Kiara, anger and confusion scrunching his heavy brow. But Patrick? He looked murderous.

"Do something!" he shouted at Lorian, getting in his face.

Not a wise move.

Lorian whirled in place, his broad hand wrapping around Patrick's neck in a blink. He lifted the boy in the air. "I promised you my wolves, nothing more," Lorian seethed, dropping Patrick like a sack of potatoes. "And I never said *I* would help, should they fail. You're already costing me much more than you know."

The god looked to me then, and I couldn't help but feel a sense of surprise float between us, an odd sort of connection that held no explanation. He, too, paused, his mouth twisting in a grimace.

"Raina," he whispered, shaking his head. His white hair grazed his shoulders with the movement. "I'd have thought she'd learned her lesson not to tangle with mortals." His gaze softened, just the slightest as he added, "You have her nose."

Ignoring my confusion, he turned to Patrick. "Our deal is done," he snapped. "You never told me what he was."

"I told you everything you needed to know!" Patrick said, pushing up and wiping at his stained clothing.

Lorian shot him a warning glare. "No, you told me he was a vessel, nothing more. I'm sorry, but I will not spill Raina's blood this night."

Patrick had said something about me being Raina's true descendant, but now that Lorian had insinuated the same, the reality of it crushed me. "What do you mean—"

Kiara's scream shook me back to reality. I whirled away from the god and charged to where she battled the final wolf. It had its claws in her shoulder, and although Jake had jumped on its back, the creature had easily shaken him off.

I took his place, but I wasn't as lucky as I'd been the first time.

Instead of focusing on Kiara trapped beneath him, the wolf thrust upward and spun. She scrambled to her feet, and for a second, I felt only gratitude.

It was short-lived.

The wolf reared back and sent me flying through the air.

I couldn't stop myself, and I silently cursed seconds before I struck a tree, my bones rattling. It cracked at the force of my body colliding with its thick wood, its mighty trunk snapping in half. Splinters cut my skin, new scars that would be added to the rest.

If the throbbing in my head was any indication, I was going to lose consciousness.

Kiara's voice sounded. I thought she called my name, but the face I saw hovering above me wasn't hers.

Patrick lowered to his knees, the Godslayer in his hand. He lifted his arm high in the air.

"Goodbye, commander," he whispered. And then his arm fell.

Chapter Fifty-Two

Kiara

Love is not the absence of self, but rather, the absence of fear,
For only the brave drop their armor and walk onto a
battlefield with their hearts exposed.

ASIDIAN PROVERB

Few people knew that the night spoke.

Even fewer knew how to answer when it did.

Right then, I didn't merely answer its call for destruction.
I roared.

Jude jerked slightly to the side as Patrick's arm dropped,
but that god-killing dagger slid into Jude's flesh with a sickening
crunch, missing his heart by a half an inch. I felt the healed
wound on my own chest pulse, a matching wound to Jude's.

Patrick grunted and yanked out the knife, preparing to bring
it back down. I knew he didn't plan on missing his target this
time. That's when the last stone in a wall holding back the power
of a goddess slipped…

I was both the night and a forgotten light.

The vast universe of black and the endless possibility of
the day.

I shattered and broke and reformed, all in that split second.

Still my eyes never left Jude, and that final, shuddering breath he took roared in my ears.

Blood pooled from where the blade had struck, and his eyes flickered shut. Death would come today and steal him away from me before we even had a chance to begin. The world, whether ruled by the moon or the sun, had been cruel to me long enough.

It was *my* turn to be cruel.

The scream that left me wasn't human. It rang through the trees and shook them until no leaves remained. It was a force greater than any wind, a song of heartache and grief and rage. I screamed for my realm, for the lost sun, but I roared for Jude, for what he represented. For what I had just lost.

Shadows unfurled from me like giant wings, and with my arms outstretched, I welcomed them to consume my enemies. My hands tingled and my chest started to burn, and gold ringed my vision, touching Jude as he lay there motionless, Patrick's dagger gleaming in my light.

Time didn't flow; it stopped to stare at me.

Not a monster, but a creature touched by the darkness and given life by the sun.

The scorching warmth expanded, trailing to my arms, to the scars on my hands, and as my shadows spread, so did my flames. That piece of me I'd locked behind years of doubt and hurt.

Freak.

Monster.

Witch.

That's what the villagers had called me. And perhaps I was all those things, but I was also Kiara Frey, and I was about to rip Patrick to shreds for the evil he had inflicted on my kingdom. On my friends. On Jude.

I commanded my gilded shadows to wrap around Patrick's wrist, holding him in place. Jude didn't move beneath him, and no more shuddering breaths left his lips.

Dead. Jude was dead.

My upper lip curled back as I stepped forward, and then so did time itself.

Patrick hissed, jerking back in shock, unable to go very far. He turned his pale-green eyes to me, a thousand questions clouding them.

"How?" he gritted out, struggling to shove down on the blade hovering above Jude's chest, his heart. He had to carve out the divinity, and I was the only person preventing him from claiming unimaginable power. "You've been touched, tainted by evil. You can't control both. It's not possible."

Sweat banded his brow, and I enjoyed his struggle. I stopped once I stood towering above, forcing him to crane his neck.

"You were once my friend, Patrick," I said, my voice coming out strange and tinny. "You know the lengths I'd go to for them."

I bent to my knees, my shadows surrounding him, holding his arms, twining about his neck like a black satin noose. I tipped my chin, and my shadows forced his head back. He sputtered, struggling for air.

A golden glow seeped from his pores as Patrick's fire met my own.

It was a battle of flames and shadows, and he refused to bend. Even as he thrashed in my hold, his sliver of Raina's power surged forth, delving beneath my flesh and trickling into my veins. I tasted the rottenness that he was, the bitterness and greed. Patrick had tainted Raina's light after decades of fueling his wrath and his unquenchable need for revenge.

I gritted my teeth as scorching heat burnt my skin, my arms, my face. Even though the two pieces belonged together, under Patrick's influence, they briefly battled, resisting one another. I felt them clash, the violent collision nearly sending me flying onto my back.

"Give. In," Patrick snarled.

My shadows hissed in reproach.

I hadn't realized I'd grabbed Jude's hand, but it was cold in mine, no longer warm or comforting. My rage burned bright, and so did my shadows.

My eyes flicked back to Patrick, spit sliding past his lips as I choked him. His power hadn't left me, and it raged inside my chest, scorching me from the inside out. I wasn't breathing, but I didn't need air. I needed revenge.

"You had *everything*," I murmured. "A love that they once wrote poetry about. Someone to share a thousand lifetimes with. And yet..."

My shadows tightened on the hand holding the Godslayer. His fingers were turning a ghastly shade of purple. "You threw away something precious, all for *more*. Always more, right? Never satisfied by what was in front of you."

I gritted my teeth as my fingers burned. Jude's limp hand glowed, a pale yellow that highlighted the onyx and blue scars beside it, his beauty shedding light on my own. In that second, we were connected, our powers one. I drew from his motionless body, and his light became mine.

Patrick cursed, the foul word coated in decades worth of misery and hatred.

"You should have just loved her back, but you were never capable of such a selfless thing, were you?" My shadows jerked the blade free and I reached out, grasping it as it flew into my open and waiting hand.

Patrick sent a wave of fire at me, and I grimaced. He wasn't going down easy.

But neither was I.

"Now you will know the same pain Raina did."

I didn't hesitate as I shoved against his wall of heat and brought down the dagger, my aim true. Patrick shrieked, only my shadows keeping him upright, trapping him in place, right where

I wanted him. Flesh tore and bones cracked, and the dagger pierced his cold, immortal heart.

"Maybe death"—I leaned close, whispering right into the shell of his ear—"will finally satisfy you."

I shoved deeper, twisting the hilt. His entire body gave a shudder, and I knew the soul within was leaving it. Drawing back, just enough to meet his clouded eyes, I felt the tremor that rattled him. I glanced down, the point of the blade aglow.

A piece of a god, now mine for the taking.

The light swelled, escaping the confines of flesh, an orb no larger than the size of an uncut gem. All I had to do was reach out, grasp it, and I'd have two of the three pieces.

But that wasn't what I did.

With Jude's cold hand still in my own, I lifted it, pushing it to the light. His body jerked when the orb connected with his skin, but I forced his fingers to curl around it, and then I pressed his closed hand to his chest, to the heart that I claimed.

I couldn't accept that he was dead. That he'd all but sacrificed himself for me.

"You never saw yourself the way I see you."

The orb sputtered in his palm. "*A good man is often the one who has known the most evil,*" I whispered, the old Asidian proverb saying everything I didn't have the words for. The light encased in his hand fluttered once more before dimming.

I thought that was it, that Raina's power had vanished just as Jude's soul had…but then I heard the most wondrous of things.

A trembling inhale.

Fingers flinching in my grip.

A groan.

The night erupted as Jude's eyes shot open. Gold poured from them, vibrant light that blinded. I thrust my hands over my face, squeezing my lids tightly as the world exploded, and for many long minutes, I saw only that piercing gold.

From far away, I heard my name, so soft and pure.

I didn't want to hope, to believe that it had come from the lips of the man who'd been lying in a pool of his own blood. If I was wrong...

"Kiara."

Warmth washed down my cheeks and I tasted salt.

"Don't cry, Kiara." Fingers traced my jaw, sliding up to my cheeks, the tender touch coaxing a choked sob from me. The blinding world dimmed, ever so slowly, that radiant light flickering out like a candle. Still, I didn't open my eyes.

"Look at me," Jude's voice begged, and the fingers grazing my cheeks lowered to my chin. "*Please*."

Maybe it was the pain lacing that one single word, but I was helpless but to comply. Jude. *My* Jude begged once more, and I snapped open my lids with a cry.

Below me, his chest rising and falling, lay the commander, his body retaining that golden sheen.

"H-how?" I choked out, gripping his hand.

He'd been killed before my very eyes. I didn't understand. I fumbled for his chest, my hands slick with his blood.

There was no gash, but I *had* left my mark. Instead of smooth skin, black veins sprouted like a gnarled tree from just below his heart. The scars were identical to mine in every way, and I realized that while I'd saved him with Raina's light, my darkness had also tarnished him forever.

"Kiara," Jude murmured, blinking as if he, too, didn't believe I was there, alive and breathing. He cupped my cheek.

My vision began to darken, and my body swayed. Hands that weren't Jude's grabbed at my waist. Jake.

"I got you, Ki," my friend said, pressing my back into his chest. I melded against him, allowing Jake to hold me.

"Is this real?" I asked, swaying as the black spots grew. Shock and exhaustion threatened to steal my consciousness, and I didn't have much fight left in me.

"I'm here, Kiara," Jude said, grunting as he sat up. "I felt myself leave, felt death grab me, but…" He paused, searching for the right words. "Then I was jerked back and my body was on fire and you were above me." He grasped both of my cheeks now.

Alive. Jude was alive.

"You brought me back," he whispered, pressing his brow to mine, our noses touching. "You fought for me."

Patrick's stolen light. It had saved him. My *monster* had saved him.

In my daze, I smiled. If anyone deserved such power, it was him. Jude had lived a life of endless pain, of cruelty even I hadn't known. I wanted him to feel peace, even if I understood what had to be done in order for him to attain it.

For him to save the world, save our friends and loved ones, he would have to take from me what I'd just taken from Patrick. But that was all right. I'd happily carve out the last piece and hand it to him as I took my final breath. For Asidia. For Jake and the recruits we'd lost. For Liam.

I would give all of me to them, to Jude, and when the day returned, I wondered if I'd be able to watch it all unfold from beyond the veil of death.

It had all been worth it.

Jude drew back, eyeing Patrick's body, a deep crease forming between his brows. Slowly, he brought his gaze back to me, pain and regret shining as clear as any sun.

My lids closed just as Jude uttered, "Kiara, what have you done?"

CHAPTER FIFTY-THREE

JUDE

*I just need him alive a little longer. Soon, he will discover
everything I've searched for, and it will be mine.*

LETTER FROM KING CIRIAN TO UNKNOWN RECIPIENT,
YEAR 47 OF THE CURSE

I held her in that clearing as she closed her eyes and slept.
Jake hovered nearby, his face riddled with scrapes and cuts,
but his eyes narrowed on the trees, ready for any danger that
might leap out at us.

I didn't care.

Kiara had given me the second piece of Raina's divinity. Her
light. She'd carved it right from Patrick's chest and given it to
me…and saved my life.

Peeling back my tattered shirt, I took in the scar across my
chest—the one from Patrick's blade—and then the tendrils of
black coiling up around it. She'd thought I'd been dead, and yet
she'd taken a chance and done the unthinkable.

She had hoped.

I groaned, taking in Kiara's matching scar, the wound I'd
healed. We were tied together, two halves of a whole.

Kiara had chosen me, and when she woke, I had no doubt

she'd hand me the Godslayer and demand I save our realm. I held two of the three keys. In order to unite all three, she would have to cut the final piece of power from herself—give up her own life—and join the three pieces together at last. I knew she would do it—she would do anything to save the realm. To save her brother. To save *me*.

And that was why I had to go.

"Jake." I cleared my throat, each swallow painful and raw. "Protect her."

I lifted my gaze to his. Seconds passed, but then he finally nodded, his jaw clenched. "You're leaving, aren't you?" he asked. It wasn't accusatory. Only understanding soothed the clouds in his eyes.

"You know what she'll do once she wakes." I looked down, memorizing her delicate and fierce beauty. For a moment I allowed myself to think of what could have been. Of the stolen kisses we'd share, the taste of her on my tongue. Of a life where she fought by my side, my partner, my friend, my lover. The heat in my chest flared, as if in warning. I ignored it.

I recalled what Patrick had mentioned during his speech. The sun priestesses and their prophecy. It was contained in my mother's book, and I'd memorized practically every single word.

The day will be restored when the darkness falls for the light.

It continued to loop around my thoughts, echoing in my head until it embedded itself beneath my flesh. I wished we could've fulfilled it, but luck didn't appear to be on our side.

"So, are we going to talk about what the hells just happened?" Jake bent into a crouch, keeping a wise distance from where I cradled Kiara.

"Which part?" I laughed, the sound brittle.

"Well, there's what Lorian said." He cocked a brow. "The whole not-being-dead thing." He held up a finger. "Oh, and the matter of you now possessing two of the three *keys*." When his eyes fell to Kiara, I growled.

"She will not die," I snapped. Unlike Raina, who was a goddess turned human by the dagger, Kiara would die should the blade pierce her heart. I'd been lucky that Patrick had missed the first time, but Kiara would not.

Jake held up placating hands. "I don't want her to die either, Maddox," he assured me. "There has to be another way." He looked to the Mist, to where Lorian had vanished. Maybe he thought we could seek out the help of the gods.

"Until I find another way, I must leave." So that she didn't do anything reckless. I wouldn't allow it.

He nodded, seeming to know her as well as I. "I'll give you a minute," Jake said, rising. He positioned himself far enough away that I could say my goodbyes in peace.

I lifted her up, placing her cheek above my heart. My fingers stroked her hair, marveling at its softness. Such a fearsome thing, my little warrior goddess.

My arms tightened as I breathed in her scent. "I'm so damned angry at you right now," I whispered, nuzzling my nose against her cheek. "You thought you would sacrifice yourself for me, eh? Give me all three pieces?" I shook my head, my eyes burning.

No one had ever looked at me like she did. Like I was a man who meant something. And apparently Kiara thought I meant *everything*. Not only to her, but to every living person in our realm.

"*When* I find another way, I'll come for you." I pressed my lips against her brow. "And after we fight about who was right and who was wrong, I'm going to kiss you senseless." I swallowed hard, memories of the glen flickering across my mind. If only we could have pretended for just a while longer.

"Thank you for seeing me, Kiara." I kissed her cheek, the

corner of her mouth. "Thank you for reminding me of the man I wish to be."

Reaching into my pocket, I retrieved the note King Cirian had given me all those days back in his council rooms. Unpinning my golden Knight's emblem from my jacket, I pierced the parchment.

Moving away, placing her gently upon the earth, might have been the hardest thing I'd ever done in my life. There had never been something to walk away from. *Someone* to walk away from.

After arranging the note and my pin in her palm, I stood.

The Godslayer lay upon the ground as if it weren't the most powerful weapon known to man. I bent over and seized it. I wasn't sure what she'd do with the blade, but I didn't want to take any chances with her life.

I didn't look back as I strode past Jake and into the dense haze of the cursed lands. If I did, I might not have had the willpower to leave, and where I planned to go, I'd need all my strength.

CHAPTER FIFTY-FOUR

KIARA

My old friend. As Kiara grows into a beautiful and strong young woman, my hatred for her destiny grows. I devoted years to the goddess, and giving her up feels cruel in return. She wasn't born to die—that can't be right. A part of me wants to keep her away from the boy, Raina's true descendant, and never tell her the truth.

LETTER FROM AURORA ADAIR TO JUNIPER MARCHANT, SUN PRIESTESS, YEAR 45 OF THE CURSE

A wave of nausea struck me, startling me awake. Warm hands were on me in a second, soft shushing sounds murmured in my ear.

"It's all going to be fine, Ki," Jake's voice said softly. "We're going to figure this mess out."

I blinked away the lingering shadows, my vision clearing. My body felt touched by both ice and fire, and my skin prickled from the conflicting powers imprisoned inside me.

"Jude?" I asked, scanning the clearing, finding nothing but those bone trees devoid of leaves. "Where is he?"

Jake shook his head. "He left," was all he said, though his gaze dipped to my hand. I hadn't realized what it held. My friend eased me into a seated position, and I took in the sight of a gleaming golden pin attached to a piece of frayed parchment.

Jude's pin.

I knew what it meant before I turned to Jake. He nodded at my unspoken question. Jude was gone. He must've known why I'd placed that second piece in his chest and he...

Damn him.

If one of us had to die, then why couldn't it have been me? I didn't fear death, and he was so much better than he believed. I had faith that if anyone could retain all of Raina's divinity, it would be him. Lorian's comment hadn't gone unnoticed. This was his destiny.

"I'd have thought she'd learned her lesson not to tangle with mortals. You have her nose," he had said.

Once Raina had fallen and become mortal, she was rumored to have lived her own life hidden among the people. I prayed she found a partner worthy of her love. They might have had children, who then had children of their own.

"Jude is Raina's true descendant, isn't he?" Jake asked, reading my thoughts.

I gave him a curt nod. "Lorian confirmed as much."

The note in my hand was wrinkled and creased, as though the owner had balled it into a fist one too many times. Proceeding to unfurl the page with great care, I brought it to my eyes and squinted at the scrawled message.

Kiara,

I'd always planned on giving you this note. I need you to be careful and trust no one. There are enemies everywhere, and not just those that lie in the cursed lands. The palace crawls with evil, and the man upon the throne is the worst of them all. If I am dead and you are reading this now, know you were the one who gave me hope of becoming a better man. I would've liked to have been that for you one day. Maybe in another life.

Forever your brooding commander,
Jude

It took great effort to keep hold of the letter.

My hands trembled as unwanted tears welled in my eyes. The page blurred into one song of heartbreak, his words ringing through my thoughts on an endless loop I couldn't turn off.

I turned the letter over, finding another scrawl, one that didn't belong to Jude.

It simply said:

Kill the girl and the other recruits in the field of Midnight Blooms. Bring me the weapon.

Slick sweat pooled at my lower back, a shrill ringing of alarm sounding in my ears.

The Godslayer. That's the weapon the writer had referred to. Whoever wrote this had wanted me dead—the missing piece of Raina inside me be damned.

Which meant...they didn't want the sun to come back at all.

"Cirian," I murmured. He'd been after something else, all along.

Jake peeked over my shoulder, reading. Jude answered to only one person. "It seems our king never wanted us to succeed after all."

He just wanted the dagger. One that could kill *gods*.

Jude had held onto this note the entire time. An order to kill me once the mission was through. And yet... This was his way of saying goodbye, while also warning me of unknown threats lurking.

I had a price on my head.

"You do realize the king will capture us the second we cross back into Asidia," Jake said, running his hands through his hair. They trembled. "He has guards posted everywhere, and if that command indeed came from the king and he wants us and the dagger, then he will post his guards all around the kingdom. We won't stand a chance."

Rising to my feet, I gripped my friend by the shoulders, my voice unwavering. Tendrils of black slithered from my fingertips, dancing down Jake's chest. Gold flickered within the smoke, shining through the murky onyx.

"Oh, Jake. Don't you know I like it when the odds are against me?" My smile was grim. "It makes winning that much more fun."

Besides, no one could kill a shadow.

EPILOGUE

JUDE

One week later

Many enter Fortuna with hope and coin
Few leave with either, if they leave at all

The city of Fortuna was where luck went to die.

Slipping past the border of the cursed lands and back into Asidia had been easier than I'd anticipated. Apparently the king had forgotten that the very person he sought was also the one who'd been in charge of his defenses.

It took me a week to make my way to the city of Fortuna, a wicked little town to the far northeast of Sciona. Home to Maliah's temple, and a place where men could remake or ruin themselves.

Well, there was another reason I ventured there.

Hidden in the corner of the ramshackle tavern aptly named The Sly Fox, I brought the glass of ale to my lips and took a large drink. My compass rested on the table, the etched claw symbol on its back staring back at me as revelers danced in a drunken stupor, while others downed liquor in hopes of forgetting their misfortune.

Fortuna boasted more than Maliah's temple.

Dozens of gambling dens and fighting pits filled the city, which smelled of blood, ale, and coin. You could find anything you wanted here, from assassins to illegal drugs or weapons. The black market had often been overlooked by Cirian, who'd claimed it was a minor inconvenience. Lucky for me.

A man wearing an obnoxious red jacket slid into the seat beside mine, his eyes trained on the band playing a raucous tune across the room. When he crossed his arms, I caught sight of a tattoo on the underside of his wrist. A single claw.

"I hear you require an audience with the Fox." It wasn't a question.

"I do," I said, sitting up and knocking back the last of my drink. The liquid courage went down smoothly, warming my already heated chest. Since that day back in the Mist, the flames inside me hadn't dissipated. They were always there, ready to be unleashed.

I shoved my pouch of stolen coins onto the table. The man snagged the bag and tucked it into his jacket. His cap rested low over his eyes, but I imagined they gleamed at the feel of the bag's weight.

"Come with me," was all he said as he stood. The Fox's minion slunk through the crowds with the ease of a man who'd been born and raised in the bedlam that was Fortuna.

I followed, my hand on my dagger's hilt.

If there was one soul in Asidia who could help me now, it would be the Fox. The very last person I ever wanted to see again.

But for her, for Kiara, I'd do just about anything. As I trailed after my guide, past the bar and through a set of doors leading to a long hall, I thought of her face. Imagined how it would look when I finally returned and held her in my arms.

"Through here," Red Coat said, grunting at the open door at

the end of the corridor. No guards were posted before it, but I suspected the Fox had other securities in place. She wasn't one to be trusted.

Nodding at the man, who slipped back into the hall, I marched over the threshold. A warm office greeted me, and tapestries from all over the realm hung on the dark-paneled walls. Statues and figurines littered small tables and ottomans, the trinkets likely worth a fortune all by themselves. The Fox was a well-known collector. A thief.

A desk sat in the center of the room, and a slight woman with brown eyes and gleaming black hair sat in its chair, her hands splayed across the polished wood surface. She never took her eyes from me, and I never gave her the satisfaction of cowering. This woman owed me a debt.

"Welcome," she said, motioning to a seat before her desk. "I was wondering when you'd come to me."

Screams sounded from the bar, muffled by the thick walls of the Fox's lair. Her grin grew predatory as I took a seat, and her gaze dipped to where my coat fell open, revealing the Godslayer blade. Her brown eyes twinkled in delight.

I lifted my chin, forcing my mask in place. How many times had I envisioned sitting right here, before her? How many years had I wondered why she'd left me, alone with a cruel man who fed off my pain?

I leaned forward, placing the compass on the table between us. Her eyes flickered down, but not a trace of emotion shone in them.

"Thought I'd return this," I said, forcing a grin. Let her see how little her presence meant to me.

She cocked her head, but she made no move to retrieve the compass.

"I believe you owe me a favor, dearest Mother."

$\mathcal{A}$CKNOWLEDGMENTS

Behind smiles, behind laughter, beneath perfect illusions, we all battle with the metaphorical night, all of us warriors in our own hearts. This story is about the masks we wear, the lies we tell, and the lies society will have us believe…but it is also about *triumphing* over them.

Kiara became my inspiration, and writing her story allowed me to seek my own light. My own strength. I thank her for being that beacon for me. And thanks to Jude, for reminding me that even in darkness, there is beauty to be found.

To my husband, Joshua. You have been my greatest support and truest friend, and I'm beyond grateful you came into my life. Thank you for your relentless faith, and for making me feel worthy, even when I couldn't see it for myself. To my children: because of you, I wanted to do better, to achieve a dream I never thought possible. It is because of you three that I finished this novel, and I pray you will be forces of great change in a world sorely in need of it.

To my mother, Nancy; I love you, and I thank you for reading everything I've ever written—including every melancholy poem that prompted you to ask, "Are you okay?"

To Jen Bouvier. I cried when I received your email telling me my story would be given life. You're the kind of editor a writer dreams of, and your support and kind words (and often hysterical ones) made this story what it is. You're brilliant and patient, and your guidance has made me a better writer. My thanks are simply not enough.

To the team at Entangled. You've given me a gift I can never reciprocate, although I will do everything I can to try. Thank you, from the bottom of my heart. You've made my dreams come true.

I wrote this story when I thought my hope was lost. But somewhere along the way, I slowly rediscovered myself. I genuinely applaud every single person out there who battles darkness of their own. You are seen. I see you. I am you.

I hope you find beauty in your dark. And I hope you shine.

In this game of cat and mouse,
she'll use every weapon she has...

Available now.

CHAPTER ONE

The Temple of Ruin has been abandoned for centuries, but it's an unspoken rule that nobody enters the looming pagoda.

There are legends of dark, dreadful *things* lurking within its depths—fanged creatures that lunge out of shadows and drag unsuspecting mortals down into the nightmarish underworld below.

And the gods do not lift a finger to help them.

Yet my lips still whisper a prayer as I eye the damned temple that Konrarnd Kalmin has deemed our mark for a midnight heist.

I am not surprised when there is no answer.

They abandoned us centuries ago, those gods, growing bored of the realm's human trifles. They are not here now. None of them are. Not even the Dokkaebi look upon this kingdom tonight.

I am alone. Completely and utterly alone, as always.

Though considering who I'm stealing from… I wince. My loneliness is, for once, a rather large blessing.

My stomach tightens with nerves as I adjust my position on the roof of the dingy wooden complex that neighbors the temple. Its scarlet color gleams tauntingly under the light of the night's half-hearted moon.

Bloodred pillars and a swirling, ink-black finial reach toward the growing storm clouds up above, determined to blot out the already-faint stars that hover over the decrepit kingdom of Sunpo.

I've snuck through almost every crevice of the Eastern Continent's dilapidated territory, every tavern and pleasure hall, every manor and slum in the four sectors. And if I hadn't, Sang or the twins had described it to me.

But neither Sang nor the twins had ever been in *there*.

Nibbling on my bottom lip, I check my suit to ensure that my single knife is sheathed at my waist. It is. I glance down at the sloping tiled roof before me with narrowed eyes and make my best effort to transform my clammy apprehension into stone-cold resolve.

For Eunbi.

I launch into action, sprinting across the ragged tiles in a rapid blur. An icy wind whips my face raw as I launch myself into open air. For a beautiful moment, I savor the feeling of utter weightlessness before my stomach drops and I'm crashing downdowndown*down*...

The pagoda's roof approaches me in a blur of crimson.

I land in a crouch, with one hand gripping a curved red roof tile and the other stretched out behind me.

My left leg, scarred and ruined from the merciless bite of a blade, screams in pain from the sudden impact. I do my best to ignore it, quelling a groan as I focus on adjusting my position to glance at the pagoda's bracket below. It's about fifteen feet underneath a dip in the red roof. *Easy.*

My boots hit the ground with a soft thud. Another jump, and I'm on the balustrade below. A moment later, I swing myself over the railing-like structure onto the awaiting wooden floor and land with a soft exhale of relief.

There's no time to waste, though.

The window I'm planning to enter through, and Kalmin's precious prize, are waiting. I touch the glass with a gloved finger and run my tongue across my front teeth. The window is certainly small, but just large enough for me to squirm through.

Hopefully.

In a swift, sure movement, I slam my gloved fist into the glass, expecting it to give way completely. Yet it only cracks, a thick sliver running down the center of the square panel.

My jaw tightens.

I've never had trouble breaking as thin a glass as this, but a year of working for Kalmin, malnourished and mistreated, has left me weakened.

And angry.

As red-hot fury heats my blood, I slam the hilt of my dagger into the window with a rough growl. The glass shatters into a storm of shards.

"Finally," I mutter and glare at the now-open entrance of the Temple of Ruin as I brush shattered glass from my hair. I peer into the inky darkness.

It's not hard to believe that the Temple of Ruin was once the place of worship dedicated to the Pied Piper—the infamous goblin who, after the gods' abandonment of our world for another, once reigned over the Three Kingdoms of the Eastern Continent as emperor of both mortals and Dokkaebi alike.

And from whom I'm now stealing.

Wonderful.

I hiss a profanity as I grip the upper windowsill and slide my legs through. I may not be able to see it, but surely there'll be a floor below. I push myself from the ledge with a slight shift of my arms.

The temple is filled with a series of barking curses as I realize that there certainly *is* a floor…just thirty feet below. I tumble through the darkness, barely managing to twist my body into a position that thankfully results in my *not* cracking my head open.

Landing on the ground and flipping myself forward on impact to soften the blow, I envision running Konrarnd Kalmin through with a particularly large sword. Godsdamn him to the depths of Jeoseung for sending me here. Godsdamn him for taking so much from me and expecting to receive pretty little prizes in return.

A burst of agony slices through my bad leg as I struggle to my feet and fish my lighter from the pocket of my stealth suit. With a hiss, it ignites, but the flickering flame barely manages to illuminate the space.

The Temple of Ruin is nothing like I expected it to be.

I anticipated a palace within the pagoda, complete with twisting, winding stairs and richly furnished rooms, haunted with whispering shadows and air thick with a sense of sinister foreboding.

Instead, I take in a simple, spacious room like that of a studio. To my dismay, it's empty—save for a thick coating of snow-like dust that now covers my suit and a small black chest in the center of the room.

There are no signs of any wailing Gwisin. No ghosts here— nothing but silence and that odd little trunk accompany me. I fight back an incredulous laugh.

The infamous Temple of Ruin is nothing more than an empty room. If anything, this temple is glaringly obvious proof that the Dokkaebi pay very little attention to the one territory they still possess. And why should they? The immortals have better things with which to occupy themselves in their own pocket realm of Gyeulcheon.

I limp my way over to the chest, in which I'm certain lies this tapestry that Kalmin so desperately desires. I blow a heavy layer of dust off the box and fight back a sneeze as the thick powder rises into the air in a cloud of white.

There is a black lock, engraved with small silver markings in a language that I don't immediately recognize. Perhaps it is the Old Language, from the time of the gods. The lock itself seems simple enough—I've picked hundreds, probably thousands, of locks before. This will be no different.

Yet I hesitate.

Stealing from the Dokkaebi…

I wonder, grimly, if I will face the wrath of the Pied Piper after this. If he will lure me away with his enchanted flute as he's done to so many mortals and slaughter me in his hidden realm. A sick sort of satisfaction creeps its way into my chest.

If the Pied Piper comes after me, I shall take an immense delight in explaining that it was Konrarnd Kalmin who sent me to the Temple of Ruin, Kalmin and his little gang of Blackbloods.

If I go down, so do they.

I smile as I jimmy the narrow tip of my blade into the trunk's keyhole. I move the blade farther into the lock, my brows furrowing in slight concentration. *Right…about…here.*

My grin grows. There we are.

The trunk unlocks with a satisfying *click.*

Slowly, I open the chest.

And realize, as my light bathes over its contents, why, exactly, the tapestry was deemed such a bother.

It is magnificent.

Washed in the glow of my flame, it shines in starbursts of vivid colors. Interwoven with threads of string, small, gleaming jewels are nestled between each stitch. Thousands of them.

I suck in a sharp breath.

With a trembling hand, I heft the tapestry out of its resting place. It must weigh the same as a small child, but judging from the number of folds, it's no bigger than a small welcome mat, and just barely as wide.

The jewels bite into my gloved fingers, slicing through the thick, padded fabric with frightening ease. My heart races.

"*Gods,*" I breathe.

These jewels are from Gyeulcheon, *their* realm, which is hidden by Dokkaebi magic. Even the jewels from the Southern Continent's kingdom of Oktari—renowned for its precious stones—do not compare to this.

Touching the jewels sends a rush of giddiness through my body and summons the image of a curly haired, gap-toothed girl with dancing eyes and an infectious laugh. *Eunbi.*

I wonder how dire the consequences would be if I take the tapestry for myself and run. Perhaps I would be able to buy out the men stationed on the Yaepak Mountains with the jewels… but no. Kalmin would give the order for his cronies to murder my sister long before I'd make it to her mountaintop school.

My throat constricts as I tuck the tapestry under one arm, quelling my fantasies of a life of freedom lived alongside my little sister. I shut the now-empty chest with a *thud* that echoes through the derelict temple.

Kalmin wants his treasure.

And so he'll get it. Just like always.

When the moon follows me home through the darkened streets of Sunpo, I can almost swear that Dalnim, its dark-haired goddess, is watching me.

*Some shadows protect you...others will kill
you in this dazzling fantasy series from
award-winning author Abigail Owen.*

THE LIAR'S CROWN

Everything about my life is a lie. As a hidden twin princess, born second, I have only one purpose—to sacrifice my life for my sister if death comes for her. I've been living under the guise of a poor, obscure girl of no standing, slipping into the palace and into the role of the true princess when danger is present.

Now the queen is dead and the ageless King Eidolon has sent my sister a gift—an eerily familiar gift—and a proposal to wed. I don't trust him, so I do what I was born to do and secretly take her place on the eve of the coronation. Which is why, when a figure made of shadow kidnaps the new queen, he gets me by mistake.

As I try to escape, all the lies start to unravel. And not just my lies. The Shadowraith who took me has secrets of his own. He struggles to contain the shadows he wields—other faces, identities that threaten my very life.

Winter is at the walls. Darkness is looming. And the only way to save my sister and our dominion is to kill Eidolon...and the Shadowraith who has stolen my heart.

Let's be friends!

🐦 @EntangledTeen

📷 @EntangledTeen

📘 @EntangledTeen

♪ @EntangledTeen

📰 bit.ly/TeenNewsletter

entangled teen

an imprint of Entangled Publishing LLC